Praise for the novels of #1 *New York Times* bestselling author Debbie Macomber

"Romantic, warm, and a breeze to read."

—*Kirkus Reviews* on *Cottage by the Sea*

"Debbie Macomber tells women's stories in a way no one else does."

—*BookPage*

"Macomber is a master storyteller."

—*Times Record News*

"With first-class author Debbie Macomber, it's quite simple—she gives readers an exceptional, unforgettable story every time, and her books are always, always keepers!"

—*ReaderToReader.com*

"Whether [Debbie Macomber] is writing lighthearted romps or more serious relationship books, her novels are always engaging stories that accurately capture the foibles of real-life men and women with warmth and humor."

—*Milwaukee Journal Sentinel*

"Macomber never disappoints."

—*Library Journal*

"Virtually guaranteed to please."

—*Publishers Weekly*

DEBBIE MACOMBER

Winter Weddings

The Sheriff Takes a Wife and *First Comes Marriage*

mira

mira™

Recycling programs for this product may not exist in your area.

ISBN-13: 978-0-7783-1162-1

Winter Weddings

This edition published by arrangement with Harlequin Books S.A.

For questions and comments about the quality of this book, please contact us at CustomerService@Harlequin.com.

Mira
22 Adelaide St. West, 41st Floor
Toronto, Ontario M5H 4E3, Canada
www.Harlequin.com

Printed in U.S.A.

Also available from Debbie Macomber and MIRA

Blossom Street

The Shop on Blossom Street
A Good Yarn
Susannah's Garden
Back on Blossom Street
Twenty Wishes
Summer on Blossom Street
Hannah's List
"The Twenty-First Wish"
(in *The Knitting Diaries*)
A Turn in the Road

Cedar Cove

16 Lighthouse Road
204 Rosewood Lane
311 Pelican Court
44 Cranberry Point
50 Harbor Street
6 Rainier Drive
74 Seaside Avenue
8 Sandpiper Way
92 Pacific Boulevard
1022 Evergreen Place
Christmas in Cedar Cove
(*5-B Poppy Lane* and
A Cedar Cove Christmas)
1105 Yakima Street
1225 Christmas Tree Lane

The Dakota Series

Dakota Born
Dakota Home
Always Dakota
Buffalo Valley

The Manning Family

The Manning Sisters
(*The Cowboy's Lady* and
The Sheriff Takes a Wife)
The Manning Brides
(*Marriage of Inconvenience*
and *Stand-In Wife*)
The Manning Grooms
(*Bride on the Loose* and
Same Time, Next Year)

Christmas Books

Home for the Holidays
Glad Tidings
(*There's Something About Christmas*
and *Here Comes Trouble*)
Christmas in Alaska
(*Mail-Order Bride* and
The Snow Bride)
Trading Christmas
Christmas Letters
The Perfect Christmas
(includes *Can This Be Christmas*)
Choir of Angels
(*Shirley, Goodness and Mercy,*
Those Christmas Angels and
Where Angels Go)
Call Me Mrs. Miracle
The Gift of Christmas
A Country Christmas
(*Kisses in the Snow* and
The Christmas Basket)

Heart of Texas

Texas Skies
(*Lonesome Cowboy* and
Texas Two-Step)
Texas Nights
(*Caroline's Child* and *Dr. Texas*)
Texas Home
(*Nell's Cowboy* and
Lone Star Baby)
Promise, Texas
Return to Promise

Midnight Sons

Alaska Skies
(*Brides for Brothers* and
The Marriage Risk)
Alaska Nights
(*Daddy's Little Helper* and
Because of the Baby)
Alaska Home
(*Falling for Him,*
Ending in Marriage and
Midnight Sons and Daughters)

This Matter of Marriage
Montana
Thursdays at Eight
Between Friends
Changing Habits
The Sooner the Better
Three Brides, No Groom
Summer Breezes
(*Fallen Angel* and *The Way to a Man's Heart*)
Seaside Springtime
(*For All My Tomorrows* and
Yours and Mine)
Fairy-Tale Forever
(*Cindy and the Prince* and
Some Kind of Wonderful)
Perfect Partners
(*Rainy Day Kisses* and
Love 'n' Marriage)
Finally You
(*All Things Considered* and
No Competition)
Winning Hearts
(*Laughter in the Rain* and
Love by Degree)
Finding You Again
(*White Lace and Promises* and
Jury of His Peers)
A Second Glance
(*Shadow Chasing* and
Yesterday Once More)
Longing for Yesterday
(*Reflections of Yesterday* and
Yesterday's Hero)
The Night We Met
(*Starlight*)
Time for Love
(*A Friend or Two* and
The Trouble with Caasi)
Their Perfect Match
(*Promise Me Forever* and
Adam's Image)
Married in Seattle
(*First Comes Marriage* and
Wanted: Perfect Partner)
Right Next Door
(*Father's Day* and *The Courtship of Carol Sommars*)
Wyoming Brides
(*Denim and Diamonds* and
The Wyoming Kid)
The Man You'll Marry
(*The First Man You Meet* and
The Man You'll Marry)
Orchard Valley Grooms
(*Valerie* and *Stephanie*)
Orchard Valley Brides
(*Norah* and *Lone Star Lovin'*)
An Engagement in Seattle
(*Groom Wanted* and
Bride Wanted)
North to Alaska
(*That Wintry Feeling* and
Borrowed Dreams)

Debbie Macomber's Cedar Cove Cookbook
Debbie Macomber's Christmas Cookbook

CONTENTS

THE SHERIFF TAKES A WIFE

One

"What do you *mean* you're in labor?" Christy Manning asked her sister.

"I didn't say that…exactly," Taylor Palmer said, her palms flattened against her protruding abdomen. She lowered her eyelashes, taking a long, slow breath.

"You can't be in labor! I just got here. My suitcases are still in the trunk of my car." Christy bolted to her feet and shoved the dark curls away from her face with both hands. She'd been driving for nearly three days to be with her sister for the birth of this baby, but she hadn't counted on the blessed event happening quite so soon.

"What do you want me to do?" she asked, regaining her poise. In her opinion, there was plenty of reason for alarm. The Lazy P, Russ and Taylor's cattle ranch, was miles outside Cougar Point, the closest town. And there wasn't a neighbor in sight.

Taylor's husband, Russ, was driving his sister, Mandy, over to a friend's house and doing a couple of errands before heading back to the ranch. At most he'd be gone only an hour, or so he'd claimed.

But a lot could happen in an hour.

"I'm not convinced this is the real thing," Taylor said in an apparent effort to reassure Christy, but her hands caressed her stomach as she spoke. "I've never been in labor before, so I'm not exactly sure what to expect."

Trying to gather her scattering wits, Christy circled the kitchen table. First and foremost, she needed to keep calm. Mentally she reviewed the recent classes she'd taken through the local library. She knew CPR and enough karate to defend herself. Great. She could knock someone out and then revive him. A lot of good either of those skills was going to do her in this situation.

She swallowed a feeling of impending panic. She wasn't even supposed to be in Montana. Her mother was the one who'd planned to make the trip, only Elizabeth Manning had taken a fall and broken her leg. She was having trouble getting around and would be little or no help to Taylor. Since Christy had a couple of weeks of vacation due, she'd volunteered to come and stay with her sister. It wasn't any sacrifice on her part; Christy and Taylor had always been close.

Unfortunately no one had bothered to tell her she was going to be stuck alone on a cattle ranch with her nine months' pregnant sister, who was "feeling funny."

It all seemed unreal. Christy had arrived late the night before. Too late to do more than greet everyone, haul her overnight bag into the guest bedroom and fall exhausted into bed.

"Stop looking like you expect to deliver this baby on your own," Taylor said, smiling up at her sister.

"But, Miss Scarlett, I don't know nothin' about birthin' no babies," Christy wailed in a Southern drawl. She might be teasing, but what she said was the honest-to-goodness truth.

None of this was supposed to be happening—at least not like this. Taylor should be living in Seattle with the rest of her family. Instead, Christy's older sister had gone to Montana a year earlier and to everyone's surprise married a cattle rancher three months later.

At the time, Christy couldn't imagine what had possessed her cultured, cosmopolitan sister to marry someone like Russ Palmer. Especially in Reno, without a single family member present.

Their father hadn't been pleased at being cheated out of the chance to walk his daughter down the aisle, but once he'd met Russ, the rancher had won him over. Russ had reassured everyone in the family without even trying. Taylor and her husband had flown to Seattle at the end of May to celebrate her parents' wedding anniversary. It was then that he'd met Christy and her three brothers.

Taylor winced and her eyes drifted shut again. Her display of pain effectively cut off Christy's thoughts. She held her breath until she saw the tension slowly ease from her sister's body. "What happened?"

"I felt a funny pain, that's all. Don't worry. It wasn't anything."

"A funny pain? And you don't want me to worry?" Christy echoed. She couldn't keep the panic out of her voice. "Then why do I have this urge to boil water?"

Taylor, forever calm and serene in a crisis, grinned. "Don't worry. I've been having these pains off and on for the past week, but…"

"But what?" Christy asked.

"But these feel…different. I don't know how to explain it." She rose haltingly to her feet. "I think it might be a good idea if I got dressed."

"Right," Christy said, as if the idea was a stroke of genius. "Me, too." With her arm around what remained of Taylor's waist, Christy led her sister down the hallway that went to the master bedroom. "Do you need any help?"

"Don't be ridiculous!" Almost before the words had left her lips, Taylor let out a cry and pressed one shoulder to the wall while clutching her stomach.

Christy was instantly alarmed. "What is it?"

"Oh…my." Wide-eyed, Taylor turned toward Christy. "Hurry and get some towels. My water just broke."

"Your water broke," Christy repeated in a stupor. She threw her hands toward the ceiling. "Her water just broke." Rushing into the bathroom, she returned with enough towels to soak up a flood.

Taylor was still leaning against the wall, breathing deeply, her eyes closed. Christy dropped the towels onto the floor, far more concerned about Taylor than she was about a little water. "Are you all right?"

Her sister answered with a nod that said otherwise.

"I'm calling the doctor," Christy told her. "Don't you dare move. Understand?" The panic was stronger than ever, but Christy managed to swallow it. Taylor needed her; there wasn't time to be concerned with her own fears.

Taylor's doctor was in Miles City, sixty miles away, and the hospital was there, too. As far as she could tell, they were an hour or more from help. Christy spoke to Dr. Donovan briefly, and when she explained what had happened, the doctor suggested Taylor come to the hospital immediately.

"I'm not going without Russ," Taylor insisted when Christy relayed her conversation. "Russ will be back any minute."

Christy started to balk. It wasn't her fault that Taylor's husband had such a bad sense of timing.

"You don't know Russ the way I do," Taylor said, even

before Christy had a chance to reason with her. "If he came home and found us gone—"

"I'll leave him a note. He'll understand. Then as soon as he's back, he can join us."

"No."

Christy had heard that tone of voice often enough to realize these was no way she could budge that stubborn streak of Taylor's. "We can't just sit here and wait," Christy moaned.

"Of course we can. Now relax!"

"Me, relax? You're the one having the baby."

"I'm fine. Baby Palmer and mother are both calm and prepared."

Baby Palmer. Her only sister was about to become a mother. This wasn't new information, but until this moment Taylor's pregnancy had seemed abstract. Yet here they were alone together, and suddenly this baby was very real. This tiny life depended on Christy, and the thought was terrifying. Yet nothing she said would convince Taylor to leave for the hospital without Russ.

The next thirty minutes felt like thirty years. Christy changed into jeans and a sweatshirt, forced down another cup of coffee and looked out the kitchen window every three seconds.

Outwardly Taylor still seemed calm, but Christy could tell from the pain that flashed on her sister's face that the intensity of the contractions was increasing.

"Maybe you should call the feed store. If Russ isn't there, then contact Cody."

"Great idea!" Christy leaped at the possibility of bringing someone else into the picture. The sooner the better. "Just a minute," she said. "Who's Cody?"

"Cody Franklin…he's the newly elected sheriff and a

good friend. I don't know what his schedule is, so try the office first. If he's not at work, his home number's written in the front of the phone book."

Calling anyone, including the National Guard, sounded like an excellent plan to Christy. She found the impossibly thin phone book in the drawer. Good grief, she'd ordered from menus thicker than this.

Christy phoned the feed store first. The lady who answered said Russ had left a half hour earlier, and she hadn't a clue where he'd gone. Christy accepted this with a shrug. At the rate things were developing, she was about to take an advanced course in childbirth.

Christy found the sheriff's home number right where Taylor said it would be. She punched it out and waited impatiently for someone, anyone, to answer.

"Hello," a groggy voice muttered on the fourth ring.

"Hi, oh, thank God you answered." Christy was so relieved, she wanted to weep. She gulped in one giant breath and rushed to explain. "You don't know me. I'm Christy Manning, Taylor Palmer's sister, and Russ left an hour ago and promised he'd be back but he isn't and Taylor's water broke and she's in labor. She keeps insisting she won't leave for the hospital until Russ comes home, but he isn't here, and I don't know anything about delivering babies."

A short silence followed. "Taylor's in labor?"

"That's what I just finished saying. The second and equally important factor is that Russ, the father of this about-to-be-born-baby, isn't here. He said he'd only be gone an hour, but he's late, and Taylor really should be leaving for the hospital."

"Where did he say he was going?"

"The feed store. But he left there thirty minutes ago and...and *disappeared.*" That might be an exaggeration, but the situation called for a minor stretching of the truth, although she realized she'd made it sound as if he'd been abducted by aliens.

"I'll find him and be there as soon as I can."

The relief that washed over Christy felt like a cool evening rain after the hottest day of summer. Taylor needed her, and the last thing Christy wanted to do was reveal how much this situation frightened her. She'd made this trip to help Taylor with the baby. As in diaper, hold, burp. Not *deliver.*

She coaxed Taylor into the living room and had her lie down on the sofa. The ease with which Christy was able to convince her revealed a great deal about Taylor's condition. Although she struggled to disguise it, her dauntless older sister was scared. The pains were obviously far stronger than Taylor was willing to admit.

A whole lifetime seemed to pass before Christy heard a car barreling down the driveway. Taylor sighed audibly and relaxed against the pillows Christy had placed behind her back. "That's Russ now."

Christy hurried to the back door. She didn't recognize the car as Russ's, but that was the least of her worries. The four-wheel-drive Cherokee hadn't even come to a stop before her brother-in-law leaped out of the front seat.

He raced up the steps. "Where's Taylor?" he demanded.

Numb with relief, Christy sagged against the doorjamb and pointed toward the living room. She was about to follow her brother-in-law when a second man climbed out of the driver's seat.

Christy couldn't pull her eyes away from this tall, long-limbed stranger. It was all she could do not to throw her arms around him in thanks. "You must be Cody."

He touched the rim of his Stetson. "At your service. You must be Taylor's sister," he said, sauntering toward her.

"Christy Manning," she said in an authoritative voice, as if she had the situation completely under control and frequently delivered babies while vacationing. She stepped forward to offer the sheriff of Custer County her hand. In truth she was so grateful he'd found Russ that she was close to tears.

A few seconds later, Russ came out, carrying Taylor. "You ready?" he asked his friend.

"Russ, put me down," Taylor insisted. "I'm too heavy."

"We'll argue later, but at the moment you're about to give birth to my son," Russ reminded her with a worried frown.

"Our baby could very well be a girl," Taylor began. "You're still so pigheaded you refuse to—"

"I swear you're the only woman on God's green earth who'd argue with me at a time like this."

"I'd think you'd be used to it by now," Taylor mumbled, but her voice faded as a fresh contraction overtook her. She closed her eyes, pressed her hands to her belly and breathed deeply.

Russ's distraught gaze connected with Christy's.

"I'll get her suitcase," Christy said as she rushed into the master bedroom. When she reappeared, Cody took the single bag from her hands and put it inside the car. Taylor and Russ were already situated in the back seat, and the passenger door was open for Christy. Without another word, she climbed inside and snapped the seat belt in place.

The ride to the hospital took a full hour. Christy didn't need to look at the speedometer to know Cody was traveling well above the speed limit. If anything, she had to stop herself from pleading with him to go even faster.

Taylor did an admirable job of disguising the extent of

her discomfort, but it was apparent to all that the sooner she was under medical supervision the better. Russ was calm and collected.

It turned out that the carburetor in Russ's truck had started acting up, and he'd pulled over to the side of the road. Cody had found him bent over the engine, trying to fix it so he could make it back to the ranch.

Christy held herself tense until they reached the outskirts of Miles City. Only then did she feel herself start to relax.

Within ten minutes of their arrival at the hospital, Taylor was in the labor room with Russ at her side. Cody and Christy were relegated to the waiting room, where they leafed through six-month-old issues of *Time* magazine.

Soon bored with those, Christy found her gaze wandering to Cody. Fine lines fanned out from the corners of his dark eyes, and sharply cut grooves bracketed his mouth. He was tanned, his skin weathered by the sun and wind. He had the kind of rich bronze coloring that others strived to achieve under a sunlamp. His hair was thick and as dark as his eyes and cut military short. He wasn't handsome or stunning or anything else she could easily put a name to, but he was beyond a doubt the most uncompromisingly masculine man she'd ever seen. Immediately she experienced a faint stirring of guilt.

James. Dear, sweet James. Always so patient and understanding. She shouldn't even be *looking* at another man, not when she had James.

Cody glanced up from his magazine, and their eyes met. Christy managed to fake a smile. He returned it with a smile of his own and went back to reading. Christy made a pretense of doing the same thing. Despite her best efforts, her gaze wandered back to the sheriff again and again. It was somewhat embarrassing to realize that she wasn't studying him as a representative of law and order but as a man. Cody Franklin was incredibly male. Incredibly…incredible. Everything about him spoke of strength and purpose: his walk, the square set of his jaw, even the way he sat with his ankle resting over his knee. Disturbed by her unintended focus on the sheriff, she flipped through the pages of a two-year-old issue of *People*. Something was definitely wrong with her. No doubt it had to do with Taylor and the baby. Babies were said to stir up lots of feelings and buried emotions. What astonished her was that she should find this man so attractive.

Enough!

More determined than ever, Christy reached for another magazine and gazed unseeing at its pages.

"I take it you just arrived in Cougar Point?" Cody surprised her by asking.

"Last night," Christy said, setting aside the dog-eared issue of *People*. "Actually, it was early this morning when I went to bed. Russ left the house about the time I came down for coffee, and the next thing I knew, Taylor was telling me she was having these 'funny' pains, only I wasn't laughing, and neither was she."

"How long after that did you call me?"

"Too long," Christy said vehemently. "Taylor claimed the pains were nothing to worry about. I knew I shouldn't have listened to her. Good grief, what does she know?"

Cody smiled, and her eyes were immediately drawn to his full sensual mouth. Frustrated with herself, she quickly looked away.

"Don't be so hard on yourself. You handled the situation exactly the way you should have." He turned back to the periodical. Christy picked up another one herself, but when she glanced up, she saw Cody studying her. "I don't mean to stare," he apologized, "but I can't get over how much you and Taylor resemble each other."

That was almost worth a laugh. She'd hardly been able to keep her eyes off Cody Franklin from the moment they got to the hospital, and *he* was apologizing for staring at *her!* As for the part about the two sisters looking alike, Christy took that as a compliment. Taylor was stunning. In fact, Christy couldn't remember a time when her sister had been more beautiful than she was right now. Taylor was the beauty, not Christy. She didn't mean to sell herself short; she knew she was reasonably attractive. Perhaps the biggest difference was that Taylor had spunk. Her older sister had always displayed such tenacity, such mettle. When it came to dealing with their headstrong father, Taylor had more courage than the rest of them put together.

Anyone looking at the two sisters would know they were related; Christy was willing to grant the sheriff that much. Their deep blue eyes were a distinct family trait, also shared by their three older brothers, as was the slightly upturned nose.

The two sisters styled their hair differently. Taylor kept her thick chestnut hair long, whereas Christy preferred hers short in a breezy wash-and-wear style.

Christy was about to make some comment along the lines of what a peaceful community Cougar Point seemed to be when they saw Russ.

Cody and Christy stood as Russ approached, his eyes slightly dazed.

"Taylor's ready to go into the delivery room."

"So soon?" Christy's heart was in her throat. "We just got here." She paused long enough to check her watch—and restrain her panic. "We've only been here twenty minutes. How could she possibly be ready for the delivery room?"

"I don't know.... The nurse told me the baby's coming *now.*"

"It wasn't supposed to be this soon."

Russ wiped a hand down his face. "You're telling me? If Cody hadn't found me when he did..." He left the rest unsaid, but the implication was obvious.

Christy slumped back into the chair, her knees about to buckle. From everything she'd read and heard, babies were supposed to take their time, especially the first one. What about those twenty-hour labors her friends had described in minute detail? What about all the talk of first labors dragging on and on? Apparently Taylor hadn't been listening.

Russ returned to the double doors, then looked back into the waiting room. He swallowed hard, and Christy realized that if she'd been shaken by the news, it had affected Russ far more profoundly.

"Are you all right?" Cody asked her.

"Of course," she lied. "I'm not the one who's having a baby minutes after I arrive at the hospital." A fact for which Christy was eternally grateful. She wasn't nearly as courageous as Taylor; in fact, when it came right down to it, she considered herself a watered-down version of her older sister. All her life Christy had admired Taylor, wanting to be more like her. Instead, she was complacent and congenial, never causing her parents a moment's concern. Their father once claimed he owed every gray hair on his head to Taylor and every laugh line to Christy. His two daughters were the joy of his life, he often said.

"You look like you're going to faint," Cody said, watching her closely.

"Don't be ridiculous," she snapped, then instantly regretted her sharp tongue. She darted Cody an apologetic smile.

"Come on," Cody suggested, "let's walk. It'll help pass the time."

"Pass what time?" she muttered. "We've been here for about twenty minutes, and already Taylor's being wheeled into the delivery room."

"Come on, you could do with some activity—get your circulation going."

Christy merely nodded. Emotions were coming at her from every direction. Her first concern was for Taylor and the baby. The thought of this precious life, created in love, stirred a realm of deep feelings inside Christy. Her stomach started churning, her palms were sweating, and her heart seemed to be doing a jig. She couldn't have uttered a word had her life depended on it.

They walked the entire length of the hallway and stopped in front of the nursery. Christy carefully studied the row of newborns swaddled in pink and blue blankets and unexpectedly found tears clouding her eyes. Normally she wasn't sentimental or weepy. She didn't dare look over at Cody. He'd assume… She hadn't a clue what he'd assume, but it wouldn't be good.

"Christy?"

"The babies are really beautiful, aren't they?" she whispered, her gaze on the five infants.

"Yes, they are," he answered softly. He stood behind her and rested his hands on the curve of her shoulders. His touch was light, but it offered her a steadiness and comfort that had been lacking all morning. He didn't say anything when she brushed the telltale moisture from her cheeks, and Christy was grateful.

She didn't know what had come over her in the past few hours. She turned to face Cody, placed her hands on his forearms and stared up at him, her eyes bright with unshed tears.

Nothing seemed real anymore. It was as if she'd been walking around in a dream. A living fantasy was beginning to unfold right before her. Perhaps she'd spent too many hours on the road. Otherwise she wouldn't be looking into the darkest brown eyes she'd ever seen and thinking the things she was thinking.

Cody was staring back at her with the same wonder and surprise. He seemed about to say something important when the doors at the other end of the hall opened and Russ stepped out, wearing a green surgical gown and a large smile. Seeing him, both Christy and Cody rushed forward.

"It's a boy," Russ announced, his eyes shimmering with tears. He let out a wild shout of joy, grabbed a shocked Christy around the waist and boisterously whirled her around.

"Congratulations," Cody said, coming forward. The two men exchanged hearty handshakes, then hugged, slapping each other on the back.

Russ didn't speak for a moment and seemed to be composing himself. "He weighed in at eight pounds, three ounces, and he's the ugliest little critter you ever saw. Taylor kept saying how beautiful he is, and all I could see was this furious pink face bawling as loud as anything. His legs were pumping like an oil rig. That boy is madder than a wet wasp."

Christy felt tears in her eyes as she pressed her fingers to her lips. "How's Taylor?"

"She's fine…more than fine. That woman's incredible. I don't know what I ever did to deserve her, but I intend to thank God every day for the rest of my life." He half turned toward the doors he'd come through. "I've got to get back.

They're taking Eric into the nursery now, and the delivery room nurse said I could watch him being washed and dressed. If I have anything to say about it, I'll do the washing and dressing myself."

"You're naming him Eric?" Christy asked as she moved one step forward.

Russ nodded. "Eric Russell, after your father and me. Taylor insists."

"That sounds like a perfectly wonderful name to me," Christy whispered, surprised at the emotion that clogged her throat. Her father would be so proud, the buttons would pop right off his shirt.

"If you two walk over to the nursery, you might be able to see him, too," Russ added excitedly. "Taylor will be out of the delivery room anytime. I know she'll want to talk to you both, so stick around for a little bit, okay?"

Christy and Cody had already started in that direction when Russ stopped them. "Hey, one last thing. Taylor and I talked it over, and we want the two of you to be Eric's godparents."

Christy exchanged a meaningful glance with Cody before they simultaneously nodded.

"We'd be honored," Cody answered for them.

"Truly honored," Christy repeated, her throat tightening even more.

In her excitement Christy whirled around to face Cody—except that she hadn't realized he was quite so close. She flattened her hands against his chest as she smiled up at him, her joy overflowing now that her nephew was safely born.

Cody returned the smile. His dark eyes were alive with emotion.

Slowly, moving as if he were hypnotized, Cody slipped

his arms around her waist and raised her from the ground. Her hands clutched his shirt collar as his eyes delved into hers.

"I believe congratulations are in order, don't you?"

"Yes," she said, hugging him, afraid he was going to kiss her, equally afraid he wouldn't.

How would she ever explain kissing another man to James? How would she rationalize allowing Cody to hold her like this when she'd promised to spend her life loving someone else?

Two

"Oh, Taylor, he's so beautiful," Christy whispered. "Russ held him up for me to see and…" She paused, unable to continue. The minute she'd seen Eric, her heart had swollen with such a profound sense of love that it had been impossible to suppress her tears.

"You're crying," Taylor said softly.

Christy rubbed her cheeks. She reached for her sister, and they hugged with an intensity she'd never felt before. This wealth of emotion, of happiness, took Christy by storm.

"I love you, Taylor. I really do. And I love Eric, too. He's beautiful, perfect. I feel absolutely ecstatic." She straightened and gave a breathy laugh. "I want to throw open the windows and tell the world my sister just had a beautiful baby boy."

"Did you get a chance to talk to Mom and Dad?"

Christy nodded. The moment her mother heard the news she'd started weeping and then her father had taken the phone. His own voice hadn't sounded all that steady, either. Russ had done most of the talking with Christy crowded close beside him. When it was her turn, she seemed to jabber on like a magpie, but couldn't stop herself.

Following the conversation, Russ and Cody had gone to

the hospital gift shop to buy a box of cigars. Christy had spent these few moments alone with her sister.

"I'm sorry I frightened you," Taylor said apologetically, "but I didn't want to leave for the hospital without Russ."

"I understood. I wasn't worried." On the contrary, Christy had been nearly frantic, but it didn't matter now that everything had turned out so well.

Her sister sighed. "I'm glad you were able to meet Cody."

At the mention of the other man's name, Christy abruptly looked away, feeling uneasy. She hadn't had the chance to tell Taylor and Russ about her engagement to James Wilkens. Unfortunately the diamond ring James had given her was still at the jeweler's being sized. If she'd been wearing the ring, it would've been a logical introduction to her announcement. She'd meant to surprise her sister and brother-in-law with the big news as soon as she'd arrived, but it had been so late and everyone was exhausted. Then, before Christy knew it, it was morning and Taylor had gone into labor.

Now the timing was all wrong. Tomorrow, she promised herself, she'd tell Taylor. Everything would be less hectic then. But even as she formed that decision, Christy hesitated, not fully understanding why.

Her head spun and her thoughts skidded to a halt. Who did she think she was fooling?

She *did* know why.

Cody Franklin had hugged her when Russ had come to tell them about Eric. Now, an hour later, the way she'd felt in his arms still caused her pulse to accelerate. He'd pulled her close, and the feeling of being held by this man was completely and utterly natural, as instinctive as breathing or sleeping. It was as if they'd known each other all their lives. As if their relationship was one of long standing.

Without his saying a thing, Christy knew he'd experienced the same lavish range of sensations. They'd stared openly at each other, neither speaking. If Russ hadn't been there, Christy couldn't help wondering what would've happened. What they would've said to each other. If anything.

But Russ had been there, and after an awkward moment, Cody had released her. He'd dropped his arms with a reluctance that sent blood pounding through her veins until she grew dizzy simply remembering.

James was her fiancé! Yet she had to struggle to bring his image to mind. Her parents had been thrilled with the news of their engagement, but Christy had known they would be. Her father had told her often enough that James, an attorney, would make her an excellent husband. They'd been dating on and off for nearly two years, almost from the first week Christy had been hired as a paralegal at James's law firm. Their relationship, however, hadn't turned serious until three months ago. Until then, their dates had been casual get-togethers with mutual friends. Then they'd started working together on an important case. It had been a real coup for James to be assigned to defend Gary Mulligan against the Internal Revenue Service, and if everything went well, it could mean a partnership for him.

"Christy?"

She turned to her sister. "Sorry. Were you saying something?"

"Just that I'm glad you met Cody today."

"He...seems very nice," Christy answered, and sighed with relief when the nurse walked into the room, distracting her sister's attention from the subject of the sheriff. The woman brought in a huge bouquet of red roses in a tall crystal vase.

"Oh, my," Taylor breathed, reaching for the card. She

tore open the small envelope and read the message. Immediate tears filled her eyes. "They're from Russ."

"How sweet."

Taylor smiled softly as a faraway look came into her eyes. Christy speculated that her sister was recalling the first time she'd met Russ and all that had happened since. Russ might not have been the man her family would've chosen for Taylor, but one fact had been clear from the instant they flew to Seattle to attend their parents' anniversary party. Russ Palmer loved Taylor. Beyond question. Beyond doubt. Whatever reservations Christy and her brothers held regarding this marriage had been quickly dissolved.

Footsteps from behind Christy told her Russ and Cody had returned.

"Russ…" Taylor held out her arms to her husband. "The roses are so beautiful. Thank you."

Christy's brother-in-law walked across the room, and his eyes closed as he took his wife into his arms. He whispered something in her ear; Taylor smiled and nodded. The scene was an intimate one, and Christy felt like an intruder. She backed away, not looking at Cody until it was impossible to avoid him.

"Hello, again," he said. His voice was low and his smile contained a warmth and depth that multiplied a hundredfold all the sensations she'd experienced earlier, the very feelings she was trying to put out of her mind. Once again Christy was struck by the possessiveness she felt looking at him, studying him. For the past hour she'd been trying to understand why she should feel anything toward him. Nothing had come to her. No insights. Nothing.

They were barely more than strangers, and yet she felt completely comfortable with him. At the same time, he rattled her composure unlike anyone she'd ever met. It seemed absurdly ironic to be so flustered by a man and still feel so sheltered.

Cody glanced toward Russ and Taylor. "Would you like to go down to the nursery to view our godson?"

She nodded, gladly accepting an excuse to leave husband and wife alone.

Together she and Cody walked down the familiar corridor until they stood in front of the large nursery window. But it wasn't the newborns that captured their attention. They made comments about little Eric and the other babies, but what interested them most was each other. After a while they gave up the pretense of looking at the newborns.

"Russ phoned the ranch and is having a couple of his hands drive a car over for him," Cody said after a while. "He's planning to spend the day with Taylor."

Once more Christy nodded. It seemed all she was capable of doing. Being this close to Cody felt like being trapped in a magnetic force field. It didn't matter how much she resisted, she was drawn to him.

With a determined effort, she diverted her attention to Eric again. The infant was sleeping, swaddled in a pale blue receiving blanket. A long-sleeved T-shirt covered his tiny arms and fists. He was so small, so adorable.

Cody's eyes followed hers, and when he spoke, his voice was filled with astonishment. "He's really something, isn't he?"

"Yes." Her voice was a whisper. "And to think we could've ended up delivering him."

"We?" Cody joked. "In all my years of law enforcement I've been spared that. Thank God."

Standing behind her, Cody's large hands held her shoulders, as if he'd been holding and touching her for a lifetime. It felt right and good to have this man so close. A small shudder skimmed down her spine at the innocent contact.

Cody must have noticed it, because he turned her around to face him, his eyes narrowing slightly. "You're trembling."

She couldn't deny it. This man she hardly knew confused her, bewildered her. The worst part was that she couldn't understand why. She'd met and dated any number of attractive, compelling men before. Yet none of them had ever overwhelmed her the way Cody did.

"Are you cold?"

"No," she answered quickly, flustered by his questions.

"What's wrong?"

How could she possibly explain something she couldn't grasp herself? "Nothing."

His eyes found hers, and she could've sworn they went several shades darker. "Does this happen often?"

"No." She shook her head. "Does it to you?" Christy swallowed, astonished she'd had the courage to ask him such a personal question.

"No," he answered after a moment. "Never."

She pulled her gaze away, baffled by his openness. His honesty. It was exactly what she'd longed to hear. And what she'd feared.

"I… I need to get back to the ranch," she said, seeking an excuse to do something, anything to end this heightened awareness between them. "Taylor asked me to make some phone calls for her."

Cody lowered his eyes to her lips, his look, unhurried and sensual, as intimate as a kiss. Christy's stomach became a churning mass of doubts, mingled with an abundance of misgivings. She wanted to blame this feeling on the chaotic events of the day.

Slowly, almost unaware of what she was doing, Christy raised her own eyes to meet Cody's. He didn't look too comfortable. In fact, he seemed as perplexed and hesitant as she.

"I need to get back myself," he murmured.

Not until that moment did Christy realize the only way she had of returning to Cougar Point was with Cody. A sinking feeling assailed her. She couldn't possibly avoid an hour or more with him in the intimate confines of his vehicle.

Cody Franklin had no idea what was happening between him and his best friend's sister-in-law. To be honest, he hadn't paid Christy Manning much attention until they were in the hospital waiting room. She'd been terribly agitated, flipping through one magazine after another. Cody doubted she'd read a single word.

Then Russ had appeared and said that Taylor was ready for the delivery room, and Cody had watched as Christy started to completely unravel.

He'd suggested they take a short walk in an effort to help her relax. He didn't know how much comfort he'd be to her, since he was a stranger, but the least he could do was try. He knew from his years as a lawman that some physical activity might help take her mind off her sister.

It was when they'd stopped to look at the babies in the nursery that Cody had felt the faint stirring of something more. Faint stirring, hell, it was like a fist to his gut!

From that moment on, some emotion had started to awaken deep within him. He experienced a lost sensation, as if he were charting unknown land, and each turn led him farther away from all that was familiar. He was suddenly at a loss for words; he'd planned to involve her in conversation, occupy her with inane chitchat about Seattle and her job to keep her from thinking about Taylor, but he hadn't asked a single question.

Every time Cody started to speak, he got lost in her eyes. He'd never seen a woman with eyes quite this blue. They reminded him of the coldest days of winter, when everything around him seemed to anticipate the promise of spring. When she smiled, those same blue eyes brightened even more, and it was like watching sunshine emerge after rain.

She'd look at him, and Cody swore he could see all the way to her soul. She was guileless and genuine and so lovely, it was all he could do not to stare at her, something he'd already apologized for once that day.

Twice he'd placed his hands on her shoulders. It wasn't his habit to comfort women with physical gestures, and he didn't understand his own actions. When he'd first held her, she'd obviously been shaken by Russ's news about Taylor, and he'd reached out in an effort to steady her.

The moment his hands had closed over her shoulders, his heart had begun racing like a runaway train. That hadn't happened since he was thirteen and had kissed a girl for the very first time.

Twenty-two years had passed, and the impact now was nearly as strong. Every minute with her he learned something new about himself, and every emotion he discovered only bewildered him more.

"I'm sorry if it's an inconvenience for you to take me out to the ranch," Christy said, sliding into the front seat of his four-wheel drive.

"It isn't a problem." The only difficulty it created was of his own making. He was caught in some mysterious web of yearning. Perhaps, in some strange way, this all had to do with Russ and Taylor. He couldn't help envying the happiness his friends had found. Taylor was the best thing that had ever happened to Russ Palmer, and now Russ was a father.

Cody paused, half expecting to feel a twinge of jealousy or resentment. When he was introduced to Taylor a year ago, he'd wanted to date her himself, but she'd already met Russ and it was clear that she was falling in love with him. Cody had stood on the sidelines and watched their romance unfold, amused at the way they'd both fought it so hard.

No, jealousy hadn't prompted these feelings; he was convinced of that. His only reaction was happiness for his friends—a pure sense of shared joy.

The drive, which had seemed like four hundred miles earlier in the day with Taylor and Russ in the backseat, went quickly on the return trip. Christy said little, but neither seemed uneasy with the silence. Occasionally Cody would look over at her, and their eyes would meet. Each time, some magic would pass involuntarily between them, some entrancement. After a while it became a challenge to discover what fascinated him about Taylor's sister, and he found his gaze repeatedly drawn to her as he attempted to analyze his attraction.

She was pretty, but no prettier than any number of women he'd dated. Not as beautiful as Becca. He paused, surprised that he didn't immediately feel a jolt of pain as he thought about her. It had been three years since Becca had turned his life upside down. He tried not to think of her at all, tried to ignore her memory as though he'd never known her at all. For the most part he succeeded… For the most part.

"Would you like to stop and get something to eat?" Cody asked as they neared Cougar Point. He wasn't hungry so much as reluctant to leave her.

He should've been exhausted. He'd had only a couple of hours sleep in the past forty-eight. Instead he felt alive. Reborn.

All he knew was that he'd met a woman, a warm, caring, generous woman, and he felt as if his life was starting over again.

"I'm starved," Christy said enthusiastically. "I was so

concerned about Taylor this morning that I forgot to eat breakfast."

"I haven't had anything, either."

"I got you out of bed when I phoned, didn't I?"

Cody nodded. Hell, he'd give his right hand to have her wake him every morning. "I worked the graveyard shift last night."

"You must be exhausted."

On the contrary, Cody had never felt more energetic. "Not at all," he said, mustering a smile to reassure her. "There are a couple of decent restaurants in town, but if you're interested in breakfast, the best place to eat is the bowling alley."

"Great."

Cody had expected her to laugh or to question his choice. She was, after all, a city girl, and he doubted that anyone in Seattle had ever taken her out to eat at a bowling alley. But she accepted his choice enthusiastically.

Since it was midafternoon by this time, the parking lot was nearly deserted. Christy didn't wait for him to come around and open the door for her, a fact that didn't surprise him. Taylor hadn't waited for him to open her door the one time he'd gone out with her, either.

Cody chose a booth toward the back of the restaurant and slid into the red vinyl seat. Christy sat across from him and reached for the menu, which was tucked between the sugar bowl and the salt and pepper shakers.

"Howdy, Cody," Mary Andrews said as she came over to the table, carrying two water glasses. She glanced curiously at Christy.

"This is Taylor's sister, Christy Manning. Christy, Mary Andrews."

"I don't suppose Taylor had her baby, did she?" Mary asked.

Christy's eyes softened as she nodded. "This morning. Eric Russell Palmer weighed in at eight pounds, three ounces."

Mary grinned from ear to ear. "That's terrific. You don't mind if I let folks know, do you?"

Christy shook her head. "Please do."

Still grinning, Mary pulled a small pad from her apron pocket. "What can I get for you two?"

"I'll have the breakfast special," Christy said, closing her menu. "With coffee."

"So will I," Cody said, sliding his own menu back into place.

Mary wrote down their order, then walked back to the kitchen.

For a long time Cody said nothing. Partly because he didn't know what to say and partly because he didn't feel the need to fill the silence with small talk. He was comfortable with Christy. He hadn't felt that way with any woman, ever. He looked over at her and wondered if she was experiencing this same sense of serenity, and instinctively knew she was. "What are you thinking?" he asked as Mary filled two cups with coffee.

Christy added cream to hers, took a sip and smiled. "If we're Eric's godparents, does that mean the two of us are related?"

A grin lit his face. "I suppose it does. I'm just not sure how."

"Me, neither."

One thing he did know: the idea of being linked to Christy pleased him immeasurably. "Tell me about yourself." He wanted to know everything there was to know about her from the time she was in preschool to the present.

"I'm the youngest of five."

"Spoiled?"

"Terribly."

He deliberately drew his gaze away from her mouth, which had fascinated him for several minutes. Beyond question, he knew he was going to kiss her. He didn't know when. Soon, if possible. Nor did he know where. Only that it was quickly becoming an obsession.

"What about you?" Christy asked, pulling a napkin from the holder and spreading it across her lap, taking time to smooth it out. She seemed to be avoiding eye contact with him. That didn't surprise Cody. He'd been blatantly staring at her every chance he got. Her mouth enthralled him as nothing ever had. Soft. Pink. Moist. Just right for kissing.

"What about you?" she repeated, and the question seemed to echo.

"I was born in Miles City," he said, focusing on his coffee. "In the same hospital as Eric, as a matter of fact."

"Was your father a rancher?"

"No. He was a lawman, just as his father was before him. The Franklins have a long tradition of upholding law and order in Custer County."

"Did you always want to work for the sheriff's department?"

"Always. For as long as I can remember I dreamed of wearing a badge."

"They must be proud of you," she said in a way that made his heart quicken. What she was said was true. But his father and grandfather would never know he'd been elected sheriff; his two younger sisters were the only family he had left.

Cody didn't want to talk about himself, not when there

was so much to learn about her. "What did *you* want to be when you were a kid?"

"Not a paralegal," she said, then looked away, as if the words had slipped out before she could stop them. "I didn't even know what they were until high school. Sad to say, my dreams were far more traditional. I wanted to be a mommy."

"And now?"

"And now," she repeated in a whisper, frowning.

She was saved from having to answer by Mary, who brought two platters to their table. Each was heaped high with steaming hash browns, scrambled eggs, sausage and toast.

Their conversation ceased as they both picked up their forks. Neither spoke for several minutes.

"I didn't realize how hungry I was," Christy said, reaching for the small container of jam. She peeled back the cover and scooped out the preserves with her knife.

"Where's Mandy?" Cody asked, remembering Russ's teenage sister, who lived with Russ and Taylor, for the first time that day.

"She's with a friend. Russ phoned from the hospital and told her about Eric. She had lots of questions and was sorry she missed all the excitement."

Cody pushed his empty plate aside. Mary stopped by the table to refill their coffee mugs and take away Cody's plate.

"You might as well take mine, too," Christy said, leaning back in the booth. She placed her hands over her flat stomach and sighed. "I can't believe I ate all that."

"Can I get you anything else?" Mary asked.

"Nothing, thanks," Cody answered for them.

Mary set the bill on the table and walked away with a quick backward wave.

They left the restaurant a few minutes later. Cody opened

the door for Christy, insisting on the courtesy because he enjoyed doing something, however small, for her.

She seemed preoccupied and anxious on the ride to the Lazy P. He started to ask her how long she planned to stay, but even before he'd finished the question, he knew she wasn't listening.

"I'm sorry. What did you say?" she asked, glancing at him.

"It wasn't important." He pulled off the main road and headed down the long, dusty driveway. This time of year the road was filled with ruts deep enough to send them both bouncing around the interior of his Cherokee if he wasn't careful to watch where he was driving. In several spots he slowed down to ten or so miles an hour. Then he was forced to ask himself if it was his car he was concerned about—or the fact that the sooner he arrived at the ranch, the sooner he'd have to leave Christy.

Once he reached the ranch yard, he turned off the engine and climbed out of the cab. Christy had opened the car door, offering him just the excuse he needed to touch her. His hands slid around her slim waist and he lifted her down.

She hadn't been expecting his help and, caught off guard, she fell forward. She made a small sound as her hands came into contact with his chest.

Neither moved. Cody couldn't believe how good it felt to have her in his arms again.

"I'm sorry," she whispered.

"I'm not." Cody had never been one to beat around the bush, as the saying went. "Not in the least," he added.

Her hands were against his chest, and he wondered if she could feel how fast his heart was beating, wondered if she had even an inkling of what he was feeling.

"Thanks for breakfast and the ride home," she murmured, but made no effort to move away from him.

Heat radiated from where her hands were touching him, warming him in ways he couldn't understand but didn't question. She tensed her fingers as if to pull away, but if that was her intention, she didn't follow through.

Cody raised his hand to the side of her neck. His fingers stroked the kitten-soft skin there, and he watched, fascinated, as she slowly closed her eyes.

Once more his gaze sought her mouth. Her lush, vulnerable mouth. Never had it looked more inviting than it did at that moment.

It seemed only natural to kiss her. Hell, he'd been thinking about doing exactly that for hours, but now that the opportunity presented itself, he hesitated. It was as if an inborn defense mechanism flashed a warning through his system. Kiss Christy Manning and you'll never be the same again, it seemed to be saying.

But the words of caution counted for nothing. Cody couldn't have stopped himself if he'd wanted to. Whatever came after, whatever life held for him, whatever the cost, he was going to kiss this woman.

Unhurriedly, deliberately, he pressed his lips over hers. She murmured something, Cody didn't know what, and he felt the movement against his mouth.

Her lips were everything Cody had dreamed they would be. Warm. Moist. Devastating. With a whimper she responded immediately. It was as if he'd never kissed a woman before this moment.

Her arms made their way around his neck as she leaned into him. Her softness melded into his hardness, and white-hot sensation seemed to explode inside him. Cody kissed her again and again, his hands in her hair, cradling the back of her head. He kissed her until his breathing became labored. Until he heard her moan, and then realized it was his own sigh of longing that echoed in his ears. Still he didn't release her. He held her against him, never wanting to let her go.

Only when Christy stiffened did Cody slacken his hold. Slowly he opened his eyes to discover her looking up at him, her beautiful eyes bright with tears. He frowned because he didn't understand. Then, in a heartbeat, he did. The kissing had affected her as profoundly as it had him.

"I know what you're thinking," he whispered, lifting her chin with his finger, dropping his mouth to hers, unable to resist.

"You don't," she said. "You couldn't possibly know."

"But I do," he countered. "You're thinking this is the craziest thing that's ever happened to you. I know because that's exactly what I'm thinking. We just met this morning, and yet I feel I've known you all my life."

Her eyes widened as if his words had hit their mark.

"All of this is because of Taylor and Russ," she told him. "Their happiness, their excitement must be rubbing off on us. Don't you see how foolish this is?"

"No." He didn't mean to be blunt or obtuse. He was nearly thirty-five years old and long past the age of playing games. Christy was younger, but she knew, the same way he did. She might choose to deny it, but he wouldn't.

"Are you saying you didn't want me to kiss you?" he asked, trusting her to be honest, because he didn't believe she could be anything else.

It took her a minute to answer him, and when she did her voice was raspy. "That's the problem.... I've never wanted anything more."

Three

Christy woke early the next morning after a restless night's sleep. She'd tossed and turned so frequently that the sheets had been pulled loose from the bed and the bedspread had slipped onto the floor. Staring up at the ceiling, Christy slowly expelled her breath while mulling over the events of the day before.

So much had happened.

Taylor's son had been born, and Christy had been introduced to the newly elected sheriff of Custer County.

However, Christy had more than *met* Cody Franklin. He'd taken her to breakfast late in the afternoon, and when he dropped her off at the ranch, he'd kissed her—and she'd let him. More than *let* him; she'd encouraged him. What she'd told him was true. She'd never wanted anyone's kiss more.

Admitting as much certainly wasn't one of her more intelligent moves, but then it hadn't been her mind doing the talking. It had been her heart.

Once again she tried to focus her thoughts on James. He'd been so sweet the evening he'd given her the engagement ring. They'd gone out for dinner, sitting at the table with candlelight flickering and soft music playing in the background. Christy had noticed that he'd barely touched his meal. He seemed nervous, then started talking nonstop. Normally James was a calm, quiet man, not easily agitated. He'd been rambling for about fifteen minutes, and Christy couldn't figure out where the discussion was leading. She'd told him so. Then James had gotten flustered.

Before Christy could react, James pulled a ring box from the inside of his suit pocket. He'd been so endearing, so wonderfully sweet as he held out the diamond, letting the ring speak for him.

By then Christy had become so flustered herself that all she could do was stare at the lovely solitary diamond glittering up at her. James had withdrawn it from its velvet bed, and without a word she'd given him her hand.

The entire thing hadn't taken more than a few seconds. She'd promised to become his wife, promised to pledge her life to him without a word of love spoken between them. James cared for her, Christy felt assured of it. He wouldn't have offered her the ring if he didn't. By the same token, she loved him. Otherwise she wouldn't have accepted his proposal.

Afterward, James had been ecstatic as he'd hugged and kissed her. The ring was too large and had nearly slipped off her finger as she'd shown it to her parents that same night. Both Eric and Elizabeth Manning had been thrilled with the news of Christy's engagement to the up-and-coming attorney.

It wasn't until two days later, just before she left for Montana, that the first of the doubts had come. She loved James, she reminded herself, repeating it again and again on the endless drive across three states.

James was a good man. He'd been a friend long before

they'd become romantically involved, and judging by everything she'd read, friends made the best husbands.

Perhaps the most convincing argument for this marriage was how comfortable Christy felt with him. Her parents thought the world of James; in fact, they seemed more excited than she was about the prospect of his joining the family. Her father talked of little else, promising Christy the wedding of the year.

But if she'd been experiencing a few niggling doubts before she left Seattle, they'd multiplied a hundredfold since she'd arrived in Montana and met Cody Franklin.

Cody.

For more reasons than she dared explore, she struggled to push every thought of the sheriff from her mind.

With a determination born of pride and a sense of fairness and truth that had been ingrained in her from birth, Christy decided to tell Russ, tell someone, anyone, about her engagement. She climbed out of bed and got dressed, then went in seach of her brother-in-law.

Russ, however, had already left the house. A note was propped against the sugar bowl, explaining he'd be with his men that morning, and she shouldn't look for him before noon. He also wrote that he wouldn't be able to visit Taylor and the baby until that evening. He signed his name, adding that Christy should make herself at home.

Defeat settled over Christy. She couldn't keep quiet about herself and James much longer and still hold her head high.

It took only an hour to straighten up the house. She cooked herself some eggs, then realized she wasn't hungry. Russ, on the other hand, had apparently fixed himself a breakfast large enough to feed five men. He'd made a minimal effort to clean the kitchen; clearly, he'd been in a rush.

With time to spare, Christy wandered outside, wanting to investigate what she could of the grounds. Since Russ was visiting Taylor that evening, she'd drive to the hospital in the afternoon.

One hand leading a chestnut horse paused and stared at her when she appeared.

"Good morning," Christy said cheerfully.

"Howdy." The lanky cowboy straightened and touched the rim of his hat. He looped the reins around a fencepost, then walked toward her. A fistful of cigars with pale blue bands was sticking out of his shirt pocket, evidence of Russ's eagerness to spread the news of his son's birth.

"You must be part of Mrs. Palmer's family."

"Christy Manning," she said, holding out her hand. "I'm Taylor's sister."

The middle-aged man took pains to remove his thick leather glove and clasped her soft palm in his callused one. "Pleased to make your acquaintance. Russ is out this morning, but I s'pect he'll be back soon. Most folks call me Billy Joe."

"Good to meet you, Billy Joe," Christy said, looking toward the barn. Several horses stuck their sleek heads over the stall doors, glancing at her with open curiosity.

"If you'll excuse me," Billy Joe said, backing away from her. His horse was saddled and waiting, prancing in place. "This gelding's anxious to be on his way."

"Of course. I'm sorry. I didn't mean to hold you up."

"No problem." He mounted the gelding in a single smooth motion. Pulling back on the reins, Billy Joe nodded at her once more, then galloped out of the yard.

Left to her own devices, Christy wandered toward the barn, stopping in front of the first stall. The name Shadow was burned into a wood plaque above the door.

"Howdy, Shadow," Christy said. "You look like a friendly horse." Friendly enough, at any rate, for her to venture petting his nose. She stroked it a few times while the gelding took pride in revealing his teeth and nickered his approval.

Seeing a large barrel of grain near the middle of the barn, Christy stepped over to it, intending to reach for a handful of oats. She didn't know much about horses, but figured a handful of oats would win approval.

"I thought I might find you in here," a deep male voice said from the barn door.

Christy's heart shot to her throat. Cody. She turned to see him silhouetted against the morning sunlight. Tall, lean and dark. He wore jeans and a western shirt with a string tie and was so strikingly handsome that for a moment all she could do was stare.

"Hello," she said, returning to her task, her hands trembling. It wasn't fair that he should have this effect on her. But then, she was learning that little in life was fair.

Her hand loaded with grain, she walked back to Shadow's stall.

"Be sure to feed that to him with your palm flat, otherwise he might inadvertently bite you," Cody warned, moving toward her.

Christy was grateful for the advice and did as he suggested. Shadow ate the oats quickly, and when he'd finished, Christy wiped her hand on her jeans. Her heart was hammering so hard, she was certain Cody could hear it.

"Did you sleep well?"

"No," she answered honestly. Her back was to him, but that didn't help. She felt warm and dizzy just knowing he was there.

"I couldn't, either." His voice was soft and raspy. Sensual. "I only had a couple of hours of sleep the night before, so I should've nodded off the minute my head touched the pillow. But I didn't. I couldn't."

Christy found a strange comfort in knowing his sleep had been as unsettled as her own. "I…tossed and turned most of the night, then finally drifted off toward morning."

"Me, too."

When he'd left her the night before, she'd stood inside the house and watched him drive away, feeling restless and uneasy. That disquiet hadn't dissipated until the moment he'd stepped into the barn. Cody spoke, and instantly the emptiness had started to leave her, as if a sense of order had been restored to her life.

Except that it wasn't right. Everything was very, very wrong.

"We need to talk."

"Yes," she whispered. She'd meant to tell Russ about James, knowing her brother-in-law would mention the fact to Cody. But this was better. She could tell Cody herself. Explain before either of them got hurt. Before things went too far.

Honesty really was the best policy. She'd grown up believing that. Practicing it.

Christy was searching for just the right words, irritated with herself for not having thought this out beforehand. There should be an easy way to say it. The truth shouldn't be this difficult.

Then Cody was behind her, so close she could feel the heat radiating from his body. His hands settled over her shoulders, his touch light and warm and reassuring. Slowly he turned her around so she faced him.

Their eyes locked, and Christy's throat went tight. His were beautiful, as dark and rich as the finest coffee. They were the eyes of a man who'd only recently learned to dream. Wistful eyes. Pensive eyes.

"Every time I'd try to sleep, all I could think about was you." His tone said that he'd struggled long and hard against allowing her to dominate his thoughts.

"It was the same with me." She shouldn't have told him that. Shouldn't admit his effect on her in one breath and then tell him about James in the next. "But I—"

"I couldn't stop thinking about how good you felt in my arms."

She knew exactly what he was saying because she'd experienced the same thing herself. He felt good to her, too, the kind of good that made everything feel right even when it was wrong. The kind of good that never diminished, never ceased.

"You felt it, didn't you?" He seemed to need confirmation from her.

She gave it reluctantly, breathlessly, lowering her eyes. "Yes."

They lapsed into silence then, as though neither of them knew what else to say. There didn't seem to be any need for words. Christy understood what Cody was thinking and feeling as clearly as if he'd spoken.

I need to kiss you again and discover if last night was real. He asked her with his eyes.

No, her heart cried. She couldn't allow it. If Cody kissed her again, she'd be forced to confront issues she dared not face. Cody Franklin was a stranger. James was her fiancé. Her friend.

I've frightened you.

No, came the cry from the farthest corner of her heart. *Yes,* she countered immediately. Cody stirred emotions she didn't know she was capable of feeling. Emotions she'd never experienced with any man. Each time they were together, her awareness of him became more intense. This shouldn't be happening to her. Not now. Not *ever.* She was engaged to another man.

Frowning, Cody took one step toward her. Christy's heart surged.

Don't, please, don't, she pleaded silently. *I can't refuse you. I can't refuse myself.*

But Cody had apparently given up listening to the cries of her heart. When she looked at him, he was both watchful and silent.

Before another second could pass, he reached for her, and whatever resistance she'd been able to muster burst like the white filaments of a dandelion in the wind. His mouth found hers, smooth and firm against her softness. She moaned in protest, but her small cry soon became a sigh of welcome, of need, of pleasure.

A tenderness blossomed within her, the sensations so exquisite they shocked her even more than they had a day earlier. It shouldn't be this good, this wonderful, she told herself over and over, wanting to weep with frustration. Yet it was better than anything she'd ever experienced.

Cody continued to kiss her with a passion and an excitement that left Christy clinging to him.

"I can't believe this," he murmured, and her mind echoed his words. She was struggling with reality, and felt lost and weak.

Cody bent his head and dropped a succession of kisses down her neck and along her jaw until she moaned. He responded with a small, throaty sound and quickly joined their mouths again, kissing hers softly.

Christy went weak with need. She was melting from the heat. Burning up with fever. Consumed with a sweet warmth that threatened to devour her. "No," she whimpered. "We can't do…this."

Cody raised his hands and held them against the sides of her face.

He was going too fast for her. Her own body was going too fast for her. She felt as though she were sitting on a runaway horse, galloping out of control, being propelled farther and farther away from reason.

"I feel as if I've been waiting for you all my life," Cody whispered, wrapping his arms completely around her. His hand reached up to smooth the hair from her temple. "I can only imagine what you must think of me coming here like this."

Her eyes remained closed, and her dark world continued to spin without restraint. Even when she opened her eyes, everything was blurred and out of focus, her thoughts hopelessly addled.

"I didn't mean to shock you," he said.

"You didn't. I shocked myself."

Cody worked his thumbs sensuously across the high curve of her cheekbones. He frowned as he felt her tears. "I hurt you?"

"No…" she murmured, looking away. Now she understood the restless feeling she'd experienced all night. She'd been haunted by his kiss, haunted by the emotions and the need he'd created within her.

All of this had to stop. Now. This instant. She pressed her forehead against his solid chest, needing his strength in order to find the courage to say what she had to say.

His hand lifted her hair, his touch gentle as though fingering strands of silk.

"I fall apart when you kiss me," she confessed.

His throaty laugh was filled with amusement and tenderness. "*You* fall apart?" He captured her hand and pressed it over his heart. "See what you do to me?"

She didn't need to touch him to realize how his pulse was churning beneath her palm. Unable to watch the disillusionment in his eyes when she told him about James, she closed her own.

"I've never felt anything for anyone as strongly as I have for you," she said softly. Then she didn't say anything more for a long moment, carefully formulating her words.

Cody obviously sensed that she felt troubled because he tucked his finger under her chin and raised her head. His gaze caressed her. "Christy?"

"Please listen," she whispered, her voice trembling. "There's something you should know, something I meant to tell you from the first, only—"

"Cody, what are you doing here?" Russ's voice echoed through the barn like thunder. "Everything's all right with Taylor, isn't it?" Christy's brother-in-law stopped abruptly when he saw Cody's arms around her waist. He removed his Stetson and wiped his forehead with the back of his hand. "I wasn't interrupting anything, was I?"

"Your timing couldn't be worse," Cody barked, glaring at his friend.

Russ didn't appear the least bit concerned. He tossed a load of baling wire into his pickup and promptly reached for another. If anything, he looked amused.

"This isn't funny."

Russ paused. "Now that's where I disagree. You just met Christy. Until yesterday you hadn't so much as set eyes on her. I don't mind telling you, Franklin, I've never known you to work so fast."

"Shut your fool mouth before you say something I'll

make you regret," Cody grumbled. His threat wasn't worth a dime and Russ knew it, but he felt he had to respond.

"She is a pretty little thing, isn't she?" Another wheel of wire landed on top of the first with a loud, discordant clang. He turned to stare at Cody when he didn't answer right away. "Isn't she?" he repeated.

"Yes," Cody admitted grudgingly.

"For a moment there, it looked like the two of you had been kissing." Once more Russ paused, a grin turning up the edges of his mouth.

"I *was* kissing her," Cody said, challenging Russ to make something of the fact if he wanted to. He was as uncomfortable as he could ever remember being with his friend. Russ was curious to learn what was going on between him and Christy, but unfortunately Cody could think of no way of explaining his feelings for Christy, especially with the mood Russ was in. His friend seemed to find the situation downright comical.

"I guessed as much." Russ wiped the sweat from his brow, but Cody had a sneaking suspicion that he did so to cover a smile. Not that Russ had any trouble poking fun at him and letting him know it.

After Russ arrived, and the three of them had exchanged pleasantries, Christy excused herself and left, saying that she was driving to Miles City to visit Taylor and Eric. Cody would have offered to go with her, but he was working swing shift and it wasn't likely that he'd be back before he was scheduled to go on duty.

"You're not going to get closemouthed with me now, are you?" Russ was asking. "I can't say I've ever seen you take to a woman the way you have to Taylor's sister. What's different about Christy?"

"What was different about Taylor?"

Russ chuckled. "Touché. But if you remember correctly, all Taylor and I could do at first was argue. Never met a woman who could irritate me as much as she did."

"You didn't stay angry at her for long."

Russ shook his head. "No, can't say I did. She'd make me so furious I couldn't think straight. Before I could stop myself, I'd say or do some fool thing I'd end up regretting. That certainly doesn't seem to be the case with you and Christy, though. You two can't seem to keep your hands off each other."

Cody decided it was best to ignore that comment. "You and Taylor worked things out, and that's what matters."

Some of the humor disappeared from Russ's dark eyes. "We did, didn't we?" A faraway expression came over him. "Did you get a good look at him, Cody?"

Before Cody could respond Russ continued. "The nurse handed me Eric, and I swear something happened to my heart. It was the craziest thing, holding that baby in my arms and loving him so much my throat got all clogged up. I couldn't have said a word if my life depended on it. Before I knew what was happening, tears were rolling down my face. *Me.* I can't remember the last time I cried. I've never felt anything as incredible as holding my son.

"You know, I loved Taylor before the baby was born, but it pales in comparison to what I felt for her as she struggled to give birth to Eric. I've always thought of women as the weaker sex, but I was wrong." He shook himself as if waking from a deep sleep, his eyes as somber as Cody had ever seen.

"You have reason to be proud."

"I bought every box of cigars the gift shop owned."

"I know. I was with you."

"Hell, I don't even smoke."

Cody laughed. "I know that, too." He hesitated, uncertain how to proceed. "About Christy… You don't have any objection to my seeing her, do you?"

"So you plan to take her to Sitting Bull Lookout?" The ridge above the town had been their favorite necking place as teenagers.

"Probably," Cody answered, trying to hold back a grin.

Russ tucked his hands in his hip pockets. "Then you really are serious?"

"I've never been more serious in my life," Cody admitted without a pause.

Taylor was sound asleep when Christy got to the hospital. Her sister's long hair spread out over the white pillows like spilled coffee. Her eyes were closed, her breathing deep and even.

Tiptoeing into the room so as not to disturb her, Christy pulled out the lone chair and sat. Although she'd been on the road for more than an hour, she remained as upset and nervous as when she'd left the house.

She felt like weeping. She felt like rejoicing. No woman should experience such conflicting emotions.

The obedient, do-what's-right-at-all-costs part of her kept reminding her of James. Loyal, hardworking James, who loved her.

All her life Christy had done what was right. She'd never been rebellious. She'd been a model child. A model sister. Respectful. Considerate. Thoughtful.

She felt none of those things now.

The look Cody had given her just before Russ stepped into the barn would be forever burned in her mind. It was the kind of look a woman dreams of receiving from a man sometime in her life. A lover's look. One so intimate and personal that it could never be explained to another.

If this intense feeling between her and Cody was wrong, then why did Christy feel so good inside? Why did she long to throw up her arms and shout for joy? If this was being rebellious or disrespectful, then all Christy could say was that she was entering puberty later than the normal teenager. About ten years later.

Taylor stirred and opened her eyes. "Christy," she said, yawning. "When did you arrive?"

"About five minutes ago."

"You should have woken me."

"And interrupted your nap?" she teased. "How are you feeling?"

"Wonderful." A soft smile touched her eyes. "Eric spent most of the morning with me. Oh, Christy, he's so adorable. We became acquainted with each other. I counted his fingers and toes, and he taught me about breast-feeding."

"You look happy."

"I am… I really am."

Christy settled farther down in the chair. Trying not to be obvious, she stared at the floor, studying the pattern in the white tile. "Cody took me out to eat when we left here yesterday."

"In Miles City?"

"No. We went to the bowling alley in Cougar Point."

"I'm glad." There was a pause. "He's a good man."

Christy knew that instinctively. "I thought so, too. I like him, Taylor. I really do."

"Why do you look so guilty?"

How could she look or feel anything else? But Taylor wouldn't understand. Her sister had no way of knowing about the lovely engagement ring being sized at the Seattle jewelers.

They chatted for a few minutes before Taylor settled back against the pillows and sighed.

"What was that all about?"

"What?"

"That sigh," Christy said.

"Oh… I was just thinking about you and Cody. I'm really pleased you like him so much. Frankly, I've been concerned about you seeing so much of James."

Christy was surprised she didn't give everything away right then and there. "Oh?" she managed.

"He's nice, don't get me wrong, but he's so boring. To be honest, I've never understood what you saw in him."

"But he's kind."

"So is Big Bird!" Taylor argued. "I think James is a nice guy, but he isn't the right one for you, and I can't understand why you continue to date him."

"How can you say that?" Christy demanded, forcing the argument. James had been a child prodigy, a recognized genius by age ten. He graduated from high school in his early teens, and from law school at twenty. At twenty-five he was close to becoming the youngest partner in Atwater and Beckham's long, distinguished history. "James is a a really nice man."

"True," Taylor agreed readily enough. "But he isn't the right one for you," she said again.

"You're wrong." A simple way to end this argument would be for Christy to announce her engagement, yet she hesitated, interested in hearing her sister's opinion.

"James is everything you say, but you're not in love with him and never have been," Taylor announced with a challenging smile.

"You sound so confident of that."

"I am. You couldn't possibly be in love with James if you're this interested in Cody Franklin."

Any objection Christy might have posed died a quick and quiet death.

"I think," Taylor said, holding out her hands to her sister, "you came to Montana at exactly the right time."

Four

"Can I hold Eric?" Mandy Palmer asked minutes after Taylor was home from the hospital. "I barely got a chance to look at him before," she added, casting an accusing glance in the direction of her older brother.

"Of course," Taylor said, leading the teenager into the living room. Russ followed, leaving Christy standing alone in the kitchen with Cody.

She busied herself at the stove, praying the sheriff would go with the others.

He didn't.

"You've been avoiding me," he said softly, leaning against the kitchen counter and crossing his arms over his chest. It was all Christy could do not to stare at him. If she did, he'd be able to read the longing in her eyes, and he'd realize she'd been miserable and unhappy and at odds with herself.

She'd needed these two days to think. To come to grips with herself. To decide.

The answers hadn't come easily. She'd wrestled with the most momentous decision of her life. The resolution had come, but not without a price. She felt exhausted, frightened and on the verge of tears.

She couldn't deny Cody's words. She *had* been avoiding him. She'd astonished herself at how clever she'd been about it. Clever enough so no one would have guessed.

Except Cody.

"Why didn't you answer my calls?" he asked.

"I came to spend time with Taylor, to help her. I've been busy...."

No one had bothered to tell her that Cody had been invited to Taylor and Eric's welcome-home dinner. She wasn't prepared for this.

From the way everyone had disappeared the minute Taylor arrived, Christy shouldn't be surprised to find herself alone with Cody. It seemed as if it had all been prearranged.

"Christy, talk to me," he pleaded, his frustration evident. "Tell me what's wrong."

"Nothing. It's just that I've been so terribly busy." So terribly confused. So terribly guilty. Cowardly, too, since she'd been juggling with her conscience, her scruples and her sense of fairness.

If anything, this time away from Cody had enlightened her. The first day she'd been trapped in the restless, lost sensation she'd experienced the night before, after he'd left.

The second day, however, she'd found peace. It was a strained peace and would be so until she went home to Seattle and talked to James. Nevertheless, she'd reached a decision.

For a good part of the afternoon, Mandy and Christy had worked together to get the house ready for Taylor's return with Eric. No one had said Cody would be returning with them.

No one had given her a word of warning. She didn't know what to say to him just now, and the truth seemed unwieldy. Awkward.

"I don't blame you if you're frightened," Cody continued, his voice low. "I'm frightened myself. The first time we kissed I felt like I'd been hit by a freight train. The second time it was even more powerful.... Deep down I'd hoped it was somehow tied up in the emotion surrounding Russ, Taylor and the baby, but it isn't."

"I don't think it is, either."

"If you're looking for an explanation of what's going on between us, I can't give you one. All I know is what I feel."

Sometimes, Christy believed, a lifetime of doing the right thing could be subverted by pure sensation. This had certainly proved true with her and Cody.

"Talk to me."

Slowly she turned, witnessing for herself the tenderness, and the confusion, in his eyes. Without uttering a word, she walked over to him and slipped her arms around his waist. He placed his own around her, anchoring her to his chest as he expelled a harsh breath.

"Can you tell me what's troubling you?"

She nodded, almost giddy with relief and release. Raising her head, she smiled up at him, longing to reassure him. Part of her yearned to put this behind them and blurt it all out. She wanted to tell him about James and the engagement and how meeting him had turned her world inside out. But there wasn't enough time to untangle this mess before dinner. They needed privacy to discuss it in detail, time to reach an understanding.

She glanced regretfully toward the living room.

"Do you want to steal away?" Cody asked. "Go somewhere else?"

That was exactly what she did want, but they couldn't leave. Tonight was an evening to celebrate. Taylor and Eric were home for the first time, and leaving would be selfish and thoughtless.

"Forget I asked that," Cody murmured. "I'll be patient."

"So will I. We'll make some excuse after dinner," she suggested, then on impulse lightly brushed her lips over his.

Cody, however, wanted more. Much more.

Placing his hands on each side of her neck, he pulled her tighter to him and wove his fingers through her short hair as he brought his mouth to hers.

"I swear," Russ exclaimed loudly, walking into the kitchen, "I can't leave these two alone for a moment." The words were followed by the sound of his laughter.

Languidly Cody eased his mouth from Christy's and slowly opened his eyes. "How about getting lost for the next few minutes?" Cody said.

"Fine with me," Russ agreed, "but I don't think that fried chicken's going to want to wait much longer."

"Oh, my," Christy said, abruptly breaking away. She'd completely forgotten about the dinner she and Mandy had so carefully planned. She grabbed a pot holder and moved the grease-spitting skillet from the burner. Heaving a sigh of relief, she brushed her bangs off her forehead.

"Need any help?" Mandy asked, sauntering into the kitchen. Russ's teenage sister lived with him and Taylor, and from everything Christy had heard, Mandy was the one responsible for bringing Russ and Taylor together. Because of a summer job and other commitments, Mandy had been away from the house during most of Christy's visit and Christy was only beginning to get to know her. And like her.

"No. I've got everything under control here."

Russ contradicted her under his breath, but Christy

chose to ignore her brother-in-law's comment. She was relieved when the two men vacated the kitchen.

With Mandy's assistance, dinner was ready fifteen minutes later. Mandy called everyone, and they gathered around the dining room table. Russ escorted his wife, his eyes tender as he seated her.

Taylor, wearing a loose pale blue dress that complemented her eye color, looked wonderful. Every woman should look so good three days after giving birth, Christy mused.

"Oh, Christy… Mandy," Taylor said, studying the table. "This is fantastic. You must've spent the whole day cooking—and in this heat!"

"It wasn't a problem," Christy said automatically.

"Yes, it was," Mandy countered smoothly. "It took all afternoon, but we had so much fun it was worth it. Your sister's great!"

"I think so, too, but you shouldn't have gone to so much trouble." Taylor gestured at the three different kinds of salads, the platter of fried chicken and two separate desserts.

"But we did," Mandy said, reaching for the potato salad, "so you might as well enjoy it."

Christy shared a secret smile with her older sister. She admired Mandy for her openness and her honesty. Had she answered, she would've quickly allowed Taylor and the others to believe she'd managed to whip up a three-course meal in a matter of minutes without the slightest trouble.

Eric stirred just as they were finishing dinner, and Taylor immediately started to rise. Russ put his hand on her arm, stopping her.

"Let me?" He made it a question.

"He probably needs his diaper changed," Taylor warned.

"So? I can do it. Just how difficult can changing a diaper be?"

Christy and Taylor exchanged a meaningful glance. When she pulled her gaze away from her sister, Christy's eyes sought out Cody. The sheriff gave her a look of exaggerated shock.

"Did I hear correctly?" he teased. "Did Russ Palmer volunteer to change a diaper?"

"Apparently so," Taylor said, pretending to be as awed as Cody.

"All right, you guys, cut it out," Russ warned, shouting from the master bedroom.

"I don't know if I can let a moment like this pass without witnessing it myself. Does anyone have a camera?"

"You're not taking any damn picture," Russ roared, his voice booming through the house. His words were quickly followed by the squalling cry of an infant. A fraction of a second later Russ shouted for Taylor.

Christy tossed her napkin aside and left the table with her sister, wondering if she could help. Mandy was the only one content to let the others deal with the baby while she finished her meal.

The three of them crowded around the bassinet where Russ struggled with the diaper and pins. He was grumbling, and his face was creased with a deep frown as if he were performing major surgery.

"I marry the most modern woman in the world. She won't let me open a car door for her, insists on paying for her own dinner when we go out on a date, but will she use disposable diapers? Oh, no, she's got to torment me with cloth ones."

"They're better for the environment," Taylor said, gently pushing her husband aside. She dealt efficiently with the diaper-changing, completely unfazed by the task.

"That's all there is to it?" Cody asked, making fun of his friend's inability to handle such an uncomplicated situation.

"If you think it's so easy, you try it."

"I will, but probably not for several years." Cody looked at Christy, and the mental image of Cody holding a baby in his arms, their baby, filled her mind. She looked away, not wanting anyone to witness the emotion she was feeling.

Russ watched as Taylor lifted the dirty diaper from the bassinet. "What are you going to do with that…thing?" He wrinkled his nose as he asked the question.

"I'm putting it in the diaper pail in the bathroom."

"You're not keeping those smelly diapers in there, are you?" he said as he followed Taylor down the hallway. Christy could hear him listing his objections.

Once more Christy and Cody were left alone, this time with Eric. The infant lay on his back, squinting his blue eyes as he gazed up at them. His mouth made small sucking motions.

Unable to resist, Christy reached into the bassinet and lifted Eric out. He gurgled contentedly in her arms as she sat on the end of the bed. Cody stood next to her, studying the newborn. He lovingly smoothed his large hand along the side of the baby's head. Eric's tiny hand closed around Cody's index finger.

"Look," Cody said excitedly, as if Eric had broken an Olympic record. "I think he recognizes us."

"And well he should! We're his godparents," Christy reminded him. She turned to smile at Cody and once more found herself lost in his eyes.

In that brief moment Christy saw a reflection of everything she was feeling. Until now, whenever they looked at each other, their eyes brimmed with questions and doubts.

But this time was different. Christy saw in Cody an

understanding. They'd each lost the need for answers or explanations.

"How long will you be in Cougar Point?" Cody asked.

"My vacation is two weeks."

Both seemed to calculate the number of days remaining before she'd need to go home.

Cody's expression told her he wanted to spend every available moment he could with her. It was what Christy wanted, too, more than she'd wanted anything in her life.

"I'm working day shift tomorrow," he told her softly, his look tender. "What about dinner?"

"I'd like that." Which was definitely an understatement.

The air between them seemed to spark with sensuality. Cody leaned toward her, and Christy knew beyond a doubt that he intended to kiss her. He hesitated a fraction of an inch from her mouth before regretfully backing away.

"I'd bet my last dollar if I kissed you, Russ would interrupt us."

"He probably would. He seems to have an incredible sense of timing, doesn't he?"

As soon as she spoke, her brother-in-law stuck his head in the doorway. "What's taking you two so long? Mandy's got the coffee poured."

"See what I mean?" Cody whispered.

Christy nodded and stood, placing Eric over her shoulder and rubbing his back. He was so tiny, so perfect, and her heart swelled anew with love for him.

Taylor and Russ were sitting in the living room when Cody and Christy appeared. Their looks were openly curious—as if they were waiting for the couple to make an announcement.

Christy didn't think it would do much good to try to disguise what was going on between her and Cody. Her sister knew her far too well, and clearly Russ was equally familiar with Cody.

Christy handed the baby over to Taylor, dropping a kiss on his forehead as she did. By tacit agreement, she and Cody sat at opposite sides of the room. Being close to each other only intensified the attraction, and no doubt the curiosity.

"So," Russ said, glancing from Cody to Christy, sporting a wide grin.

"Russ," Taylor warned in a low whisper.

"What?"

"Do you have to be so obvious?"

Russ blinked, apparently at a loss to understand his wife's censure. "I didn't say anything, but if I did venture to mention the obvious, I'd say something along the lines of how happy I am that my best friend and your sister have apparently hit it off so well."

"To tell you the truth, I couldn't be more pleased myself," Taylor added, smiling.

Cody crossed his legs and picked up his coffee. "I'm glad to hear Christy and I have made you two so happy."

Russ chuckled at that, amusement glistening in his eyes. "Do you remember that time in the sixth grade?" Russ asked.

"I'm not likely to forget it."

"What are you two mumbling about now?" Taylor demanded.

"We were eleven."

"You were eleven," Cody corrected. "I was ten."

"Right," Russ agreed. "We'd been good friends for several years and had started to notice some of our other buddies turning traitor."

"Turning traitor?" Christy repeated.

"Liking girls."

Since Christy was the youngest of the five Manning children, she couldn't recall her brothers sharing similar feelings. "What did you two do?" she asked.

"The only thing we could," Russ explained, grinning again. "We were losing our best friends left and right, so Cody and I made a pact and became blood brothers. We made a solemn vow never to associate with any of the guys who'd turned traitor and liked girls."

"Especially pretty ones with dark hair and bright blue eyes," Cody remarked, looking at Christy, who possessed both. His mouth quivered, and she realized he was only a breath away from laughing outright.

"And which of you broke this sacred vow first?"

"Cody did," Russ said.

"Russ," Cody responded, the two speaking almost simultaneously.

"Boys, please," Taylor said in what Christy was sure was her best schoolteacher voice.

"Cody gave Mary Lu Hawkins a valentine that year," Russ reminded him.

"My mother forced me to do it," Cody insisted. "I never liked Mary Lu Hawkins, and you know it."

"That's not what I heard."

Listening to Cody and Russ was like being present at an exchange between her own brothers. A strong sense of family was an integral part of who she was. She loved their frequent get-togethers and had missed Taylor dreadfully over the past year.

"Is it always like this between these two?" Christy asked her sister.

"Sometimes worse," Taylor answered.

"Russ was the ultimate traitor," Cody said, setting his

coffee mug aside. "He married a dark-haired, blue-eyed woman, and worse, I wasn't even invited to the wedding."

"No one was," Mandy inserted as she came in from the kitchen, drying her hands on her apron skirt. "Not even me. Russ's very own sister."

"I swear you're never going to forgive me for that, are you?" Russ grumbled. "Just wait till you fall in love, little sister, then you might be more understanding."

Mandy straightened her spine and threw back her shoulders. Her eyes narrowed as she glared across the room at her brother. She reminded Christy so much of her older sister confronting their father that she nearly laughed out loud.

"It may come as a shock to you, big brother, but I've been in love several times." Mandy evidently considered herself a woman of the world.

Russ didn't hide his opinions on *that* issue. He rolled his eyes.

"Russ," Taylor said softly.

"Now what did I do?" he asked. At the rate he was going, his foot would remain permanently in his mouth. "All right, all right, I—*we* made a mistake by not including you in the wedding ceremony. There. Are you satisfied?"

"No. I want you to admit that I'm old enough to be in love."

"Mandy!"

"Admit it." It was clear that brother and sister were often at odds, yet Christy sensed the deep and abiding love they shared.

"Don't look at me, Russ Palmer," Taylor said bluntly. "You got yourself into this."

"I suppose that at fifteen a mature teenage girl may have experienced her first taste of love."

"May have?" Mandy repeated. "That's not good enough."

"Hey, the girl wants blood," Cody murmured.

"She's likely to get it, too," Taylor said, apparently for Christy's benefit.

"All right, I'll admit it. There! *Now* are you satisfied?"

Mandy smiled graciously and nodded. "Thank you, brother dearest."

"You're welcome, sister sweetest." He turned his attention away from Mandy. "Listen," Russ said, looking at Cody and Christy and then back at his friend. "If you two ever get married, whether it's to each other or anyone else, take my advice and don't elope."

"If Mandy was upset about not being at the wedding, that was nothing compared to how strongly Mom and Dad felt about it," Taylor said. "Dad seemed to feel I'd cheated him out of an important part of fatherhood by not letting him escort me down the aisle."

From somewhere deep inside, Christy forced a smile. This talk about weddings was making her decidedly uncomfortable. What her sister said was true enough; her parents had been bitterly disappointed not to hold a large wedding for their oldest daughter. It was one of the reasons they were so pleased when Christy announced that she and James would be getting married. Almost immediately they'd started talking about the church ceremony, with a reception and dance to follow.

"I think it's time for us to go, don't you?" Cody said to Christy, unfolding his long legs and standing. He walked across the room in three strides. "See you later, Taylor, Eric. Oh, and you, too." He nodded at Russ with a grin. "Thanks for dinner, everyone."

"Where are you two headed?" Russ wanted to know, making no effort to disguise his interest.

"Out." Cody turned to Christy, and his smile was like

the warm fingers of sunlight in winter. They'd known each other such a short while, and it seemed inconceivable that she could feel like this. But she did. The feelings she and Cody shared were too complex to put into words.

"When will you be back?" Russ asked his sister-in-law, as if he wasn't completely convinced his best friend was safe in her company.

"Who appointed you my guardian angel?" Cody asked sarcastically, his eyebrows raised.

"I'm only looking out for your best interests," Russ explained, continuing the game. "Good grief, man, she's pretty with dark hair and blue eyes. We learned way back in the sixth grade that those are the ones to watch out for. You've got to be careful. Look what happened to me!"

"What did happen to you?" Taylor asked, her brow wrinkling with the question.

"You should know. Before I realized it, I was saddled with a wife. I don't mind telling you, Franklin, I'm worried about you."

"If I'm responsible for the security of an entire county, you can trust me to take care of myself."

"Saddled?" Taylor asked, her voice ominously low. "You found yourself *saddled* with a wife?"

Russ instantly looked guilty. "Maybe saddled wasn't the best word."

"Then I suggest you search for another."

"Ah..." Russ rubbed his hand across his neck.

"He's talking off the top of his head," Cody said, defending his friend. He turned toward Russ. "If I were you, I'd plead for leniency and remind her how crazy in love you are."

"How about I was *favored* with a wife?" Russ muttered. He seemed quite pleased with his choice of word.

Taylor glanced at Christy, a smile playing at the corners of her mouth, then shook her head. "You'll have to do better than that."

"Taylor, come on, I'm having a serious discussion with my friend here. All I'm trying to do is impart a few words of wisdom before Cody makes the same…before he ends up…"

"Ends up what?" Taylor prompted.

It took Russ a moment to answer. "Blessed?" he offered, confident he'd smoothed things over.

"Blessed is an acceptable word."

"I think we should get out of here while the getting's good, don't you?" Cody asked, reaching for Christy's hand, entwining their fingers.

"I couldn't agree with you more." The solid ground beneath her feet seemed to shift as she realized that once they were alone she'd need to explain about James. Dragging in a steadying breath, she looked at Taylor. "I won't be gone long."

"If I get worried, I'll call the sheriff," Taylor teased.

The phone rang, and Mandy shot out of the living room.

Russ escorted Christy and Cody to the back door.

Mandy appeared, stretching the long telephone cord into the kitchen. She seemed confused as she held out the receiver to Russ. "I think it must be a wrong number. Maybe you should talk to him."

"All right."

Cody chuckled. "I never thought I'd be grateful for a phone call. I had the impression Russ was going to make us listen to more of his pearls of wisdom."

They were all the way down the steps when the back door swung open with enough force to send it crashing shut.

"Christy." Russ stood on the top of the steps, hands on his hips, his eyes squinting against the setting sun.

"Yes?" She turned to face her brother-in-law. The humor in his eyes had been replaced with a fierce anger that transformed his handsome features.

Cody took a step forward. "What is it?"

"The phone," Russ said. "It's for Christy. Someone named James Wilkens."

She gasped softly before she could stop herself.

"He claims he's her fiancé."

Five

"Cody, please," Christy began, her heart in her eyes. "I can explain."

"You mean it's true?" Russ shouted.

"It's not as bad as it sounds—if you'd take the time to listen." Both of her hands gripped Cody's forearm as she boldly held on to him, not wanting to let him go for fear she'd never see him again.

"Are you engaged or not?" Cody asked. His dark eyes burned into hers, searing her conscience far more deeply than any words he could've spoken.

"I was going to tell you about James…."

Cody's face tensed as though she'd delivered a crippling blow to his abdomen. He lowered his gaze to her hands, which clenched his arm tightly.

"I see." The two words were cold, his voice remote.

She moistened her lips, unsure she could trust her voice. "Please let me explain."

"What's there to say? It's simple, isn't it? Either you're engaged or you're not." He pulled himself free and turned his back to her.

"Cody." She tried once more, hating the way her voice wobbled as she pleaded for patience and understanding.

One stern look told her he wasn't willing to grant her either. Her heart seized painfully as she slowly dropped her hands and stepped away from him.

Without another word, Cody climbed inside his Cherokee, slammed the door and drove away as if the very demons of hell were in hot pursuit.

Christy went completely still. She couldn't move. Couldn't breathe.

How long she stood there, Christy had no idea. Nor could she put order to her thoughts. Just a few minutes ago she'd been sitting across the room from Cody, laughing with him, sharing secret smiles, her whole being permeated with gladness and joy. How natural it had seemed to be together. As natural as the sun setting. As natural as rain.

"Are you going to talk to your fiancé or not?" Russ demanded, his voice sharp with censure.

Christy stared at him for a moment before she realized James was still on the phone. Nevertheless, she stood where she was and watched the plume of dust that trailed behind Cody's vehicle. After a while it faded away, taking with it the promise of something wonderful.

Russ waited for her at the top of the porch steps. Christy lowered her eyes as she moved past him. He didn't need to say anything for her to feel his reprimand.

The telephone receiver was resting on a small table in the hallway. Christy dragged in a deep, calming breath and reached for it. "Hello, James." She prayed her voice revealed none of her turmoil.

"Christy. How are you?" He sounded anxious, concerned.

"Fine, just fine. Taylor had the baby, but I suppose you've heard about that already. I doubt Mom and Dad could keep quiet about Eric. He really is precious." She knew she was chattering but couldn't seem to make herself stop. "Montana is a beautiful state. I haven't seen much of Cougar Point yet, except the bowling alley. I had breakfast there the other morning, only it was really the middle of the afternoon—the day Eric was born, actually."

"You ate breakfast at a bowling alley?"

"There's a restaurant there and the food's good—excellent, in fact."

"That's nice."

"How are you?" Christy felt obliged to ask.

"Fine. I miss you." He dropped his voice slightly as if he'd admitted something he shouldn't. "The office seems empty with you away."

James wasn't a man who was comfortable with expressing his emotions. Showing affection was difficult for him. The fact that he'd called and said he missed her was practically equivalent to another man standing on a rooftop and shouting at the top of his voice that he was madly in love.

"I… I've been busy."

"I was hoping you'd call me."

His disappointment echoed in each word.

"I'm sorry, James, really I am. It's just that everything happened so fast. I didn't even have a chance to unpack my bags before Taylor went into labor. She came home from the hospital today, and we…we were just having dinner." That was a slight exaggeration, but she needed an excuse to get off the phone before she did something stupid like weep uncontrollably or tell him about Cody.

"You're having dinner? Why didn't you say something sooner? No wonder it took you so long to get to the phone."

Christy leaned against the wall, closed her eyes and swallowed. She felt guilty about by her minor deception, contaminated by the way she was deceiving him in an effort to cut short this painful conversation.

James deserved so much more than this. The guilt was killing her, and it demanded all the self-control she possessed to keep from blurting everything out.

"I'll let you go, but before I do I want you to know I got the diamond back from the jeweler. It'll be ready when you return from your sister's."

"Oh, g-great," she stammered, trying to inject some enthusiasm into her voice.

"Goodbye, Christy. Give my regards to Taylor and her husband and congratulate them both for me."

"I will. Bye, James. Don't work too hard."

"No, I won't."

She replaced the receiver, her fingers curled tensely around it as she waited for the recriminations to rain down on her. She felt an overwhelming sense of wrongdoing, a surge of remorse.

Raised voices came at her from inside the living room.

"The least you can do is listen to her," Christy heard Taylor shout.

"What possible explanation could she have? Either she's engaged or she isn't."

"Listen to me, Russ Palmer. I won't have you yelling at my sister. Whatever's happening between her and Cody is her business. It doesn't have anything to do with us."

"Like hell I'm going to stay out of it. We're talking about Cody here—my best friend. I thought he was your friend, too."

"He is."

"Then you can't expect to sit idly by and watch him get hurt."

"Please," Christy said, stepping into the room. She couldn't bear to have them arguing over her. "Please...don't fight."

The room went silent, a silence so intense it seemed to throb like a giant heart. Taylor's gaze, clouded with doubt and uncertainty, locked with Christy's. Russ's eyes were filled with reproach.

Russ and Taylor continued to stare at her. Russ was angry and made no effort to disguise his feelings. Taylor, usually so strong and confident, couldn't hide her confusion.

Christy suspected her sister was as troubled as her husband. Only Taylor wouldn't allow herself to voice her misgivings because of family loyalty.

"Sit down," Taylor suggested. She motioned toward the recliner where Christy had sat earlier. "You're so pale. Are you sure you're all right?"

"Why didn't you tell us you were engaged?" Russ asked, barely giving her time to compose herself. "And if you and James are getting married, why aren't you wearing a ring?"

"Russ, please," Taylor said, "let her answer one question before hitting her with another." Directing her attention to Christy, Taylor widened her eyes. "We're waiting."

Folding her hands in her lap, Christy squeezed her fingers so tightly they hurt. "James asked me to marry him two days before I left Seattle."

"He didn't give you an engagement ring?"

"Of course...it's being sized now."

"I see," Taylor said, frowning. "And you didn't mention it to anyone? Do Mom and Dad know? I'm your sister, for heaven's sake! The least you could've done was mention it to me."

"Taylor," Russ said gruffly, then reminded her of her own words. "She can only answer one question at a time."

"I didn't have a chance to tell you when I first arrived. Remember? Then first thing the next morning you went into labor and… I met Cody."

"You had no business leading him on," Russ snapped.

"I didn't mean to," she cried, and raked her fingers though her short hair, praying Taylor and Russ wouldn't condemn her. "It just…happened. We were both so excited about the baby and afterward we went out to eat. Then Cody drove me home and…and I knew he was going to kiss me. I realize it was a mistake not to say anything to him, but I was afraid…" Afraid that if she *had* said something he wouldn't have touched her, and she'd wanted his kiss so much.

Unable to meet her sister's eyes, she glanced at the coffee table as the tears spilled down her cheeks.

"Who's this James character, anyway?" Russ asked Taylor. "Did we meet him?"

She nodded. "He's the attorney Christy introduced to us last summer."

"Not the…" He hesitated.

"Why didn't you tell me?" Taylor apparently considered it a personal affront that Christy had kept the news to herself. "We had plenty of time to talk while I was in the hospital and you were there every day."

"I tried," Christy said in her own defense. "But every time I mentioned James, you changed the subject. And when I finally managed to drag him back into the conversation, you started telling me how dry and boring you think he is and what a mismatched couple we are. What was I supposed to do? Tell you I'd agreed to marry the man you'd just finished criticizing?"

"Oh, dear," Taylor whispered. "Now that you mention

it, I do remember you trying to bring James into the conversation."

"Fine. You two got that settled, but what about Cody?" Russ stalked to the other side of the room and stared out the front window. "I can't, I *won't* let this happen to him a second time. Not when it's in my power to prevent it." Gradually he turned around, his shoulders squared and his jaw tightly clenched.

"A second time?" Christy echoed.

When Russ didn't respond right away, she looked at her sister, who was busy with Eric. Either that or she was avoiding eye contact. "Taylor?"

"It happened several years ago," Russ began grudgingly. "A woman by the name of Rebecca Morgan moved into town. She was from somewhere in the south and had the sweetest manners you can imagine. She was the type of woman a man could fall in love with. Becca was perfect. Beautiful. Demure. Charming and…" Russ shook his head. "Who would've guessed?"

"Guessed what?" Christy asked.

"Becca made it obvious from the moment she moved into town that she was attracted to Cody. Every time he turned around there she was, batting her eyes at him, doing those things you women do to let a man know you're interested."

"I could make a comment here, but I won't," Taylor muttered.

"Soon Becca and Cody were seeing a lot of each other. You have to understand, Cody isn't easily taken in, especially by a pretty woman. Until recently." He frowned at Christy as he said it. "But Becca did more than interest him. For the first time in his life, Cody was in love. It showed in everything he said and did.

"Cody's always been popular with the folks around here,

and his happiness seemed to rub off on everyone. Most folks liked Becca, too. They couldn't help it. There was plenty of talk about the two of them getting married." Russ walked over to the ottoman and sat down. "A month or so after she moved into town, a series of baffling robberies started happening."

"You don't mean to say Becca…"

"Not her personally. She was part of a team. They worked a scam in small cities all across the western states. Apparently the heat was on in several of the larger cities, and she and her partner decided to try their hand in smaller towns. They were successful, too. Becca would move someplace and get involved with a deputy from the local sheriff's office. One way or another she'd get information about shipments of money to the town banks. Then she'd pass that information to her partner. It was all cleverly done. Whenever a shipment of cash was due to arrive, Becca would make sure she was nowhere nearby. Two banks were robbed, and a couple of stores lost valuable equipment all within the second month she was in town. But no one suspected her. How could they? She was just as sweet as honey."

"How long did it take Cody to realize it was Becca?"

"Not long, a few weeks, but he felt like the biggest fool who ever lived and you'll never convince him differently. He took responsibility for everything, blamed himself for not picking up on the scam sooner."

"But he loved her. Trusted her."

Russ's dark gaze collided with Christy's. "I know. He arrested her and her partner and testified against them."

"Surely no one blamed Cody!"

"No, everyone in town was as taken in by her as he was. But Cody felt as responsible as if he'd personally handed over the money. It's his job to protect and to serve and he felt he'd let the entire county down, although he worked his fool head off until every penny was returned. Even that wasn't enough. Cody felt he had to resign from the department."

"No." Christy's response was immediate. True, she'd only known Cody a short while, but in that time she'd learned how important law enforcement was to him.

"Thankfully some of us were able to talk some sense into him. He made the mistake of falling in love with the wrong woman—but then again, it was all due to his efforts that Becca and her friend were caught. If it hadn't been for Cody, no one knows how long their little scam would've worked or how many other communities would've been bilked. Unfortunately Cody didn't see it that way."

"He's only human." Christy felt a burning need to defend him.

"Becca used him. But worse than that, she made him feel like an idiot. It's taken three years for him to live it down, at least in his own mind. The way most folks figure it, Cody did Montana a good deed by putting Becca Morgan and her partner behind bars."

"That's why he wouldn't run for sheriff until last year?" Taylor asked, shifting the baby in her arms.

"It's been his life's dream to be elected sheriff of Custer County, but it took all this time for him to agree to run. I suppose he felt he had to prove his worth all over again. The crazy part is that he could've won hands down *any* year, including the year he was involved with Becca."

"I didn't know," Taylor said softly.

"It's not something that's talked about a lot," Russ explained. "The subject is such a painful one, it's best forgotten."

"Then Becca's still in prison?" Christy managed to ask.

Learning how Cody had been deceived was painful for her, too. The knowledge that justice had been done somehow made it easier to accept.

"From what I understand, she's tried to contact Cody a few times, claiming she really was in love with him, and still is. To hear her tell it, she was a helpless pawn in all this. She says she was a victim of blackmail. But Cody won't have anything to do with her."

"I can certainly understand that," Taylor said.

"You aren't comparing me to Becca, are you?" Christy asked bluntly, feeling even more wretched.

"You're no thief," Russ said abruptly. "I'm not worried about you bilking the good citizens of Cougar Point, if that's what you think. No..." He rubbed the back of his neck. "After Becca something changed in Cody. He rarely dated. He closed himself off, became more pensive, introspective. It was as if he'd lost trust in women."

Taylor nodded. "I can't say I really blame him."

"I don't, either," Christy added, realizing as she did so that she was condemning herself.

Russ frowned. "That's why I was so pleased about what happened after he met you. When he looked at you, it was like seeing the old Cody all over again, the man who smiled and joked and didn't take everything so seriously. I don't know what went on between you." He hesitated and glanced at his wife. "Taylor's right when she says it isn't any of my business, but I won't stand by and let you take advantage of him."

"I wouldn't... I couldn't."

"Then why didn't you tell him you were engaged?"

Christy felt as if she'd been backed into a corner. "I planned to. I never intended to keep it a secret, but I needed time to think. You may not believe this, but I'd hoped to talk to Cody about James tonight. I was going to tell him everything."

"Are you planning on marrying James?" Taylor asked, her eyes seeking Christy's.

The question came as a shock. "No. I couldn't—not after meeting Cody."

"Then why didn't you break the engagement when you had the chance?" Russ asked. "You were just talking to him. It would've been a simple matter to tell him then."

"I can't do it over the phone," Christy said, jerking her head upward. "James is a good man. He deserves better than that. He hasn't done anything wrong. I hate to hurt him…." She paused when hot tears threatened to spill down her face. Biting her lower lip, she drew in a shuddering breath.

"Christy's right." Taylor's words cut through the emotion of the moment. "This is a delicate situation. You can't expect her to call James and break off the engagement. That would be heartless. This is best done in person. James may be a bit dull, but he's a decent human being."

"Is…is there any chance Cody will talk to me?" Christy wanted to drive into town and explain that she had no intention of going through with the marriage.

"I doubt he'll have anything to do with you," Russ answered, confirming her worst fears.

"Wait until tomorrow," Taylor advised. "Give him an opportunity to think everything through."

"He asked me out to dinner…. But I'm not sure if he'll show up."

"He won't," Russ said. "I know him better than anyone, and I can tell you, as far as he's concerned, whatever was between you is over."

Christy's shoulders sagged with defeat. "I was afraid of that."

"Don't make it sound so hopeless," Taylor muttered.

"She's engaged, for crying out loud. What do you expect Cody to do?" Russ said. "Ignore it? He isn't going to do that."

"But I have every intention of breaking off the engagement."

"I doubt that'll make any difference to him. I'll be surprised if he even listens to you."

"That's not true," Taylor said confidently. "Cody's a reasonable man, and it's obvious that he's attracted to you."

"He isn't anymore." Russ shook his head for emphasis.

Taylor shot daggers at her husband. "Russ Palmer, kindly allow me to finish."

"Feel free, but you've got to understand. After Becca, Cody doesn't have a lot of trust in the opposite sex."

"My sister isn't another Becca," Taylor insisted.

"You and I know that."

A short silence followed before Christy said, "Cody's smart enough to know it, too." She wanted to believe that. Needed to believe it. But whether that was the case or not was something she'd soon discover.

Cody slammed his fist against the steering column. He was parked on the ridge that overlooked Cougar Point and had been sitting there for the past hour, collecting his thoughts.

Frustration and anger mounted with each passing minute. Drawing in a deep breath, he rubbed his face with both hands, certain he'd almost made a world-class fool of himself for the second time.

When was he going to learn? Women weren't to be trusted. Especially pretty blue-eyed ones who looked as pure as freshly fallen snow. On the outside they were all sweetness, but inside… His thoughts skidded to an abrupt halt despite his best efforts to think badly of Christy.

He couldn't compare Becca with Taylor's sister. The two women had little, if anything, in common. Becca was a con artist. Christy wouldn't know how to deceive anyone.

But she had.

She'd deceived him.

Once more he rubbed his hand down his face. Had she really? Hadn't she said there was something she needed to tell him? He'd stood in Russ's kitchen, looked into her beautiful eyes and had seen for himself the turmoil inside her. He'd been unable to grasp what was troubling her.

But right now all Cody could think about was himself. For the first time in years he'd been able to feel again. For the first time in years he'd been whole.

The only thing he felt now was an ache that cut far deeper than anything he'd known before. His feelings for Christy had been a cruel joke.

"You don't honestly expect Cody's going to come, do you?" Taylor asked as Christy sprayed her carefully styled hair. She'd spent the past half hour fussing with her makeup and hair, hoping that if she looked her best, it would lend her confidence.

"No. But I want to be ready in case he does."

"You've been restless all day," her sister said.

"I know. I can't help it. Oh, Taylor, I can't bear to let things end this way between Cody and me. Everything felt so…so right with us."

"It's hard, isn't it?"

She nodded, fighting the need to rush to him and make him understand. "His eyes were so cold. I didn't know anyone could look so…" She couldn't think of a word strong enough to describe her fears.

For much of the night she'd wrestled with the sheets and blankets, trying to find a comfortable position. Once she did and closed her eyes, the disdainful look on Cody's face would pop into her mind. Her eyes would fly open, and the need to explain to him would dominate her thoughts again.

She'd spent most of the night composing what she was going to say. All day she'd been mentally rehearsing it so when the time came she'd be ready.

But she didn't feel ready now. She felt uneasy and scared, as if nothing she could say or do would make a difference.

"If he doesn't come, what do you plan to do?"

"Go to him," Christy said firmly. "He made a date, and he's going to keep it whether he wants to or not."

A quick smile flashed from Taylor's eyes, and her lips quivered with the effort to suppress it. "I see."

"I mean it. If Cody isn't man enough to give me a chance to explain, then he deserves what he's going to get."

"And what's that?"

"I haven't decided yet, but I'll think of something."

"Yes, I'm sure you will," Taylor said on her way out of the bathroom.

Once she was finished, Christy joined her sister, who was busy with dinner preparations. "Let me help," she insisted, feeling guilty that Taylor was stuck with the cooking. The very reason Christy was in Montana was to help with the household chores while Taylor recuperated.

"Don't be silly. I'm perfectly fine. Besides, you might mess up your makeup." Leaning against the counter, Taylor surveyed Christy's attire. "Personally I'm betting Cody's not going to be able to take his eyes off you."

"Oh, Taylor, do you really think so?" Looking her best

was important to Christy. If Cody was going to slam the door in her face, which was a distinct possibility, then she wanted him to know what he was missing.

"There's something different about you," Taylor went on to say, her expression somber. She crossed her arms and cocked her head to one side.

"You mean the eyeliner. I'm using a different shade."

"No, this doesn't have anything to do with eyeliner. You're not the same Christy I left when I moved away from Seattle."

"I'm older," Christy said, "and hopefully more mature."

Taylor paused to consider that. "I suppose that's part of it, but there's more."

"Oh?"

"You were always the 'good daughter.'"

"You make it sound like you were the bad one, and that isn't the least bit true."

"But we both know I love an argument," Taylor said, "and Dad was always willing to comply. We were so often at odds."

"But you and Dad loved and respected each other. It wasn't like some families."

"I know. It's just that we're so different. About the worst thing I can remember you doing was running around the house with a pair of scissors in your hand."

"I did go swimming in the community pool without a bathing cap that one time, remember?"

"Ah, yes, I'd forgotten about that. You renegade!"

They laughed. Taylor was right; Christy had never caused a problem, never been in trouble. The good daughter. Too good, in some ways.

"You realize Mom and Dad are going to be disappointed when they find out you aren't going to marry James."

"Probably more disappointed than James," Christy joked.

Taylor frowned slightly. "Are you sure you're doing the right thing?"

The question was unexpected. "Of course. Very soon after I met Cody, I knew I should never have agreed to marry James. I..."

"Then why did you?"

"Well...because we're friends and we'd been working together a lot, and it just seemed...like a good idea."

"Your decision had nothing to do with Mom and Dad?"

"I...ah..."

"I don't mean to pressure you or sound like a know-it-all, but if you check your motives, I think you might discover that you accepted James's proposal for all the wrong reasons. It suited Mom and Dad for you to marry him, and you went along with it because you were trying to please them. Am I right?"

"I..." Christy lowered her eyes as a tingling extended from her stomach to her arms and down her fingers. She loved her parents so much and wanted to make them proud of her. Her marrying James would certainly have done that. Christy had been so concerned about doing what her parents thought was right that she'd never considered if it was best for her.

"Christy?"

"You make me sound so weak, so insecure."

"You're not. You're loving and gentle and good. James is a fine young man, but he's not the one for you."

Without question her parents would be upset with her, but in time they'd realize she was doing what was best for both her and James.

Christy left the Lazy P soon afterward, not waiting to

see if Cody was going to come for her or not. From the way he'd left the evening before, she suspected he had no intention of keeping their dinner date.

She found his place without a problem and parked her car. She took several minutes to compose herself before making her way to the front door.

An eternity passed before he answered her knock. "Christy?"

"I believe we have a dinner date," she said boldly, damning her voice for shaking. She didn't want him to guess how terribly nervous this confrontation made her.

"A dinner date? You and me? Forget it, sweetheart. If you want to go out, call your fiancé."

Six

"I'm not going to marry James," Christy explained in a voice that demanded Cody listen to her and at the same time begged for his understanding. Cody wasn't in the mood to do either. From the moment he'd left Christy the night before, he'd fought to push every thought of her from his mind.

With very little success.

"Who you marry or don't marry is none of my business," he said, his words sharp and abrupt.

Christy flinched at his disdain, and it was all Cody could do to keep from reaching for her and asking her forgiveness.

"Please, if you'd give me a chance to explain...."

She was so beautiful, with her cobalt-blue eyes and sweet, innocent face. Until he'd met Christy and Taylor, Cody had never seen eyes that precise shade of blue.

He groaned inwardly, struggling against the need to take her in his arms and bask in her softness. Equally strong was the instinctive urge to protect his heart and his orderly life from the havoc she was sure to bring.

Cody was the sheriff-elect, but there was little that could terrify him the way this woman did. It was essential to keep his eyes off her. Everything about her was sensual and provocative. It was difficult enough to fight her, but the battle grew even fiercer as he struggled with his own desires. This was much harder than he'd ever imagined it would be.

"At least talk to me."

Her voice was soft and compelling. The mere sound could drive him straight through the bounds of what was fast becoming his limited self-control.

"I think you should leave."

There, he'd said it. He didn't mean it, but he'd said it, and that little bit of resistance lent him a sense of control, which had been sadly lacking to this point. Christy wasn't aware of that, but he was.

"I'm not leaving until you've listened to me."

"Then you're going to have to do your talking from the street." It astonished him how forcefully he came across. He blocked the doorway as he leaned indolently against the jamb, trying his best to suggest that he hadn't a care in the world.

She hesitated, then surprised him by nodding. "Fine. If that's what it takes, I'll shout at you from the middle of the street, loud enough for the entire block to hear."

"You're wasting your time." He'd played these games with another woman once, and he wasn't about to fall into that trap a second time.

Feeling suddenly confident, he straightened, leaned forward and braced his hands against her shoulders, keeping her at arm's length. It was a risk to touch her, but one he was prepared to take. Perhaps he felt the need to convince himself that he could be close to her and not want to kiss her....

His plan backfired the instant she looked directly up at him. To complicate matters, she flattened her hands on his chest. His heart reacted immediately, and he was sure she could feel the effect she had on him. Maybe touching her wasn't such a smart move, after all.

"I meant what I said." He narrowed his eyes, hoping she'd take the hint and leave. In the same breath he prayed she wouldn't.

"You have every right to be angry," Christy continued, her eyes pleading with him. "I don't blame you. I intended to tell you about James and me. Remember when we were in the kitchen before dinner? I told you there was something I had to talk to you about."

She didn't give him a chance to answer. Not that it mattered; he did remember, all too well.

"It was never my intention to mislead you. I would've explained everything except James phoned before I had the chance."

Cody felt himself weakening. This wasn't supposed to be happening. He should be a tower of strength. A bastion of fortitude. With little more than a shrug of his shoulders he ought to send her packing. One woman had mercilessly used him before. Only an idiot would allow it to happen again.

"I realized the first time you kissed me that I could never marry James," she persisted. "Maybe even before then. I know it should've been a simple decision, but it wasn't. I had to think everything through. The answer was so obvious, so clear—but it frightened me."

She was frightened! Cody was shaking in his boots!

He dropped his hands; touching her had been a tactical error.

"So you've broken it off?" he asked, hating the way his hopes rose at the possibility that she was free.

Christy dropped her eyes. "Not exactly. But I promise you I will the minute I get back to Seattle."

Cody's blood turned to ice. So she intended to string him along. At least she was honest about it, but frankly that didn't count for much.

"I know it sounds bad," she said softly. "You might think it'd be better if I told James now. I thought so myself, but then I realized it wouldn't be right. James doesn't deserve to be treated so heartlessly. He's a good man—it would be wrong to call him and just tell him I'd met someone else. It's cruel to do it over the phone."

Cody snorted a soft laugh. She was a candidate for the loony bin if she expected him to buy into that. Either she was engaged to James or she wasn't. Either the wedding was on or it was off. As simple as that.

"All right," she said, and he could see her fighting to hold on to her composure. "If you can't accept that, I'll phone James and talk to him right now."

"Fine." He led her into the house and didn't stop until he reached the kitchen phone. Feeling slightly cocky, he lifted the receiver and handed it to her, fully expecting her not to go through with the call. She was putting on a brave front, but he was sure she had no intention of following through.

She stared at the receiver for a moment before taking it out of his hand. When she did, Cody saw how deathly pale she'd gone.

She offered him a quick, reassuring smile. "You're right," she said weakly. "I shouldn't be thinking about James's feelings at a time like this. You have feelings, too. It's probably best to get this over with now. James will understand. I know he will." As if her fingers weighed a thousand pounds, she lifted her hand and slowly punched out a series of numbers, then closed her eyes as she waited. "He's probably still at the office."

After what seemed like an inordinate amount of time,

and a short conversation with the receptionist, Christy replaced the receiver. "James already left. He must be home by now. I'll try there—only…" She looked up at him, her eyes wide and full of tension. She was willing to do this because Cody demanded it of her, but it was so hard. To know she was humiliating *James,* causing him pain…

"Only what?" he prompted.

"Could you kiss me? I seem to need it right now."

His mouth found hers even before she'd finished speaking. He'd planned to brush his lips gently across hers. This wasn't the time for anything more.

To be on the safe side, he kissed her again—just so he'd know for a fact that he could walk away from her in the blink of an eye.

That was Cody's second tactical error of the evening.

She tasted like heaven, sweet and warm. His mouth continued to move over hers until her lips parted. She sighed deeply and sagged against him. Then she buried her face in the curve of his neck. Her breathing was as hard and uneven as his own. His hands were splayed across her back, and he held on to her with what little strength he'd managed to reserve.

"Give me a moment and I'll phone James at his house," she whispered, her voice raspy.

Cody framed her face in his hands. "No," he whispered.

"No?"

"I'm not happy with the situation, but you're right. Breaking the engagement by phone would be insensitive. I can wait until you get back to Seattle and talk to him face-to-face."

She lowered her eyes in gratitude, her thick lashes sweeping her cheek. "Thank you."

He nodded.

"Oh, Cody, please believe me, I'm going to end it. I'm being as completely honest as I can."

"I know."

"You do?"

He nodded. He wrapped his arms around her and rested his chin on her head. "I don't know where that leaves us," he said. "Or even where we go from here."

"I don't, either," Christy whispered, but he felt her sigh of contentment as she relaxed against him.

"You're as jumpy as a grasshopper," Russ teased three days later. "I swear you keep looking out that window as though you expect the Mounted Police to come riding over the hill."

"Not the Mounted Police, just one handsome sheriff."

"Ah, so you're seeing Cody again."

"I've seen him every night this week." Christy could feel herself blush as she said it, which was exactly the reaction her brother-in-law was looking for.

"Quit teasing my sister," Taylor said. She was sitting at the kitchen table, Eric nestled in her arms, nursing greedily.

Every time Christy watched her sister with the baby, she felt astonished at how easily Taylor had taken to motherhood. She acted as though she'd been around infants all her life. She seemed so comfortable, so *confident* with her son, whether she was breast feeding him or diapering or rocking him to sleep.

"Where's Cody taking you this afternoon?" Taylor asked, glancing up at her.

"He wouldn't say. It's supposed to be a surprise, but I have a sneaking suspicion we're headed into the wild blue yonder." At her sister's raised eyebrows, she explained. "I think he's planning to take me for a plane ride. He told me earlier that he has his private license and twice now he's mentioned flying."

"I thought you were afraid of planes," Taylor commented. When it was first decided that Christy would come to Montana, she'd immediately rejected the idea of flying into Miles City. Driving to Montana appealed to her far more. Neither Taylor nor their mother had pressed the issue.

"I'm not excited about flying," Christy admitted.

"But you don't mind going up in a plane with Cody?"

"No." She trusted him beyond question. Enough to place her life in his hands.

"If I were you, I'd make sure his little surprise doesn't involve horses," Russ warned, and his eyes connected with his wife's as though they were sharing some well-kept secret.

"Cody doesn't ride that often."

Russ poured himself a cup of coffee and joined Taylor at the kitchen table. He smiled at his son while speaking to Christy. "You certainly seem to know a great deal about the sheriff's habits."

"I..." Christy could feel warmth invade her cheeks. She hated the way she blushed whenever the subject of Cody was introduced.

She and Cody had spent every available moment together. With her vacation vanishing like melting snow, each day was more precious than the one before. It was as if they were cramming several months of a relationship into two short weeks.

Cody wasn't pleased that she remained technically engaged to James, but he'd graciously accepted the situation. It wasn't easy for him, but he never questioned her about the other man, or brought James into their conversation.

For his part, Cody had never said anything to Christy

about Becca and the way he'd been duped by the other woman. Knowing what she did made her more sensitive to his needs, made her love him all the more.

Christy did love Cody. This wasn't infatuation or hormones or anything else. For some reason, unknown to them both, they were meant to be together. She knew it. He knew it. Yet Christy never spoke of her feelings, and neither did Cody.

She understood his hesitancy. He couldn't talk freely about their relationship while James was still part of her life.

Once she was back in Seattle and had broken the engagement to James, then and only then would she tell Cody she loved him. And he in turn would be free to tell her what she already knew.

Christy would've liked to hear it sooner, but if Cody could display this much patience, she could do no less.

"I don't know when we'll be back," Christy said. "Is there anything I can do for you before I leave?" she asked, looking at Taylor.

Her sister grinned. "Just have a good time."

"I will." She was already having the time of her life.

"I was in town earlier today," Russ said. He paused to be sure he had their full attention.

"So? You go into town at least twice a week," Taylor reminded him.

"Noah Williams, who works at the insurance agency, stopped me." Once more he hesitated as if this news was significant.

"Old Man Williams stops anybody who'll listen to him," Taylor interjected. "That man is the biggest gossip in three counties, and you know it."

Russ rubbed the side of his jaw. "Yeah, I suppose I do."

"Would you say what's on your mind and be done with it?" Taylor grumbled.

Russ chuckled. "All right. Noah claimed he'd heard that the sheriff's about to take a wife. A pretty one, too. He said word has it she's a relative of mine."

"Oh?" Christy asked, willingly playing into his hands. "And did this relative of yours have a name?"

Christy remembered Cody introducing her to the town's sole insurance agent. He'd also told her that Noah Williams was well acquainted with most folks' business, whether they were his clients or not.

"Said he didn't recall the name, but he thought it was something like Cathy or Christine. Or Christabel."

"Funny. Very funny," Christy muttered, looking out the window, hoping to see Cody's truck.

"I'm telling you right now," Russ said, chuckling again, "the secret's out. The sheriff's gonna take himself a wife."

The next afternoon, Christy was lying on her back in a meadow not far from the ranch house, chewing on a long blade of grass. Cody had taken her flying the previous day, just as she'd guessed, and the experience had been exhilarating, not frightening at all. He lay beside her now, staring at the darkening sky. A series of clouds was rolling in, obliterating the sun, but they'd both decided to ignore the threat of rain.

"Looks like there's a storm coming," Cody said.

"Let it. I don't mind, do you?"

"That depends." He rolled onto his stomach and leaned on his elbows as he gazed lovingly down at her. He didn't seem any more eager to leave the site of their picnic than Christy.

The afternoon had been ideal. Cody had arrived at the

house early in the day, and Christy had met him with a basket full of goodies. Russ complained that she was taking enough food to feed a small army...of ants.

"Depends on what?" she asked, smiling up at him.

"On who I'm with." As if he couldn't stop himself, he leaned over her and pressed his mouth to hers. Then his lips moved along the side of her face and into her hair. He paused and went still as he breathed in the scent of the cologne she'd dabbed behind her ears.

Other than the few kisses they'd exchanged over the past days, Cody hadn't touched her. It wasn't that he didn't desire her, didn't need her. But he held himself back—held himself in check.

Christy understood and in many ways approved.

The physical attraction between them was more powerful than either had ever experienced. It wasn't something to be trifled with.

He kissed her again lightly, softly, gently.

Christy slid her hands up his chest and put her arms around his neck. He kissed her again, his breath hot and quick. "We should stop now," he warned but made no effort to move away from her.

"Yes, I know," she concurred.

He brushed his thumb back and forth over her moist lips as if gathering the needed resolve to pull away from her. She gazed up into his dark, troubled eyes and saw his hesitation. His hands were trembling as he started to roll away from her.

"No." Her cry was instinctive. Urgent.

"Christy..."

"Shh." She sank her fingers into his hair at the sides of his lean, rugged face, raised her head from the soft patch of grass and touched her mouth to his.

His hands tangled with her short curls as he moved the upper half of his body over hers, anchoring her to the ground. Their frenzied kissing seemed to go on and on.

"Enough," he said breathlessly. "We have to stop."

Christy wanted him so desperately; the hunger to love him all but consumed her, and she moved fitfully beneath him.

"Christy," he said, "we're headed for trouble if we don't stop…*now.*"

"I thought sheriffs were trained to deal with any kind of trouble." Her tongue outlined his mouth even as she spoke.

Cody moaned.

Christy sighed.

There didn't seem to be anything strong enough in this world or the next to pull them apart. Christy felt as if she'd been created for this man, for this moment. The love between them was as inevitable as the setting sun. As natural as the ocean waves caressing the shore or the wind stirring the trees. Her blood seemed to vibrate in sympathy, a vibration that grew more insistent—until she realized something was amiss. It wasn't her blood that was pounding in her veins, but rain that was pounding the earth. The clouds burst over them, drenching Christy within seconds.

Cody brought his hands to her face, framing it as he slowly raised his head. His eyes sought hers.

"Cody, it's pouring!"

He responded by kissing her again. "You taste too sweet to move."

"You're getting soaked."

"So are you." He grinned. "And I don't mind if you don't."

"I don't."

"Good." Once more his mouth connected with hers.

A moment later, Christy leaned against him. “We…almost made love.”

“I promised myself we wouldn’t,” he whispered. “And this is a promise I mean to keep.” His hands closed around her upper arms. “Understand?”

Christy nodded.

“I mean it, Christy.”

“Yes, sir.” She teased him with a salute.

Deftly he reversed their positions, smoothly rolling over and taking her with him so she was poised above him. She straddled his hips and arched her head back as the rain pummeled her face. Brushing away her hair, she smiled at the dark, angry sky.

“I suppose I should be grateful,” Cody murmured.

“For the rain? Why?”

“You know why.”

“Yes,” she whispered, “but in some ways I wish…” She let the rest fade, because they were aware of what would have happened if Mother Nature hadn’t intervened when she did.

Seven

"You're *sure* you want to babysit?" Taylor asked, as though she expected Christy to change her mind.

"You're going," Christy said, ushering her older sister to the kitchen where Russ was waiting impatiently. It was the first time Taylor had left Eric, and she was having second thoughts.

"This night is for you and Russ."

"I know but—"

"I have the phone number to the restaurant, the home nurse, the doctor and the hospital. If anything the least bit out of the ordinary occurs, I'll phone someone, so quit worrying."

"Eric's never had a bottle," Taylor protested.

"It's still Mama's milk. He's a smart baby. He'll adjust." After Taylor had spent a long—and hilarious—afternoon learning how to operate the breast pump, each ounce was more precious than gold.

"Christy, I'm not convinced this is such a good idea, after all."

"Don't be ridiculous. Eric will probably sleep the entire time you're away."

"Are you going to let me take you to dinner or not?" Russ's voice boomed from the kitchen. "I'd like to remind you the reservation is for six." After a hard day on the ranch, Russ got too hungry to wait much beyond that for the evening meal.

Cody was the one who'd come up with the idea of the two of them babysitting Eric while Russ and Taylor took an evening for themselves. It was Christy's last night in Cougar Point. First thing in the morning she'd start the long drive across three states. Although she'd been gone less than two weeks, it felt as if an entire lifetime had passed.

"Cody's here," Russ called out. "Just how long does it take you women to put on a little war paint, anyway?" His voice lowered, and Christy could hear him conversing with the sheriff. Her brother-in-law was saying that Taylor and Christy were the two most beautiful women in the county as it was. He contended that they didn't need makeup, and he was having a heck of a time understanding why they bothered with it.

"Hold your horses," Taylor cried, poking her head out the bathroom door and calling down the hallway into the kitchen. "I'll only be a minute."

"Famous last words if I ever heard 'em," Russ grumbled.

As it turned out, her brother-in-law was right. Taylor spent an extra five minutes fussing with her hair and adding a dash of perfume to her wrists. When she'd finished, she checked Eric, gave Christy and Cody a long list of instructions, then reluctantly left the house with her husband.

Cody brought his arm around Christy as they stood on the back porch, watching Russ hold open the car door for Taylor. Christy smiled when Russ stole a lengthy kiss.

"Well," Cody said after Russ had pulled out of the yard, "they're off."

"I don't think they'll win any races."

"No," he chuckled, "I doubt they will." He turned her into his arms and kissed her softly.

"Oh, honestly," Mandy said, scooting past them and down the porch steps. "You two are as bad as Russ and Taylor. If it was me doing these PDAs, you can bet I'd be in big trouble. It seems to me that people over twenty-one get away with a whole lot more than they should."

"PDAs?" Christy asked. "What's that?"

"Public Displays of Affection," Cody whispered close to her ear. As if the temptation were too strong to resist, he caught her lobe between his teeth.

"Cody," she cried, "behave yourself."

"Hey, where are you going?" Cody demanded when Mandy started toward the barn. "I thought you were planning to stick around and chaperone the two of us."

"I'm going to the movies."

"In the barn?"

"Don't be cute with me, Cody Franklin. Just because you've been elected sheriff doesn't mean you can control *my* life."

"You're not the one I want to get cute with."

"Obviously. I figured you two would appreciate a little privacy. Billy Joe's driving me over to Melissa's, and I'm going to the movies with her. She got her license last week."

"I heard rumors along those lines," Cody said with a grin.

"Just don't go sending Bud or any of the other deputies out to tail us." Mandy wagged an accusing finger in Cody's direction. "I know you'd do it, too. Melissa's still a little nervous, and the last thing she needs is a sheriff's car following her into town."

"You think I'd radio for someone to follow her?" Cody

sounded aghast that Mandy would even hint at something so dastardly.

"You'd do it if you thought you could." But she was smiling as she spoke.

Billy Joe, Russ's ranch foreman, stepped out from the barn, freshly shaved. His hair was wet and combed down against the sides of his head. "You ready?"

"Yup," Mandy said, walking toward his battered red pickup.

Taylor had explained that the foreman was interested in Melissa's widowed mother and had been seeing her for the past few months. Apparently Mandy and Melissa were working together to stage an evening alone for the two adults.

Eric wailed loudly, and after bidding Mandy farewell, Christy hurried inside the house and into the master bedroom. Eric was lying in the bassinet waiting for someone to answer his summons.

"What's the matter, big boy?" she asked, reaching for him. His damp bottom answered that question. "So you wet your diaper, did you?" she chided playfully, giving him her finger, which he gripped fiercely.

"I'll change him," Cody said from behind her.

Christy arched her brows in feigned shock. "This I've got to see."

"I'll have you know I've changed more than one diaper in my lifetime."

"That may be true, but it seems to me you took great delight in teasing Russ when he offered to change Eric."

"I've had more practice than Russ, that's all." Cody took a fresh diaper from the pile of folded ones on the dresser. "Both of my sisters have children, and being the generous uncle I am, I've helped out now and then. It's not nearly as difficult as Russ seems to think."

"All right, since you're so sure of yourself, go ahead and I'll see to our dinner." Carefully she handed Cody the baby, then walked to the kitchen.

Taylor had set a frozen pepperoni pizza on the kitchen counter. The only place in Cougar Point that served pizza was the bowling alley; Taylor could go without a lot of luxuries, but she needed her pizza. Every time she was in Miles City, she bought three or four pepperoni pizzas from a nationwide chain, brought them home and promptly froze them.

"I hope you're in the mood for pizza," Christy called, setting the gauge on the oven to the right temperature.

"You mean Taylor's willing to share one of hers? Without us having to ask?"

"I didn't even have to bribe her."

"I may volunteer to babysit more often," Cody said as he entered the kitchen, holding Eric against his shoulder. His large hand was pressed against the infant's tiny back.

Christy paused when she saw them, and her heart beat so fast, it actually hurt. Cody looked so natural with a baby in his arms. As natural as any father. Turning away in an effort to disguise her emotions, she clasped the counter with both hands and waited for the aching tenderness to pass.

She was engaged to an attorney in Seattle, a good friend she'd known for several years, and not once had she pictured him as a father. The fact that they'd likely have children someday had barely crossed her mind.

Yet here she was with Cody and her nephew, and the sight of this big, rugged man holding this precious child was enough to bring tears to her eyes.

"Christy, could you give me..." He hesitated when she didn't immediately respond. "Christy?"

She swallowed the lump in her throat, smeared the tears across her cheek and turned, smiling as brightly as she could. She doubted she'd be able to fool Cody, but she intended to try.

"What's wrong?" His question was filled with concern.

"Nothing..."

"If that's the case, then why are you crying?"

She didn't know how she could explain it, not without sounding as though she required long-term therapy. She was crazy in love with one man, and engaged to another. In a few hours she'd be leaving Cody behind. There were no guarantees, no pledges, no promises between them.

Nothing.

There couldn't be anything while she was engaged to James.

James. Two weeks away from him and she had trouble remembering what he looked like. Inconsequential details occurred to her—that he drank his tea with milk and hadn't worn a pair of jeans since he was thirteen years old. He was endearing, hardworking and brilliant.

And he loved her. At least he thought he did, the same way she'd once assumed she loved him.

The phone rang, startling Eric, who let out a loud wail. Cody whispered reassurances while patting the baby's back.

"I'll get that," Christy said, grateful for the intrusion. "It's probably Taylor calling to check up on us." She hurried into the hallway, wanting to catch the phone before it rang again and frightened Eric a second time.

"Hello," she sang out cheerfully. "This is Palmer's Pizza Parlor. May I take your order?" Taylor would get a kick out of that.

Silence followed.

"It appears I've dialed the wrong number," a male voice said stiffly.

"James? Oh, dear… I thought it was Taylor. This is Christy."

Cody heard Christy's laughter end two seconds after she answered the phone. He knew almost immediately that the man on the other end of the line was her fiancé.

Cody was instantly overwhelmed by confusion and an equally large dose of good old-fashioned jealousy. He was so resentful of Christy's engagement that a long painful moment passed before he could clear his head. He'd never been the jealous type, and now he was all but blinded by it.

He shouldn't have been surprised that James—he had trouble thinking about the other man without tightening his jaw—would call Christy. If Cody was the one engaged to her and she was a thousand miles away, he'd phone her, too. Frequently.

That realization, however, was no comfort. Before many more hours passed, Christy would be leaving Cougar Point. In another two days she'd be back with James. Her weeks with him in Montana would be little more than a fading memory.

Cody wasn't willing to kid himself any longer. There was no use trying to hide from it, or deny it or ignore it. He was in love with Christy Manning. He'd pledged a thousand times that he'd never allow this foolish emotion to take hold of his life again. So much for all the promises he'd made himself. So much for protecting his heart.

Dammit all, he was in love!

But Cody was realistic enough to put their relationship in the proper perspective. Or at least try. Christy was engaged to a hotshot Seattle attorney. He, on the other hand, was a backwoods sheriff. Christy might be infatuated with him now, but once she returned to the big city that could easily change. Believing these few days together meant more to her could be dangerous.

She was going to break the engagement. Or so she claimed. But now something was troubling her. Cody had sensed it when she was fussing with the pizza. When he'd first arrived, she'd been her usual warm, happy self. She'd joked with him as though she hadn't a care in the world.

Cody frowned. Since the afternoon of their picnic when they'd gotten caught in the downpour, Cody had noticed subtle changes in her. She seemed more spontaneous, more open with him.

He was willing to admit there'd been numerous intricate transformations in their relationship over the past ten days. They'd spent hours together, getting to know each other, growing to love each other.

And for most of that time, Cody had to struggle to keep his hands off her.

He found himself studying her at every opportunity, and whenever he did he liked what he saw. She captivated him. When they were alone together, he'd learned how dangerous it was to kiss her—and how difficult it was to stop. She'd press her soft body against his, and it was a test by fire of his limited control.

In the distance Cody heard the anxiety in her voice as her phone conversation with the other man continued. Not wanting to listen in, Cody opened the screen door and walked outside, carrying the baby. He sat on the top step and let his gaze wander across the acres of prime pastureland.

"See all those pesky cattle, Eric?" he whispered to the baby held securely against his shoulder. "It'll all belong to you someday. Take some advice, though, boy…" He was about to tell Russ's son not to get involved with women because all they did was cause a man grief.

But he stopped himself. Christy hadn't caused him grief or trouble. If anything, she'd brought him the truest joy he'd ever felt. He hadn't realized how lonely he was. Nor had he known how isolated his life had become until she'd walked into it, bold as could be.

Okay, he mused, sighing deeply. He was in love. It wasn't supposed to happen, but it had. Damned if he knew what to do next. For a man in his thirties he'd had precious little experience with it. The one other time he'd committed his heart to a woman, it had cost him dearly. He hadn't been willing to place himself at risk again. Not until he met Christy.

Fifteen minutes passed before Christy finally joined him. He heard her moving behind him in the kitchen and felt the swish of the screen door as it opened.

"That was James," she said as she sat down on the step beside him.

"I heard." He didn't mean to be, but he sounded flippant, uncaring.

"He…he's called two other times."

"That's none of my business," he informed her curtly.

"I know, but I want to be honest with you. Are you angry?"

"No."

"You sound angry."

"I'm not." And pigs fly, he told himself.

For a long moment Christy didn't say anything. She sat there looking like an angel, smelling like something out of a rose garden. How was a man supposed to resist her when she gazed at him with those large blue eyes of hers?

"I…almost told him about you. It was on the tip of my tongue to try to explain. But James seemed so preoccupied. He was visiting my parents, and I spoke to them, too, and…" She shrugged. "It was impossible."

"Why's that?" He made a determined effort to take the starch out of his voice.

She hesitated before answering. "My mom and dad like James a lot."

"I'm sure he's perfect son-in-law material."

Christy ignored that comment, which was probably best. He knew he wasn't dealing with this situation well. In fact, he was making a real jackass of himself.

"Now…now that I've had these two weeks with you, I think I accepted his proposal more to please my parents than because I was in love with James."

"I see." Several questions popped into his mind. Christy was a kind person, affectionate and empathetic, someone who tried to please others. Her parents, James, *him.*

"They like Russ, too," she hurried to add.

Cody didn't know what that proved, and frankly he wasn't in the frame of mind to ask.

"Or at least they do now. At first—" She stopped abruptly, as if she'd already said too much.

Cody didn't doubt that the week to come, when she confronted James and her family, would be one of the most difficult of her life. If she went through with it, if she decided to break off the engagement, after all.

"I…can't bear for us to spend our last night together arguing," she whispered.

Cody forced himself to relax. He couldn't bear it, either. He lifted his free arm and placed it around her shoulders, drawing her closer to him and Eric. She turned and smiled shyly up at him. With unhurried ease he lowered his head until their mouths met. The kiss was long and slow and when he raised his head, Cody felt dizzy with yearning.

"Oh, Cody," she moaned, her fingers clutching his shirt collar, her eyes closed. "I hate to leave you."

He hated it, too, feared it more than he'd feared anything. He dreaded the moment she'd drive away from him.

Fear and dread. Fighting those emotions wasn't how he wanted to spend their last hours together.

"Are you sure you haven't forgotten anything?" Taylor asked for the tenth time. They stood beside Christy's car, Taylor in her housecoat, Christy in her traveling clothes—a comfortable pair of faded jeans and a long-sleeved T-shirt.

"I'm positive I've got everything." She'd checked the house twice, and even if she'd inadvertently left something behind, she'd be back. Soon, she hoped. As soon as she could clear up the situation with James. As soon as she was free.

Taylor hugged her, and Russ stepped forward, holding Eric. He placed his free arm around Christy and squeezed tight.

"Drive carefully," Taylor said, "and phone the minute you arrive in Seattle. You know I'll worry until I hear from you." Tears brimmed from her sister's eyes as she reached for Christy one last time. "I really hate to see you go."

"I'll phone," Christy promised. As for the part about hating to leave, that went without saying.

"Where's Cody?" Russ asked, frowning.

"He's got the day shift," Christy explained. Although she'd spent until the wee hours of the morning saying goodbye to the sheriff, she half expected Cody to come barreling down the driveway before she headed out.

"Be a good little baby," she whispered to Eric, kissing

his brow. "Remember your Aunt Christy." With no more reason to delay, she opened her car door and climbed inside.

As she was driving toward the road, Christy looked in the rearview mirror and caught sight of Taylor slipping her arm around her husband's waist. She rested her head on his broad chest and leaned against him, as though she needed his strength, his support.

The scene was a touching one, and Christy found herself blinking back tears.

She was still sniffling as she headed for the highway that would connect her with the interstate. It would be a straight shot to Seattle after that.

Christy planned to make the best time she could. The sooner she got home, the sooner she could set her life in order.

Reaching across the seat, she located the thermos of coffee Taylor had insisted she take with her. Holding it between her legs, she struggled to unscrew the cap. It was difficult to do with one hand. She'd just about given up when a flashing blue and red light was reflected in her rearview mirror.

Cody.

Christy eased to the side of the road, turned off the engine and threw open the door. It was impossible to hold her emotions at bay a moment longer.

Her gaze was blurred with tears, but it didn't matter. Cody had come to her.

By the time she'd climbed out of her car, he was out of his. Not waiting for an invitation, she rushed toward him, sobbing, so grateful he'd come.

He caught her, encircling her waist with his arms and lifting her from the ground. His lips found hers, their mouths connecting with such force that it threw her head back. Christy didn't mind; she was as needy as Cody. As hungry. As lost.

He continued to kiss her, saying with his body what he couldn't with words. That he loved her, needed her and was desperately afraid of losing her.

Christy understood and responded to each doubt.

"There's a side road about two miles back. Do you know where I mean?"

She nodded, remembered having driven past it minutes earlier.

"Meet me there?"

"Yes."

By the time she climbed back into her car, Christy was trembling from the inside out. Her stomach felt tight, and her heart was pounding. Cody made a U-turn and led the way. Christy followed willingly.

He pulled onto the dirt road, stirring up layers of fine dust, partially obliterating his vehicle. He drove past a wide curve, then he parked at the side. Christy watched as he reached for his radio. She got out of her car and waited for him.

"I told dispatch I wouldn't be available for the next fifteen minutes," he explained, his dark eyes holding hers. "I know it's not long enough to say what I want to say, but it's all the time I dare take."

Christy nodded.

He brushed his fingertips over her damp cheek. "You've been crying."

"I…couldn't get the thermos open."

"That's why?" he asked softly.

"No, of course it's not. I don't want to go. Oh, Cody, it's so much harder to leave you than I thought it would be." She tried unsuccessfully to swallow a sob.

"Don't cry," Cody pleaded. He held her against his chest and lowered his head. When he kissed her, it was with desperation and urgency, his mouth slanting over hers. She clung to him, giving as much as she took.

He kissed her neck, nuzzled it. Christy let her head fall back, allowing him to do whatever he wished. She was his for this moment, this hour, this day.

His warm mouth skimmed the length of her throat, planting moist kisses along her shoulder blade…then lower, much lower.

Slowly, as if he was calling upon all the self-control he possessed, Cody raised his head. "Letting you go is the hardest thing I've ever done," he whispered. He smoothed the hair away from her face and kissed her again.

A well-modulated voice came over the radio of the patrol car, reminding them both who and what Cody was. A man who'd pledged to serve and protect. As much as he would've liked to stay with her, the time had come for them to return to their separate lives.

"I'll follow you to the county line," he told her. He held open her car door, looking very much like the dignified sheriff he was. There was little evidence of the loving interlude that had passed between them.

A nod was all Christy could manage. She slid into the driver's seat. Her hand closed around the key. Cody held on to her door, his eyes trained directly ahead.

"I guess this is goodbye," she said hoarsely. "At least for now."

He nodded. "For now. You'll drive carefully?"

"Of course."

Again he nodded, closed her door and then stepped back. He seemed about to say something else, but then changed his mind.

Christy waited for him to enter his patrol car before starting her engine. She sent him a smile and glanced in her rearview mirror as she entered the main road.

True to his word, Cody followed her for several miles. In the distance she read the sign that stated she was leaving Custer County. An immediate knot formed in her throat, making it difficult to swallow.

Her rearview mirror showed Cody's red and blue lights flashing. She pulled over and stopped. Cody eased the patrol car in behind her.

He was out of his vehicle before she had a chance to free her seat belt. Lowering her window, she looked at him expectantly.

"One last thing before you go." His voice was deep and gravelly. "I love you, Christy. Come back to me."

Eight

"James," Christy said quietly, "you know I consider you one of my dearest friends. I've always heard good friends make the best husbands…no," she mumbled, her hands tightening around the steering wheel. "That doesn't sound right. Think, Christy, think!"

She'd just crossed the Idaho-Washington border and was within six hours of Seattle and home. Every mile, every minute, led her closer to the confrontation with James and her parents.

For the past two days Christy had carefully rehearsed what she planned to say, outlining her speech, inordinately conscious of each word.

James would be devastated, her parents shocked.

When it came right down to it, Christy was more worried about confronting her parents than she was James, especially her father, whom she adored. Eric Manning always seemed to think he knew what was best for her; for the most part, Christy had agreed with him. And he'd decided James would be the perfect husband for his youngest daughter.

The hours sped past, far too quickly to suit Christy. As she approached the outskirts of Seattle she found that she was traveling well below the speed limit, which produced several heated stares from her fellow travelers.

Once she'd arrived at her apartment building and had unloaded her car, Christy paced her living room restlessly. She'd assumed that once she was surrounded by everything that was familiar, some of the uneasiness would leave her.

It didn't. In fact, she was more agitated now than ever.

Gathering her courage, she decided to call her family and deal with them first. She planned to ask if it was convenient for her to come over, hoping it would be. The she could quickly put an end to this madness.

Once she was alone with her parents, she'd tell them she intended to break her engagement. Her argument was prepared, her decision unshakable.

Her first choice would've been to do it over the phone, but that would be the cowardly way out. Her only option was to confront them together. Once that was finished she'd go and see James.

As she reached for her phone, her stomach tensed. She wasn't sure what to expect from her parents or James and tried not to dwell on how they'd react to her news. She closed her eyes and prayed someone would answer before she lost her courage and hung up the phone.

"Hello."

"Jason?" He was her second-oldest brother and the handsomest of the lot, or so he liked to claim. At thirty-two he was a "catch," only he enjoyed playing the field far too much to settle down with any one woman.

"Christy? When did you get back?"

"Just a few minutes ago." How odd she sounded. Christy prayed Jason wouldn't notice. "What are you doing there? Are Mom and Dad around?"

"I'm here 'cause I took the day off. Mom and Dad are

out but they'll be back any minute." He paused. "You don't know yet, do you?"

"Know what?" Jason loved playing games, dangling bits of information in front of her like bait, making her hungry for more.

"Never mind."

"Jason, I've been on the road for two days, and to be frank, I'm not up to any of your trick questions." Under normal circumstances Christy would have been amused and played along, but not now.

"Hey, sweetie, no trick questions with this one. All I can say is you have a real surprise waiting for you. Mom's slaved every day since you've been gone, so if I were you, I'd make my presence known soon."

"Thank you so much," Christy muttered sarcastically. "Talking to you is like looking through a telescope with the lens cap on."

"Always happy to oblige," Jason responded with a light chuckle. "Just drop by the house soon.... In fact, the sooner the better."

Christy intended on doing exactly that. "I'll be over in fifteen minutes. By the way, how's Mom?" Breaking her leg had kept Elizabeth Manning at home for several weeks, and Christy knew how terribly disappointed her mother had been about missing this important time with her eldest daughter and newborn grandson.

"Mom's doing great. Especially now..." He didn't finish the enigmatic statement, and Christy refused to fall into his hands by asking what he meant. "If you don't mind, I'll stick around for a while, too. I'd like to get a look at your face once you find out what's been going on around here. Mom's in seventh heaven. At the rate things are going, you're likely to end up in one of those celebrity magazines."

"Cute, Jason, very cute." Christy had no idea what he was talking about, but that was typical of her older brother. Over the last few years, his comments had taken on a biting edge. Christy didn't know what his problem was, but she wished he'd straighten out whatever was wrong.

In an attempt to delay the unavoidable, Christy played back the messages on her answering machine while she leafed through two weeks' worth of mail. Anyone who mattered wouldn't have phoned because they'd know she was out of town, but she couldn't help being curious.

There were several beeps, indicating that whoever had called had hung up before leaving a message. Probably salesmen.

Deciding it was a waste of time, Christy started for her front door when Taylor's voice, hesitant and unsure, came over the tinny speaker. "Christy, call me as soon as you get home. Something's come up that we need to discuss."

There was an uncharacteristic note in her sister's voice, an uncertainty that suggested something was terribly amiss.

Puzzled, Christy returned to the phone and placed a long-distance call to Cougar Point. Mandy answered, sounding as cheerful as ever.

"Taylor's not here," Russ's sister explained. "She drove into Miles City for Eric's first appointment with the pediatrician. Do you want me to have her call you once she gets back? I don't think it'll be too much longer. I know she was anxious to talk to you."

"No. I'm headed to my parents' house now. I'll phone again later." Hopefully by that time everything would be settled. She could contact Taylor and Russ and then talk to Cody. The mere thought of him made her go weak. Seemingly by accident they'd found each other and unexpectedly discovered what it meant to fall in love. Neither of them had been looking for this, neither of them fully understood why it had happened, but it was right. Right for Cody. Right for Christy.

After two long days on the road, she was physically exhausted and mentally depleted. She'd considered delaying this confrontation until she was well-rested and relaxed, but she knew she couldn't do that. The engagement to James hung over her head and she wouldn't find peace until all the obstacles were cleared out of the road that would lead her back to her sheriff.

Her parents' luxury vehicle was in the driveway when Christy drove up. Jason's car was in the street, and Christy parked her own behind his. Even before she'd turned off the engine, her father had opened the front door and was walking toward her, arms outstretched.

Eric Manning embraced his daughter, hugging her tight. From the time she was little Christy had always felt a special closeness to her parents. Most of her friends had rebelled in one way or another against their families, but never Christy. She'd never felt the need.

"When did you get back?" her father asked.

"Not even half an hour ago." She slipped her arm around his thickening waist and they walked toward the sprawling brick house. The lawn was a soft, lush green. Many a happy hour had been spent racing across this very same grass. Echoes of her childhood laughter seemed to mock her now.

Elizabeth Manning stood in the entryway, her left leg encased from her foot to just below her knee in a hot pink cast. She broke into a broad smile as Christy approached the front door.

"Sweetheart, it's so good to have you home."

"It's good to be home, and before you ask, yes, I brought tons of pictures of Eric."

"Oh, that's wonderful, I can't tell you how excited we are that Russ and Taylor named him after your father."

Christy stepped into the house. It was a large home built into a hill overlooking the freeway that cut a wide path through the heart of Seattle. The basement opened onto an enormous, landscaped yard with a profusion of flower beds and space for a vegetable garden, whose bounty spilled over to friends and neighbors every summer.

"How's the leg?"

"Better," Elizabeth said, dismissing her daughter's concern with a quick shake of her head. She was walking with a cane now, leaning heavily upon it. Christy knew her mother well enough to realize Elizabeth Manning would never want to burden her children with the fact that she was in pain. But her mother did look much healthier, Christy mused. The sparkle was back in her eyes, and a flush of excitement glowed from her cheeks. Christy couldn't remember how long it'd been since she'd seen her mother so happy. No doubt the birth of their third grandson was responsible.

"You're looking terrific," Christy said, kissing her mother's cheek.

"Actually, sweetie, we have you to thank for that," her father murmured, sharing an enigmatic smile with his wife.

"Me?" Apparently they were playing the same game as Jason.

"Eric, let's not discuss this in the entryway."

Her father chuckled, and Christy noted that his eyes seemed brighter, too. He certainly was in one of his better moods. Christy would like to think it was all due to her arrival and the fact that she'd brought pictures of their grandson. But somehow she doubted it, especially after having spoken to Jason.

Her second-oldest brother was sitting in the family room

in front of the television when Christy walked in. He was wearing a Seattle Mariners baseball cap, which he had on much of the time.

"Welcome home, little sister," he greeted her. He stood and hugged her, then stepped back, wiggling his eyebrows.

"All right, you guys," Christy said, claiming the easy chair next to Jason. "What's going on around here?"

Her father's mouth started to quiver, as though he was having difficulty holding back his excitement. He shared another look with his wife of thirty-five years.

"If you'll recall, your mother's spirits were low after she fell and broke her leg. Missing out on this special time with Taylor and Russ depressed her."

"I didn't even realize how melancholy I'd become until Eric mentioned it," Elizabeth said. "Sometimes I swear he knows me better than I know myself."

Christy felt herself nod.

"Your father's the one who came up with the idea for an engagement party."

"An...engagement party," Christy echoed, coming half-way out of her chair, appalled and dismayed.

Her mother pressed her fingers to her lips, almost giddy with delight. "We knew you'd be pleased."

"I... I..." Christy was at a complete loss for words. Somehow she managed a smile and slumped back into the cushions of the overstuffed chair.

"You can't imagine what fun we've had," Elizabeth continued, her voice animated. "I'm afraid your father got carried away. He insisted we order the best of everything. We've rented the Eagles Hall, got the invitations mailed—engraved ones. Oh, sweetie, I can hardly wait for you to see them. We spent hour after hour with the caterers. I can't even *begin* to tell you what a fabulous time I—we—

had planning every detail of this party. I can't help feeling proud of everything we accomplished in such a short time."

"It was just what your mother needed," Christy's father inserted smoothly, looking equally delighted. "Elizabeth's been like a kid again from the moment we decided to go through with this."

"I see." Christy went completely numb. It seemed impossible that no one was aware of it.

"I suppose we're a pair of old fools, but when Taylor married Russ in Reno, your father and I felt cheated out of a large family wedding. We've been looking forward to throwing one for years."

"When?" It was torture getting the word past the tightness that all but blocked her throat.

"That's the crazy part," Jason told her. "Mom and Dad put this entire thing together in two weeks."

Christy still didn't understand; not much of the conversation made sense. Her look must have conveyed her confusion.

"The party's tomorrow night," Elizabeth said, her face radiating her excitement.

"Tomorrow night?"

"I know it sounds crazy, and we took a chance booking it so close to the end of your vacation, but there were only a few dates available at the Eagles Hall, and it was either tomorrow night or three months from now."

"In fact, the only reason we were able to get the hall is because of a last-minute cancellation," Eric said. "I had no idea we'd need to book this sort of thing so far in advance."

"James?" No one seemed to notice she was having trouble speaking, which Christy supposed was a blessing of sorts.

"He knows, of course, but we decided to keep it a secret for you. A welcome-home surprise."

Christy nodded, hating the way she continued to sit in her parents' home, saying nothing when it felt as if the foundations of her world were crumbling at her feet. Her mother and father and Jason were all looking at her, waiting for some response, but for the life of her, Christy couldn't give them one.

Her eyes met with her brother's.

He winked broadly. "Mom and Dad are sparing no expense. If the wedding's half as elaborate as the engagement party, then your big day's going to be spectacular."

Eric Manning chuckled. "It isn't every father who has a daughter as special as Christy."

Christy forced a smile although she longed to stand up and beg them to put an end to this craziness. She didn't love James. She loved Cody. She couldn't possibly go through with an engagement to a man she didn't intend to marry.

She glanced from her mother to her father, both of them staring at her with bright, eager smiles, as though waiting for her to burst into a song of praise for their efforts.

"I… I…" The words froze on her lips.

"Honey, look," Elizabeth murmured devotedly to her husband. "Christy's speechless. Oh, sweetie, you don't need to say anything. Your father and I understand. If anyone should be giving thanks, it's me. I was so miserable after my fall. Planning this party was the best thing in the world for me. I've loved every minute of it. Keeping it a surprise has been so much fun."

There had to be a plausible excuse she could use to avoid this farce of an engagement party. "I don't have a dress." The words escaped her lips almost as quickly as they formed in her mind.

"Not to worry," Elizabeth said, her eyes glowing even brighter. "I thought of everything, if I do say so myself.

I went shopping the other day and picked out a dress for you. If you don't like it, or it doesn't fit, we can exchange it first thing in the morning."

First thing in the morning. The words echoed in her ears. "I… I'm supposed to go back to work." That sounded reasonable to her. After two weeks away from the law firm, Christy was expected back. They needed her. They were short-staffed without her. She couldn't demand additional time off to exchange a party dress.

"No need to worry about that, either," Eric said. "James has that covered. He talked it over with the office manager, and she's given you two extra days off with pay."

"Tomorrow, of course, will be filled with all the last-minute details for the party," Elizabeth rattled on, rubbing her palms together.

"You didn't tell Taylor?" Her older sister would've said something to her; Christy was sure of it.

"Well, not right away. I mailed her a long letter and an invitation so it would arrive the day you were scheduled to leave Montana. I'm guessing she has it by now. I couldn't take the chance of mailing it any sooner for fear you'd find it, and I didn't want to say anything when we phoned in case she inadvertently let the cat out of the bag. I wanted to keep this a surprise."

"I see," Christy murmured.

"Your father and I don't expect Taylor to fly home for the party, not so soon after having the baby. She and Russ will come out for the wedding. Which is something else we need to discuss. Talk to James, sweetie—the sooner we have a date, the better. There's so much to do, and I so want this wedding to be carefully planned. I can't tell you how much I've learned in the past two weeks. Right after the party tomorrow night, we're going to sit down and discuss the wedding."

Christy nodded, simply because she lacked the courage to explain there would never be a wedding, at least not one in which James was the bridegroom.

"You are surprised, aren't you?" Jason demanded, looking exceptionally cocky, as though he was the person responsible for pulling this whole affair together.

Surprise was too mild a word for what Christy was experiencing. Even shock and dismay were too mild.

Horror and panic more aptly described her feelings.

James! She needed to talk to James. He'd help her. He'd understand, and then together they'd clear up this mess. Together they could confront her parents and make *them* understand.

She stood before she realized what she was doing. Everyone in the room seemed to be staring holes straight through her. Glancing around, she offered them each a weak smile.

Always dutiful. Always obedient. Never causing a concern or a problem. Christy was about to destroy her good-girl image.

But first she had to talk to James.

Two messages were waiting for Christy on her answering machine when she returned late that afternoon. The first was from Cody and the second from Taylor.

Christy didn't answer either.

Instead she sat in her living room, staring into space, weighed down by guilt, pressured beyond anything she'd ever experienced and entangled in circumstances beyond her control.

How long she stayed there Christy didn't know. Here she was safe. Here she was protected. Here she could hide.

That small sense of security, however, quickly disintegrated. Knowing there was nothing else she could do to stop the progression of events, she stood and walked into the kitchen. She paused in front of the phone, then abruptly picked it up before she had a change of heart.

Cody wasn't home, and she left an all-too-brief message. Her next call was to Taylor.

"Christy, what's going on?" Taylor burst out the instant she recognized her younger sister. "I got this crazy letter from Mom about a surprise engagement party for you. What's happening?"

"You mean about the party?" Christy asked. Her voice lacked any level of emotion. She had none left.

"Of course I mean the party," Taylor cried. "Do you mean to say you're going through with it?"

"I don't have any choice."

"Christy, you can't be serious! What about Cody? I thought you were in love with him. I may be out of line here, but I could've sworn you…" She inhaled deeply. "I'd better stop before I say something I shouldn't. Just answer me one question. Do you or do you not love Cody Franklin?"

Christy wiped the tears from her face and nodded wildly. "You know I do."

"Then it seems to me you're allowing Mom and Dad to dictate your life."

"You don't understand," Christy whimpered.

"What's there to understand?"

"Mom broke her leg—" She couldn't go on, wondering if she should even try to describe this hopeless mess. Even if she did it was doubtful Taylor would understand.

"I know about Mom's accident," Taylor returned impatiently.

"She was terribly depressed afterward. I saw it, we all did, but apparently it didn't go away like everyone expected it would. Then Dad came up with the brilliant idea of planning this engagement party."

"Oh, dear."

"Mom put everything she had into it, and now—"

"Christy, I know it's difficult, but you've got to remember Mom and Dad planned this party without consulting you."

That was true enough, but it didn't change the facts. "I can't humiliate them. I thought if I talked to James, told him about Cody, everything would work out, but then I discovered I couldn't do that, either. I wanted us to face Mom and Dad and make some kind of decision together about the party, but that's impossible now. Everything's so crazy.... I can't believe this is happening."

"Do you mean to say James doesn't know about Cody yet?"

Christy closed her eyes.

"Christy?"

"I...couldn't tell him." She stiffened, waiting for the backlash of anger that was sure to follow.

After a short silence, Taylor said, "You *couldn't* tell James about Cody?"

The trouble she had forming the words was painfully obvious. "You heard me."

There was another silence. "I see."

"How could you possibly *see?*" Christy demanded, keeping her voice level, when she wanted to scream at the accusation she heard in her sister's voice. "I went to him, fully intending to tell him everything."

"Then why didn't you?"

"For two months James has been preparing for the most important trial of his career."

"You mean to say you're worried about James's *career?* At a time like this?"

Christy ignored her sister's outburst. "A businessman from Kirkland… You must know Alfred Mulligan. He's the one who does all those crazy television ads. Anyway, he's been charged with cheating on his taxes. The whole case is extremely complicated, and you know as well as I do how messy this kind of thing can get when the federal government is involved." She waited for Taylor to agree with her.

"What's that got to do with anything?"

Christy hated the angry impatience she heard in her sister's voice. It was all too clear that Taylor was upset with her. Christy felt Taylor's disapproval as strongly as a slap. All her life she'd experienced love and approval, especially from her family, and it hurt more than she could bear to feel such overwhelming censure from her only sister.

"You don't understand," Christy tried again. "James has been working day and night for weeks to get ready for this trial. It was scheduled for the first of next month, but he learned this afternoon they've called the case early. He's making the opening statement tomorrow morning."

"I'm afraid I don't understand the relevance of all this."

"I don't expect you to. James has worked himself into a frenzy. I've never seen him like this. So much hangs in the balance for him."

"That's fine, but I still don't—"

"He has a chance to win this case, but it's going to be difficult," Christy went on, cutting off her sister's protest. "James knows that. Everyone does, but if by some miracle he can pull this off, it could mean a partnership for him."

"Oh, Christy," Taylor said with a groan.

"If I broke off the engagement now, it could ruin everything for him."

"That's James's problem, not yours."

"Maybe it is his problem. I don't know anymore. I do know that I can't do this to him. Not on the eve of the most important trial of his career. Not when James has finally been given the chance to prove himself. If anything went wrong, I'd always blame myself."

The silence hummed as Taylor considered her words. "What about Cody?" she asked finally. "Have you given any thought to *his* feelings?"

"Yes." Christy had thought of little else. Never in her life had she asked more of a person than she was asking of Cody. Another woman had destroyed his trust, and there was nothing to assure Christy that he'd want anything to do with her after this.

As painful as it was, as difficult, she found she couldn't humiliate her parents and risk destroying James's chances with this case.

Even if it meant she lost Cody.

Nine

Something was wrong. Cody felt it instinctively, all the way to the marrow of his bones. Christy had left two separate messages on his answering machine, and every time he'd played them back, he'd felt an achy, restless sensation. It wasn't what she'd said, but how she'd said it. She sounded lighthearted and cheerful, but beneath the facade, Cody heard unmistakable confusion.

He'd tried to phone her back, but to no avail. Unable to sleep, he rose in the early morning hours and drove around the back roads outside town, trying to make sense of what was happening. Or not happening.

He couldn't find the answers, not when he didn't understand the questions.

His greatest fears were about to be realized. Once again he'd fallen in love, involved his life with a woman who couldn't be trusted.

Christy isn't Becca, his heart shouted, but Cody had virtually given up listening.

The sun had barely crested the hill as Cody sat in his Cherokee, looking at the valley below, pondering what he should do. If anything. Dammit all, he should never have let this go so far. Becca had taught him everything he needed to know about women and love.

Dawn burst over the hillside, with golden rays of sunlight splashed against the rugged landscape, and small patches of light on the horizon.

Cody released a jagged sigh, then started his car. As much as he'd like to turn his back on the entire situation and pretend the past two weeks with Christy hadn't happened, he knew the effort would be futile.

He glanced at his watch, knowing Russ and Taylor would be up and about. He needed to talk.

The light from the kitchen window glowed as Cody approached the ranch house. He pulled in to the yard, turned off the engine and waited until the door opened and Russ appeared on the back porch.

Climbing out of the car, Cody joined his friend.

"I thought that was you," Russ said, opening the door in mute invitation.

Cody removed his hat and set it on the peg while Russ walked over to the coffeepot and automatically poured him a mug.

"Taylor's feeding Eric," Russ said. "She'll be out in a few minutes."

Cody nodded and straddled a high-backed wooden chair.

Russ sat across from him. "Personally I don't think this thing with Christy is as bad as it sounds. Although, to be honest, if I was in your shoes, I don't know what I'd do."

Cody hadn't a clue what his friend was talking about but decided not to say anything, hoping Russ would explain without him having to ask.

"How're you holding up?"

"Fine." Cody was about to drop the charade and ask his friend what was going on when Taylor came in, wearing a long pink housecoat. Her hair was mussed and fell to the middle of her back. She offered Cody an apologetic smile, and once more he was left to interpret the meaning. His gut was tightening, and he didn't know how much longer he could go on pretending.

"Good morning, Cody," Taylor greeted him, helping herself to a cup of coffee. It seemed to Cody that her smile conveyed more concern than welcome.

It was all Cody could do not to leap to his feet and demand someone tell him what was happening.

"I suppose you're here to talk about Christy?" she asked gently. If Russ hadn't said a word, Cody would've guessed something was wrong just from the way Taylor was looking at him—as if she wanted to put her arms around him and weep.

"Christy's been on my mind," he answered brusquely.

"You realize she doesn't have any choice, don't you?" Taylor added. Her eyes, so like Christy's, appealed to him to be open-minded. "Russ and I've gone round and round about this and—"

"Any choice about what?" Cody demanded. His friends exchanged a surprised look.

"You mean Christy didn't get hold of you?"

"No."

"Then you don't know about the engagement party?"

"All I got was two messages in which she sounds like Mary Sunshine. I *knew* she wasn't telling me something. I sensed that right away."

It took a moment for the news to hit him. Engagement party? That meant she was still involved with… If he hadn't already been sitting down, Cody would have needed a chair fast. He'd heard of men who'd had their feet kicked out from under them, but he'd never understood the expression until then.

"Oh, dear." Taylor reached for her coffee and it was clear that she was upset. Her hands trembled, and her eyes avoided meeting his.

Cody transferred his attention to Russ, who looked as uncomfortable as his wife. "What's going on?" Cody asked in a deceptively calm voice.

Once more, husband and wife exchanged glances as if silently deciding between themselves who would do the talking. Apparently Russ presented his wife with the unpleasant task, because she swallowed, then turned to Cody. "My sister's caught in a series of difficult circumstances."

"What the hell does that mean?"

"Apparently my mother took the two weeks while Christy was here in Montana to plan an elaborate engagement party. It seems her spirts needed a boost, and my father thought involving her in planning a party would help. Unfortunately he was right. Mom threw herself into the project and arranged the event of the year, starring Christy and James."

"Are you telling me she's going through with it?"

"She doesn't have much of a choice. The celebration's scheduled for this evening."

This second bit of information hit Cody with the same impact as the first. "You've got to be kidding!"

"I wish we were," Russ said, his expression annoyed. "My in-laws mean well, but Christy's trapped in this fiasco simply because there isn't time to cancel it now."

"What about James?" Cody asked, stiffening as he mentioned the other man's name. Every time he thought about the Seattle attorney, he struggled with anger and jealousy. James Wilkens had far more claim to Christy than he did.

They both loved her, but it was James who'd given her an engagement ring. It was James her parents wanted her to marry.

"James is another problem," Taylor whispered.

Cody didn't understand. "You mean he's refusing to release her from the engagement?"

"He doesn't know Christy intends to break it off," Russ said without preamble.

Cody would've accepted just about anything more readily than he did this news. Christy had played him for a fool, used him the same way Becca had, for her own selfish purposes—whatever they might be.

"She's going to tell James everything," Taylor said heatedly in her sister's defense.

Cody didn't bother to comment, still reeling from this last news.

"When I talked to her, she'd just returned from seeing James. She'd gone to him with the best of intentions, wanting to tell him about you and break off the engagement before it went any further. She was hoping the two of them could discuss the engagement party and decide what could be done."

"She didn't say a word about me to James, did she?" At Taylor's wilted look, Cody decided that was all he needed to know. He stood, emptied the contents of his mug into the sink and set it on the counter so hard that it almost shattered.

"She couldn't tell him," Taylor cried. "If you love Christy the way you claim, you'll listen long enough to find out why."

Cody did love Christy, but he didn't know how much more battering his heart and his pride could take. He stood frozen, waiting for Taylor to continue.

"If she told James about you, she might put his entire career in jeopardy." For the next ten minutes Russ and Taylor took turns explaining the situation as best they could.

"Christy doesn't have any choice but to follow through with this farce of a party, don't you see?"

Taylor did an admirable job of presenting her sister's case; Cody would give her that.

She kept her pleading eyes focused on him. "If it'd been up to her, she would've ended the engagement five minutes after she got home."

Cody didn't respond, although it was apparent his friends were waiting for him to say something.

"You've got to appreciate the situation Christy's in," Taylor went on. "What would *you* have done had the circumstances been reversed?"

Cody closed his eyes, pondering the dilemma. What would he do?

He just didn't know.

"Oh, sweetheart!" Christy's mother exclaimed, stepping back to examine the effect of the full-length layered blue dress. "You look like an angel. Eric, come and see."

Eric Manning, wearing a white tuxedo with a pale blue cummerbund the same shade as Christy's dress, stepped gingerly into the living room. He eyed his youngest daughter and nodded approvingly. "You make an old man proud," he said with a warm smile.

"You've never looked lovelier," her mother added.

Christy managed a smile. She had no idea how she was going to make it through this party. She might be able to fool her parents, but surely someone would notice. Rich would. Of her three brothers, she'd always been closest to

Rich. He'd take one look at her and immediately guess that something was wrong.

Not that it would make any difference. She'd stand before family and friends and pretend to be madly in love with James, pretend to be an eager bride-to-be. But the only thing Christy was eager for at the moment was to put this evening behind her.

"I'd like to propose a toast to the happy couple, my sister Christy and the love of her life, James Wilkens." Rich Manning raised his champagne glass to the couple.

Christy grinned at her brother and fought the urge to empty her champagne glass over his head. Of all the guests, she'd expected him to realize how miserable she was. Instead, he'd unwittingly made things even worse.

Smiling faces nodded appreciatively at her brother's words before the party-goers sipped the vintage champagne. The round of toasts had been going on for several minutes. Christy wasn't sure how much more of this she could endure.

Her father had proposed the first toast, followed by her uncles and all three of her brothers. Each seemed to add something to the list of blessings they wished for her and James.

Christy swallowed another sip of champagne as her fiancé stood at her side, tall and debonair. She could barely look at him without being overwhelmed with guilt. They'd spent two hours in each other's company, and neither had spoken more than a handful of sentences.

In retrospect Christy wondered how she could possibly have agreed to spend the rest of her life with James. He was wonderful, but it was increasingly obvious that they were painfully mismatched.

Hoping she wasn't being conspicuous, Christy scanned the gathering, wondering if it was possible for anyone to read her thoughts. Not that it would do any good.

"Would you like something to eat?" James asked, glancing toward the linen-draped tables where trays of hors d'oeuvres lay waiting.

Christy shook her head, positive she wouldn't be able to keep down a single bite. "Nothing for me, thanks. What about you?"

"I'm fine," James answered.

The music started, and a handful of couples were making their way to the gleaming wooden floor. "I've always been terrible at this sort of thing," James confessed, reaching for Christy's hand. "But I suppose it's expected of us."

Christy nodded, wanting nothing more than to escape. A path was cleared as James led her to the dance floor and slipped his arm around her waist, careful to maintain a respectable distance between them. The music was slow and melodious, a love ballad, whose words seemed to ridicule her more than anything that had preceded the dancing.

James smiled into Christy's eyes as they moved across the floor. Soon other couples joined them.

Her fiancé seemed to relax a little more now that they weren't the only two on the floor. For that matter so did Christy. "I'm sorry I haven't been myself this evening," James murmured regretfully.

Christy was ashamed to admit she hadn't noticed. Her whole attention had been focused on simply getting through this ordeal.

"The Mulligan case is going to take up a lot of my time over the next few weeks, and I can only hope you'll be patient with me."

Christy was horrified to realize she'd forgotten all about

the trial and how important it was to him. "Oh, James, I'm so sorry. I didn't even ask how everything went this morning."

"Not as well as I'd hoped," he mumbled under his breath.

"I'm sorry," she said again. "But I understand you're going to be busy. In fact, it might actually work out for the best. You see, I met—" She wasn't allowed to finish.

"I knew you'd be understanding," he said, cutting her off. He smiled gently and drew her toward him. "You always have been."

"You, too," she whispered sarcastically, but James didn't respond.

Closing her eyes, she tried to pretend it was Cody's arms around her. That was the only way she'd be able to continue this farce. Keeping his image in her mind gave her a sense of purpose, a means of enduring this disastrous night.

After a respectable number of dances, James escorted her off the floor. Until then Christy hadn't noticed how tired and defeated he looked. Several family members insisted on dances with her, and Christy found herself on the floor with a number of uncles, her brothers and longtime family friends.

James was doing his duty, as well, keeping the women from both families occupied. She did see that he managed to do so without dancing with any of them, and that made her smile, however briefly.

It wasn't until the end of the evening, when Christy decided she just might survive, that her aunt Lois, her mother's youngest sister, asked the impossible question. "When's the date for the wedding?"

The whole room went silent. The music ceased, and everyone turned to stare at Christy and James. They were sitting together in a long row of folding chairs against the wall. It was the first time they'd sat down that evening.

Christy felt like a cornered animal. The cracker in her mouth seemed to go down her throat whole.

"You don't have an engagement party without letting those you love know when you're planning the wedding," Aunt Lois said.

James glanced at Christy. "We haven't had a chance to discuss a date, have we, darling?"

"No," Christy muttered. It wouldn't look good to announce that she was counting the days until she could break the engagement. If she was going to discuss a wedding date with anyone, it would be with Cody. But he hadn't asked her, and after he learned about this evening, Christy doubted he'd ever want to see her again.

"Springtime is always lovely for a wedding." Aunt Lois stood directly in front of her, waving her arms, demanding the attention of Christy and everyone else. "George and I were married in May, and the flowers were gorgeous." Pressing her gloved hands together, she released a slow sigh of remembered happiness.

"But May's almost a year away," Elizabeth Manning objected loudly, walking across the dance floor to join this all-important discussion. "Why wait so long? I was thinking more along the lines of November."

"November?" Christy echoed.

"The leaves are always so pretty then. You know how I love orange, brown and yellow," she said, looking at her daughter.

Already Christy could see her mother's mind working, plotting and planning. She'd enjoyed making the arrangements for the engagement party so much that she couldn't wait to start on all the pomp and ceremony of a formal wedding.

"With your dark coloring, Christy, an autumn theme would be perfect."

"Personally I favor a December wedding," Eric Manning shouted. He'd obviously had more than his share of champagne.

"December?" Elizabeth shrieked, shaking her head. "Never."

"All right," Eric countered. "Let's ask Christy and James which date they prefer. This is, after all, their wedding."

"Ah." Christy couldn't think. Her mind froze along with her hands, which were raised halfway to her mouth, her fingers clutching a delicate artichoke canapé. In a panic she looked at James, her eyes wide in speechless appeal. If ever she needed rescuing, it was now.

"What do you say, sweetheart?" her mother asked.

By some miracle Christy managed to lower the cracker to her plate. "I… I haven't given the matter much thought."

"When George and I decided to marry, we couldn't do it fast enough," Aunt Lois informed the group.

"November," James said decisively. "Your aunt's right. There's no need to put off the wedding."

"We don't have to choose a date *now,* do we?" Christy asked. "Not when you're so busy with the Mulligan case."

His hand patted hers gently. "This trial will be over soon enough, and I've been selfish not to consider your feelings. Naturally you and your mother will want to start making all the necessary arrangements."

"November would be perfect." Elizabeth Manning opened her purse and withdrew a small appointment calendar. "Let's pick the date right now. How does the twelfth sound?"

Once more Christy found herself speechless. "Ah…"

"The twelfth sounds grand," James said triumphantly, and lightly touched his lips to Christy's cheek. "Isn't that right, darling?"

The whole world came to an abrupt halt, awaiting Christy's reply. The walls seemed to be falling in around her, until she could hardly breathe.

"Christy?" her mother probed, eyeing her curiously. "November 12 would be a beautiful day for a wedding, don't you agree?"

Cody slowly patrolled the deserted streets of Cougar Point, but his mind wasn't on the job. The crime wave of the century could be happening before his very eyes, and Cody doubted he would've noticed.

How could he? The only reason he'd agreed to take this shift was in an effort to forget that Christy was with James tonight.

While Cody dutifully served his constituents, Christy was sipping champagne with her attorney fiancé. No doubt his diamond was firmly placed on her ring finger and she was having the time of her life.

It hurt.

The pain was as real as anything he'd ever endured. Except that it hurt more. There wasn't a thing he could do to alter the chain of events that had led Christy into this predicament. Apparently there wasn't much she could do, either.

He tried to remind himself that the woman he loved would go to great lengths not to hurt others, even if it meant hurting herself. But Christy wasn't the only one suffering.

Cody felt like a casualty of circumstance. And there was nothing he could do….

It was late when he rolled into the station—after eleven. He got out of the patrol car and saw Russ's pickup truck parked out front. Frowning, he made his way inside.

Russ Palmer unfolded his long legs and stood. "About time you got here."

"Problems?"

Russ nodded. "A few. I thought it might be a good idea if we talked."

The anxiety that had been following him around all night grew more intense. "I'll meet you in ten minutes."

Since the bowling alley was the only restaurant in town that stayed open this late, Cody didn't need to mention where they'd meet.

Russ was already in the booth, holding a white ceramic mug, when Cody walked inside. Cody slid in across from him, wondering how his friend had come to pick the same booth he'd sat in with Christy. He'd been in love with her then and hadn't even known it.

"What's so all-fired important to bring you out this time of night?" Cody asked.

"Taylor."

That didn't explain a lot.

The cook brought out a second mug for Cody and returned to the kitchen. Russ stared after the other man.

"You don't mean Taylor, you mean Christy, right?"

Russ nodded glumly.

"What did she do now? Run off with Gypsies? Marry the garbageman?"

"Worse."

"I suppose this has to do with the engagement party."

Once more Russ nodded. "Apparently no one guessed her real feelings. It seems everyone was too concerned about how much liquor made it into the punch bowl to ask Christy how *she* felt about the whole thing."

"I should be grateful for that?"

"No," Russ answered. "She went through the evening like a real trooper. She loves her family, and she did this for their sake, but she didn't like it."

"She's not the only one."

"I can well imagine," Russ said with a sympathetic sigh. "I know how I'd feel in the circumstances."

"I'm not sure what to do anymore." Cody rubbed his face wearily. "Tell me what happened. I can deal with that better than not knowing."

Russ seemed uncertain where to begin.

"Just spit it out," Cody said, trying to persuade himself he should forget he'd ever met Christy Manning.

"She's sick. Started throwing up at the party. Taylor talked to her and said Christy's in pretty rough shape."

For all his effort to portray disinterest, Cody's heart raced at the news. "What's wrong?"

"It's not what you think."

"If she's feeling as bad as you say, then why didn't she contact me?"

"She's been trying to reach you for two days."

"I've been busy. What was I supposed to do? Phone her and suggest she enjoy her engagement party? I have some pride left, and frankly I'm holding on to it."

"She needs to talk to you. Call her."

Cody shrugged.

"If you've been avoiding her, don't. She doesn't deserve this. Not now."

"I've tried phoning," Cody confessed, as if admitting to a shortcoming in his character. "She's never there."

"You didn't leave a message?"

"No," he answered reluctantly. What was there to say in a message that would help their situation? As far as he could see, nothing.

"She's at her apartment now. Take my advice and put each other out of this misery. Talk to her."

Ten minutes later Cody unlocked his front door, turned on the light and walked into his living room. He scowled at the phone—but he didn't know who he was trying to kid. He practically lunged at it, he was so hungry for the sound of Christy's voice.

He dialed the Seattle number Russ had given him, and Christy answered even before the first ring had finished.

"Cody?" Her voice caught on his name before he had a chance to speak.

"Hello, Christy," he said in a voice that, to his own ears, sounded stiff and cold.

"Thank you for calling me."

Before he could respond, she asked, "Did Taylor tell you?"

"Tell me what?"

"What happened at the party."

"No." There was more? "Russ came into town and asked me to call you. He alluded to something but never said exactly what. Go ahead and tell me."

A slight hesitation followed. "I…it isn't easy."

"Dammit, Christy, what's going on now?" The possibilities that came to mind did little to put him at ease.

"I want to be honest with you," she said, her voice shaking. "I…" She paused, and Cody could hear her drag a deep breath through her lungs. "Something happened at the party tonight…something I never intended."

Cody wanted to come across as nonchalant, but he

couldn't. He expelled his breath, trying to think of what she might have done that would make him stop loving her.

Nothing. She could do nothing. Even if she were to inform him that she'd given in to the pressure and married James that very night, it wouldn't be enough. He'd still love her. He'd always love her.

"November 12," she whispered.

"I beg your pardon?" She'd gone from guessing games to riddles.

"The wedding's set for November 12."

Ten

Christy rolled over and glanced at the illuminated dial of her clock radio. It was 10:00 a.m.

This was supposed to be her first day back at the office, but she'd had to phone in sick. A flu bug was what she'd told Marcia, the office manager, who was sympathetic enough to suggest Christy stay home. But it wasn't the flu that was making her ill.

It was something else entirely. Christy was heartsick, afraid she'd lost Cody forever. She felt trapped, doing what was right for everyone but herself.

Now she was wide awake, and the day stretched out before her. She could occupy herself with mindless game shows on television, but that would only use up an hour or two. Reading would help pass the time—if she could concentrate. She might even give some thought to phoning Cody.

No.

That was out of the question. Cody didn't want to talk to her, not anymore. She'd said everything she could to make him understand her predicament two nights earlier. The conversation had gone reasonably well until she'd told him she'd been forced to set a date for the wedding.

An unexpected sob tore through her throat, and fresh tears flooded her eyes. She'd done a lot of weeping over the past days. Damp, crumpled tissues lay scattered across her bedspread where she'd carelessly discarded them.

She loved Cody, and nothing she'd been able to say had convinced him of that. Cody, being a sheriff, saw life in terms of black and white. Either she'd agreed to the wedding date or she hadn't. Unfortunately Christy had sanctioned November 12, more or less, when pressured by James and her entire family. As soon as she confessed as much, her telephone conversation with Cody had ended abruptly.

She'd pleaded with him for understanding, tried to assure him she'd never willingly marry James, but it hadn't helped. They'd hung up with Cody promising to contact her after he'd had time to think.

Nearly thirty-four hours had passed. Surely he'd had adequate opportunity to come to some kind of decision.

The doorbell chimed, and sniffling, Christy reached for another tissue. She blew her nose before tossing aside her covers and climbing out of bed. She intended to send her visitor, whoever it was, away. She was in no mood for company.

With her luck, it was probably her mother wanting to discuss color schemes for the bridesmaids' dresses. If her car hadn't been parked directly in front of her door, she wouldn't even bother answering.

"Who is it?" she asked, squinting through the peephole and seeing no one.

"Cody Franklin."

"Cody…oh, Cody." Christy threw open the door. For one wild second she did nothing but stare into his wonderful face, convinced he'd been conjured up by her imagination. Before another second could pass, she launched herself into his arms.

Cody dropped his suitcase, clasping her around the waist with both arms. He hauled her to him with joyful abandon. Their mouths met in a kiss so fierce, it threatened to steal her breath. He held her as if he was starving for the taste of her, and meant to make up for every minute of every day they'd been apart.

Christy's arms encircled his neck, her mouth finding his. She kissed him over and over in an agony of need.

With a shudder Cody tore his mouth from hers and spread a wildfire of kisses over her face. His arms were around her waist, and her feet dangled several inches off the ground as his chest heaved with deep breaths.

Weeping for joy, Christy pressed her head against his shoulder, feeling completely at ease for the first time since she'd left Montana. She was in Cody's arms. Nothing could hurt her again.

"It might be a good idea if we went inside," he whispered.

Christy nodded. Slowly he released her, and she slid down.

"How'd you get here?" she asked, searching the parking lot for signs of his Cherokee.

"I flew," he explained as his hand stroked the tumbling curls away from her face. "I couldn't leave things between us the way they were. At least not without talking this out face-to-face. I took three days' vacation, hoping we could put an end to this craziness."

Christy was hoping for the same thing. She took his wrist and pulled him inside her small apartment. She closed the door, then turned to face him, her hands behind her.

From the moment she'd come home, she'd stood alone

against what seemed like overwhelming forces. Her mother needed her. James needed her. Everyone wanted a part of her until she felt as if she were being torn in two.

"How…how'd you know I was home?" she asked once her mind had cleared enough to process her thoughts.

"I phoned the law firm from the airport. They told me you were out with the flu."

Christy couldn't believe what she was hearing. Cody had phoned her at the office!

"You disapprove?" His eyes narrowed.

"No." But her heart was thumping loudly. It wasn't likely anyone had given his inquiry a second thought. Even if they had, she wouldn't be around to answer their questions.

"But the fact that I talked to someone who knew you *and* James upset you, didn't it?" He started to pace her living room. Four long strides covered the entire length of it. He buried one hand in his back pocket while the other massaged the muscles of his neck. "You're so afraid your precious James is going to find out about me."

"That's not true," she denied vehemently. Too late, Christy realized she probably was the most pathetic sight he'd ever seen.

Her eyes were red and swollen, and she wasn't even dressed. The five-year-old pajamas she was wearing were as sexy as dishcloths. Not that any of this seemed to bother Cody, who was apparently far more interested in arguing with her than ravishing her.

In her emotionally fragile condition Christy was much too weak to withstand a heated verbal exchange. She'd already heard from Taylor, who knew without a doubt what would be best. Russ, too. But they weren't listening to *her.* It was easy for them to dish out advice when they were a thousand miles from the situation.

She was the one on the front line, the one who'd have to face their parents. She seemed to be the only one who appreciated the long years of hard work that had led James to this point in his career. She couldn't, *wouldn't,* ruin his chances now.

If Cody Franklin expected her to buy their happiness at another's expense, then he didn't really know her at all.

He turned to face her. Boldly she met his eyes, staring down the hot accusation she saw in them.

Suddenly Christy felt his anger start to dissolve, replaced with doubt and pain. Defeated, he expelled a harsh breath. His shoulders sagged. "Forget I ever mentioned James. I didn't come here to fight about him."

"Why did you come?"

He didn't seem to have an answer, or if he did, he wasn't willing to supply it just yet. He looked away from her and plowed his fingers through his hair. "To talk some sense into you and end this confusion before we both go insane."

How Christy wished it was that simple.

"This isn't as complicated as you're making it," he said. "Either you're serious about loving me or you aren't. It should be a matter of setting the record straight, but—"

"I do love you."

"Then why are you wearing another man's ring?" he demanded. He stalked toward her and pulled her hand from behind her back. He frowned as he found her ring finger bare.

"I've only worn James's diamond once. The night of the engagement party," she said, surprised by how strained her voice sounded. "I took it off the minute I walked in the door and haven't put it on since."

Cody's large, callused hand curled over her fingers as he shut his eyes. The muscles in his jaw clenched. Then, moving slowly, as though hypnotized, he lowered his mouth to hers.

Her lips trembled under his and Christy closed her eyes as hard as she could, wanting to shut out the realities that kept them apart. She longed to block out everything, except the man who was holding her so gently.

"We need to talk," he whispered.

"Isn't 'I love you' enough?" she asked. Although he struggled to hold her at bay, Christy spread nibbling kisses at the curve of his neck. She wanted him so much....

Cody released a ragged sigh and propelled himself away from her. He moved so fast and so unexpectedly that Christy nearly stumbled. Bewildered, she caught herself just in time.

By then Cody had put the full distance of the living room between them. "In case it's slipped your mind, I'd like to remind you that you're an engaged woman."

It seemed she was allowed to forget that when she was in Cody's arms. She blinked back her pain. Throwing this farce of an engagement at her now was cruel and unfair.

"If you flew all those miles to remind me of that, then you made a wasted trip." Humiliation tainted her cheeks and it was all she could do not to cover her face with both hands and turn away from him.

For several minutes neither of them spoke. She sensed that they both needed time to compose themselves. Cody continued pacing, while Christy stood rooted, leaning against the door, requiring its solidity to hold her upright. It was a shock to discover how badly she was trembling.

"I need to ask you to do something," Cody said crisply, as if whatever he was about to say didn't involve him.

"All right."

"Break the engagement to James." His dark eyes cut into her with sharp, unquestioning demand.

"Of course. You know I will as soon as I can—"

"I want you to do it now. Today."

Full of anguish and regret, Christy shut her eyes. This had tormented her from the moment she got home and talked to James. Surely Cody realized she didn't want to stay engaged to another man.

"Christy?"

"I…can't break it off. Not yet. You know that. James has been working for three months getting ready for this trial. He was as prepared as any attorney could be, and yet one thing after another has gone wrong for him. I can't add to his troubles by—"

"We have no business seeing each other," Cody interrupted. "We didn't when you were in Montana, and we have even less of an excuse now that you're home."

"But I love you."

Her words fell into an uncomfortable silence. Cody didn't answer for so long that she began to worry. His expression told her nothing.

"Love doesn't make everything right," he said, his eyes darkening with bitterness. "I wish it did, but the way we feel about each other doesn't alter one damn thing. You're promised to another man, and that's all there is to it."

"But… Cody—"

"Not only do you have his ring, you've set a wedding date."

"I explained all that," she whispered, feeling utterly defenseless.

"There's something you don't seem to understand," Cody said, frowning heavily. "I'm a man of honor, a man of my word…"

She nodded. "I couldn't love you as much as I do without knowing the kind of man you are."

"Then you must realize that I can't continue this. You must know how it makes me feel."

She stared at him, barely able to believe she'd been so stupid and selfish. Cody wasn't being possessive or jealous. It wasn't his pride that was injured or his ego. It was his sense of fairness. A matter of honesty.

He slowly shook his head. "For both our sakes, I wish I could be different. I'd like nothing better than to steal away with you for a few days, hold you, kiss you. More than anything else in this world I want to make love to you, but I can't allow that to happen."

Christy wanted all those things, too.

"The fact that you were committed to James bothered me when you were staying with Russ and Taylor. The fact that you didn't want to break the engagement over the phone wasn't unreasonable and I understood it."

Christy now wished she'd put an end to everything two weeks ago. If she had, her life would be so much simpler.

"It wasn't easy to keep my hands off you then, and it's a lot more difficult now." His voice was tight, and he didn't slacken his stride as he continued to pace. "I can't do this any longer. Either you break it off with James, right now, today, or it's over. I'll fly back to Montana and this will be the last time I see you."

Christy felt as if the entire ceiling had come crashing down on her head.

"The last time?" she repeated, struggling to keep her voice from rising.

"Christy, look at it from my point of view."

"I am. All I'm asking for…all I need is for you to be a little more patient. The trial will be over soon."

"I've been more than patient already."

"But it'll only be for a while. I swear to you," she said urgently, "I'll break it off with James at the first opportunity. But I can't do it now."

Once again her words fell into a void and she was left to wonder at his thoughts. "Cody…please," she whispered when she couldn't tolerate the silence anymore.

He pivoted sharply. "I know you. You're warm and loving, and you won't do anything that might hurt another person. You refuse to disappoint anyone—except yourself."

If he understood her so well, then surely he'd be patient just a little longer. She was about to say that when he added, "You've allowed your parents to manipulate you all your life."

"That's not true," she burst out, wanting to defend herself, angry that he'd even suggest it.

"They handpicked a husband for you, and you went along with it."

Her shoulders slumped, but her indignation had yet to cool.

"You didn't love James then and you don't love him now. Or so you claim."

"I love *you,*" she cried. "How many times do I have to say it?"

"Yet when James offered you an engagement ring, you accepted his proposal."

"I… I…" Her outrage went limp for lack of an argument. Everything he said was true, but it had happened before she'd met Cody.

"You're so eager to take care of everyone else you're willing to sacrifice your own happiness."

"All I need is a few more days, just until this trial…" She

didn't finish, since nothing she said was going to change his mind.

"Frankly I have a strong suspicion that you're going to wake up one fine morning married to dear old James and not realize how it happened."

"That's ridiculous." She folded her arms to ward off an unexpected chill. "I swear to you that will never happen."

"You swore to me you were going to break the engagement when you arrived back in Seattle, too. Remember?"

His eyes challenged her to deny it. She couldn't. He met her stare, but it was Christy who looked away first, Christy whose gaze flickered under the force of the truth.

"But how could I have known about the engagement party?" she asked weakly. Then, gaining conviction, she said, "You're not being fair. To even suggest I'd go ahead with the wedding is—" she searched for the right word "—ludicrous."

"Is it really?"

"Of course it is! You make me sound like some weak-willed… I can't imagine why you'd want anything to do with me if that's how you feel."

"I love you, Christy, and it's going to hurt like crazy to walk away from you. My request isn't unreasonable, although I know you don't agree with that."

She leaned against the door frame. "You can't ask me to make that kind of decision! Not right this minute. I need time…." In the back of her mind she was desperately praying the Mulligan case would be thrown out of court that afternoon and this whole regrettable affair could be laid to rest.

She might win the lottery, too, but she couldn't count on it.

"Is the decision that difficult?" Cody asked, frowning.

"That on its own says something, whether you admit it or not."

Christy shut her eyes and took a deep breath. The man she loved, her entire future, was about to walk out the door, and she knew of no way to stop him short of destroying another person's happiness.

Straightening, she glared at Cody across the room. "I don't know what's right anymore," she said defiantly. "How can I? All everyone does is make demands of me. First it's Mom and then James and now…you."

Then she started to cry. She couldn't help it. Her shoulders shook and her chest heaved as the sobs convulsed her and tears cascaded down her cheeks.

She heard Cody mutter a swear word. "Christy, please, I can't stand to see you cry," he whispered hoarsely.

He could break her heart, but he couldn't stand to see her cry. Christy found the thought almost laughable.

Cody moved across the room and took her in his arms. His hands stroked the hair away from her brow. With him she felt secure. With him she felt warm and protected. She hid her face in his shoulder as the emotion worked through her. He held her until she was able to draw in a deep, shaky breath. Christy could feel her control slipping back into place.

Still Cody held her, his hands caressing her back. For the longest time he said nothing. He continued to hold her close, and after several minutes Christy became aware of how intimate their position was.

She sighed longingly and tested her discovery by tenderly kissing his neck. A moment passed in which she waited for him to protest or ease himself away.

Experiencing a small sense of triumph when he didn't,

she leisurely investigated the warm, tantalizing skin, making slow, moist circles over the hollow of his throat.

"Kiss me," she whispered. "Oh, please, Cody, just kiss me. I'll be all right if you do that."

He didn't immediately comply; in fact, he seemed inclined to ignore her, as if nothing would be proved, nothing would be solved by kissing.

He froze when she placed her hands on each side of his strong face, sliding her lips up his jawline and over his chin until their mouths were joined.

Cody pulled his mouth from hers. His whole body seemed to be shaking as he inhaled. He walked over to her sofa and sat on the edge, his elbows on his knees. "What are we going to do?" He shook his head in despair. "I'm not strong enough to walk away from you," he said starkly. "I thought I could."

"I won't let you go." She sat next to him, resting her forehead on his shoulder, and sighed. "I love you so much.... I'd give anything to marry you today."

Cody went stock-still. "What did you just say?"

Eleven

"I won't let you go, Cody. I can't," Christy repeated.

"Not that," he said, bolting to his feet. He started pacing again, and when she didn't immediately speak, he added, "It was after that."

She frowned. "I love you?"

"Not that, either. The part about marrying me today."

"I would." She didn't feel any hesitation in saying as much. Almost from the first day she'd met the sheriff of Custer County, she'd known she was going to love him all the days of her life.

"Will you marry me, Christy?" His expression was so open and sincere that she felt tears stinging her eyes.

"Oh, yes," she whispered. She'd probably be the only woman in the world engaged to two men at the same time, but that couldn't be helped.

"I mean now."

"Now?"

"I'd like us to be married this afternoon."

Her heart responded with a quick, wistful beat, but Christy didn't see how a wedding, that day, would be possible.

"Maybe it's different in Montana, but Washington state

has a three-day waiting period after we apply for the license."

A satisfied smile lifted the corners of his mouth. "Idaho doesn't."

"That may be, but Idaho's over 350 miles from here. If you're only going to be in Seattle three days, we'll end up spending two of them on the road."

"That's easily fixed. I'll rent a plane." He smiled a breathtaking smile that was so appealing, she thought she'd die a slow death if he didn't make love to her soon. "Am I going too fast for you?"

"No," she rushed to assure him, although her mind was abuzz. "It's just that I'm having trouble understanding. What about James?" She hated mentioning fiancé number one, but she had to be sure they were doing the right thing for the right reasons.

"What about him?"

"Will I…do I have to tell him about the wedding? I mean, it won't make much difference if he learns I've married you a couple of days from now or even next week. I'm only suggesting I delay telling him because of the trial."

Some of the happy excitement left Cody's eyes. "I'll leave that up to you. As far as James is concerned, I don't know what's right or wrong anymore. All I know is that I love you more than I thought it was possible to love any woman. It scares me to think I could lose you."

"There isn't the slightest chance of that."

His smile was sad. "I meant what I said earlier about being afraid you'd end up married to James. I've had nightmares about it, wondering if I'd get a call in the middle of the night. I actually dreamed that you phoned to explain how everything got out of your control and you'd married

James before you could come up with a way to stop the ceremony."

"I would never allow such a thing."

He gave her a distrusting look, and although it injured her pride to admit it, Christy could understand Cody's concern.

"I feel a whole lot better making *sure* that couldn't happen." The warmth in his eyes removed the sting his words might have inflicted. "I learned a long time ago to cover all my bases. Marrying like this might not be the best thing, but we're making a commitment to each other, and heaven help me for being so weak, but I need that."

Heaven help *him!* Christy felt herself go soft. "Oh, Cody, I love you so much."

"Good," he said, his voice slightly husky, "because you're about to become my wife."

He smiled, completely disarming her. If Christy had a single argument, which she didn't, one of those devastating smiles would have settled it.

"How soon can you be ready?"

"An hour?"

"I'll check the phone book and make the arrangements while you dress." He took her hands and helped her to her feet, pausing long enough to plant a kiss on her unsuspecting lips.

In a daze Christy walked into her bedroom and searched through her closet for something special enough for her wedding. Smiling to herself, she walked to the door and leaned idly against it. "The whole thing's off. I don't have anything decent to wear," she said, teasing him.

Cody sat at her kitchen table, leafing through the impossibly thick yellow pages. He glanced up and chuckled.

"Don't worry about it. Whatever you put on is going to come off so fast it'll make your head spin."

Christy chose a soft pink suit she'd purchased the year before at Easter. Carrying it into the bathroom, she closed the door. Quite by accident she caught her reflection in the mirror above the sink and gasped at the pitiful sight she made.

Leaning over the sink, she studied the woman who stared back at her. Her short dark hair was a mess, as if it hadn't been combed in weeks. Her eyes were another thing. Christy had always considered her distinctive blue eyes to be her best feature. Now they were red-rimmed and bloodshot as if she'd been on a two-day drunken spree. Her lips were red and swollen, although she attributed that to Cody's kisses. That man could kiss like nobody's business. She went weak all over again, remembering the feel and taste of his mouth on hers.

Bracing her hands against the sink, she was forced to admit that she was probably among the most pathetic creatures on earth. Yet Cody had looked at her as if she was gorgeous.

The man definitely loved her. That worked out well, since she definitely loved him.

Cody couldn't keep still. He couldn't seem to make himself stop pacing Christy's living room. Four steps, turn, four more steps, turn again.

He glanced at his watch. She was already five minutes past the hour she'd told him she'd need. What could be taking her so long? She'd locked herself in the bathroom, and he hadn't heard a peep since. His mind was beginning to play cruel tricks on him. Perhaps she'd changed her mind about going through with the wedding and, not wanting to hurt his feelings, she'd climbed out the bathroom window.

That thought revealed the shocking state of his mental condition more than anything he'd said or done in the past two hours. He'd flown into Seattle with one purpose. Either he'd settle this craziness between him and Christy or he'd end their relationship.

He hadn't counted on her enthusiasm. She'd been giddy with happiness when he'd arrived. Okay, he was the giddy one. He'd had no idea she was going to throw herself into his arms the moment she opened the door. Not that he'd minded… A slow smile relaxed his mouth. Everything had progressed naturally from there.

Cody had always considered himself a strong man. Not muscular or brawny, although he could hold his own and often had. His real strength, he felt, was his stubborn determination. He liked to think he had a will of iron.

Christy had proved him wrong in world-record time.

During the early-morning flight, he'd given himself a pep talk, outlining everything he intended to say. He'd planned to meet with her, explain his position and ask her as calmly and unemotionally as possible to make her decision.

It was either James or him.

If she chose the attorney, Cody was prepared to accept her choice serenely and walk out of her life.

Other than the rocky beginning of that conversation, everything had gone as he'd hoped. Never mind that Christy had managed to break down his resolve within five seconds. The instant she was in his arms, he could feel himself start to weaken.

No woman, not even Becca, had ever had as much control over him.

Now he and Christy would be flying into Coeur d'Alene,

Idaho, and getting married. Smiling, Cody settled against the back of the sofa. He recalled when Russ and Taylor had come back to Cougar Point after serving as chaperones for the drill team, traveling with a busload of high school girls to Reno. They'd left town barely speaking to each other and arrived home a few days later married.

Cody could still remember how surprised everyone was. Most folks agreed Taylor was the best thing ever to happen to the opinionated Russ Palmer, but there'd been skeptics, too.

Understandably. Taylor was a city girl. Russ was a rancher. Taylor had only been in town three months.

But when folks in Cougar Point learned that Cody had married Christy after knowing her less than *one* month, there'd be even more raised eyebrows.

That didn't disturb Cody in the least. He loved Christy beyond a doubt, and next month when he stood before the citizens of Custer County to be sworn in as sheriff, she'd be at his side. It would be the proudest moment of his life, and he wanted her with him.

The bathroom door opened, and Christy stepped out. Cody turned around to inform her that she was twelve minutes late. His teasing comment wilted before ever making it to his lips.

She was stunningly beautiful, dressed in a pink linen suit. Her hair was perfect, her makeup flawlessly applied. Christy Manning was so beautiful, Cody couldn't help staring at her. It took more effort than he could believe just to close his mouth. He was too tongue-tied to utter a single word.

"Do I look all right?" she asked, gazing at him expectantly.

For the life of him, all Cody could do was nod.

Christy smiled and held out her hand. "Then let's get this show on the road."

* * *

The ceremony itself took place later that evening in a wedding chapel overlooking the crystal blue waters of Lake Coeur d'Alene. Between the time they obtained the license, purchased a pair of gold bands and made the arrangements for the wedding itself, Cody half expected Christy to express some doubts.

She didn't. When she repeated her vows, Christy's strong, clear voice had sounded so confident and poised, he couldn't help marveling—and feeling both humbled and honored by her love.

The flight back to Seattle brought them into the airport shortly before midnight. In the space of one day Cody had traveled from Montana to Washington state, then had flown a two-seater Cessna from Seattle to Coeur d'Alene and back again. He should've been exhausted, but he wasn't. In fact, he felt more alive than he could ever remember being in his life. All he had to do was glance at Christy, who delighted in flashing him a sexy, slightly naughty smile, to feel the blood shoot through his veins.

They returned the Cessna to the hangar and headed toward his rental car. He held the door for her and pressed a light kiss on her lips when she climbed inside. She leaned against him, and it took all his restraint not to deepen the kiss right then and there.

He needed a moment to let his mind clear. "Where to, Mrs. Franklin?" he asked, sliding behind the wheel of the car.

She responded with a blank look.

"Choose any hotel you'd like." He wanted the best Seattle had to offer for Christy. A honeymoon suite. Champagne. Silk sheets. Room service.

"But I didn't pack anything," she protested.

Cody was about to comment that she wouldn't need any clothes, but he didn't get the chance.

"I have this white silk baby doll gown. Would you mind if we went back to my apartment so I could put a few things together?"

"Your wish is my command, Mrs. Franklin."

Resting her head against his shoulder, Christy sighed audibly and murmured, "I like that in a man."

At the apartment complex, he went inside with Christy. His own suitcase was still there.

Christy hurried into the bedroom, then reappeared a moment later. She walked shyly up to him, then placed her hands on his chest. Cody gazed down at her as she slipped her arms around his neck and kissed him soundly.

Cody's response was immediate. He cradled the back of her head as he returned her kiss—and then some. Soon she was weak and pliant in his arms.

"What was that for?" he asked when he found his breath.

"Because I'm so happy to be your wife."

Cody locked his hands at the small of her back and glanced longingly toward her bedroom.

Christy reached up, kissed his cheek and deftly removed the Stetson from his head. Cody frowned when she tossed it Frisbee fashion across the room. It landed on a chintz-covered cushion as neatly as if he'd set it there himself.

Next her fingers were busy working loose the knot of his tie. "Christy?" Her name tumbled from his lips. "What are you doing?"

"Undressing my husband. I've decided I don't want to go to a hotel room, not when we're both here. Not when I can't wait another minute for us to act like a married couple."

"You're sure?" He didn't know why he was questioning her; he wanted her so much that he was trembling.

"Very sure." After discarding his tie, she began to unfasten his shirt buttons.

Cody's hands roved her back, his fingers seeking and not finding a zipper.

She peeled open his shirt and lightly ran her long nails down his bare chest. Shudders swirled down his spine as she nuzzled his neck, nibbling and sucking and licking her way to the throbbing hollow of his throat.

"Christy," he pleaded, his hands on her bottom. "Where's the zipper to your skirt?"

Smiling, she broke away long enough to remove the suit jacket and kick off her heels, which went flying in opposite directions. She twisted around and unfastened the button at her side, then slid the zipper open so the skirt could fall past her hips and pool at her feet. Stepping out of it, she reached behind her for the row of buttons that ran down the back of her silk blouse.

"I can do that," he said eagerly. His fingers fumbled awkwardly with the tiny buttons, but he managed. Her blouse and her lacy bra followed the path of his shirt, landing on the carpet somewhere between the sofa and television.

Unable to wait a second longer, Cody kissed her, his tongue surging into her mouth. The minute she leaned into him, Cody felt his body heat rise to the boiling point.

Slipping her arms around his neck, Christy let her head fall back, grazing his bare chest with her breasts.

He groaned, fighting the rising flames of his passion. She was slowly, surely, driving him out of his mind.

"Christy," he begged, not knowing exactly what he was pleading for. Not for her to stop, that much he knew. *More*, he decided. He needed more of her.

Tucking his arms behind her knees, he lifted her up and

carried her into the bedroom. The only light was the soft illumination from the single lamp in the living room.

Gently he placed her on the bed, and they hastily finished undressing each other. Cody looked down on her, nestled in the thick folds of a lavender comforter. She was so beautiful that for a moment he was lost to everything but the woman before him. He longed to tell her what he felt, and knew it would be impossible to put into words.

Lightly he ran his hands over her breasts and smiled....

Afterward he lay on his back with Christy beside him, her head on his shoulder, her arm draped over his chest. Cody sighed as she cuddled her body intimately against his.

Her eyes remained closed, her smile dreamy. "I guess I'm not a good girl anymore."

"Oh, yes, you are. Very good, indeed..."

"What are you doing now?" Cody murmured.

He was half asleep, Christy saw as she caught his earlobe between her teeth. "I'm making a citizen's arrest."

"Oh, yeah? What's the charge?"

"I'll trump something up later."

"Christy, hey, what are you wearing?"

"My new silk nightgown."

"I like you better with nothing on."

Ignoring his complaints, she straddled his hips and leaned forward to kiss his chin.

"Mmm, you smell good...flowers, I think."

"Remember, you're the one who emptied an entire bottle of bubble bath into my tub."

"You didn't object."

"How could I? You were doing your husbandly duty and pampering me...only..." She paused and drew in a soft breath as he closed his hands over her breasts. "I didn't realize it could be done in a tub."

"It?" he teased.

"Cody, I was supposed to be the one arresting you, remember?"

"Say it." He raised the silk gown high on her leg and began to caress her thighs with both hands.

"It embarrasses me to say it… Cody," she whimpered as his finger executed the sweetest of punishments.

"You *are* going to say it."

She couldn't utter a single word. She hadn't known her body was capable of giving her any more pleasure than it already had.

"I love it when you blush," he murmured.

Christy rested her head on his chest, listening to the steady, even beat of his heart. "Are we ever going to sleep?" she asked.

"Nope. The way I figure it we've got about forty-eight hours before my planc leaves, and at the rate we're going we can make love—"

"I'm too tired."

Christy felt him smile against her hair. "I am, too." he said. "We'll make up for lost time in the morning."

"In the morning," she echoed as her eyes slowly drifted closed.

A horrible racket woke Christy several hours later. She bolted upright and glanced at her clock radio. Just after 4:00 a.m.

Cody was already out of bed and reaching for his pants.

"Christy?"

The slurred voice belonged to none other than her brother

Rich. She'd given him an extra key to her apartment. He stopped in often, but had always phoned first.

"It's my brother. He has a key. Stay here. I'll get rid of him."

"Your brother?"

"Shh." She grabbed her robe, then kissed Cody before hurrying into the living room.

Rich stood by the door, looking like an errant schoolboy. "Hi," he said, raising his right hand.

"I don't suppose you know what time it is?"

"Late," he offered.

"How about early."

"How early?"

"Too early," she told him, praying he wouldn't notice the two sets of clothes spread from one end of the living room to the other. She marched across the room and gripped his elbow, turning him toward the door.

He gave her a hurt look. "You're sending me back into the cold?"

"Yes."

"I didn't drive here. I couldn't," he said. "I know you probably can't tell, but I've had a teeny bit too much to drink."

"I noticed."

"I was hoping you'd make me some coffee, listen to my woes and let me sleep on your couch."

"I have to be at work in a few hours." A slight exaggeration. Besides, when she didn't show up at the office, everyone would assume she was still home with the flu.

"Pamela cheated on me," Rich blurted. "I need some advice and I need it from a woman. Just hear me out, okay?"

Not knowing what else she could do, Christy moved into her kitchen and started making a pot of coffee. Rich pulled out a stool at her kitchen counter and plopped himself down. "Apparently she's been seeing him all along."

"Who?"

"Pamela."

"No, who's she been seeing?" This conversation was frustrating Christy.

"Hell if I know his name. Some jerk."

"It isn't like you were crazy about her."

"Maybe not, but I always thought she was crazy about me. What is it with women these days? Isn't anyone faithful anymore?" he said plaintively.

"Ah…"

Rich squinted into the darkened living room. "Hey, what's going on here?" Standing, he walked over to the chintz-covered chair and picked up Cody's Stetson. He glanced back at his sister.

"I can explain," she said in a weak voice.

Frowning, he returned to the kitchen and carefully placed the Stetson on her head. Several sizes too large, it rested well below her hairline in the middle of her forehead.

"Is there something you wanted to tell me?" he asked.

Twelve

"Who the hell are you?" Rich demanded.

Christy shoved the Stetson farther back on her head to find Cody walking out of the bedroom.

"It sounded like you might need a little help explaining things," her husband said casually.

Rich pointed at his sister and his mouth fell open. His eyes had narrowed, and disdain and disbelief marked his handsome features.

"It's not as bad as it looks," Christy said, ignoring his censure. Acting as nonchalant as she could, she poured him a cup of coffee.

Swiveling his gaze between Cody and Christy, Rich shook his head. "It looks pretty darn bad, little sister." He stared at the trail of clothing on the living-room carpet. His mouth twisted with disgust as he started toward the front door. "In fact, I don't think I've got the stomach to listen to you."

"You'll listen to her," Cody warned grimly, striding toward Rich. The two men stood no more than two feet apart, glaring at each other ferociously.

"And who's going to make me? You?" Rich's sarcasm

was sharp. "If that's what you think, I've got news for you, cowboy."

"Rich, shut up," Christy said. "The least you can do is hear what I have to say."

"I don't listen to—"

"Don't say it," Cody interrupted, his words so cold they almost froze in midair. "Because if you do, you'll live to regret it."

Rich mocked him with a smile. "Listen, Mr. Marlboro Man, I've taken about enough from—"

"Stop it, both of you!" Christy marched out from her kitchen. She stood between her husband and her brother, a hand on each man's chest, and glanced up at Rich. "I'd like to introduce you to my husband, Cody Franklin. Cody, this stupid oaf is my third-youngest brother, Rich."

"Your husband!"

"My husband," she echoed softly. She dropped her hands and slipped her arm around Cody's waist, leaning against him, needing his solid strength.

"I'll have you know," Cody muttered, "you interrupted my wedding night."

"Your husband," Rich repeated a second time, stalking across the room. He retrieved Christy's bra from the floor and twirled it around on one finger. "I don't suppose James knows about this?"

Christy snatched her underwear out of her brother's hand. "As a matter of fact, he doesn't."

"This is getting even more interesting." Sitting on the sofa, he picked up Cody's shirt and made a soft tsking sound with his tongue. "What about Mom and Dad?"

"They don't know, either," Cody said forcefully.

"Aha," Rich snickered, "the plot thickens."

"I'm so pleased you find this amusing." Christy moved

hastily about the room, picking up pieces of discarded clothing, more embarrassed than she could ever remember being.

Cody poured himself a cup of coffee and joined Rich, sitting on the opposite end of the sofa. "I'm a good friend of Russ Palmer's," he said by way of explanation.

Rich nodded. "So my dear, sweet sister met you when she was in Montana visiting Taylor?"

"Cody's the one who drove her to the hospital," Christy added. She sat on the side of the sofa and curved her arm around Cody's broad shoulders.

"Then this was what you'd call a whirlwind courtship." Rich studied the two of them. "Exactly how long have you known each other?"

"Long enough," Cody answered, making it plain he didn't much care for this line of questioning.

"We didn't mean to fall in love so fast," Christy continued, wanting to untangle any doubts Rich had about her relationship with Cody. "It just happened."

"You might have mentioned it to James."

"I probably should've phoned and told him while I was still in Montana, but it seemed wrong to break the engagement over the phone, and then when I got home—"

"The surprise engagement party," Rich said, groaning loudly. "I can see that you were trapped. Mom put her heart and soul into that party. You couldn't back out without humiliating her. Not at the last minute like that."

"I wanted to tell James right away, but that didn't work out, either." The hopelessness of the entire situation nearly overwhelmed her. "The Mulligan trial was called early, and he's immersed himself in the most complicated case of his career. He's got to be emotionally and physically at his peak for that."

"Yeah, that's right," Rich commented. "I'd forgotten about that."

"The timing couldn't be worse. I can't tell James about Cody and me until he's through with the trial. And yet..."

Rich released a long, sympathetic sigh. "You do seem to have your problems, little sister."

Cody leaned against the back of the sofa. "You can imagine how I felt when I learned she'd been roped into that engagement party. To complicate matters, she set a date for the wedding."

Rich did a pitiful job of disguising a smile. "November 12, wasn't it?"

"That's not funny, Rich, so cut the comedy, will you?" Christy playfully punched his upper arm.

"You have to admit, it's kind of amusing."

Christy found very little of this amusing. She was deliriously pleased to be Cody's wife, but he was flying out of Seattle in another day, and she'd have to return to her job and live a complete lie with James and her parents. She wouldn't be able to keep up this charade for long.

"Perhaps this predicament is comical to someone else," Cody said grudgingly, "but trust me, it isn't if you're one of the parties involved."

Rich was quick to agree. "So the two of you decided to take matters into your own hands and get married."

Christy nodded. Her eyes met Cody's, and they exchanged a loving look. His fingers linked with hers. "It must sound crazy."

"Hey, it works for me," Rich said, "but I wouldn't be in your shoes for all the tea in China when you tell Mom and Dad what you did."

"Why not?" Cody asked with a dark frown.

"They were cheated out of one wedding when Taylor

married Russ without a single family member present. I can only speculate what they'll say when they hear Christy did the same thing."

"They'll skin me alive," she muttered. In all the excitement, in all her enthusiasm, Christy had forgotten how much her mother was looking forward to planning her wedding—which would be far more elaborate than the engagement party. As they left the Eagles Hall that dreadful night, Elizabeth Manning had been filled with ideas and opinions and excitement.

"Your parents won't do any such thing," Cody insisted.

"Cody, you don't know them." Christy felt a return of the nausea that had overtaken her at the party. Elizabeth Manning might never forgive her, and she'd always done what her mother thought best. Until now.

"They won't say a word," he said softly, "because I won't let them."

"But you don't understand—"

"If your parents are looking for someone to blame, they can deal with me. I was the one who insisted you marry me now. You just went along with it."

"Because I'm crazy in love with you and because I want to be your wife more than I've ever wanted anything."

"Hey," Rich said, raising both hands, "if both of you want to stand in front of the firing squad, I'm not going to stop you."

A chill descended on the room. "I take it there was a reason for this unexpected visit," Cody said pointedly.

"I was having woman problems," Rich mumbled.

"I thought there was something bothering you the night of the party." Although Rich hadn't enlightened her with the details, Christy should've known something was amiss.

Otherwise he would have noticed how upset she was that evening.

"I may be having a few problems," Rich continued. "But they're nothing compared to what you two are facing. Married to one man while engaged to another—that, little sister, takes the cake."

"How kind of you to point it out." Yawning, she covered her mouth with her hand. "I'll make you a bed on the sofa and you can spend the rest of the night there."

"And interrupt your honeymoon?"

"It's already been interrupted," Cody reminded him. "If there's any justice in this world, I'll be able to return the favor someday."

"No chance of that. I'm swearing off women. The whole lot of them," Rich said with an emphatic shake of his head.

"Oh?" Christy had heard that song before.

"It's true. They're fickle, money-hungry, materialistic—"

"Thank you very much," Christy said, standing.

"With a few exceptions." He eyed his sister and smiled in apology.

"Now where was it you said you wanted to go for dinner?" Cody asked, reaching for his suit jacket.

"What's the matter with eating here?" Christy asked, not wanting to leave the apartment. Everything had been idyllic, and she was almost light-headed with happiness. To walk outside these protected walls might well invite trouble, and she'd had enough of that to last her a lifetime.

"I thought you wanted to dine out?"

"Not really." At the time he'd made the suggestion, Christy hadn't been able to think of an excuse. Now her mind overflowed with them, only she doubted Cody would consider any of them sensible.

She checked her freezer and extracted a package of pork chops. “I could wrestle us up some grub in no time.” She turned around and grinned. “Am I beginning to sound like a Montana woman?”

“No. You’re beginning to sound like a cattle thief.” He moved behind her, slid his arms around her waist and nuzzled the curve of her neck.

“I’m a good cook.”

“I know.”

“How could you? Every time I go to make something for us, you interrupt me with…you know.”

“Are you still having trouble saying the words?”

“No…” She giggled softly. “You’ve cured me of that.” Twisting around, she leaned against the refrigerator door with her hands primly linked in front of her. “I can talk about making love about as often as you want to do it.”

“Then let’s get out of here before you give me any ideas.”

“I like giving you ideas.”

Cody glanced at his watch. “It’s well past dinnertime and I’m hungry.”

She moistened her lips. “You want me to say some of the other words you taught me?”

“Christy…no.”

“Come here.” She beckoned him with her index finger. “I’ll whisper a couple of humdingers in your ear.”

Cody ignored her. “I’m not going to let you sidetrack me.”

“Oh, but I enjoy sidetracking you.”

“That’s the problem,” Cody said. “I like it, too.” He cleared his throat and changing tactics, grabbed his hat. “As your husband, I command that we leave for dinner now.”

"You command?" She couldn't help laughing.

"That's right," he said, his mouth quivering with a suppressed smile. "I've got to teach you that I'm wearing the pants in this family."

"If that's the case, then why are they so often unzipped?"

Cody actually blushed, and Christy smiled.

"Because I'm a needy husband," he said gruffly. "Are you complaining?"

"Oh, no." She sent him a saucy grin. "Because I happen to be a needy wife. In fact, I seem to be experiencing a need right now. Is it hot in here to you?"

"Christy?" Cody's voice contained a low note of warning.

"It seems very hot…much too hot for all these clothes." She jerked the light sweater over her head and let it fall to the floor. Next she lowered the straps of her bra. "There," she said with a deep sigh, offering Cody what she hoped was a tantalizing display of her assets. "That feels better."

Cody stood his ground for a couple of minutes. Then he removed his hat and sent it flying across the room.

Silently Christy rejoiced.

"What about those jeans? Aren't they making you hot, too?" Cody asked.

"Maybe they are. Only I can't seem to open the snap." He didn't seem to notice that she hadn't tried.

"I see." He stepped over to her and made short work of her bra, then cupped Christy's breasts, his hands firm and insistent.

Sighing, Christy closed her eyes, giving herself over to a host of delightful sensations. Cody used one hand to stroke her breast, his other hand busy at the opening of her jeans. The zipper purred, and Christy was filled with another small sense of triumph.

She shivered helplessly as Cody slid her jeans down her hips. Her bikini underwear followed and that was the last thing she noticed for some time. Other than Cody, of course…

Christy's gaze fell reluctantly on Cody's luggage, which lay open on her bed. The lump in her throat seemed to grow larger every minute, until she could hardly swallow. She'd decided earlier that she wasn't going to be emotional when he left. They'd talked everything out earlier, planned for their future as best they could.

"You called the office?" Cody asked, putting a clean shirt in the suitcase.

"Yes… I told them I still had the flu." Lying didn't come easy to Christy. She felt as though she'd dug herself into a deep pit.

"What did they say?"

"Marcia, she's the office manager, said it's a slow week and not to worry about it, but she did make a point of asking me if I'd be in on Friday, which seemed a little odd."

"What about James?"

"He was at the courthouse." Her eyes widened at the unexpectedness of the question.

"When's the last time you heard from him?"

"Ah…" She had to stop and think. "The day after the engagement party. We talked briefly, and he explained that he wouldn't be able to keep in touch while the trial's going on." Under normal circumstances she would've seen him at the office, even if it was only for a few minutes, every morning. The fact that he hadn't made an effort to contact her said a good deal about their relationship.

"I see." Cody was obviously surprised.

"He's very intense and single-minded."

"Do you think he'll get an acquittal?"

"I don't know," she said.

"Whatever happens, this can't go on much longer. You realize that, don't you?"

"It won't be more than a few days." In discussing the situation they'd agreed on a time limit. Even if the trial dragged on for more than a week, Christy had promised to return James's ring and tell her parents that she and Cody were married.

"I still think we should tell your parents now."

"Not yet," she pleaded. The way Christy figured it, she'd start dropping hints so the fact that she'd married Cody wouldn't come as such a shock. After Cody flew back to Montana, she intended to drop by the family home and casually point out that James hadn't called her once since the party. She was hoping her parents would conclude that perhaps he wouldn't be the best husband for her, after all.

"Christy, I'm worried." Cody stood in front of her, his face concerned. "I don't like leaving you, especially under these circumstances."

"You know I love you."

His mouth curved into a sensual smile. "Beyond a doubt."

"Good." She put her arms around his waist and hugged him close. His heart beat strongly and evenly, offering her reassurance. In time they'd look back on these bleak days and laugh, she told herself. Someday, but not now.

"I'll phone you twice a day," he promised in a husky whisper. "Morning and night."

"I'll need that."

"So will I."

A sigh of regret rumbled through his chest as he dropped his arms. "It's time to go."

Neither of them seemed inclined to talk on the ride to

the airport. Once Cody had checked in at the airline counter, he hugged Christy and kissed her lightly. It was as if he dared not kiss her the way they both enjoyed for fear he wouldn't be able to walk away. She understood all too well.

"Take care of yourself," she whispered.

"You, too."

She nodded, barely conscious of the way she clung to him. "Of course. We'll talk tonight. And before we know it, we'll be together."

"Together for good," he added. "I've got to go."

She closed her eyes tightly to keep from crying.

Cody kissed her again, only this time his mouth was fierce and wild. He released her by degrees, his reluctance tearing at her heart. With everything in her, Christy longed to board the plane with him. How much easier it would be to leave with Cody and then call James and her parents. But Christy knew she couldn't abandon her responsibilities. Cody understood that, too; she was sure of it. Christy Manning Franklin had always done the right thing, even if it was sometimes for the wrong reasons.

The next morning Christy returned to work for the first time since she'd left for vacation. What a difference a few weeks could make. She wasn't the same woman anymore.

"Christy." James's voice rose as he hurried over to her desk. "You're back. I hope you're feeling better."

For all his brilliance, James had very little experience of life. That was even more obvious to Christy now, and it made her feel oddly protective of him. She smiled as he reached for her hand, squeezing her fingers. Kissing her, even in an empty office, would have been unthinkable. He'd never been openly affectionate, but he was tender and good, and Christy couldn't ignore her guilty conscience.

"I'm much better, thanks. How's the Mulligan case going?"

He frowned and briefly looked away before responding. "Not too well."

"How much longer do you think it's going to be?"

"I'm hoping to wrap everything up by the end of next week."

"That long?" She couldn't keep the disappointment out of her voice.

James frowned again. "I didn't realize how negatively this case was affecting you."

"It's just that..." She couldn't very well announce that she was looking for the right moment to tell him she was married to someone else.

"I know, darling." He said the last word softly, as though fearing someone might overhear him. "This is a difficult time for us both, but it'll soon be over, and we can get on with our lives."

Now that Christy had a chance to study him, she saw that he seemed exhausted. Deep lines were etched around his eyes and mouth. Clearly James wasn't sleeping well.

"The case is going worse than you expected, isn't it?"

James sighed. "It's difficult to hide something like this from the one you love. Yes, it's going much worse."

"Is there anything I can do?" Christy found herself asking.

"Nothing," he said, giving her a rare smile. "But your concern is greatly appreciated." He looked at his watch. "It's time I left for the courthouse. I won't be back for the rest of the day."

Christy nodded.

"I suppose we should meet for dinner. After all, it's been a long time since we've gone out. But—"

"Don't worry," Christy interrupted. "I understand." If

she was having trouble dealing with a short conversation as James was walking out the door, an entire evening in each other's company would've been unbearable.

"Have a good day," he said gently.

"You, too."

He nodded, but his expression was somber. It was all too apparent that he didn't think he'd be having anything resembling a satisfactory day.

At lunchtime Christy looked up to find Marcia standing at her desk. The office manager had been with the firm for over fifteen years and was one of the finest women Christy knew.

Christy smiled. "Do you need something, Marcia?" After a three-week absence, her desk was piled high with folders.

"Can you come into one of the conference rooms for a minute?"

"Sure."

Leading the way, Marcia paused in front of the wide oak doors and grinned sheepishly. "It's good to have you back from vacation, Christy. It made all of us appreciate how much your bright smile adds to our day." With that she opened the door.

Christy was greeted with a chorus of "Surprise" from her fellow workers. A large cake sat in the center of the table, surrounded by several gaily wrapped packages. She must have looked stunned, because Marcia placed one hand on her shoulder and explained. "It's a wedding shower for you and James."

Thirteen

A week had passed since Cody had come back to Cougar Point. By far the longest week of his life. He wanted Christy with him, hungered for her smile and the way her eyes darkened when she looked up at him in that suggestive way.

He loved Christy, and marrying her had helped him cope with the ridiculous set of circumstances in which they found themselves trapped.

He wasn't pleased that she was still engaged to James, but there seemed little he could do about it. If it had been up to him, he'd have settled it before flying out of Seattle, but Christy had been adamant that she was doing the right thing in waiting. Cody wasn't convinced, but the decision had been hers, and he didn't feel he could go against Christy's wishes.

So they were husband and wife. Cody *felt* married. It was as if he'd lived his entire life waiting for this woman. In the too-brief days they'd been together, Cody knew he'd changed. His life's purpose had been focused on his career, and in many ways it still was. Christy, however, added a new dimension to his personality.

She'd taught him to dream.

Unlike Russ, who'd always planned on marriage, Cody had given up hope of ever finding the right woman. It hadn't been a conscious decision; in fact, he wasn't fully aware of it until he met Christy.

He was getting downright philosophical, he mused. Christy gave his life a deeper meaning, and their marriage made everything else more…important, somehow.

Someone brighter than he was would have guessed what was happening the first time they'd kissed. He still recalled feeling lost and bewildered. When he learned she was engaged to marry James, Cody had been even more shaken than he dared to admit.

James. The other man's name brought a grim frown. Reluctantly Christy had shown him a picture of the attorney. He looked clean-cut, professional, intelligent. But he guessed that James Wilkens lacked passion. It was difficult to imagine James allowing a little thing like falling in love to overcome his inhibitions.

Throwing off his anxiety about Christy's engagement, he stood, moved into his kitchen and poured a cup of coffee. He was supposed to be packing, getting ready for his move to Miles City, but because of everything that had happened between Christy and him, he'd delayed until the last minute.

Almost everything in the living room was inside cardboard boxes, and Cody headed absently toward the bedroom, intent on getting as much accomplished that evening as he could.

He recognized his mistake immediately.

Christy had never slept on his bed, never even been in this room, but the fires she sparked to life within Cody were more evident there than anywhere else.

Feeling helpless, missing her so much, Cody sat on the end of the bed. He'd married himself one little hellcat. A smile tempted his mouth. She was a seductress in bed, and an angel out of it.

His need for her was insatiable. Half the time they were so impatient for each other that they hadn't bothered to use any birth control. They'd discussed that; if she were to get pregnant, Cody wouldn't mind. In many ways it would please him tremendously, although he admitted the timing would be all wrong for her. Christy had enough pressures on her already.

A week. They'd been apart for seven days, and it felt like an eternity. Dammit all, he wanted her with him.

Now. Not two days from now.

Not next week. *Now.*

His patience was wearing paper-thin. He picked up the phone and called the number he knew by heart. Christy answered on the second ring.

Her voice softened when she heard his. "Soon," she promised in a seductive whisper that nearly drove him crazy.

"How soon?" he demanded.

"A couple more days."

"Forgive me for saying this, but didn't you claim it would be 'a couple of days' a couple of days ago?" His voice was sharp despite his best efforts.

"Yes, but there are complications."

"Aren't there always?"

"Cody, please, don't be angry with me..."

"I called because I love you."

"I love you, too," she said, sounding a little bewildered. Cody realized he'd probably pushed too hard and backed off, spending the next few minutes telling his wife he loved her.

When he replaced the receiver, he was more frustrated than ever.

* * *

Cody was enjoying breakfast in the bowling alley early the following morning when Russ showed up. It wasn't unusual for Russ to eat in town, but rarer since he'd married Taylor.

The rancher slid into the booth across from Cody. "I thought I'd find you here."

"You looking for me?" he asked.

"You could say that." Russ turned over the ceramic mug and waited until the waitress came by and filled it for him. He reached for the menu. "You look like hell."

"Nice of you to say so," Cody muttered.

"I didn't come here to pick a fight."

Their friendship was too good for this kind of bickering. "I haven't been sleeping well," Cody admitted reluctantly, sipping his own coffee. Truth be known, he hadn't had a decent night's sleep since he'd flown home from Seattle.

"How's Christy holding up?"

"A lot better than I am." She always managed to sound cheerful, as if it was perfectly normal for a couple to be married three days and then separated for weeks.

"You sure about that?"

Russ's question caught Cody off guard. He narrowed his eyes, wondering if Russ knew something he didn't. Russ's attention seemed to be on the menu.

"I'm not sure of anything," Cody answered thoughtfully. "What makes you ask?"

Typically Russ shrugged. "Nothing in particular." He set aside the menu, declined to order breakfast when Mary delivered Cody's and sat there looking superior. "Go ahead and eat," he said, motioning toward the plate of sliced ham, eggs, hash browns and toast.

"I wasn't planning on letting my meal get cold," Cody

informed him frostily. His nerves were shot, and the last thing he needed was his best friend dropping obscure hints.

Cupping the mug with both hands, Russ leaned back in the booth. "Who else knows you and Christy are married?" he asked after a moment.

"Everyone except James and her parents." Christy's three older brothers were all aware of the fact that they'd eloped. Cody had spoken to the two oldest brothers, Paul and Jason, before he'd left Seattle. Rich had been the first to discover their secret, of course, and he'd quickly let the others in on it.

"Should I thank you for the fact that Mrs. Simmons stopped me in the street yesterday with a jar of her watermelon pickles?" Cody asked, eyeing Russ. "She says she heard the sheriff had taken himself a wife and wanted to give me a small gift."

"Ah… I might've mentioned something to Mrs. Simmons," Russ said, hiding a smile. Mrs. Simmons handed out homemade preserves at every opportunity. Each family in town ended up with at least one jar every year.

Russ took another drink of his coffee. "I guess you and everyone else in town figured out Taylor got pregnant on our honeymoon."

Cody was having trouble following this conversation. "What's that got to do with anything?"

"Nothing," he said with an enigmatic smile.

"Listen, Russ, if you know something I don't, spit it out, would you? I'm in no mood for games. Is something going on with Christy that I don't know?"

"Did she tell you about the wedding shower?"

Cody scowled. "No. When was this?"

"Last week. The girls in the office held it for her, threw it as a surprise."

"That was nice."

"It wasn't for you and Christy," Russ barked. "What's with you, man? The shower was for Christy and James."

Cody rubbed his face. She hadn't said a word, not a single word about any wedding shower. And now that he knew, Cody thought that, maybe, just maybe, Christy did sound a little less cheerful than usual. He was fast losing his perspective.

"I bet she hasn't told you something else, either."

Cody resented having his brother-in-law tell him things Christy hadn't even mentioned. "You mean there's more?" he asked darkly. "Did her mother take her shopping and spring for a five-thousand-dollar wedding dress?"

"Nothing quite so drastic," Russ said with a hint of a smile. "I overheard Taylor on the phone last night. She was talking to Christy."

"What did Christy say?"

"I don't know. I only heard half the conversation."

Cody had talked to Christy, too. He'd hung up with a restless feeling he couldn't identify, but he'd attributed it to the fact that she was still in Seattle when he wanted her in Montana.

"And?"

"And when I asked Taylor, she seemed reluctant to say much. But I heard her discuss symptoms."

"Symptoms?"

"I tried to tell you earlier," Russ informed him with a look that questioned Cody's intelligence, "but you got so damn defensive, I shut up." Russ shook his head. "Taylor got pregnant in Reno. Think about it, Cody. Taylor and Christy are two of *five* children. Doesn't it seem obvious to you that the Manning women are a fertile lot?"

"Christy's not pregnant," Cody said with a confidence he wasn't feeling. He felt his head start to spin.

"You're sure of that?"

"She'd say something if she even suspected. I'd bet on it."

"Of course. She tells you everything."

"I'd like to think she'd confide in me," Cody said, growing more uncertain.

"If she didn't tell you about the wedding shower, you can damn well wager she wouldn't mention that she's hanging her head over a toilet every morning."

Cody felt as if he'd been kicked in the stomach. Christy was pregnant and too concerned about protecting her parents and James to risk telling him.

Hell, she *couldn't* tell him. He hadn't made it easy for her, had he? Missing her the way he did, Cody was irritable and impatient while Christy carried the brunt of the load.

Hastily he slid out of the booth and put on his hat. He'd been looking for an excuse to put an end to this nonsense, and now he had one.

"Where you going?" Russ demanded, reaching across the table for Cody's untouched breakfast plate. He leaned forward and retrieved the salt and pepper shakers.

"Seattle."

Chuckling, Russ nodded. "That's what I thought."

"Enjoy your breakfast," Cody muttered sarcastically.

"Thanks," he responded between bites, "I will."

Christy had been feeling blue all day. Cody wasn't home when she'd tried to call, and that depressed her even more. Nothing made sense. Nothing. She felt weepy and excited. Confused and elated. Engaged to one man. Married to another. She might be pregnant. It might be the beginning of an ulcer. She didn't know which.

She couldn't sleep, although she desperately needed to.

Her appetite was nil. After going through the bother of fixing herself spaghetti and a salad for dinner, her meal sat uneaten on her kitchen table.

Feeling wretched, she sank down in front of the television and turned on the movie channel, silently chastising herself for not writing thank-you notes to her friends from the office. Sending notes of appreciation for gifts she intended to return seemed a ridiculous thing to do.

A 1940s war movie with an incredibly young John Wayne and Maureen O'Hara was on, and she was soon caught up in the fast-paced action. How minor her troubles seemed compared to those on the screen.

Damp tissues crowded her end table. She was sniffling ingloriously when her doorbell chimed.

Whoever was on the other side was certainly impatient. The doorbell rang a second time before she was halfway across the carpet. "Hold your horses," she said peevishly. She wasn't interested in company.

Christy quickly changed her mind.

"Cody," she whispered when she saw her husband. "Oh, Cody." Without another word she broke into tears and flew into his arms.

Seconds later, his mouth was on hers in that urgent, hungry way that was so familiar between them. Cody directed her into the living room, then closed the door with his foot, all the while kissing her.

Christy's hands roamed his face when he released her. She giggled and locked her arms around his neck, holding on to him for everything she was worth.

"Oh… Christy, I missed you," he breathed. His hands

caressed her face. Then he was kissing her again and again as if he'd never get enough of the taste of her.

"I've been so miserable without you," Christy admitted, feeling weepy and jubilant at the same time.

"Me, too, love." He looked at her for a long moment, frowning, then smiling, then frowning again.

"What is it?" Christy asked, reacting to his confusion but not understanding it. She sensed a wonder in him, too, as if he couldn't quite believe they were married.

Christy believed it. Their love was the only thing that had gotten her through the trauma of the past week.

"Are you pregnant?" he asked without preamble, running his splayed fingers through her hair. His hold on her tightened, but Christy doubted he was aware of it.

Involuntarily her eyes widened at his question. "I… I don't know yet."

"You've been ill?"

"Yes… How'd you know that?" Usually she'd been sick in the mornings, but often in the afternoons, too. If she was looking for a pattern, there wasn't one. She was confused and anxious, and not knowing where to turn, she'd called her sister. "Taylor?" Christy had never dreamed that her older sister would say anything to Cody. She'd counted on Taylor to be discreet.

"No," Cody admitted, scowling. "I had breakfast with Russ this morning. Rather Russ ate *my* breakfast while he cheerfully pointed out that Taylor got pregnant while they were still in Reno and—"

Christy interrupted him. "You came because of that?"

"No." Cody dropped his hands and stepped away. "Well, not completely. I did come in part because I was afraid…no, afraid's the wrong word. I was concerned for you. I came for another reason, too."

He was so sincere, so forthright. "Yes?"

His eyes darkened. "You didn't tell me about the wedding shower."

Christy's gaze fell. "I couldn't."

"I realize that now, and I realize a whole lot more. This has to be the end of it, Christy." His eyes burned into hers. "As your husband—the man that loves you—I can't let you continue this charade any longer."

Spontaneous tears filled her eyes as she nodded. "I don't think I can pull it off another day. I…thought I was doing what was best for everyone involved, but I see now that I was only prolonging the agony—mostly my own. You were right, so right. There'll never be a good time to tell Mom and Dad. I did us both a terrible disservice by refusing to acknowledge that."

Cody's lips brushed her forehead. "Don't be so hard on yourself."

"There's no one else to blame. It's just that it's really difficult for me to disappoint my parents. I love them both so much, and they're so fond of James."

"But they don't have the right to pick your husband for you."

"I know." She exhaled softly. "I would've liked to have spared James this, but he has to know. I… I did him a disservice by not telling him the afternoon I came home. James isn't as emotionally fragile as I've made him out to be."

Cody's eyes flared briefly before he spoke. "How soon can we get you in to see a doctor?"

"A doctor?" she asked. "Why?" Sure, she'd been overprotective of James and reluctant about telling her parents the truth, but that didn't mean she needed medical help.

"If you're pregnant—"

"Oh, that," she said, relieved. "Taylor recommended I buy one of those home pregnancy test kits, which I did this afternoon. Only I decided I could deal with *not* knowing better than I could handle knowing. Does that sound crazy?"

Cody chuckled. "No. But do you mind satisfying my curiosity? I, for one, am anxious to find out if I'm going to become a father."

"You definitely are," she said, loving the way Cody's face brightened at her words. "The only question is whether or not it's going to be nine months from now."

Cody's arms were around her, his eyes filled with a tenderness that made her knees grow weak. "The test takes about twenty minutes," she said, sliding her hands up the front of his shirt.

"Twenty minutes," Cody repeated.

She moistened her lips, thrilled when her husband's narrowed gaze followed the seductive movement of her tongue.

"Are you suggesting what I think you're suggesting?" he whispered.

Christy nodded.

"But if you're pregnant, will it hurt the baby?" His voice was hoarse, and a dark flame seemed to leap to life in his eyes.

"Not according to Taylor."

"You're sure?"

"Positive. Besides, it'll do this baby's mother a whole lot of good."

Christy lay contentedly in his arms, her long, sleek body nestled intimately with his. If they spent the next ten years exactly like this, Cody wouldn't have a single complaint. He loved this woman. He loved everything about her.

"Are you disappointed?" she asked softly, rolling over so she could look at him when he answered.

He kissed her, his mouth clinging to hers, his hands caressing her. "You've got to be kidding."

They'd been on fire for each other from the moment he'd arrived. Their hands had trembled as they'd hurriedly undressed each other, their mouths eager, filled with promises and pleas.

Raising herself on one elbow, Christy smiled dreamily down on him and lovingly traced her fingers over the hard angles of his face as though memorizing every feature. To Cody's way of thinking, that was unnecessary. He never planned to leave her again.

"I wasn't talking about the lovemaking," she said. "I was referring to the pregnancy test."

His arm curved around her trim waist. "No. When the time's right, we'll start our family and not because we were in too much of a hurry to—"

"May I remind you how much of a hurry we were in a few minutes ago?"

"No, you may not." He clasped her around the waist and they both dissolved into laughter.

A woman he could love *and* laugh with—how did he get so lucky?

"It might be a good idea if I went over to my parents' house alone," Christy said. She looked up at him beseechingly. "Please, Cody?"

"I won't hear of it, Christy," he answered in a voice that brooked no dissent. "We're in this together."

"But…"

"You phoned James?"

"You know I did. He'll arrive at my parents' within the hour." James had sounded surprised to hear from her, and even more perplexed when she explained she needed to speak with him urgently. He'd offered to come to her apartment, but when she'd suggested they meet at her family home in an hour, he'd agreed.

"How did Rich find out we're telling your parents?" Cody asked, frowning.

Her scoundrel of a brother had been visiting their parents when Christy called and in fact had answered the phone. There must have been something in her voice that conveyed her intent, because Rich had made it clear he planned to stay around for the fireworks display. That comment reminded Christy that the coming scene was bound to evoke plenty of emotion. Christy wished Cody would wait for the worst to pass before he presented himself as their latest son-in-law.

"Don't even think of arguing with me," he said. "We're doing this together."

"All right," she murmured, holding in a sigh. "The way I figure it, we'll have forty-five minutes to explain everything to my parents before James arrives."

"Good." Cody nodded.

"Are you ready?" she asked, and her voice trembled despite every effort to maintain an optimistic facade. Her heart felt frozen with fear. Although she'd wanted to handle this on her own, she was grateful Cody had chosen to go with her.

They spoke infrequently on the drive to her parents' home. When they did, it was to murmur words of encouragement, or reinforce how much they loved each other.

As they pulled in to the driveway, another car came in after them. "Oh, no," Christy breathed.

"What's wrong?"

"It's James." Christy climbed out of the car, not waiting for Cody. She turned to face her fiancé. "You're early," she said, struggling to keep the annoyance out of her voice.

"I called your parents, and they suggested I come now." James's gaze narrowed as Cody came to stand behind her and rested his hand on her shoulder.

It was clear that James took offense at the familiar way Cody touched her. His eyes went cold as he demanded, "Who is this?"

Fourteen

Christy felt Cody's hand tighten involuntarily. The two men glared at each other like hostile dogs who'd inadvertently strayed into each other's territory. She supposed it wasn't a complimentary analogy, but it seemed fitting.

"James, this is Cody Franklin," she said, hating the unexpected way her voice squeaked.

"So the gang's all here," Rich shouted, coming out the front door, ready to greet the two men. "I suppose you're wondering why I've called this meeting." He laughed, obviously in a playful mood.

Christy glared at him, wondering what he was doing.

"Do you mind waiting a few minutes?" Rich asked. "Jason and Paul are on their way."

"As a matter of fact, I do mind," Christy snapped. She gripped Rich hard by the elbow and forced him back into the house. "Please introduce Cody to Mom and Dad," she said.

Rich's mouth fell open. "Me? No way, little sister. I happen to value my neck."

"I'll take care of everything," Cody said, slapping Rich on the back. "You have nothing to fear but fear itself."

"James," Christy said reproachfully, turning to face the attorney, "it would have helped matters if you'd come when I suggested, but since you're here now, we'll settle this in the kitchen."

She walked into the house and passed her mother, who was watching her curiously.

"We'll talk in the kitchen," Christy reminded James when he hesitated in front of Elizabeth Manning and shrugged.

"Christy?" her father called. "What's going on here?"

"I'll explain everything in a few minutes, but first I have to clear something up with James."

"Actually, I'll be more than happy to explain," Cody said, stepping forward. He offered Eric Manning his hand, and they exchanged a brief handshake as Cody introduced himself.

"Exactly what's going on?" James wanted to know as they entered the kitchen.

Christy stopped at the huge round oak table. She pulled out a chair and sat down, then gestured for James to do the same.

He complied, but with some hesitation. "You never answered my question. Who is that man?"

"Cody Franklin."

"That doesn't explain much."

"No, it doesn't," she agreed readily. With a sigh, she wondered where she should even begin. "He's from Montana."

"Ah, that accounts for the cowboy hat."

"We met when I went to spend time with Taylor. Cody's the new sheriff of Custer County."

James nodded, urging her to go on. She'd explained the easy part; everything else was hard.

Unable to stay seated, Christy surged to her feet and frowned as she organized her thoughts. "Sometimes, not often I think, but sometimes when two strangers meet something happens…something special." She paused and looked at James, hoping, praying she'd see a glimmer of understanding. She didn't.

"You're talking about fairy tales," he said, and laughed as though she'd made a poor joke. "Are you going to break into song next?"

Christy ignored the question. "A special magic, a chemistry that flows between the two of them," she went on. "There was magic when Taylor met Russ. At first they both resisted it and—"

"Yes, yes," James interrupted, "but what have your sister and her husband got to do with anything?"

"Cody and I experienced that same…chemistry," she announced, astonished this genius attorney could be so obtuse. "Neither of us was expecting to fall in love."

"You didn't," James said flatly, dismissing her claim.

"But I did."

"You can't be in love with Franklin. It isn't possible when you're in love with me."

"James, please, let me explain—"

He interrupted with an upraised hand. "Christy, darling, what you experienced for this man is a simple case of homesickness. It's perfectly understandable, and forgivable. We were only engaged a day or two, and after working so hard for all those weeks, it only makes sense that you'd look to another man for companionship."

"James," she said, taking both of his hands in her own, "that's not the case. I wish it was that simple, but it isn't."

"Nonsense." James hadn't been touted as a brilliant attorney without reason. With infuriating ease, he twisted everything she said around to suit his own purposes.

"I love Cody." She said it forcefully enough, she prayed, for James to accept it as truth.

"As I already said, that isn't possible." He stood, placing his hands on her shoulders, his look indulgent. "You love me, remember? Otherwise you wouldn't have agreed to become my wife."

"I agreed to your proposal because I *like* you. And because it pleased my mother and father," she cried.

"Christy." He said her name softly, as if she were a petulant child. "I'm sure you're mistaken."

"I'm not." Her hands on his forearms, she stared directly into his eyes. "I love Cody Franklin so much I married him."

It hurt Christy to watch the transformation come over his face. She hated the pain she saw. The disbelief. The humiliation.

"It's true," she said before he could question her.

Anger flickered in his eyes. He jerked his arms free from her and dropped them to his sides.

"When?"

"Does it matter?"

"No, I guess not." His eyes drifted briefly shut. That said more than any words he could have spoken.

She took a moment to open the clasp of her purse and take out the diamond ring he'd given her. When she handed it back to him, James stared at the velvet box as if he'd never seen it before. "Keep it."

"No, I can't."

He removed it from her hand and turned away long enough to shove it into his coat pocket. When he looked at her again, he was able to mask the pain, but she knew him well enough to realize how deeply she'd hurt him. Causing him such intense suffering was the most difficult thing she'd ever had to do. James didn't deserve to be treated this way.

"I intended to tell you the minute I got home from Montana," she said in her own defense, the words coming so fast they nearly blended together.

"The engagement party," he supplied for her. "You tried to tell me then, didn't you?" He didn't wait for her to answer. "I sensed something was wrong and trapped you into setting a wedding date." He scowled. "On a subconscious level I ignored the obvious, immersed myself in my work, hoping whatever had happened with you would pass. I know I made it difficult to talk to me. But am I that unreasonable that you couldn't have told me the truth?"

"That wasn't it." Christy felt it was important to correct that impression. "I just didn't feel I could. You were so heavily involved in the Mulligan case and I didn't want to—"

"I'm still involved."

"I know. But the worst of it's over, and I couldn't go on pretending. I'm sorry, James, sorrier than you'll ever realize."

He snickered, but didn't openly contradict her.

"I'm terribly fond of you and I'd give anything to—"

"Fond." He spit out the word as if it were an obscenity.

His vehemence was a shock. James wasn't a passionate man. Rarely had Christy seen him reveal any emotion, in or out of a courtroom.

Once more she tried to explain. "I don't expect you to understand how difficult this was for me. That would be asking too much of you." She knew she sounded shaken, but she couldn't help that. "If there was any possible way I could've done this without hurting you, I would have."

He didn't respond.

"You're a wonderful man, James, and someday a woman will come into your life—the right woman. And you'll know what I mean."

"You were the right woman. Or so I believed."

"I'm sorry. So very sorry."

He shook his head as if he didn't quite believe her. His hand was buried in his pocket, and Christy guessed he'd made a tight fist around the diamond.

"I only wish you the best," she whispered.

He breathed deeply, then nodded, although Christy had the impression he didn't agree with her. She was about to say something more when a thunderous shout came from the direction of the living room.

"Your father?" James asked.

Christy nodded. "Cody must have told him."

James's gaze continued to hold hers. "You'll be all right?"

"Of course."

He seemed to accept that. "Can I kiss you, one last time?"

In response she opened her arms to him, her eyes brimming with unshed tears. James reached for her, his touch gentle. He held her close for just a moment, then pressed his mouth to hers.

He broke away, and his finger touched her cheek, his eyes clouded. "Be happy, Christy."

"I will."

With that he turned and walked out of the kitchen. Christy stood by the window and watched him move down the walkway, then climb inside his car. For what seemed an eternity, James sat in the driver's seat with his hands gripping the steering wheel as he stared straight ahead.

Christy couldn't delay the confrontation with her family any longer. Squaring her shoulders, she walked into the living room to find her brothers, Paul, Jason and Rich, perched on bar stools as though viewing a stage performance.

"Christy," her mother sobbed, dabbing a tissue under her nose, "tell us it isn't true."

She moved next to Cody and sat on the arm of the chintz-covered chair. She slipped her hand into his. "Cody and I were married last week."

"Married!" Her father stormed to his feet as if she'd desecrated the Constitution of the United States.

Confused, Christy's eyes went to Cody's.

"I hadn't gotten around to telling them that part yet," he told her.

"Married," her mother repeated. "It can't be true. Christy would never do anything so… We have a wedding to plan. You couldn't possibly have gone off and gotten married without telling your own mother and father. It isn't like you to do something so underhanded."

"I thought they knew," she whispered, bewildered. "I heard Dad shout, and I thought… I assumed."

"All I said," Cody explained, "was that you wanted a little privacy with James so you could return his engagement ring."

"Oh." She swallowed and closed her eyes for a moment. "Well, Mom and Dad," she said brightly, looking at them once more, "I see you've met your new son-in-law."

"Welcome to the family," Paul said, holding up a soft drink can in tribute. "From what Rich said, you're a friend of Russ's."

Cody nodded.

"But you couldn't possibly be married," her mother

whimpered, turning to Eric as though he could explain everything.

"Trust me, Mom, we're married."

"They're married," Rich said, saluting them with his own can of soda. "I should know. I was at their wedding night."

"Hear, hear," Jason cried, wearing the ever-present baseball cap. "Wait a minute. At their *wedding* night?"

"I don't find any of this humorous or in good taste," Eric roared. "Your sister's turned down the best man in three states for some…some small-town lawman. Bad enough that Taylor had to marry a country boy, but Christy, too? Never!"

"Dad," Christy reminded him softly, "the deed is done."

"But, Christy," Elizabeth wailed, "I bought the material for the bridesmaids' dresses and we've put down a deposit on the hall for the reception, and—"

"I didn't mean to cheat you out of a wedding, Mom. I really didn't."

"What will we say to our friends?" Her mother appeared to be in a state of shock. She'd gone deathly pale, and her shoulders jerked as she tried to gain control of her emotions.

"If you're worried about what to tell your friends," Paul said, sounding knowledgeable, "I'd suggest the truth."

"Stay out of this," Eric shouted, dismissing his eldest son with a shake of his head. "We're in one hell of a mess here."

"How's that?" Cody asked.

"Christy's married to you is how," Eric informed him none too gently. "My daughter doesn't belong in the country. She was born and raised in the city. We've already got Taylor living out in the sticks. I won't allow Christy to be out there slopping hogs or whatever you do in that backwoods community."

"Dad!" Christy was outraged. "It's *my* decision. And Cougar Point isn't any backwoods community. Besides, we won't be living there."

"You're moving to Washington state?" Elizabeth asked Cody, her eyes wide and hopeful.

"Sorry, no."

Her mother drooped against the back of the sofa and reached for a fresh tissue. She wadded it up and pressed it over her eyes as if to block out this horrible scene.

"Cody's the sheriff," Christy said, wanting to impress both of her parents with the fact that he was a responsible citizen. "We'll be living in Miles City once he's installed."

"A sheriff should please them," Jason said under his breath, speaking to his two brothers.

"I think they prefer an attorney over a sheriff," Rich concluded when neither parent responded to Christy's announcement.

"I recognize that this is all rather abrupt," Cody said in a reasonable voice. "I don't blame you for being shocked. I can't even blame you for being concerned. You wouldn't have raised a daughter as wonderful as Christy if you weren't the kind of people who'd care about her happiness."

"That's good," Paul whispered to Jason. "He's going to win them over with flattery."

"Will you three shut up," Eric yelled, infuriated with his sons and not bothering to disguise it.

"Dad, please try to understand," Christy tried again. "I fell in love with Cody."

"Falling in love is one thing, but marrying him on the sly is another."

"While she was engaged to James, I might add." Rich apparently didn't know when to keep his mouth closed.

Both Eric and Cody sent daggers his way. Guarding his face with his hands, Rich pretended to ward off their attack.

"I can only say I love you both," Christy said. "I'd never intentionally do anything to hurt you. In fact, most of my life I've done everything I can to please you, right down to becoming engaged to James."

"I can't believe I'm hearing this," Eric said to his wife. "We raised her the best we knew how, and now this."

"Darling, we thought you loved James," her mother pleaded.

"I thought I did, too, until I met Cody." Her hand clasped Cody's, and she smiled down at him. "I know I made mistakes, lots of them."

"*We* made mistakes," Cody corrected, his gaze holding hers.

"No one's making a list," her father mumbled, "but if I were—"

"Nothing on this earth will ever convince me I made a mistake marrying Cody." Her father obviously wasn't willing to accept what they'd done. As Christy suspected, her family would need time to come to terms with her marriage and the fact that she'd be leaving the Seattle area.

"I gave my week's notice when I returned from vacation," Christy said. It had been one of the low points of her life, telling Marcia she was quitting her job in order to prepare for her wedding. The lie had all but choked her.

"You're leaving your job?"

"She couldn't very well continue working with James," Eric muttered to his wife. "And from the sounds of it, she intends to live in Montana."

"Poor James," Elizabeth said with a regretful sigh. "He would've made such a good husband."

"I'll make Christy a good husband, too," Cody promised. "I love your daughter."

An awkward silence followed Cody's words. "My daughter doesn't belong in Montana, and she deserves a decent wedding with her family around her. Christy's not the type of girl a man takes to a justice of the peace."

"We were married by a minister." Christy knew even before she spoke that there was little she could say to appease her father. He wasn't accustomed to having his authority challenged. Not even by a sheriff.

"It might be best if we gave your parents a chance to get used to the idea," Cody suggested.

Christy agreed, but leaving her family home was one of the most difficult tasks of her life.

Paul, Jason and Rich followed them outside.

"They'll come around," Paul said to Cody as they exchanged handshakes. Paul was tall and silver-blond, the only one in the family who'd inherited that coloring.

"Just give 'em a year or three," Rich said with less than diplomatic cheer. "Grandkids will be sure to win 'em over. There *will* be children, won't there?" He was eyeing Christy as if a good stare would tell him if she was in the family way.

"Don't worry about a thing," Jason said, throwing his arm over Cody's broad shoulders. "Mom and Dad will accept your marriage before you know it."

"They've got two days," Cody said darkly.

"Two days?" Christy echoed, a little stunned, although she shouldn't have been. Cody's life was in Miles City, and he'd recently taken three days of his vacation to spend with her. He couldn't afford to take off any more, not during this important period of transition.

"Is that too soon for you?" he asked, his eyes revealing

his concern. "I figured that would give us enough time to get your things packed and shipped."

She nodded, slipping her arms around his waist. Her life was linked to Cody's now, and there was no turning back.

They hadn't gone through airport security yet, but Christy delayed, glancing around the terminal building, certain if she stayed there long enough her parents would rush in and throw their arms around her, telling her how much they loved her and how they wished her and Cody well.

Only they hadn't come.

"Honey," Cody said patiently. "They aren't coming. We have to go."

"I know, but I'd hoped. I…thought they'd at least want to say goodbye."

Christy hadn't heard from them in the two hectic days they'd spent packing up her apartment. She'd tried not to let it affect her, but she'd always been close to her parents, and being shunned this way hurt more than anything they could have said.

"Give them time," Cody said—he'd been saying that a lot—and it seemed as if her pain belonged to him, too.

Christy offered him a brave smile and nodded.

They joined the security line, then hurried to their departure area, arriving just as their flight was called. Christy realized there was nothing left to do but board the plane that would take her away from everything that was familiar and bring her to a whole new life.

"You're not sorry, are you?" Cody asked once they were seated and about to take off.

"No." Beyond a doubt Christy knew she was meant to be with Cody. She would've preferred to have her parents' blessing. But if she had to do without it, then she'd learn to accept that.

Cody was her love. And now he was her life.

Since Paul, Jason and Rich all worked days and hadn't been able to come to the airport to say their goodbyes, the three of them had taken Christy and Cody to dinner the night before.

Everyone had made an effort to have a good time, and they all had.

Only something vital had been missing. No one said anything. No one had to.

Eric and Elizabeth Manning weren't there. And what was missing was their love. Their blessing. Their approval.

Christy didn't know when she'd see her parents again.

"Oh, Cody," Christy whispered, stepping back to study her husband in his full dress uniform. "You look…wonderful."

They'd been in Miles City, Montana, a week. In that time they'd moved into their first home, unpacked their belongings and gone about making a place for themselves in the community.

"When will Russ and Taylor get here?"

"Oh," she said, still a little awed by how handsome Cody looked. "I forgot to tell you Taylor phoned. They're going to meet us at the courthouse for the installation."

"Good." He straightened the sleeves of his crisp uniform jacket. "Well, I'm ready."

"I'm not," Christy told him. "In case you haven't noticed, I'm not dressed yet."

Cody wiggled his eyebrows suggestively. "All the better to seduce you, my dear."

Christy giggled. "I do believe you've seduced me in

every room of this house, Sheriff Franklin. More than once."

"There's time—"

"There most certainly is not." She scurried past him. She wasn't quick enough, and with little effort, Cody caught her in his arms.

"Cody," she warned him. "We…can't. You don't want to be late for your own installation. And I don't want to arrive at the ceremony looking like a disheveled mess."

Cody hesitated. "Well…"

She entwined her arms around his neck and kissed him soundly.

"Shameless hussy," he said with a grin as he unwound her arms. "Get dressed before I change my mind."

"Yes, sir." Mockingly she saluted him.

A half hour later they entered the courthouse. Judge Carter would be doing the honors, and the room was filled to capacity. Christy was escorted to the front row of reserved seats. Many of the citizens of Cougar Point were in the audience.

The ceremony was about to begin when Taylor, carrying Eric, and Russ slipped into the chairs to her right. That left two empty seats on her left. Christy was so busy greeting her sister that she didn't notice the vacant chairs had been filled. She turned to smile and introduce herself to her seatmates, and to her astonishment saw her parents.

"Mom. Dad." Without warning, tears flooded her eyes. She looked at Cody, who was standing at the podium with Judge Carter. When she nodded toward her family, Cody's face brightened.

"Are you willing to forgive your father for being a stubborn old cuss?" Eric asked in a low voice.

Christy nodded, shaken by the intensity of her relief.

She hugged him and then her mother, who was as teary-eyed as Christy.

When the ceremony was over, Cody joined them. Christy's husband and father faced each other. Eric Manning offered his hand first, and the two exchanged a hearty shake.

Judge Carter came forward to introduce himself a few minutes after that, and soon they were all talking at once.

A small reception followed, and Cody held Christy's hand as he led the way.

"Thank you," she whispered.

He shook his head. "Honey, as much as I'd like to take credit for bringing your parents out here, I can't."

"Not that," she said, smiling up at him from the very depths of her soul. "Thank you for loving me."

"That," he said softly, "was the easiest thing I've ever done."

"Eric Manning," Christy could hear her father say over the din of raised voices. "I'm the sheriff's father-in-law. We're proud of the boy. Glad to have him in the family."

"Not as glad as he is to be part of it," Cody murmured, smiling at his wife.

* * * * *

FIRST COMES MARRIAGE

One

"You must be Zachary Thomas," Janine said breathlessly as she whirled into the office. "Sorry I'm late, but I got hung up in traffic on Fourth Avenue. I didn't realize they'd torn up the whole street." Still a little winded, she unfastened her coat, tossed it over the back of the visitor's chair and threw herself down, facing the large executive desk.

The man on the other side blinked twice as though he didn't know quite what to think.

"I'm Janine Hartman." She drew in a deep breath. "Gramps said if he wasn't back from his appointment, I should introduce myself."

"Yes," Zachary said after a moment of strained silence. "But he didn't tell me you'd be wearing—"

"Oh, the bandanna dress," Janine said, smoothing one hand over her lap. The dress had been constructed of red and blue bandannas; it featured a knee-length zigzag hemline and closely hugged her hips. "It was a gift. And since I'm meeting the girl who made it later, I thought I should wear it."

"And the necklace?"

Janine toyed with the colored Christmas-tree lights

strung between large beads on a bootlace that dangled from her neck. "It's a bit outrageous, isn't it? That was a gift, too. I think it's kind of cute, don't you? Pamela is so clever."

"Pamela?"

"A teenager from the Friendship Club."

"I…see," Zach said.

"I do volunteer work there and the two of us hit it off as soon as we met. Pam's mother doesn't live in the area and she's at that awkward age and needs a friend. For some reason she took a liking to me, which was fine because I think she's wonderful."

"I see," he said again.

Janine doubted he did.

"The necklace is *different* I'll grant you," Zach was saying—which wasn't admitting to much. His dark eyes narrowed as he studied it.

Now that she'd met Zachary Thomas, Janine could understand why her grandfather was so impressed with him—if appearances were anything to judge by. In his well-tailored suit, he was the very picture of a high-powered executive, crisp, formal and in control. He was younger than she'd assumed, possibly in his early thirties, but it was difficult to tell. His facial features were attractive enough, but he wasn't strikingly handsome. Still, she found herself fascinated by the strength of character she saw in the uneven planes of his face. His dark hair was cut military short. His jaw was strong, his cheekbones high and his mouth full. That was the way she'd describe him physically, but there was apparently much more to this man than met the eye. At least, her grandfather was convinced of it.

Several months earlier Anton Hartman had merged his well-established business-supply firm with the fast-expanding company owned by Zachary Thomas. Together the two men had quickly dominated the market.

For weeks now, Gramps had wanted Janine to meet Zachary. His name had popped up in every conversation, no matter what they were discussing. To say her grandfather thought highly of his partner was an understatement.

"Gramps has spoken…well of you," she said next.

A hint of a smile—just the merest suggestion—touched his mouth, giving her the impression that he didn't smile often. "Your grandfather has one of the keenest business minds in the country."

"He's incredible, isn't he?"

Zachary's nod betrayed no hesitation.

There was a polite knock on the door and a tall middle-aged woman wearing a navy-blue pin-striped suit stepped into the room. "Mr. Hartman phoned," she announced primly. "He's been delayed and asked that you meet him at the restaurant."

Zach's lean dark face tightened briefly before he cast Janine an uneasy glance. "Did he say when he was going to get there?"

"I'm sorry, Mr. Thomas, but he didn't."

Janine looked at her watch. She was supposed to meet Pam at three. If they were delayed much longer, she'd be late.

She scowled at Zach's apparent reluctance to entertain her in Gramp's absence. "Maybe it would be best if we rescheduled for another day," she offered brightly. She wasn't any happier about the prospect of waiting in a restaurant, just the two of them, than he was. "Gramps is held up, I'm meeting Pam, and you're obviously a busy man."

An uncomfortable silence followed her remark. "Is it

your habit not to show up when your grandfather's expecting you?" he asked sharply.

Janine bristled. "Of course not." She swallowed the words to defend herself. Her suggestion hadn't been unreasonable and he had no right to insinuate that she was inconsiderate and rude.

"Then I feel we should meet your grandfather at the restaurant as he requested," he finished stiffly.

"By all means," she said, forcing a smile. She stood and reached for her coat, watching Zach from the corner of her eye. He didn't like her. That realization had a peculiar effect on Janine. She felt disappointed and a little sad. Zach hadn't said much, and actually there hadn't been time for a real conversation, but she'd sensed his attitude almost from the first. He thought of her as spoiled and frivolous, probably because he knew she didn't hold a responsible job and loved to travel. Part of her longed to explain that there were good reasons she'd chosen the lifestyle she had. But from the looks he was sending her, it would be a waste of breath.

Besides, it was more important to maintain the peace, however strained, for Gramps's sake. She'd have enjoyed getting to know Zach, perhaps even becoming friends, but that didn't seem likely.

That morning, before Gramps had left the house, he'd been as excited as a little boy about their luncheon date. He'd come down the stairs whistling when he'd joined her for breakfast, his blue eyes sparkling. When she'd refused the use of the limousine, he'd spent the next fifteen minutes giving her detailed directions, as though she'd never driven in downtown Seattle.

Almost as an afterthought, he'd mentioned that he had a morning meeting with an important client. If he hadn't returned by the time she arrived, she was to go directly to Zach's office, introduce herself and wait for him there.

Shrugging into a raincoat, Zachary moved toward the door. "Are you ready?"

She nodded, burying her hands in her pockets.

Thankfully the restaurant her grandfather had chosen was close by. Without further discussion, they began to walk the few short blocks, although Janine had trouble matching her stride with Zach's much longer one.

Struggling to keep up with him, Janine studied Zachary Thomas, trying to determine exactly what disturbed her about the man. His height was a good example. He wasn't tall—under six feet, she guessed—and since she was almost five-eight there wasn't more than a few inches' difference between them. Why, then, did he make her feel much shorter?

He must have sensed her scrutiny because he turned and glared at her. Janine gave him a feeble smile, and felt the color rise in her cheeks. Zach's dismissive glance did nothing to boost her ego. She wasn't vain, but Janine knew she was attractive. Over the years, plenty of men had told her so, including Brian, the man who'd broken her heart. But she could have warts on her nose for all the notice Zachary Thomas gave her.

If he found the bandanna dress disconcerting, he was probably put off by her hairstyle as well. She wore it short, neatly trimmed in the back with extra-long bangs slanted across her forehead. For years Janine had kept her hair shoulder-length, parted in the middle. One afternoon a few weeks earlier, for no particular reason, she'd decided to have it cut. She was in the mood for something radical and the style she now sported seemed more appropriate to the pages of a fashion magazine. Pam had been crazy about the change, insisting she looked “phenomenal.” Janine wasn’t convinced. Her one comfort was that, given time, her hair would grow back.

Janine suspected Zach had characterized her as flamboyant, if not downright flashy. She, in turn, would describe him as austere and disciplined, perhaps solitary. Her grandfather saw all that, she knew, and a good deal more.

“Mr. Hartman is waiting for you,” the maître d’ informed them when they entered the plush waterfront restaurant. He led them across the thick carpet to a high semicircular booth upholstered in blue velvet.

“Janine, Zach.” Anton Hartman smiled broadly as they approached. The years had been kind to her grandfather. His bearing was still straight and confident, although his hair had grown completely white. His deep blue eyes, only a little faded, were filled with warmth and wisdom. “I apologize for the inconvenience.”

“It wasn’t any problem,” Zach answered for both of them before Janine could respond—as if he’d expected her to complain!

Ignoring him, Janine removed her coat and kissed her grandfather’s leathery cheek.

“Janine,” he began, then gasped. “Where did you get that…dress?”

“Do you like it?” She threw out her arms and whirled around once to give him the full effect. “I know it’s a bit unconventional, but I didn’t think you’d mind.”

Gramps’s gaze flickered to Zach, then back to her. “On anyone else it would be scandalous, but on you, my dear, it’s a work of art.”

“Honestly, Gramps,” she said, laughing softly. “You never could lie very well.” She slid into the booth next to her grandfather, forcing him into the center, between her and Zach. Gramps looked a bit disgruntled, but after her turbulent first encounter with Zach, she preferred to keep her distance. For that matter, he didn't seem all that eager to be close to her, either.

She glanced at him and noted, almost smugly, that he was already studying the menu. No doubt he found ordinary conversation a waste of time. Janine picked up her own menu. She was famished. At breakfast she'd only had time for coffee and a single piece of toast, and she had every intention of making up for it now.

When the waiter came to take their order, Janine asked for the seafood entrée and soup *and* salad. She'd decide about dessert later, she said. Once he'd left, Gramps leaned toward Zach. "Janine never has to worry about her weight." He made this sound as if it was a subject of profound and personal interest to them both. "Her grandmother was the same way. How my Anna could eat, and she never gained an ounce. Janine's just like her."

"Gramps," Janine whispered under her breath. "I'm sure Zach couldn't care less how much I weigh."

"Nonsense," Gramps said, gently patting her hand. "I hope you two had the chance to introduce yourselves."

"Oh, yes," Janine returned automatically.

"Your granddaughter is everything you claimed," Zachary said, but the inflection in his voice implied something completely different to Janine than it did to her grandfather. She guessed that to Anton, he seemed courteous and complimentary. But he was telling Janine he'd found her to be the spoiled darling he'd long suspected. He didn't openly dislike her, but he wasn't too impressed with her, either.

Unfortunately, that was probably due to more than just the dress and the lightbulb necklace.

Janine watched for her grandfather's reaction to Zach's

words and she knew she was right when his gaze warmed and he nodded, obviously pleased by his partner's assessment. Zachary Thomas was clever, Janine had to grant him that much.

"How did the meeting with Anderson go?" Zach asked.

For a moment her grandfather stared at him blankly. "Oh, Anderson… Fine, fine. Everything went just as I'd hoped." Then he cleared his throat and carefully spread the linen napkin across his lap. "As you both know," he said, "I've been wanting the two of you to meet for some time now. Janine is the joy of my life. She's kept me young and brought me much happiness over the years. I fear that, without her, I would have turned into a bitter old man."

His look was so full of tenderness that Janine had to lower her eyes and swallow back a rush of tears. Gramps had been her salvation, too. He'd taken her in after the sudden deaths of her parents, raised her with a gentle hand and loved her enough to allow her to be herself. It must've been difficult for him to have a six-year-old girl unexpectedly thrust into his life, but he'd never complained.

"My only son died far too young," Anton said slowly, painfully.

"I'm sorry," Zachary murmured.

The genuine compassion Janine heard in his voice surprised her. And it definitely pleased her. Zach's respect and affection for her grandfather won her immediate approval—even if the man didn't seem likely to ever feel anything so positive toward *her.*

"For many years I mourned the loss of my son and his wife," Anton continued, his voice gaining strength. "I've worked all my life, built an empire that stretches across these fifty states, and in the process have become a wealthy man."

Janine studied her grandfather closely. He was rarely

this serious. He wasn't one to list his accomplishments, and she wondered at his strange mood.

"When Zach brought his business into the area, I saw in him a rare gift, one that comes along seldom in this life. It's said that there are men who make things happen, those who watch things happen and those who wonder what happened. Zachary is a man who makes things happen. In many ways, the two of us are alike. That's one of the primary reasons I decided to approach him with a proposal to merge our companies."

"I'm honored that you should think so, sir."

"Sir," Anton repeated softly and chuckled. He raised his hand, motioning for the waiter. "You haven't called me that in six months, and there's no reason to start again now."

The waiter returned with a bottle of expensive champagne. Soon glasses were poured and set before them.

"Now," Anton continued, "as I said earlier, I have the two people I love most in this world together with me for the first time, and I don't mind telling you, it feels good." He raised his glass. "To happiness."

"Happiness," Janine echoed, sipping her champagne.

Her eyes met Zach's above the crystal flute and she saw a glint of admiration. If she were dining on it, she'd starve—to quote a favorite expression of her grandfather's—but it was just enough for her to know that he'd think more kindly of her because of her love for Anton.

Her grandfather chuckled and whispered something in his native tongue, a German dialect from the old country. Over the years she'd picked up a smattering of the language, but when she'd repeated a few phrases to a college German professor, he'd barely recognized the words. Gramps paused and his smile lingered on Janine, then went to Zach.

Whatever Gramps was muttering appeared to please him. His blue eyes fairly twinkled with delight.

"And now," he said, setting his glass aside, "I have an important announcement to make."

He turned to Janine and his face softened with affection. "I feel as though I've been an impossible burden to you, child, what with running this company." He shook his head. "Never in all my dreams did I expect to accumulate so much in a single lifetime. I've stayed in the business far longer than I should. It's time for me to retire and do a little traveling."

"It's past time," Janine said. For years, she'd been urging her grandfather to lessen his heavy work schedule. He'd often spoken of revisiting his birthplace and the surrounding countries. He talked at length of cousins and friends he'd left behind in the small German settlement. It was located in what was now part of Russia.

"This is where Zachary comes into the picture," Anton explained. "I know myself all too well. Full retirement would be impossible for me. If I stopped working, I'd shrivel up and die. That's just the way I am," he said simply.

Neither Janine nor Zachary disputed his words.

"I'll never be able to keep my fingers out of the business, yet I want to enjoy my travels. I couldn't do that if I was fretting about what was going on at the office." He paused as if he expected one of them to contradict him. "I believe I've come upon a solution. As of this afternoon, Zachary, I'm handing the reins to you. You will assume my position as chairman of the board. I realize this is sooner than we discussed, but the time is right and I hope you'll agree."

"But, Anton—"

"Gramps—"

Anton held up his hand. "I've thought about this long

and hard," he said confidently. "I find Zach's honesty unquestionable, his loyalty certain and his intelligence keen. He's shrewd, perceptive and insightful. I can think of no better man, and there's no better time."

Janine noticed that Zach seemed uncomfortable with the praise. "Thank you," was all he said.

"A share of this company will belong to you someday, Janine," Anton said next. "Do you have any objections to this appointment?"

She opened her mouth, but nothing came out. Of course she approved. What else could she do? "Whatever you decide is fine with me."

Anton turned his attention to the other man. "Zachary, do you accept?"

Although their acquaintance had been brief, Janine knew instinctively that it took a lot to fluster this man. But her grandfather had managed to do so.

Zachary continued to stare at him as though he couldn't quite believe what he was hearing. But when he spoke, his voice was well modulated, revealing little emotion. "I'm honored."

"For the next few months, we'll be working closely together, much as we have in the past, but with a difference. No longer will I be showing you the ropes. I'll be handing them to you."

The first course of their lunch arrived, and after that, the conversation flowed smoothly. Her grandfather made sure of it. He was jubilant and entertaining, witty and charming. It would have been impossible not to be affected by his good humor.

When they'd finished the meal, Zachary looked at his watch. "I'm sorry to leave so soon, but I have an appointment."

Janine took a last sip of her coffee. "I should be leaving, too." She reached for her purse and coat, then slid out of the booth, waiting for her grandfather to join her.

"If neither of you objects, I'm going to linger over my coffee," Anton said, nodding toward his steaming cup.

"Of course." Janine leaned over to kiss him goodbye.

Zachary walked out to the street with her. Before he left, he shook her hand. "It's been a pleasure, Ms. Hartman."

"You're sure?" she teased, unable to stop herself.

"Yes." His eyes held hers and he smiled. She walked away feeling oddly excited about their meeting. Zach wasn't an easy person to know, but she suspected he was everything her grandfather claimed and more.

Gramps's mood remained cheerful when he got home later that evening. Janine was in the library sipping herbal tea with her feet tucked under her as she watched the local news.

Sitting in the wingback leather chair next to her, Gramps crossed his legs and chose one of his Havana cigars. Janine shook her head affectionately as he lit it; she loved her grandfather dearly and wished he'd stop smoking, though she no longer bothered to express that wish. He was the kind of man who did exactly as he chose, got exactly what he wanted. He was obviously pleased with the way their luncheon had gone, and she wondered briefly if Zach had said anything about her afterward. Somehow she doubted it.

"Well," he said after a moment, "What do you think of Zachary Thomas?" He blew a steady stream of smoke at the ceiling while he awaited her answer.

All afternoon, Janine had prepared herself for his question. Several complicated answers had presented themselves, clever replies that would sidestep her true feelings, but she used none of them now. Her grandfather expected the truth, and it was her duty to give it to him.

"I'm not sure. He's a very…reserved man, isn't he?"

Anton chuckled. "Yes, he is, but I've never known you to walk away from a challenge. The boy's a little rough around the edges, but on the inside, he's pure gold."

Janine hadn't thought of Zach in those terms—a challenge. Frankly, she doubted there'd be much reason for her to have any future contact with him. Gramps and Zach would be working closely together, but she had almost nothing to do with the business.

"I've earned his trust, but it took time," Gramps was saying now.

"I'm glad you've decided to retire," she said absently, half listening to the weather report.

"Zachary will change," her grandfather added.

He had her full attention now. "Gramps," she said patiently, holding in a laugh. "Why should he? He's achieved considerable financial success. Everything's looking good for him. What possible reason could there be for him to change?"

Anton stood and poured himself a liberal dose of brandy, swirling it slowly in the bottom of the snifter. "You're going to change him," he said after a thoughtful moment.

"Me?" Janine laughed outright. "*I'm* going to change Zachary Thomas?" she repeated in wide-eyed disbelief. That would be the day!

"Before you argue with me, and I can see that's what you're dying to do, I have a story I want to tell you. A rather sad one as it happens."

Janine picked up the remote control and snapped off the television. She'd often listened to her grandfather's parables. "So tell me."

"It's about a boy, born on the wrong side of the tracks to an alcoholic father and a weak mother. He never had much of a chance in life. His father was abusive enough for the state to remove the lad and his younger sister. He was barely eight and subjected to a long series of foster homes, but he refused to be separated from his sister. He'd promised her he'd always take care of her.

"Once, there wasn't any alternative and the two were sent to separate homes. Beside himself with worry for his sister, the young boy ran away. The authorities were in a panic, but three days later, he turned up two hundred miles away at the home where they'd placed Beth Ann."

"He probably felt responsible for her."

"Yes. Which made matters much worse when she drowned in a swimming accident. He was twelve at the time."

"Oh, no." A pain squeezed Janine's heart at the agony the boy had suffered.

"He blamed himself, of course," Anton said softly.

"The poor kid."

"This lad never seemed to belong to anyone after that," Gramps said, staring into his brandy. "He never quite fit in, but that wasn't entirely his fault." He paused to take another puff of his cigar. "His mother died a month after his sister. They were the only ones who'd ever truly loved him. He lost contact with his father, which was probably for the best. So his family was gone and no one seemed to want this troubled, hurting boy."

"Did he turn into a juvenile delinquent?" It made sense to Janine that he would; she'd dealt with a number of troubled teenagers through her volunteer work and was familiar with the tragic patterns that so often evolved in cases like this.

"No, I can't say he did." Gramps dismissed her question with a shake of his head, more interested in continuing his tale than getting sidetracked by her questions. "He drifted through adolescence without an anchor and without ever being allowed to enjoy those formative years."

"Gramps—"

He raised his hand to stop her. "When he was eighteen, he joined the military. He did well, which isn't surprising, considering his intelligence and the fact that he had little regard for his own well-being. There was no one to mourn if he died. Because of his courage, he advanced quickly, volunteering for the riskiest assignments. He traveled all over the world to some of the most dangerous political hot spots. His duties were often top secret. There's no telling how far he might have gone had he chosen to remain in the armed services, but for some reason, he resigned. No one understood why. I suspect he wanted to start his life over. This was when he opened a business-supply company. Within a year, he had my attention. His methods were aggressive and creative. I couldn't help admiring the way he handled himself and the company. Within five years, he'd become one of my most serious rivals. I saw a strength in him that age had stolen from me. We met. We talked. As a result of these talks we joined forces."

"Obviously you're telling me about Zachary's life."

Anton grinned and slowly sipped his brandy. "You noticed his remoteness quickly. I thought knowing all this would help you. Zach's never had the security that a caring home and family provide. He's never really experienced love, except what he shared with his sister, Beth Ann. His life has been a long progression of painful experiences. By sheer force of will, he's managed to overcome every obstacle placed in his path. I realize Zachary Thomas isn't going to win any Mr. Personality contests, but by heaven, he's earned my respect."

Janine had rarely heard such emotion in her grandfather's voice. "Zach told you all this?"

Anton's laughter echoed through the room. "You're joking, aren't you? Zach has never spoken of his past to me. I doubt that he has to anyone."

"You had him investigated?"

Gramps puffed on his cigar before answering. "It was necessary, although I'd guessed early on that his life hadn't been a bed of roses."

"It's all very sad, isn't it?"

"You're going to be very good for him, my dear."

Janine blinked. "Me?"

"Yes, you. You're going to teach him to laugh and enjoy life. But most important, you're going to teach him about love."

She hesitated, uncertain of her grandfather's meaning. "I don't think I understand. I realize Zach and I will probably see each other now and then since he's assuming your responsibilities with the company, but I don't see how I could have any great impact on his life."

Gramps smiled, a slow lazy smile that curved the corners of his mouth. "That's where you're wrong, my dear. You're going to play a very big role in Zach's life, and he in yours."

Janine was still confused. "Perhaps I missed something this afternoon. I thought you made Zach the chairman of the board."

"I did." A lazy swirl of smoke circled his head.

"I don't understand where I come into the picture."

"I don't suppose you do," he said softly. "You see, Janine, I've chosen Zachary to be your husband."

Two

For a stunned moment, Janine said nothing. "You're teasing, aren't you, Gramps?"

"No," he said, lighting a second cigar. He paused to stare at the glowing tip, his eyes filled with mischief—and with something else, less easily defined. "I'm serious."

"But..." Janine's thoughts were so jumbled she couldn't make sense of them herself, let alone convey her feelings to her grandfather.

"I've been giving the matter serious consideration for some time now. Zach's perfect for you and you're the ideal complement to him. You're going to have beautiful blond-haired children."

"But..." Janine discovered she was absolutely speechless. One minute she was listening to a touching story, and the next her grandfather was telling her about the husband he'd arranged for her—and even the color of her children's hair.

"Once you think about it," Gramps said confidently, "I'm sure you'll agree with me. Zach is a fine young man, and he'll make you an excellent husband."

"You... Zach talked...agreed?" The words stumbled over the end of her tongue.

"Do you mean have I suggested this arrangement to Zach?" Gramps asked. "Heavens, no. At least not yet." He chuckled as if he found the thought amusing. "Zach wouldn't appreciate my blatant interference in his personal affairs. With him, I'll need to be far more subtle. To be honest, I considered making this marriage part of my handing over the chairmanship, but after thinking it through, I changed my mind. Zach would never have agreed. There are other ways, I decided, better ways. But I don't want you to worry about it. That's between Zach and me."

"I…see." At this point, Janine wasn't sure *what* she saw, other than one determined old man caught between two worlds. In certain respects, the old ways continued to dominate his thinking, but his success in America allowed him to appreciate more modern outlooks.

Gramps inhaled deeply on his cigar, his blue eyes twinkling. "Now, I realize you probably find the idea of an arranged marriage slightly unorthodox, but you'll get used to it. I've made a fine choice for you, and I know you're smart enough to recognize that."

"Gramps, I don't think you fully understand what you're suggesting," she said, trying to gather her scattered wits, hoping she could explain the ridiculousness of this whole scheme without offending him.

"But I do, my child."

"In this country and in this age," she continued slowly, "men and women choose their own mates. We fall in love and then marry."

Gramps frowned. "Sadly, that doesn't work," he muttered.

"What do you mean, it doesn't work?" she cried, losing her patience. "It's been like this for years and years!"

"Look at the divorce rate. I read in the paper recently that almost fifty percent of all marriages in this country fail. In the old country, there was no divorce. Parents decided whom a son or daughter would marry, and their decision was accepted without question. First comes marriage, and then comes love."

"Gramps," Janine said softly, wanting to reason this out with him. Her grandfather was a logical man; surely, if she explained it properly, he'd understand. "Things are done differently now. First comes love, then comes marriage."

"What do you young people know about love?"

"A good deal, as it happens," she returned, lying smoothly. Her first venture into love had ended with a broken heart and a shattered ego, but she'd told Gramps little if anything about Brian.

"Pfft!" he spat. "What could you possibly know of love?"

"I realize," she said, thinking fast, "that your father arranged your marriage to Grandma, but that was years ago, and in America such customs don't exist. You and I live *here* now, in the land of the free. The land of opportunity."

Gramps gazed down into his brandy for a long moment, lost in thought. Janine doubted he'd even heard her.

"I'll never forget the first time I saw my Anna," he said in a faraway voice. "She was sixteen and her hair was long and blond and fell in braids to her waist. My father spoke to her father and while they were talking, Anna and I sat at opposite ends of the room, too shy to look at each other. I wondered if she thought I was handsome. To me, she was the most beautiful girl in the world. Even now, after all these years, I can remember how my heart beat with excitement when I saw her. I knew—"

"But, Gramps, that was nearly sixty years ago! Marriages aren't decided by families anymore. A man and a woman discover each other without a father introducing them. Maybe the old ways were better back then, but it's simply not like that now." Gramps continued to stare into his glass, lost in a world long since enveloped by the passage of time.

"The next day, Anna's parents visited our farm and again our two fathers spoke. I tried to pretend I wasn't concerned, determined to accept whatever our families decided. But when I saw our fathers shake hands and slap each other on the back, I knew Anna would soon be mine."

"You loved her before you were married, didn't you?" Janine asked softly, hoping to prove her point.

"No," he returned flatly, without hesitation. "How could I love her when I'd only seen her twice before the wedding? We hadn't said more than a handful of words to each other. Love wasn't necessary for us to find happiness. Love came later, after we arrived in America."

"Wasn't it unusual for a marriage to be arranged even then? It wasn't *that* long ago." There had to be some point for her to contend, Janine mused.

"Perhaps it was unusual in other parts of the world, but not in Vibiskgrad. We were a small farming community. Our world had been ravaged by war and hate. We clung to each other, holding on to our own traditions and rituals. Soon our lives became impossible and we were forced to flee our homes."

"As I said before, I can understand how an arranged marriage—back then—might be the best for everyone involved. But I can't see it working in this day and age. I'm sorry to disappoint you, Gramps, but I'm not willing to accept Zachary Thomas as my husband, and I'm sure he'd be equally unwilling to marry me."

Briefly Gramps's face tensed with a rare display of disappointment and indignation, then quickly relaxed. Janine had seldom questioned his authority and had never openly defied him.

"I suppose this is a shock to you, isn't it?" he said.

If it astonished *her,* she couldn't wait to hear what Zachary Thomas thought! They'd only met once, but he hadn't disguised his opinion of her. He wouldn't take kindly to Gramps's plan of an arranged marriage—especially to a woman he viewed as spoiled and overindulged.

"All I'm asking is that you consider this, Janine," Gramps said. "Promise me you'll at least do that. Don't reject marriage to Zach simply because you think it's old-fashioned."

"Oh, Gramps…" Janine hated to refuse him anything. "It isn't just me. What about Zach? What about *his* plans? What if he—"

Gramps dismissed her questions with an abrupt shrug. "How often do I ask something of you?" he persisted.

Now he was going to use guilt. "Not often," she agreed, frowning at him for using unfair tactics.

"Then consider Zach for your husband!" His eyes brightened. "The two of you will have such beautiful children. A grandfather knows these things."

"I promise I'll think about it." But it wouldn't do any good! However, discretion was a virtue Janine was nurturing, and there'd never been a better time to employ it than now.

Gramps didn't mention Zach Thomas or even hint at the subject of her marrying his business partner again until the following evening. They'd just sat down to dinner, prepared to sample Mrs. McCormick's delicious fare, when Gramps looked anxiously at Janine. "So?" he asked breathlessly.

From the moment he'd walked into the house that afternoon, Gramps's mood had been light and humorous. Grinning, he handed her the platter of thinly sliced marinated and grilled flank steak. It happened to be one of Janine's favorite meals. "So?" he repeated, smiling at her. "What did you decide?"

Janine helped herself to a crisp dinner roll, buttering it slowly as her thoughts chased each other in frantic circles. "Nothing."

His smile collapsed into a frown. "You promised me you'd consider marrying Zach. I gave you more time than Anna's father gave her."

"You have to know now?"

"Now!"

"But, Gramps, a simple yes or no isn't an appropriate response to something as complex as this. You're asking me to decide on a lifelong commitment in less than twenty-four hours." She was stalling for time, and Gramps had probably guessed as much. Frankly, she didn't know what to tell him. She couldn't, wouldn't, marry Zach—even if he was willing to marry her—but she hated disappointing her grandfather.

"What's so difficult? Either you marry him or not!"

"I don't understand why you've decided to match me up with Zach Thomas," she cried. "What's wrong with Peter?" She'd been dating the other man casually for the last few months. Her heart was too bruised after what had happened with Brian for her to date anyone seriously.

"You're in love with that whitewashed weakling?"

Janine signed loudly, regretting the fact that she'd introduced Peter into their conversation. "He's very nice."

"So is chocolate mousse!" Gramps muttered. "Peter Donahue would make you a terrible husband. I'm shocked you'd even think about marrying him."

"I hadn't actually thought about him in those terms,"

she said. Peter was witty and fun, but Gramps was right; they weren't suited as husband and wife.

"I thank the good Lord you've been given some sense."

Janine took a deep breath and finally asked a question that had been nagging at her all afternoon. "Did—did you arrange my father's marriage?"

Gramps lowered his eyes, but not before he could disguise the pain there. "No. He fell in love with Patrice while he was in college. I knew the match wasn't a good one, but Anna reminded me that this was America and young people fell in love by themselves. She convinced me they didn't need a father's guiding hand the way we did in the old country."

"Do you think he would've listened if you'd wanted to arrange a marriage?"

Her grandfather hesitated, and his hand tightened on his water glass. "I don't know, but I'd like to believe he would have."

"Instead he married my mother."

Neither spoke for a long moment. Janine remembered little of her parents, only bits and pieces of memory, mostly unconnected. What she did recall were terrible fights and accusations, a house filled with strife. She could remember hiding under her bed when the shouting started, pressing her hands to her ears. It was her father who used to find her, who comforted her. Always her father. Her memory included almost nothing of her mother. Even pictures didn't jar her recollection, although Janine had spent hour upon hour looking at photographs, hoping to remember *something.* But the woman who'd given birth to her had remained a stranger to her in life and in death.

"You're the only consolation I have from Steven's marriage," Anton said hoarsely. "At least I had you after Steven and Patrice died."

"Oh, Gramps. I love you so much and I hate to disappoint you, but I can't marry Zach and I can't see him agreeing to marry me."

Her grandfather was silent after that, apparently mulling over her words as he finished his dinner. "I suppose I seem like a feeble old man, still trying to live the old ways."

"Gramps, no, I don't think that at all."

He planted his elbows squarely on the table and linked his fingers, gazing at her. His brow was puckered in a contemplative frown. "Perhaps it would help if you told me what you want in a husband."

She hesitated, then glanced away, avoiding eye contact. Once she'd been so certain of what she wanted. "To be perfectly honest, I'm not sure. Romance, I suppose."

"Romance." Gramps rolled the word off his tongue as though he was tasting an expensive wine.

"Yes," she said with a nod of her head, gaining confidence.

"And what exactly is romance?"

"Well..." Now that she'd been called upon to define it, Janine couldn't quite put that magical feeling into words. "It's...it's an awareness that comes from the heart."

"The heart," her grandfather repeated, smacking his palm against his chest.

"Romance is the knowledge that a man would rather die than live his life without me," she said, warming to the subject.

"You want him to die?"

"No, just to be willing."

Gramps frowned. "I don't think I understand."

"Romance is forbidden trysts on lonely Scottish moors," she added, thinking of an historical romance she'd read as a teenager.

"There aren't any moors in the Seattle area."

"Don't distract me," she said, smiling, her thoughts gaining momentum. "Romance is desperate passion."

He snorted. "That sounds more like hormones to me."

"Gramps, please!"

"How can I understand when all you say is ridiculous things? You want romance. First you claim it's a feeling in the heart, then you say it's some kind of passion."

"It's more than that. It's walking hand in hand along the beach at twilight and gazing into each other's eyes. It's speaking of love without ever having to say the words." She paused, feeling a little foolish at getting so carried away. "I don't know if I can adequately describe it."

"That's because you haven't experienced it."

"Maybe not," she agreed reluctantly. "But I will someday."

"With Zach," he said with complete assurance and a wide grin.

Janine didn't bother to argue. Gramps was being obstinate and arguing with him was pointless. The only recourse she had was time itself. Soon enough he'd realize that neither she nor Zach was going to fall in with his scheme. Then, and only then, would he drop the subject.

A week passed and Gramps hadn't said another word about arranging a marriage between her and Zachary Thomas. It was a cold windy March evening and the rain was coming down in torrents. Janine loved nights like this and was curled up in her favorite chair with a mystery novel when the doorbell chimed. Gramps had gone out for the evening and she wasn't expecting anyone.

She turned on the porch light and looked out the peephole to discover Zach standing there, a briefcase in his hand. His shoulders were hunched against the pelting rain.

"Zach," she said in surprise, throwing open the door.

"Hello, Janine," he said politely, stepping inside. "Is your grandfather here?"

"No." She held the book against her chest, her heart pounding hard. "He went out."

Zach frowned, clearly confused. "He asked me to stop by. There were some business matters he wanted to discuss. Did he say when he'd be home?"

"No, but I'm sure if he asked you over, it'll be soon. Would you care to wait for him?"

"Please."

She took his raincoat, then led him into the library where she'd been reading. A fire was burning, and its warmth hugged the room. The three-story house, situated in Seattle's Mt. Baker district, was a typical turn-of-the-century home with high ceilings and spacious rooms. The third floor had once housed several servants. Charles was their only live-in help now, and his quarters had always been an apartment over the carriage house. He worked exclusively for Gramps, driving the limousine. Mrs. McCormick arrived early in the mornings and was responsible for housekeeping and meal preparation.

"Can I get you something to drink?" she asked, once he was comfortably seated.

"Coffee, if you have it."

"I made a fresh pot about twenty minutes ago."

Janine brought him a cup from the kitchen, then sat across from Zach, wondering what, if anything, she should say about Gramps and his idea of an arranged marriage.

She doubted that Gramps had broached the subject yet. Otherwise he wouldn't be sitting there so calmly sipping coffee. He'd be outraged and infuriated, and studying him now, she concluded that he wasn't even slightly ruffled. It was on the tip of her tongue to warn him about what was coming, but she decided against it. Better that he learn the same way she had.

Lacing her fingers together, she smiled, feeling awkward and a little gauche. "It's nice to see you again."

"You, too. I'll admit I'm a bit disappointed, though."

"You are?"

"On the drive over, I was trying to guess what you'd be wearing this time. A dress made from bread sacks? A blouse constructed out of men's socks?"

She muttered under her breath, annoyed by his teasing. He had the uncanny ability to make her feel fifteen all over again. So much for any possibility that they'd ever be compatible. And Gramps seemed to think he knew them both so well.

"I'll admit that an Irish cable-knit sweater and jeans are a pleasant surprise," he said.

A flicker of admiration sparked in his dark eyes, something that had been missing the first time they met.

In that instant, Janine knew.

She went stock-still, almost dizzy with the realization. Not only had Gramps approached Zach, but they'd apparently reached some sort of agreement. Otherwise Zach would never have been this friendly, this openly appreciative. Nor would he arrive unannounced when Gramps had specifically stated that he'd be gone for the evening.

They were obviously plotting against her. Well, she had no intention of putting up with it. None. If Zach and Gramps thought they could lure her into marriage, they had a real shock coming.

Squaring her shoulders, she slid to the edge of her chair.

"So you gave in to the pressure," she said, shooting him a scalding look. Unable to stay seated, she jumped to her feet and started pacing, rubbing her palms together as she cornered her thoughts. "Gramps got to you, didn't he?"

"I beg your pardon?" Zach stared up at her, his eyes curious.

"And you agreed?" She threw up her hands and groaned, "I don't believe it, I simply don't believe it. I thought better of you than this."

"What don't you believe?"

"Of all the men I've met over the years, I would've sworn you were the type who'd refuse to be bought. I'm disappointed in you, Zach."

He remained calm and unperturbed, which infuriated her more than anything he could have said or done.

"I haven't got the slightest idea what you're talking about," was all he said.

"Oh, sure, play the innocent," she snapped. She was so incensed that she continued to pace. Standing still was impossible.

In response, Zach merely glanced at his watch and drank his coffee. "Does your grandfather know you suffer from these bouts of hysteria?"

"Funny, Zach, very funny."

He exhaled an exaggerated sigh. "All right, I'll take the bait. What makes you think I've been bought? And what exactly am I getting in exchange?"

"Technically you're not getting anything, and I want that understood this very minute, because *I* refuse to be sold." Arms akimbo, she turned to glare down at him with the full force of her disdain. "What did he offer you? The entire company? Lots of money?"

Zach shrugged. "He's offered me nothing."

"Nothing," she repeated slowly, feeling unreasonably insulted. "He was just going to *give* me away." That was enough to deflate the billowing sails of her pride. Stunned, she sat down again. "I thought the bride's family was supposed to supply some kind of dowry. Gramps didn't even offer you money?"

"Dowry?" Zach repeated the word as if he'd never heard it before.

"Gramps's family received a cow and ten chickens from my grandmother's family," she said, as if that explained everything. "But apparently I'm not even worth a single hen."

Zach set his coffee aside and sat straight in his chair. "I think we'd better begin this conversation again. I'm afraid I lost you back there when you said something about cracking under pressure. Perhaps you should enlighten me about what I'm supposed to have done."

Janine just glared at him.

"Humor me."

"All right, if you insist. It's obvious that Gramps talked to you about the marriage."

"Marriage," he echoed in a shocked voice. His face went blank. "To whom?"

"Me, of course."

Zach flung himself out of the chair, bolting to his feet. "To you?"

"Don't look so horrified! My ego's taken about all it can for one evening. I'm not exactly the Wicked Witch of the West, you know. Some men would be more than happy to marry me." Not Brian, and certainly not Peter, but she felt it was important that Zach think she was sought after.

"Marriage between us is…would be impossible. It's completely out of the question. I don't ever plan to marry—I have no use for a wife or family."

"Tell that to Gramps."

"I have every intention of doing so." His face tightened and Janine guessed her grandfather was due for an earful when he got home. "What makes that crazy old man think he can order people's lives like this?" he asked angrily.

"His own marriage was arranged for him. Trust me, Zach, I argued until I was exhausted, but Gramps hasn't given up his old-country beliefs and he thinks the two of us—now this is really ridiculous—are perfect for each other."

"If you weren't serious, I'd find this highly amusing."

Janine noticed that he seemed rather pale. "I appear to have jumped to the wrong conclusion earlier. I apologize for that but, well, I thought… I assumed Gramps had spoken to you already and you'd agreed."

"Was that when you started mumbling about a cow and a few chickens?"

She nodded and her long bangs fell over her eyes. Absently she pushed them aside. "For a moment there, I thought Gramps was offering me to you gratis. I know it's silly, but I felt insulted by that."

For the first time since they'd entered into this conversation, Zach's face softened and he granted her a faint smile. "Your grandfather loves you, no question."

"I know." Feeling self-conscious, she threaded her fingers through her hair. "I've used every argument I could come up with. I explained the importance of romance and told him how vital it is for men and women to fall in love with the person of their choice. However, he refused to accept any of it."

"He wouldn't listen to you?"

"He listened," she replied, feeling defeated, "but he disputed everything I said. Gramps says the modern version of love and marriage is a complete failure. With the divorce rate what it is, I'm afraid I don't have much of an argument."

"That's true enough," Zach said, looking frustrated.

"I told him men and women fall in love and then decide to get married, but Gramps insists it's better if marriage comes first."

Zach rubbed a hand over his face. "Now that I think about it, your grandfather's been introducing you into every conversation, telling me how wonderful you are."

Janine gasped softly. "He's done the same to me about you. He started weeks before we even met."

Pressing his lips together, Zach nodded. "A lot of things are beginning to make sense."

"What should we do?" Janine wondered aloud. "It's perfectly obvious that we'll have to agree on a plan of action. I hate to disappoint Gramps, but I'm not willing to be married off like...like..." Words failed her.

"Especially to me."

Although his low words were devoid of emotion, Janine recognized the pain behind his statement. Knowing what she did about his past, the fact that he'd experienced only brief patches of love in his life and little or no approval tugged at her heart.

"I didn't mean it to sound like that," she insisted. "My grandfather wouldn't have chosen you if he didn't think you were pretty special. He prides himself on his ability to judge character, and he's always been impressed with you."

"Let's not kid ourselves, Janine," Zach returned, his voice hardening. "You're an uptown girl. We're totally unsuited."

"I agree with you there, but not for the reasons you assume. From the minute I stepped into your office, you made it clear that you thought of me as some kind of snob. I'm not, but I refuse to waste my breath arguing with you."

"Fine."

"Instead of hurling insults at each other," she suggested, crossing her arms in a show of indignation, "why don't we come up with a plan to deal with Gramps's preposterous idea?"

"That isn't necessary," he countered. "I want no part of it."

"And you think I do?"

Zach said nothing.

Janine expelled her breath loudly. "It seems to me the solution is for one of us to marry someone else. That would quickly put an end to this whole thing."

"I already told you I have no intention of marrying," he said emphatically. "You're the one who insinuated you had plenty of men hanging around just waiting for you to say 'I do.'"

"None that I'd consider marrying, for heaven's sake," she grumbled. "Besides, I'm not currently in love with anyone."

Zach laughed, if the sound that came from his throat could be called a laugh. "Then find a man who's current. If you fall in and out of love that easily, surely there's got to be at least one prospect on the horizon."

"There isn't. *You're* going to have to come up with someone! Why don't you go out there and sweep some sweet young thing off her feet," she muttered sarcastically.

"I'm not willing to sacrifice my life so you can get off scot-free." His words were low and furious.

"But it's perfectly all right for *me* to sabotage mine? That makes a lot of sense."

"Okay," he said after a tense moment. He paused, shaking his head. "That idea's obviously not going to work. I guess we'll have to come up with something better."

"Okay, then." Janine gestured toward him. "It's your turn."

He glared at her, seeming to dislike her even more. In all honesty, Janine wasn't too pleased with the way she was behaving, either. She'd been sarcastic and needlessly rude, but then, Zach had driven her to it. He could be the most unpleasant man.

Still, Janine was about to say something conciliatory when the sound of the front door opening distracted her. Her gaze flew to Zach and he nodded, reassuring her that he'd handle the situation.

They'd returned to their chairs and were seated by the time Gramps appeared in the library doorway.

"Zach, I'm sorry for the delay. I'm glad to see Janine entertained you." Her grandfather smiled brightly as if to tell her he approved and hoped she'd taken advantage of this hour alone with Zach.

"We did manage to have a stimulating conversation," Zach said, his eyes briefly meeting Janine's.

"Good. Good."

Zach stood and reached for his briefcase. "There were some figures you wanted to go over with me?"

"Yes." Looking satisfied with himself, Gramps led the way out of the room. Zach followed him, with a glance back at Janine that said he'd get in touch with her later.

Later turned out to be almost a week. She was puttering around outside, trimming back the rosebushes and deciding where to plant the geraniums this year, when Mrs. McCormick came to tell her she was wanted on the phone.

"Hello," Janine said cheerfully.

"We need to talk," Zach said without preamble.

"Why?" she demanded. If he was going to keep her

hanging for six anxious days, then she wasn't going to give the impression that she was thrilled to hear from him.

"Your grandfather laid his cards on the table this afternoon. I thought you might be interested in hearing what he's offering me to take you off his hands."

Three

"All right," Janine said, bracing herself. "What's he offering you? Huge bonuses?"

"No," Zach said quickly.

"Cash? I want to know exactly how much."

"He didn't offer me money."

Janine frowned. "What then?"

"I think we should meet and talk about it."

If her grandfather had openly approached Zach with the arranged-marriage idea, Janine knew darn well that Gramps would've made it worth Zach's while. Despite his claims to the contrary, it wouldn't have surprised Janine to discover that the newly appointed chairman of the board of Hartman-Thomas Business Supply had taken the bait.

"You want us to meet?" she repeated in a faltering voice.

"There's a restaurant on University Way—Italian 642. Have you heard of it?"

"No, but I'll find it."

"Meet me there at seven." Zach paused, then added, "And listen, it might not be a good idea to tell your grandfather that we're getting together. He might misunderstand."

"I won't say anything," she promised.

Zach hesitated once more. "We have a lot to discuss."

Janine's heartbeat accelerated, and she felt the perspiration break out on her forehead. "Zach," she began, "you haven't changed your mind, have you? I mean, you're not actually considering this ridiculous idea of his? You can't… We agreed, remember?" She swiped at her forehead with the back of her free hand as she waited for him to answer.

"There's nothing to worry about," he finally said.

Replacing the receiver, Janine had the sudden horrible sensation of being completely at her grandfather's mercy. He was an unshakably stubborn man who almost always got what he wanted. Faced with a mountain, Anton Hartman either climbed it, tunneled through it or forged a path around it; failing such active alternatives, he settled down in the foothills and waited for the mountain to dissolve. He claimed he won a majority of his battles by simply displaying patience. Janine called it not knowing when to pack up and go home.

She knew her grandfather's methods, but then so did Zach. She hoped Anton's candidate for her husband would at least be able to withstand a few bribes, however tempting. Apparently he did, because he'd told her she had nothing to worry about. On the other hand, he sounded downright eager to discuss the subject with her.

"He *says* he never wants to get married," she muttered aloud in an effort to reassure herself. Indeed, Zachary Thomas was the last man who'd be humming "The Wedding March"—especially when someone else was directing the band.

Janine was waiting in the library, coat draped over her arm, when her grandfather got home at six-thirty. He kissed her dutifully on the cheek and reached for the evening paper, scanning the headlines as he settled into his big leather chair.

"Zach called," she said without thinking. She hadn't intended to mention that to Gramps.

Anton nodded. "I thought he might. You meeting him for dinner?"

"Dinner? Zach and me?" she squeaked. "No, of course not! Why would you even think I'd agree to a dinner date with…him?" Darn, she'd nearly forgotten her promise to keep their meeting a secret. She detested lying to her grandfather, but there was no help for it.

"But you are dining out?"

"Yes." She couldn't very well deny that, dressed as she was and carrying her coat.

"Then you're seeing Peter Donahue again?"

"No. Not exactly," Janine said uncomfortably, "I'm meeting a…friend."

"I see." The corners of Gramps's mouth quirked into a knowing smile.

Janine could feel the telltale heat saturating her face. She was a terrible liar and always had been. Gramps knew as surely as if she'd spelled it out that she was meeting Zach. And when she told Zach she'd let it slip, he'd be furious with her, and rightly so.

"What did Zach want?"

"What makes you think he wanted anything?" Janine asked fervently. Her heart was thundering as she edged toward the door. The sooner she escaped, the better.

"You just said Zach phoned."

"Oh. Yes, he did, earlier, but it wasn't important. Something about…something." Brilliant! She rushed out of the house before Gramps could question her further. What a fool she was. She'd blurted out the very thing she'd wanted to keep secret.

By the time Janine located the Italian restaurant in the University district and found a parking place, she was ten minutes late.

Zach was sitting in a booth in the farthest corner of the room. He frowned when he saw her and glanced at his watch, just so she'd know she'd kept him waiting.

Ignoring his disgruntled look, Janine slid onto the polished wooden bench, removed her coat and casually announced, "Gramps knows."

Zach's frown deepened. "What are you talking about?"

"He knows I'm having dinner with you," she explained. "The minute he walked in the door, I told him you'd called—I just wasn't thinking—and when he asked why, I told him it had to do with *something*. I'm sure you'll be able to make up an excuse when he asks you later."

"I thought we agreed not to say anything about our meeting."

"I know," she said, feeling guiltier than ever. "But Gramps asked if I was going out with Peter and he just looked so smug when I told him I wasn't." At Zach's sudden movement, she burst out, "Well, what was I supposed to do?"

He grunted, which wasn't much of an answer.

"If I wasn't going out with Peter, I'd have to come up with another man on the spot, and although I'm clever, I don't think *that* fast." She was breathless with frustration when she'd finished.

"Who's Peter?"

"This guy I've been seeing off and on for the past few months."

"And you're in love with him?"

"No, I'm not." Doubtless Zach would suggest she simply marry Peter and put an end to all of this annoyance.

Zach reached abruptly for the menu. "Let's order, and while we're eating we can go over what we need to discuss."

"All right," Janine said, grateful to leave the topic of her blunder. Besides, seven was later than she normally dined, and she was famished.

The waitress appeared then, and even as she filled Janine's water glass, her appreciative gaze never strayed from Zach. Once more Janine was struck by the knowledge that although he wasn't handsome in the traditional sense, he seemed to generate a good deal of female interest.

"I'll have the clam spaghetti," Janine said loudly, eyeing the attractive waitress, who seemed to be forgetting why she was there. The woman was obviously far more interested in studying Zach than in taking their order.

"I'll have the same," Zach said, smiling briefly at the waitress as he handed her his menu. "Now, what were you saying?" he asked, returning his attention to Janine.

"As I recall, you were the one who insisted we meet. Just tell me what my grandfather said and be done with it." No doubt the offer had been generous; otherwise Zach wouldn't have suggested this dinner.

Zach's hand closed around the water glass. "Anton called me into his office to ask me a series of leading questions."

"Such as?"

Zach shrugged. "What I thought of you and—"

"How'd you answer him?"

Zach took a deep breath. "I said I found you attractive, energetic, witty, a bit eccentric—"

"A bandanna dress and a string of Christmas-tree lights doesn't make me eccentric," Janine said, her voice rising despite herself.

"If the Christmas-tree lights are draped around your neck it does."

They were attracting attention, and after a few curious stares, Zach leaned closer and said, "If you're going to argue with everything I say, we'll be here all night."

"I'm sure our waitress would enjoy that," Janine snapped, then immediately regretted it. She sounded downright *jealous*—which, of course, was ridiculous.

"What are you talking about?"

"Never mind."

"Shall we return to the conversation between your grandfather and me?"

"Please," she said, properly chastised.

"Anton spent quite a long time telling me about your volunteer work at the Friendship Club and your various other community activities."

"And I'll bet his report was so glowing, I rank right up there with Joan of Arc and Florence Nightingale."

Zach grinned. "Something like that, but then he added that although you were constantly busy, he felt your life lacked contentment and purpose."

Janine could see it coming, as clearly as if she were standing on a track and a freight train was heading toward her. "Let me guess. He probably said I needed something meaningful in my life—like a husband and children."

"Exactly." Zach nodded, his grin barely restrained. "In his opinion, marriage is the only thing that will fulfill you as a woman."

Janine groaned and sagged against the back of her seat. It was worse than she thought. And to her chagrin, Zach actually seemed amused.

"You wouldn't look so smug if he said marriage was the only thing that would fulfill you as a *man,*" she muttered.

"Honestly, Zach, do I look like I'm wasting away from lack of purpose?" She gestured dramatically with her hands. "I'm happy, I'm busy…in fact I'm completely delighted with my life." It wasn't until she'd finished that she realized she was clenching her teeth.

"Don't take it so personally."

Janine rolled her eyes, wondering what his reaction would be if he was on the receiving end of this discussion.

"In case you didn't know it, Anton's a terrible chauvinist," he remarked, still smiling. "An old-fashioned word, perhaps, for an old-fashioned man."

"That's true, but he *is* my grandfather," she said. "And he's so charming, it's easy to forgive him."

Zach picked up his wineglass and gazed at it thoughtfully. "What I can't figure out is why he's so keen on marrying you off now. Why not last year? Or next year?"

"Heavens, I don't know. I suppose he thinks it's time. My biological clock's ticking away and the noise is probably keeping him awake at night. By age twenty-four, most of the women from the old country had four or five children."

"He certainly seems intent on the idea of seeing you married soon."

"Tell me about it!" Janine cried. "I'd bet cold cash that when he brought up the subject he said you were the only suitable man he'd found for me."

"Anton also said you have a generous heart, and that he feared some fast-talker would show up one day and you'd fall for him."

"Really?" she asked weakly. Her heart stopped, then jolted to life again. Anton's scenario sounded exactly like her disastrous romance with Brian. She sighed deeply. "So then he told you he wants me to marry someone he respects, someone he loves like a son. A man of discretion and wisdom and honor. A man he trusts enough to merge companies with."

Zach arched his brows. "You know your grandfather well."

"I can just imagine what came next," Janine added scathingly and her stomach tensed at her grandfather's insidious cleverness. Zach wasn't someone who could be bought, at least not with offers of money or prestige. Instead, Gramps had used a far more subtle form of inducement. He'd addressed Zach's pride, complimented his achievements, flattered him. To hear Gramps tell it, Zachary Thomas was the only man alive capable of taking on the task of becoming Janine's husband.

"What did you tell him?" she asked, her voice low.

"I told him no way."

Janine blinked back surprise mingled with a fair amount of indignation. "Just like that? Couldn't you at least have mulled it over?" Zach was staring at her as though he thought someone should rush over and take her temperature. "Forget I said that," she mumbled, fussing with her napkin in order to avoid meeting his eyes.

"I didn't want to encourage him."

"That was wise." Janine picked up her water glass and downed half the contents.

"To your grandfather's credit, he seemed to accept my answer."

"Don't count on it," Janine warned.

"Don't worry, I know him, too. He isn't going to give up easily. That's the reason I suggested you and I meet to talk about this. If we keep in touch, we can anticipate Anton's strategy."

"Good idea."

Their salads arrived and Janine frowned when the waitress tossed Zach another suggestive glance. "So," she began in a conversational tone once the woman had left, "Gramps was smart enough not to offer you a large incentive if you went along with his scheme."

"I didn't say that."

She stabbed viciously at her salad. "I hadn't expected him to stoop that low. Exactly what tactics did he use?"

"He said something about family members having use of the limousine."

Janine's fork made a clanging sound as it hit the side of her salad bowl. "He offered you the limousine if you married me? That's all?"

"Not even that," Zach explained, not bothering to disguise his amusement, "only the *use* of it."

"Why…why, that's insulting." She crammed some salad into her mouth and chewed the crisp lettuce as though it were leather.

"I considered it a step above the cow and ten chickens you suggested the first time we discussed this."

"Where he came from, a cow and ten chickens were worth a lot more than you seem to realize," Janine exclaimed, and immediately regretted raising her voice, because half the patrons in the restaurant turned to stare. She smiled blandly at those around her, then slouched forward over her salad.

She reached for a bread stick, broke it in half and glared at it. "The use of the limo," she repeated, indignant.

"Don't look so upset." He grinned. "I might have accepted."

Zach was deriving far too much pleasure from this to suit her. "Your attitude isn't helping any," she said, frowning righteously.

"I apologize."

But he didn't act the least bit apologetic. When she'd first met Zach, Janine had assumed he was a man who rarely smiled, yet in the short time they'd spent together today, he'd practically been laughing outright.

The waitress brought their entrées, but when Janine took her first bite, she realized that even the pretense of eating was more than she could manage. She felt too wretched. Tears sprang to her eyes, which embarrassed her even more, although she struggled to hide them.

"What's wrong?" Zach surprised her by asking.

Eyes averted, Janine shook her head, while she attempted to swallow. "Gramps believes I'm a poor judge of character," she finally said. And she was. Brian had proved it to her, but Gramps didn't know about Brian. "I feel like a failure."

"He didn't mean any of it," Zach said gently.

"But couldn't he have come up with something a little more flattering?"

"He needed an excuse to marry you off, otherwise his suggestion would have sounded crazy." Zach hesitated. "You know, the more we discuss this, the more ludicrous the whole thing seems." He chuckled softly and leaned forward to set his elbows on the table. "Who would've believed he'd come up with the idea of the two of us marrying?"

"Thank you very much," Janine muttered. He sat there shredding her ego and apparently found the process just short of hilarious.

"Don't let it get to you. You're not interested in me as a husband, anyway."

"You're right about that—you're the last person I'd ever consider marrying," she lashed out, then regretted her reaction when she saw his face tighten.

"That's what I thought." He attacked his spaghetti as though the clams were scampering around his plate.

The tension between them mounted. When the waitress arrived to remove their plates, Janine had barely touched her meal. Zach hadn't eaten much, either.

After paying for their dinner, Zach walked her to her car, offering no further comment. As far as Janine was concerned, their meeting hadn't been at all productive. She felt certain that Zach was everything Gramps claimed—incisive, intelligent, intuitive. But that was at the office. As a potential husband and wife, they were completely ill-suited.

"Do you still want me to keep in touch?" she asked when she'd unlocked her car door. They stood awkwardly together in the street, and Janine realized they hardly knew what to say to each other.

"I suppose we should, since neither of us is interested in falling in with this plan of his," Zach said. "We need to set our differences aside and work together, otherwise we might unknowingly play into his hands."

"I won't be swayed and you won't, either." Janine found the thought oddly disappointing.

"If and when I do marry," Zach informed her, "which I sincerely doubt, I'll choose my own bride."

It went without saying that Janine was nothing like the woman he'd want to spend his life with.

"If and when *I* marry, I'll choose my own husband," she said, sounding equally firm. And it certainly wouldn't be a man her grandfather had chosen.

"I don't know if I like boys or not," thirteen-year-old Pam Hudson admitted over a cheeseburger and French fries. "They can be so dumb."

It'd been a week since Janine's dinner with Zach, and

she was surprised that the teenager's assessment of the opposite sex should so closely match her own.

"I'm not even sure I like Charlie anymore," Pam said as she stirred her catsup with a French fry. Idly she smeared it around the edges of her plate in a haphazard pattern. "I used to be so crazy about him, remember?"

Janine smiled indulgently. "Every other word was Charlie this and Charlie that."

"He can be okay, though. Remember when he brought me that long-stemmed rose and left it on my porch?"

"I remember." Janine's mind flashed to the afternoon she'd met Zach. As they left the restaurant, he'd smiled at her. It wasn't much as smiles went, but for some reason, she couldn't seem to forget how he'd held her gaze, his dark eyes gentle, as he murmured polite nonsense. Funny how little things about this man tended to pop up in her mind at the strangest moments.

"But last week," Pam continued, "Charlie was playing basketball with the guys, and when I walked by, he pretended he didn't even know me."

"That hurt, didn't it?"

"Yeah, it did," Pam confessed. "And after I bought a T-shirt for him, too."

"Does he wear it?"

A gratified smile lit the girl's eyes. "All the time."

"By the way, I like how you're doing your hair."

Pam beamed. "I want it to look more like yours."

Actually, the style suited Pam far better than it did her, Janine thought. The sides were cut close to the head, but the long bangs flopped with a life of their own—at least on Janine they did. Lately she'd taken to pinning them back.

"How are things at home?" Janine asked, watching the girl carefully. Pam's father, Jerry Hudson, was divorced and had custody of his daughter. Pam's mother worked on the East Coast. With no family in the area, Jerry felt that his daughter needed a woman's influence. He'd contacted the Friendship Club about the same time Janine had applied to be a volunteer. Since Jerry worked odd hours as a short-order cook, she'd met him only once. He seemed a decent sort, working hard to make a good life for himself and his daughter.

Pam was a marvelous kid, Janine mused, and she possessed exceptional creative talent. Even before her father could afford to buy her a sewing machine, Pam had been designing and making clothes for her Barbie dolls. Janine's bandanna dress was one of the first projects she'd completed on her new machine. Pam had made several others since; they were popular with her friends, and she was ecstatic about the success of her ideas.

"I think I might forgive Charlie,"she went on to say, her look contemplative. "I mean, he was with the guys and everything."

"It's not cool to let his friends know he's got a girlfriend, huh?"

"Yeah, I guess…."

Janine wasn't feeling nearly as forgiving toward Zach. He'd talked about their keeping in touch, but hadn't called her since. She didn't believe for an instant that Gramps had given up on his marriage campaign, but he'd apparently decided to let the matter rest. The pressure was off, yet Janine kept expecting some word from Zach. The least he could do was call, she grumbled to herself, although she made no attempt to analyze the reasons for her disappointment.

"Maybe Charlie isn't so bad, after all," Pam murmured, then added wisely, "This is an awkward age for boys, especially in their relationships with girls."

"Say," Janine teased, "who's supposed to be the adult here, anyway? That's my line."

"Oh, sorry,"

Smiling, Janine stole a French fry from Pam's plate and popped it into her mouth.

"So when are you leaving for Scotland?" Pam wanted to know.

"Next week."

"How long are you going to be gone?"

"Ten days." The trip was an unexpected gift from her grandfather. One night shortly after she'd met Zach for dinner, Gramps had handed her a packet with airline tickets and hotel reservations. When she'd asked why, his reply had been vague, even cryptic—something about her needing to get away. Since she'd always dreamed of visiting Scotland, she'd leapt at the chance.

It wasn't until she'd driven Pam home that Janine thought she should let Zach know she was going to be out of the country. It probably wasn't important, but he'd made such a point of saying they should keep in touch....

Janine planned her visit to the office carefully, making sure Gramps would be occupied elsewhere. Since she'd been shopping for her trip, she was carrying several department and clothing store bags. She was doing this for a reason. She wanted her visit to appear unplanned, as if in the course of a busy day, she'd suddenly remembered their agreement. She felt that dropping in would seem more spontaneous than simply calling.

"Hello," she said to Zach's efficient secretary, smiling cheerfully. "Is Mr. Thomas available? I'll only need a moment of his time."

The older woman clearly disapproved of this intrusion,

but although she pursed her lips, she didn't verbalize her objection. She pushed the intercom button and Janine felt a tingle of awareness at the sound of Zach's strong masculine voice.

"This is a pleasant surprise," he said, standing as Janine breezed into the room.

She set her bags on the floor and with an exaggerated sigh, eased herself into the chair opposite his desk and crossed her legs. "I'm sorry to drop in unannounced," she said casually, "but I have some news."

"No problem." His gaze fell to the bags heaped on the floor. "Looks like you had a busy afternoon."

"I was shopping."

"So I see. Any special reason?"

"It's my trousseau." Melodramatically, she pressed the back of her hand against her forehead. "I can't take the pressure anymore. I've come to tell you I told my grandfather to go ahead and arrange the wedding. Someday, somehow, we'll learn to love each other."

"This isn't amusing. Now what's so important that it can't—"

"Mr. Thomas," his secretary said crisply over the intercom, "Mr. Hartman is here to see you."

Janine's eyes widened in panic as her startled gaze flew to Zach, who looked equally alarmed. It would be the worst possible thing for Gramps to discover Janine alone with Zach in his office. She hated to think how he'd interpret that.

"Just a minute," Zach said, reading the hysteria in her eyes. She marveled at how composed he sounded. He pointed toward a closed door and ushered her into a small room—or a large closet—that was practically a home away from home. A bar, refrigerator, microwave, sink and other conveniences were neatly arranged inside. No sooner was the door slammed shut behind her than it was jerked open again and three large shopping bags were tossed in.

Janine felt utterly ridiculous. She kept as still as she could, afraid to turn on the light and almost afraid to breathe for fear of being discovered.

With her ear against the door, she tried to listen to the conversation, hoping to discover just how long Gramps intended to plant himself in Zach's office.

Unfortunately, she could barely hear a thing. She risked opening the door a crack; a quick glance revealed that both men were facing away from her. That explained why she couldn't understand their conversation.

It was then that Janine spotted her purse. Strangling a gasp, she eased the door shut and staggered away from it. She covered her mouth as she took deep breaths. When she found the courage to edge open the door and peek again, she saw that all her grandfather had to do was glance downward.

If he shuffled his feet, his shoe would catch on the strap and he'd drag it out of the office with him.

Zach turned away from the window, and for the first time Janine could hear and see him clearly.

"I'll take care of that right away," he said evenly. He was so calm, so composed, as though he often kept women hidden in his closet. He must have noticed Janine's purse because he frowned and his gaze flew accusingly toward her.

Well, for heaven's sake, she hadn't purposely left it there for Gramps to trip over! He wasn't even supposed to be in the building. That very morning, he'd told her he was lunching at the Athletic Club with his longtime friend, Burt Coleman. Whenever Gramps ate lunch with his cronies, he spent the afternoon playing pinochle. Apparently he'd changed his habits, just so her hair would turn prematurely gray.

Several tortured minutes passed before Zach escorted Gramps to the door. The instant it was shut, Janine stepped into the office, blinking against the brightness after her wait in the dark. "My purse," she said in a strangled voice. "Do you think he saw it?"

"It would be a miracle if he didn't. Of all the stupid things to do!"

"I didn't purposely leave it out here!"

"I'm not talking about that," Zach growled. "I'm referring to your coming here in the first place. Are you crazy? You couldn't have called?"

"I...had something to tell you and I was in the neighborhood." So much for her suave, sophisticated facade. Zach was right, of course; she *could* have told him just as easily by phone.

He looked furious. "For the life of me I can't think of a solitary thing that's so important you'd do anything this foolish. If your grandfather saw the two of us together, he'd immediately jump to the wrong conclusion. Until this afternoon, everything's been peaceful. Anton hasn't mentioned your name once and, frankly, I appreciated that."

His words stung. "I... I won't make the mistake of coming again—ever," she vowed, trying to sound dignified and aloof. She gathered her purse and her bags as quickly as possible and hurried out of the office, not caring who saw her leave, including Gramps.

"Janine, you never did say why you came." Zach had followed her to the elevator.

Janine stared at the light above the elevator that indicated the floor number, as though it was a message of the utmost importance. Her hold on the bags was precarious and something was dragging against her feet, but she couldn't have cared less. "I'm sorry to have imposed on your valuable time. Now that I think about it, it wasn't even important."

"Janine," he coaxed, apparently regretting his earlier outburst. "I shouldn't have yelled."

"Yes, I know," she said smoothly. The elevator opened and with as little ceremony as possible, she slipped inside. It wasn't until she was over the threshold that she realized her purse strap was tangled around her feet.

So much for a dignified exit.

Four

"The castle of Cawdor was built in the fifteenth century and to this day remains the seat of the earl of Cawdor," the guide intoned as Janine and several other sightseers toured the famous landmark. "In William Shakespeare's *Macbeth,* the castle plays an important role. Macbeth becomes the thane of Cawdor…"

For the first few days of Janine's visit to Scotland, she'd been content to explore on her own. The tours, however, helped fill in the bits and pieces of history she might otherwise have missed.

The castle of Cawdor was in northeastern Scotland. The next day, she planned to rent a car and take a meandering route toward Edinburgh, the political heart of Scotland. From what she'd read, Edinburgh Castle was an ancient fortress, built on a huge rock, that dominated the city's skyline. Gramps had booked reservations for her at an inn on the outskirts of town.

The Bonnie Inn, with its red-tiled roof and black-trimmed gables, had all the charm she'd expected, and more. Janine's room offered more character than comfort, but she felt its welcome as if she were visiting an old friend.

A vase filled with fresh flowers and dainty jars of bath salts awaited her.

Eager to explore, she strolled outside to investigate the extensive garden. There was a chill in the April air and she tucked her hands in her pockets, watching with amusement as the partridges fed on the lush green lawn.

"Janine?"

At the sound of her name, she turned, and to her astonishment discovered Zach standing not more than ten feet away. "What are you doing here?" she demanded.

"Me? I was about to ask you the same question."

"I'm on vacation. Gramps gave me the trip as a gift."

"I'm here on business," Zach explained, and his brow furrowed in a suspicious frown.

Janine was doing her own share of frowning. "This is all rather convenient, don't you think?"

Zach took immediate offense. "You don't believe I planned this, do you?"

"No," she agreed reluctantly.

Zach continued to stand there, stiff and wary. "I had absolutely nothing to do with this," he said.

"If you hadn't been so rude to me the last time we met," she felt obliged to inform him, with a righteous tilt to her chin, "you'd have known well in advance that Gramps was sending me here, and we could have avoided this unpleasant shock."

"If you hadn't been in such an all-fired hurry to leave my office, you'd have discovered I was traveling here myself."

"Oh, that's perfect! Go ahead and blame me for everything," she shrieked. "As I recall, you were furious at my being anywhere near your precious office."

"All right, I'll admit I might have handled the situation

poorly," Zach said, and the muscles in his jaw hardened. "But as you'll also recall, I did apologize."

"Sure you did," she said, "after you'd trampled all over my ego. I've never felt like more of a fool in my life."

"You?" Zach shouted. "It may surprise you to know that I don't make a habit of hiding women in my office."

"Do you think I enjoyed being stuffed in that…closet like a bag of dirty laundry?"

"What was I supposed to do? Hide you under my desk?"

"It might've been better than a pitch-black closet."

"If you're so keen on casting blame, let me remind you I wasn't the one who left my purse in full view of your grandfather," Zach said. "I did everything but perform card tricks to draw his attention away from it."

"You make it sound like I'm at fault," Janine snapped.

"I'm not the one who popped in unexpectedly. If you had a job like everyone else—"

"If I had a job," she broke in, outraged. "You mean all the volunteer work I do doesn't count? Apparently the thirty hours a week I put in mean nothing. Sure, I've got a degree. Sure, I could probably have my pick of a dozen different jobs, but why take employment away from someone who really needs it when so many worthwhile organizations are hurting for volunteers?" She was breathless by the time she finished, and so angry she could feel the heat radiating from her face.

She refused to tolerate Zach's offensive insinuations any longer. From the moment they'd met, Zach had clearly viewed her as spoiled and frivolous, without a brain in her head. And it seemed that nothing had altered his opinion.

"Listen, I didn't mean—"

"It's obvious to me," she said bluntly, "that you and I are never going to agree on anything." She was so furious she couldn't keep her anger in check. "The best thing for us to do is completely ignore each other. It's obvious that you don't want anything to do with me and, frankly, I feel the same way about you. So, good day, Mr. Thomas." With that she walked away, her head high and her pride intact.

For the very first time with this man, she'd been able to make a grand exit. It should have felt good. But it didn't.

An hour later, after Janine had taken the tourist bus into Edinburgh, she was still brooding over her latest encounter with Zachary Thomas. If there was any humor at all in this situation, it had to be the fact that her usually sage grandfather could possibly believe she and Zach were in any way suited.

Determined to put the man out of her mind, Janine wandered down Princes Street, which was packed with shoppers, troupes of actors giving impromptu performances and strolling musicians. Her mood couldn't help but be influenced by the festive flavor, and she soon found herself smiling despite the unpleasant confrontation with her grandfather's business partner.

Several of the men who passed her in the street were dressed in kilts, and Janine felt as if she'd stepped into another time, another world. The air swirled with bagpipe music. The city itself seemed gray and gloomy, a dull background for the colorful sights and sounds, the excitement of ages past.

It was as Janine walked out of a dress shop that she bumped into Zach a second time. He stopped, his eyes registering surprise and what looked to Janine like a hint of regret—as though confronting her twice in the same day was enough to try anyone's patience.

"I know what you're thinking," he said, pinning her with his dark intense gaze.

"And I'm equally confident that you don't." She held her packages close and edged against the shop window to avoid hindering other pedestrians on the crowded sidewalk.

"I came here to do some shopping," Zach said gruffly. "I wasn't following you."

"You can rest assured I wasn't following *you*."

"Fine," he said.

"Fine," she repeated.

But neither of them moved for several nerve-racking seconds. Janine assumed Zach was going to say something else. Perhaps she secretly hoped he would. If they couldn't be friends, Janine would've preferred they remain allies. They should be uniting their forces instead of battling each other. Without a word, Zach gestured abruptly and wheeled around to join the stream of people hurrying down the sidewalk.

A half hour later, with more packages added to her collection, Janine strolled into a fabric store, wanting to purchase a sizable length of wool as a gift for Pam. She ran her fingertips along several thick bolts of material, marveling at the bold colors. The wool felt soft, but when she lifted a corner with her palm, she was surprised by how heavy it was.

"Each clan has its own tartan," the white-haired lady in the shop explained. Janine enjoyed listening to her voice, with its enthusiastic warmth and distinct Scottish burr. "Some of the best-known tartans come in three patterns that are to be worn for different occasions—everyday, dress and battle."

Intrigued, Janine watched as the congenial woman walked around the table to remove a blue-and-green plaid. Janine had already seen that pattern several times. The shop owner said that tourists were often interested in this particular tartan, called Black Watch, because it was assigned to no particular clan. In choosing Black Watch, they weren't aligning themselves with any one clan, but showing total impartiality.

Pleased, Janine purchased several yards of the fabric.

Walking down the narrow street, she was shuffling her packages in her arms when she caught sight of Zach watching a troupe of musicians. She started to move away, then for no reason she could name, paused to study him. Her impression of him really hadn't changed since that first afternoon. She still thought Zach Thomas opinionated, unreasonable and…fine, she was willing to admit it, attractive. *Very* attractive, in a sort of rough-hewn way. He lacked the polish, the superficial sophistication of a man like Brian, but he had a vigor that seemed thoroughly masculine. He also had the uncanny ability to set her teeth on edge with a single look. No other man could irritate her so quickly.

The musicians began a lively song and Zach laughed unselfconsciously. His rich husky tenor was smooth and relaxed as it drifted across the street toward her. Janine knew she should've left then, but she couldn't. Despite everything, she was intrigued.

Zach must have felt her scrutiny because he suddenly turned and their eyes locked before Janine could look away. The color rose to her cheeks and for a long moment, neither moved. Neither smiled.

It was in Janine's mind to cross the street, swallow her pride and put an end to this pointless antagonism. During the past several weeks her pride had become familiar fare; serving it up once more shouldn't be all that difficult.

She was entertaining that thought when a bus drove past her belching a thick cloud of black smoke, momentarily blocking her view of Zach. When the bus had passed, Janine noticed that he'd returned his attention to the musicians.

Disheartened, she headed in the opposite direction. She hadn't gone more than a block when she heard him call her name.

She stopped and waited for him to join her. With an inquiring lift of one eyebrow, he reached for some of her packages. She nodded, repressing a shiver of excitement as his hand brushed hers. Shifting his burden, he slowed his steps to match Janine's. Then he spoke. "We need to talk."

"I don't see how we can. Every time you open your mouth you say something insulting and offensive."

Only a few minutes earlier, Janine had been hoping to put an end to this foolish antagonism, yet here she was provoking an argument, acting just as unreasonable as she accused him of being. She stopped midstep, disgusted with herself. "I shouldn't have said that. I don't know what it is about us, but we seem to have a hard time being civil to each other."

"It might be the shock of finding each other here."

"Which brings up another subject," Janine added fervently. "If Gramps was going to arrange for us to meet, why send us halfway around the world to do it?"

"I used to think I knew your grandfather," Zach murmured. "But lately, I'm beginning to wonder. I haven't got a clue why he chose Scotland."

"He came to me with the tickets, reminding me it'd been almost a year since I'd traveled anywhere," Janine said. "He told me it was high time I took a vacation, that I needed to get away for a while. And I bought it hook, line and sinker."

"You?" Zach cried, shaking his head, clearly troubled. "Your grandfather sent me here on a wild-goose chase. Yes, there were contacts to make, but this was a trip any of our junior executives could've handled. It wasn't until I arrived at the inn and found you booked there that I realized what he was up to."

"If we hadn't been so distracted trying to figure out who was to blame for that fiasco at your office, we might've been able to prevent this. At least, we'd have guessed what Gramps was doing."

"Exactly," Zach said. "Forewarned is forearmed. Obviously, we have to put aside our differences and stay in communication. That's the key. Communication."

"Absolutely," Janine agreed, with a nod of her head.

"But letting him throw us together like this is only going to lead to trouble."

What kind of trouble, he didn't say, but Janine could guess all too easily. "I agree with you."

"The less time we spend together, the better." He paused when he noticed that she was standing in front of the bus stop.

"If we allow Gramps to throw us together, it'll just encourage him," she said. "We've got to be very firm about this, before things get completely out of hand."

"You're right." Without asking, he took the rest of the packages from her arms, adding them to the bags and parcels he already carried. "I rented a car. I don't suppose you'd accept a ride back to the inn?"

"Please." Janine was grateful for the offer. They'd started off badly, each blaming the other, but fortunately their relationship was beginning to improve. That relieved her. She'd much rather have Zachary for a friend than an enemy.

They spoke very little on the twenty-mile ride back to the Bonnie Inn. After an initial exchange of what sights they'd seen and what they'd purchased, there didn't seem to be much to say. They remained awkward and a little uneasy with each other. And Janine was all too aware of how intimate the confines of the small rented car were. Her shoulder and her thigh were within scant inches of brushing against Zach, something she was determined to ignore.

The one time Janine chanced a look in his direction, she saw how intent his features were, as if he was driving a dangerous, twisting course instead of a straight, well-maintained road with light traffic. His mouth was compressed, bracketed by deep grooves, and his dark eyes had narrowed. He glanced away from the road long enough for their eyes to meet. Janine smiled and quickly looked down, embarrassed that he'd caught her studying him so closely. She wished she could sort out her feelings, analyze all her contradictory emotions in a logical manner. She was attracted to Zach, but not in the same way she'd been attracted to Brian. Although Zach infuriated her, she admired him. Respected him. But he didn't send her senses whirling mindlessly, as Brian had. Then again, she didn't think of him as a brother, either. Her only conclusion was that her feelings for Zach were more confusing than ever.

After thanking him for the ride and collecting her parcels, she left Zach in the lobby and tiredly climbed the stairs to her room. She soaked in a hot scented bath, then changed into a blue-and-gold plaid kilt she'd bought that afternoon. With it, she wore a thin white sweater under her navy-blue blazer. She tied a navy scarf at her neck, pleased with the effect. A little blush, a dab of eye shadow and she was finished, by now more than ready for something to eat.

Zach was waiting to be seated in the dining room when she came downstairs. He wore a thick hand-knit sweater over black dress slacks and made such a virile sight she found it difficult not to stare.

The hostess greeted them with a warm smile. "Dinner for two?"

Janine reacted first, flustered and a little embarrassed. "We're not together," she said. "This gentleman was here before me." Anything else would negate the agreement they'd made earlier.

Zach frowned as he followed the hostess to a table set against the wall, close to the massive stone fireplace. The hostess returned and directed Janine to a table against the same wall, so close to Zach that she could practically read the menu over his shoulder. She was reading her own menu when Zach spoke. "Don't you think we're both being a little silly?"

"Yes," she admitted. "But earlier today we agreed that being thrown together like this could lead to trouble."

"I honestly don't think it would hurt either of us to have dinner together, do you?"

"No… I don't think it would." They'd spend the entire meal talking across the tables to each other, anyway.

He stood up, grinning. "May I join you?"

"Please." She couldn't help responding with a smile.

He pulled out the other chair, his gaze appreciative. "Those colors look good on you."

"Thanks." She had to admit he looked good—darkly vibrant and masculine—himself. She was about to return his compliment when it dawned on her how senselessly they were challenging fate.

"It's happening already," she whispered, leaning toward him in order to avoid being overheard.

"What?" Zach glanced around as though he expected ghostly clansmen to emerge from behind the drapes.

"You're telling me how good I look in blue and I was about to tell you how nice *you* look and we're smiling at each other and forming a mutual admiration society. Next thing you know, we'll be married."

"That's ridiculous!"

"Sure, you say that now, but I can see a real problem here."

"Does this mean you want me to go back to my table and eat alone?"

"Of course not. I just think it would be best if we limited the compliments. All right?"

"I'll never say anything nice about you again."

Janine smiled. "Thank you."

"You might want to watch that, as well," he warned with a roguish grin. "If we're too formal and polite with each other, that could lead us straight to the jewelers. Before we know what's happening, we'll be choosing wedding bands."

Janine's lips quivered with a barely restrained smile. "I hadn't thought about that." They glanced at each other and before either could hold it in, they were laughing, attracting the attention of everyone in the dining room. As abruptly as they'd started, they stopped, burying their faces in the menus.

After they'd ordered, Janine shared her theory with Zach, a theory that had come to her on their drive back to the inn. "I think I know why Gramps arranged for us to meet in Scotland."

"I'm dying to hear this."

"Actually, I'm afraid I'm the one responsible." She heaved a sigh of remorse. Every part of her seemed aware of Zach, which was exactly what she didn't want. She sighed again. "When Gramps first mentioned the idea of an arranged marriage, I tried to make him understand that love wasn't something one ordered like…like dinner from a menu. He genuinely didn't seem to grasp what I was saying and asked me what a woman needed to fall in love."

"And you told him a trip to Scotland?" Zach's eyes sparkled with the question.

"Of course not. I told him a woman needed romance."

Zach leaned forward. "I hate to appear dense, but I seem to have missed something."

Pretending to be annoyed with him, Janine explained, "Well, Gramps asked me to define romance…"

"I'd be interested in learning that myself." Zach wiped the edges of his mouth with his napkin. Janine suspected he did it to cover a growing need to smile.

"It isn't all that easy to explain, you know," Janine said. "And remember this was off the top of my head. I told Gramps romance was forbidden trysts on Scottish moors."

"With an enemy clan chieftain?"

"No, with the man I loved."

"What else did you tell him?"

"I don't remember exactly. I think I said something about a moonlight stroll on the beach, and…and desperate passion."

"I wonder how he'll arrange that?"

"I don't think I want to find out," Janine murmured. Considering how seriously Gramps had taken her impromptu definition, she almost dreaded the thought of what he might do next.

When they'd finished, their plates were removed by the attentive waiter and their coffee served. To complicate her feelings, she was actually a little sad their dinner was about to end.

They left the dining room, and Zach escorted her up the stairs. "Thank you for being willing to take a risk and share dinner with me," he said, his voice deadpan. "I enjoyed it, despite the, uh, danger."

"I did, too," Janine said softly. More than she cared to admit. Against her better judgment, her mind spun with possible ways to delay their parting, but she decided against each one, not wanting to tempt fate any more than she already had.

Zach walked her to her room, pausing outside her door. Janine found herself searching for the right words. She longed to tell him she'd enjoyed spending the evening with him, talking and laughing together, but she didn't know how to say it without sounding like a woman in love.

Zach appeared to be having the same problem. He raised one hand as though to touch her face, then apparently changed his mind, dropping his hand abruptly. She felt strangely disappointed.

"Good night," he said curtly, stepping back.

"Good night," she echoed, turning to walk into her room. She closed the door and leaned against it, feeling unsettled but at a loss to understand why.

After ten restless minutes she ventured out again. The country garden was well lit, and a paved pathway led to rocky cliffs that fell off sharply. Even from where she stood, Janine could hear the sea roaring below. She could smell its salty tang, mixed with the scent of heath. Thrusting her hands into her blazer pockets, Janine strolled along a narrow path into the garden. The night air was cool and she had no intention of walking far, not more than a few hundred feet. She'd return in the morning when she planned to walk as far as the cliffs with their buffeting winds.

The moon was full and so large it seemed to take up the entire sky, sending streaks of silvery light across the horizon. With her arms wrapped around her middle, she gazed up at it, certain she'd never felt more peaceful or serene. She closed her eyes, savoring the luxurious silence of the moment.

Suddenly it was broken. "So we meet again," Zach said from behind her.

"This is getting ridiculous." Janine turned to him and smiled, her heart beating fast. "Meeting on the moors..."

"It isn't exactly a tryst," Zach said.

"Not technically."

They stood side by side, looking into the night sky, both of them silent. During their meal they'd talked nonstop, but now Janine felt tongue-tied and ill at ease. If they'd been worried about having dinner together, they were placing themselves at even greater risk here in the moonlight.

Janine knew it. Zach knew it. But neither suggested leaving.

"It's a beautiful night," Zach said at last, linking his hands behind his back.

"It is, isn't it?" Janine replied brightly, as if he'd introduced the most stimulating topic of her entire vacation.

"I don't think we should put any stock in this," he surprised her by saying next.

"In what?"

"In meeting here, as if we'd arranged a tryst. Of course you're a beautiful woman and it would be only natural if a man...any red-blooded man were to find himself charmed. I'd blame it on the moonlight, wouldn't you?"

"Oh, I agree completely. I mean, we've been thrust together in a very romantic setting and it would be normal to...find ourselves momentarily...attracted to each other. It doesn't mean anything, though."

Zach moved behind her. "You're right, of course." He hesitated, then murmured, "You should've worn a heavier jacket." Before she could assure him that she was perfectly comfortable, he ran his hands slowly down the length of her arms, as though to warm her. Unable to restrain herself, Janine sighed and leaned against him, soaking up his warmth and his strength.

"This presents a problem, doesn't it?" he whispered, his voice husky and close to her ear. "Isn't moonlight supposed to do something strange to people?"

"I…think it only affects werewolves."

He chuckled and his breath shot a series of incredible light-as-air sensations along her neck. Janine felt she was about to crumple at his feet. Then his chin brushed the side of her face and she sighed again.

His hands on her shoulders, Zach urged her around so that she faced him, but not for anything would Janine allow her gaze to meet his.

He didn't say a word.

She didn't, either.

Janine experienced one worry after another, afraid to voice any of them. Zach apparently felt the same way, because he didn't seem any more eager to explain things than she did. Or to stop them…

After a moment, Zach pressed his hands over her cheekbones. Leisurely, his thumbs stroked the line of her jaw, her chin. His eyes were dark, his expression unreadable. Janine's heart was churning over and over, dragging her emotions with it. She swallowed, then moistened her lips.

He seemed to find her mouth mesmerizing. Somewhere deep inside, she discovered the strength to warn him that her grandfather's plan was working. She opened her mouth to speak, but before she could utter a single word, Zach's arms came around her and drew her close against him. She felt his comforting warmth seep through her, smelled the faint muskiness of his skin. The sensations were unlike anything she'd ever known. Then he lowered his mouth to hers.

The immediate shock of pleasure was almost frightening. She couldn't keep from trembling.

He drew back slightly. "You're cold. You should've said something."

"No, that's not it." Even her voice was quivering.

"Then what is?"

In response she kissed him back. She hadn't meant to, but before she could stop herself, she slipped her arms around his neck and slanted her mouth over his.

Zach's shoulders were heaving when at last she pulled her mouth away and hid her face against his chest.

"What are we doing?" he whispered. He broke hastily away from her.

Janine was too stunned to react. In an effort to hide his effect on her, she rubbed her face as though struggling to wake up from a deep sleep.

"That shouldn't have happened," Zach said stiffly.

"You're telling me," she returned raggedly. "It certainly wasn't the smartest move we could've made."

Zach jerked his fingers roughly through his hair and frowned. "I don't know what came over me. Over us. We both know better."

"It's probably because we're both tired," Janine said soothingly, offering a convenient excuse. "When you stop to think about it, the whole thing's perfectly understandable. Gramps arranged for us to meet, hoping something like this would happen. Clearly the power of suggestion is stronger than either of us realized."

"Clearly." But he continued to frown.

"Oh, gee," Janine said glancing at her watch, unable to read the numbers in the dark. Her voice was high and wavering. "Will you look at the time? I can't believe it's so late. I really should be getting back inside."

"Janine, listen. I think we should talk about this."

"Sure, but not now." All she wanted was to escape and gather some perspective on what had happened. It had all started so innocently, almost a game, but quickly turned into something far more serious.

"All right, we'll discuss it in the morning." Zach didn't sound pleased. He walked through the garden with her, muttering under his breath. "Damn it!" he said, again shoving his fingers through his hair. "I knew I should never have come here."

"There's no need to be so angry. Blame the moonlight. It obviously disrupts the brain and interferes with wave patterns or something."

"Right," Zach said, his voice still gruff.

"Well, good night," Janine managed cheerfully when they reached the staircase.

"Good night." Zach's tone was equally nonchalant.

Once Janine was in her room, she threw herself on the bed and covered her eyes with one hand. *Oh, no,* she lamented silently. They'd crossed the line. Tempted fate. Spit in the eye of common sense.

They'd kissed.

Several minutes later, still shaking, Janine got up and undressed. She slid under the blankets and tried to find a relaxing position. But she didn't feel like sleeping. Tomorrow she'd have to make polite conversation with Zach and she didn't know if she could bear it. She was sure he'd feel just as uncomfortable with her. She'd seen how he could barely look at her when they entered the inn.

Tossing aside the blankets, Janine decided she had only one option. She'd leave Scotland, the sooner the better.

Grabbing the phone, she called the airport, booked a seat on the earliest flight home and immediately set about packing her bags.

Not bothering to even try to sleep, she crept down the stairs a little before midnight and checked out.

"You're leaving sooner than you expected, aren't you, Miss Hartman?" the night manager asked after calling for a cab.

"Yes," she said.

"I hope everything was satisfactory?"

"It was wonderful." She pulled a folded piece of paper from her purse and placed it on the counter. "Would you see to it that Mr. Thomas receives this in the morning?"

"Of course." The young man tucked it in a small cubbyhole behind him.

Satisfied that Zach would know she was leaving and wouldn't be concerned by her hurried return to Seattle, she sat in a chair in the small lobby to wait for her cab.

About fifteen minutes later, Janine watched silently as the cabdriver stowed her luggage in the trunk. She paused before climbing in the backseat of the car and glanced one last time at the muted moonlit landscape, disappointed that she wouldn't have an opportunity to visit the cliffs.

The ride to the airport seemed to take an eternity. She felt a burning sense of regret at leaving Scotland. She'd fallen in love with the country during her short visit and hoped someday to return. Although the memory of her evening stroll through the garden would always bring with it a certain chagrin, she couldn't completely regret that time with Zach. In fact, she'd always remember the fleeting sense of contentment she'd felt in his arms.

Janine arrived at the airport long before her flight was scheduled to leave. She spent an hour drinking coffee and leafing through fashion magazines, several of which she took with her to give to Pam later.

A cup of coffee in one hand, she approached the airline counter with her passport in the other. The bag she had draped over her shoulder accidentally collided with the man standing next to her. An automatic apology formed on her lips, but before she could voice it, that same man turned to face her.

“Zach,” she cried, nearly dropping her coffee in shock. “What are you doing here?”

Five

"You think this is intentional, don't you?" Zach demanded. "It's obvious *you're* the one running after me. You found the note I slipped under your door and—"

"I checked out just before midnight so I couldn't possibly have read your note," she said angrily. "And furthermore I left a message for you."

"I didn't get it."

"Then there's been a misunderstanding."

"To say the least," Zach muttered. "A misunderstanding…" His tone was doubtful, as if he suspected she'd purposely arranged to fly home with him. She launched into an indignant protest.

"Excuse me, please."

The interruption was from a uniformed airline employee who was leaning over the counter and waving in an effort to gain their attention.

"May I have your ticket and passport?" she asked Janine. "You're holding up the line."

"Of course. I'm sorry." The best thing to do, she decided, was to ignore Zach completely. Just because they were booked on the same flight didn't mean they had to have anything to do with each other. Evidently they'd both panicked after their encounter in the garden. He was as eager to escape as she was.

Okay, so she'd ignore him and he'd ignore her. She'd return to her life, and he'd return to his. From this point forward, they need never have contact with each other again. Then they'd both be satisfied.

The airline clerk punched something into her computer. "I can give you your seat assignment now," she remarked, concentrating on the screen.

Standing on tiptoe, Janine leaned toward the woman and lowered her voice to a whisper. "Could you make sure I'm as far from Mr. Thomas's seat as possible?"

"This flight is booked solid," the attendant said impatiently. "The only reason you and your…friend were able to get seats was because of a last-minute cancellation. I'll do the best I can, but I can't rearrange everyone's seat assignments just before the flight."

"I understand," Janine said, feeling foolish and petty. But the way her luck had been going, Zach would end up in the seat beside hers, believing she'd purposely arranged that, too.

They boarded the flight separately; in fact, Zach was one of the last passengers to step onto the plane.

By that time, Janine was settled in the second row of the first-class section, flipping through the in-flight magazine. Zach strolled past her, intent on the boarding pass clutched in his hand.

Pretending she hadn't seen him seemed the best tactic, and she turned to gaze out the window.

"It seems I'm sitting here," Zach announced brusquely, loading his carry-on luggage in the compartment above the seats.

Janine had to bite her tongue to keep from insisting she'd had nothing to do with that. She'd even tried to prevent it, but she doubted Zach would believe her.

"Before you claim otherwise, I want you to know I didn't arrange this," he said, sitting down beside her.

"I know that."

"You do?"

"Of course," Janine told him. "The fates are against us. I don't know how my grandfather arranged our meeting at the airport or the adjoining seats, any more than I know why I stumbled on you my first day at the Bonnie Inn. We might never have crossed paths. But somehow, some way, Gramps is responsible." That didn't sound entirely reasonable, but she thought it best not to mention their stroll in the moonlight.

"So you're not ready to unleash the full force of your anger on me?"

"I don't see how I can be upset with you—or the reverse. Neither of us asked for this."

"Exactly."

Janine yawned loudly and covered her mouth. "Excuse me. I didn't sleep last night and now it's catching up with me."

Her yawn was contagous and soon Zach's hand was warding off his own admission of drowsiness. The flight attendant came by with coffee, which both Zach and Janine declined.

"Frankly, I'd be more interested in a pillow," Janine said, yawning again. The attendant handed her one, as well as a blanket, then offered the same to Zach. He refused both, intending to work on some papers he'd withdrawn from his briefcase. The minute the plane was safely in the air,

Janine laid her head back and closed her eyes. Almost immediately she felt herself drifting into a peaceful slumber.

She stirred twice in the long hours that followed, but both times a gentle voice soothed her back to sleep. Sighing, she snuggled into the warmth, feeling more comfortable than she had in weeks.

She began to dream and could see herself walking across the moors, wearing traditional Scottish dress, while bagpipes wailed in the background.

Then, on the crest of a hill, Zach appeared, dressed in a Black Watch kilt and tam-o'-shanter; a set of bagpipes was draped over his shoulder. Their eyes met and the music ceased. Then, out of nowhere, her grandfather appeared, standing halfway between the two of them, looking distinctly pleased. He cupped his hands over his mouth and shouted to Janine."Is this romance?"

"Yes," she shouted back.

"What else do you need?"

"Love."

"Love," Gramps repeated. He turned to Zach, apparently seeking some kind of assistance.

Zach started fiddling with his bagpipes, avoiding the question. He scowled as he concentrated on his task.

"Look at the pair of you," Gramps called. "You're perfect together. Zach, when are you going to wake up and realize what a wonderful girl my Janine is?"

"If I do get married, you can be sure I'll choose my own bride," Zach hollered.

"And I'd prefer to pick out my own husband!"

"You're falling in love with Zach!" Gramps declared, obviously elated.

"I—I—" Janine was so flustered she couldn't complete her thought, which only served to please her grandfather more.

"Look at her, boy," Gramps directed his attention to Zach again. "See how lovely she is. And think of what beautiful children you'll have."

"Gramps! Enough about babies! I'm not marrying Zach!"

"Janine." Zach's voice echoed in her ear.

"Keep out of this," she cried. He was the last person she wanted to hear from.

"You're having a dream."

Her eyes fluttered open and she saw Zach's face close to her own, her head nestled against his chest. "Oh..." she mumbled, bolting upright. "Oh, dear... I am sorry. I didn't realize I was leaning on you."

"I hated to wake you, but you seemed to be having a nightmare."

She blinked and tried to focus on him, but it was difficult, and to complicate matters her eyes started to water. She wiped her face with one sleeve. Then, straightening, she removed the pillow from behind her back and folded the blanket, trying to disguise how badly her hands were trembling.

"You're worried about what happened after dinner last night, aren't you?"

Janine released a pent-up breath and smiled brightly as she lied. "Nothing really happened."

"In the garden, when we kissed. Listen," Zach said in a low voice, glancing quickly around to ensure that no one could overhear their conversation, "I think it's time we talked about last night."

"I... You're right, of course." She didn't feel up to this, but she supposed it was best dealt with before she had to face her grandfather.

"Egos aside."

"By all means," Janine agreed. She braced herself, not

knowing what to expect. Zach had made his views on the idea of an arranged marriage plain from the first; so had she. In fact, even her feelings about a marriage based on love weren't all that positive at the moment. Brian had taught her a valuable lesson, a painful lesson, one she wouldn't easily forget. She'd given him her heart and her trust, and he'd betrayed both. Falling in love had been the most shattering experience of her life, and she had no intention of repeating it anytime soon.

"I'd be a liar if I didn't admit how nice kissing you was," Zach said, "but I wish it had never happened. It created more problems than it solved."

Janine wasn't exactly flattered by his remark. Keeping egos out of this was harder than it sounded, she thought ruefully. Her expression must have revealed her thoughts because Zach elaborated. "Before I arrived in Scotland, we hardly knew each other. We met that first afternoon over lunch—with Anton—and talked a couple of times, but basically we were strangers."

"We had dinner one night," Janine reminded him, annoyed that he could so casually dismiss it.

"Right," he acknowledged. "Then we met at the Bonnie Inn and, bingo, we were having dinner together and walking in the moonlight, and before either of us knew how it happened, we were kissing."

Janine nodded, listening quietly.

"There are several factors we can take into account, but if we're going to place blame for that kiss, I'm the one at fault."

"You?"

"Me," he confirmed with a grimace. "Actually, I'm prepared to accept full responsibility. I doubt you were aware of what was going on. It didn't take me long to see how innocent you are, and—"

"Now just a minute," Janine snapped. Once again he was taking potshots at her dignity. "What do you mean by that?"

"It's obvious you haven't had a lot of sexual experience and—"

"In other words I'm so incredibly naive that I couldn't possibly be held accountable for a few kisses in the moonlight?"

"Something like that."

"Oh, brother," she muttered.

"There's no need to feel offended."

"I wasn't exactly raised in a convent, you know. And for your information, I've been kissed by more than one man."

"I'm sure you have. But we're getting sidetracked here—"

"I'm sorry you found me so inept. A man of your vast worldly experience must've been sorely disappointed by someone as unsophisticated as me, and—"

"Janine," he said firmly, stopping her. "You're putting words in my mouth. All I was saying is that we—*I*—let matters get out of hand and we can't blame your grandfather for what happened."

"I'm willing to accept my part in this. I can also see where this conversation is leading."

"Good," Zach said. It was clear that his composure was slipping. "Then you tell me."

"You think that because I enjoyed spending time with you and we shared this mildly romantic evening and—"

"*Mildly* romantic?"

"Yes, you did say egos aside, didn't you? I'm just being honest."

"Fine," he said, tight-lipped.

"You seem to think that because you have so much more

experience than I do, there's a real danger I'll be *swooning* at your feet." She drew out the word, enjoying her silliness, and batted her eyelashes furiously.

"Janine, you're behaving like a child," he informed her coldly.

"Of course I am. That's exactly what you seem to expect of me."

Zach's fingers tightened on the armrest. "You're purposely misconstruing everything I said."

"Whatever you're trying to say isn't necessary. You figure we had a borderline interest in each other and now we've crossed that border. Right? Well, I'm telling you that you needn't worry." She sucked in a deep breath and glared at him. "I'm right, aren't I? That's what you think, isn't it?"

"Something like that, yes."

Janine nodded grimly. "And *now* you think that since you held me in your arms and you lost your control long enough to kiss me, I'm suddenly going to start entertaining thoughts of the M word."

"The… M word?"

"Marriage."

"That's ridiculous," Zach said, jamming the airline magazine back into the seat pocket in front of him.

"Well?"

"All I mean is that the temptation might be there and we should both beware of it."

"Oh, honestly, Zach," she said sarcastically, "you overestimate yourself."

"Listen, I wasn't the one mumbling about babies."

"I was having a dream! That has absolutely nothing to do with what we're talking about now."

"Could've fooled me." He reached for the same magazine he'd recently rejected and turned the pages hard enough to rip them in two. "I don't think this discussion is getting us anywhere."

Janine sighed. "You were right, though. We did need to clear the air."

Zach made a gruff indistinguishable reply.

"I'll try to keep out of your magnetic force field, but if I occasionally succumb to your overwhelming charm and forget myself, I can only beg your forgiveness."

"Enough, Janine."

He looked so annoyed with her that she couldn't help smiling. Zach Thomas was a man of such colossal ego it would serve him right if she pretended to faint every time he glanced in her direction. The image filled her mind with laughter.

Zach leaned his head back and closed his eyes, effectively concluding their conversation. Janine stared out the window at the first signs of sunrise, thinking about all kinds of things—except her chaotic feelings for the man beside her.

Some time later, the pilot announced that the plane was approaching Seattle-Tacoma International Airport. Home sounded good to Janine, although she fully intended to have a heart-to-heart talk with her grandfather about his matchmaking efforts.

Once they'd landed, she cleared customs quickly. She struggled with her two large pieces of luggage, pulling one by the handle and looping the long strap of her carry-on bag over her shoulder. Zach was still dealing with the customs agent when she maneuvered her way outside into the bright morning sunlight, joining the line of people waiting for cabs.

"Here," Zach said, from behind her, "I'll carry one of those for you." He'd managed to travel with only his briefcase and a garment bag, which was neatly folded and easily handled.

"Thank you," she said breathlessly.

"I thought we'd agreed to limit our expressions of gratitude toward each other," he grumbled, frowning as he lifted the suitcase.

"I apologize. It slipped my mind."

Zach continued to grumble. "What'd you pack in here, anyway? Bricks?"

"If you're going to complain, I'll carry it myself."

He muttered something she couldn't hear and shook his head. "Once we get a cab—"

"We?"

"We're going to confront your grandfather."

"Together? Now?" She was exhausted, mentally and physically. They both were.

"The sooner the better, don't you think?"

The problem was, Janine hadn't given much thought to what she was going to say. Yes, she intended to challenge Gramps but she'd planned to wait for the most opportune time. And she'd hoped to speak to him privately. "He might not even be home," she argued, "and if he is, I'm not sure now would really be best."

"I want this settled once and for all."

"So do I," she said vehemently. "But I think we should choose when and how we do this more carefully, don't you?"

"Perhaps…" His agreement seemed hesitant, even grudging. "All right, we'll do it your way."

"It isn't my way. It just makes sense to organize our thoughts first. Trust me, Zach, I want this cleared up as badly as you do."

His reply was little more than a grunt, but whether it

was a comment on the weight of her suitcase or her tactics in dealing with Anton, she didn't know.

"And furthermore," she said, making a sweeping motion with her arm, "we've got to stop doubting each other. Nobody's following anyone and neither of us is in any danger of falling in love just because we were foolish enough to kiss."

"Fine," Zach murmured. He set her suitcase down as a cab arrived and the driver jumped out.

"How is it that we always seem to agree and yet we constantly find ourselves at odds?" she asked.

"I wish I knew," he said, looking weary in body and spirit. The cabdriver opened the trunk, storing her suitcases neatly inside. Zach threw his garment bag on top.

"We might as well still share this taxi," he said, holding the door for her.

"But isn't the Mt. Baker district out of your way?"

"I do need to talk to your grandfather. There're some estimates I need to give him."

"But can't it wait until tomorrow? Honestly, Zach, you're exhausted. One day isn't going to make any difference. And like I said, Gramps might not even be at the house."

Zach rubbed his eyes, then glanced irritably in her direction. "Honestly, Janine," he mocked, "you sound like a wife."

Biting her tongue to keep back her angry retort, Janine crossed her arms and glared out the side window. Indignation seeped through her with every breath she drew. Of its own accord, her foot started an impatient tapping. She could hardly wait to part company with this rude, unreasonable man.

Apparently Zach didn't know when to quit, because he added, "Now you even act like one."

She slowly turned to him and in a saccharine voice inquired, "And what's that supposed to mean?"

"Look at you, for heaven's sake. First you start nagging me and then—"

"Nagging you!" she exploded. "Let's get one thing straight, Zachary Thomas. I do *not* nag."

Zach rolled his eyes, then turned his head to gaze out the window on his side.

"Sir, sir," Janine said, sliding forward in the seat. She politely tapped the driver on the shoulder.

The middle-aged man glanced at her. "What is it, lady?"

"Sir," she said, offering him her warmest, most sincere smile. "Tell me, do I look like the kind of woman who'd nag?"

"Ah… Look, lady, all I do is drive a cab. You can ask me where a street is and I can tell you. If you want to go uptown, I can take you uptown. But when it comes to answering personal-type questions, I prefer to mind my own business."

"Are you satisfied?" Zach asked in a low voice.

"No, I'm not." She crossed her arms again and stared straight ahead.

The cabdriver's eyes met hers in the rearview mirror, and Janine tried to smile, but when she caught a glimpse of herself, she realized her effort looked more like a grimace.

"Me and the missus been married for near twenty years now," the driver said suddenly, stopping at a red light just off the James Street exit. "Me and the missus managed to stay married through the good times and the bad ones. Can't say that about a lot of folks."

"I don't suppose your wife is the type who nags, though, is she?" Zach made the question sound more like a statement, sending Janine a look that rankled.

"Betsy does her fair share. If you ask me, nagging's just part of a woman's nature."

"That's absurd," Janine countered stiffly. She should've known better than to draw a complete stranger into the discussion, especially another male who was sure to take Zach's side.

"I'll tell you the real reason me and the missus stayed together all these years," the cabbie continued in a confiding tone. "We never go to bed mad. I know I look like an easygoing guy, but I've got a temper on me. Over the years, me and Betsy have had our share of fights, but we always kiss and make up."

Janine smiled and nodded, sorry she'd ever gotten involved in this conversation.

"Go on," the cabbie urged.

Janine's puzzled gaze briefly met Zach's.

"Go on and do what?" Zach wanted to know.

"Kiss and make up." The cabbie turned for a moment to smile at them and wink at Janine. "If my wife was as pretty as yours, mister, I wouldn't be hesitating."

Janine nearly swallowed her tongue. "We are *not* married."

"And have no intention whatsoever of marrying," Zach added quickly.

The driver chuckled. "That's what they all say. The harder they deny it, the more in love they are."

He turned off Broadway and a few minutes later pulled into the circular driveway that led to Janine's house. As the talkative cabbie leapt from the car and dashed for the trunk, Janine opened her door and climbed out.

Apparently, Zach had no intention of taking her advice, because he, too, got out of the cab. It was while they were tussling with the luggage that the front door opened and Mrs. McCormick hurried outside.

"Janine," she cried, her blue eyes lighting up with surprise. "What are you doing back so soon? We weren't expecting you for another two days."

"I missed your cooking so much, I couldn't bear to stay away any longer," Janine said, throwing her arms around the older woman in a warm hug. "Has Gramps been giving you any trouble?"

"Not a bit."

Zach paid the driver, who got back in his cab, but not before he'd winked at Janine again. "Remember what I told you," he yelled, speeding off.

"How much was the fare?" Janine asked, automatically opening her purse.

"I took care of it," Zach said, reaching for his garment bag and the heavier of Janine's two suitcases. He said it as though he expected an argument from her, but if that was the case, Janine didn't plan to give him one.

"Is Gramps home?" Janine curved her arm affectionately around the housekeeper's waist as she spoke.

"He went out early this morning, but he should be back soon."

"Good," Zach mumbled, following them into the house.

"I imagine you're both starved," Mrs. McCormick said, heading toward the kitchen. "Let me whip up something for you that'll make you both glad you're home."

Left alone with Zach, Janine wasn't sure what to say to him. They'd spent almost twenty-four hours in each other's company. They'd argued. They'd talked. They'd laughed. They'd kissed.

"Janine—"

"Zach—"

They spoke simultaneously, then exchanged nervous smiles.

"You first," Zach said, gesturing toward her.

"I… I just wanted to say thanks for everything. I'll be in touch," she said. "By phone," she assured him. "So you don't need to worry about me dropping by the office unannounced."

He grinned sheepishly. "Remember, communication is the key."

"I agree one hundred percent."

They stood facing each other in the foyer. "You wanted to say something?" she prompted after a moment.

"Yes." Zach exhaled sharply, then drew a hand along the side of his jaw. "What that cabbie said is true—even for us. I don't want us to part with any bad feelings. I shouldn't have said what I did back there, about nagging. You don't nag, and I had no right to say you did."

"I overreacted." The last thing she'd expected from Zach was an apology. His eyes, dark and tender, held hers, and without even realizing what she was doing, Janine took a step forward. Zach met her and she was about to slip into his arms when the sound of the front door opening drove them apart.

"Janine," Anton cried, delighted. "Zach. My, my, this is a pleasant surprise." He chuckled softly as he removed his coat. "Tell me, was your tryst on the moors as romantic as I hoped?"

Six

"Our best bet is to present a united front," Janine said to Zach four days later. They'd met at her house early in the afternoon to outline their strategy. Gramps was gone for the day, but by the time he returned, Zach and Janine planned to be ready to talk him out of this marriage idea. The sooner Anton understood that his ploy wasn't working, the better. Then they could both get on with their lives and forget this unfortunate episode.

"It's important that we stand up to him together," Janine said when Zach didn't comment. From the moment he'd arrived, he'd given her the impression that he'd rather not be doing this. Well, she wasn't overjoyed about plotting against her grandfather, either, but in this instance it was necessary. "If we don't, I'm afraid Gramps will continue to play us against each other."

"I'm here, aren't I?" Zach grumbled. He certainly wasn't in one of his more charming moods.

"Listen, if you're going to act like this—"

"Like what?" he demanded, standing up. He walked over to the polished oak sideboard and poured himself a cup of coffee. When he'd finished, he ambled toward the fireplace and leaned against the mantel.

"Like you're doing me a big favor," Janine elaborated.

"You're the one who's left *me* dangling for three days. Do you realize what I've been forced to endure? Anton kept giving me these smug smiles, looking so pleased with himself and the way things worked out in Scotland. Yesterday he went so far as to mention the name of a good jeweler."

Before Janine could stop herself, she was on her feet, arms akimbo, glaring at Zach. "I thought you were going to call me! Weren't you the one who said communication is the key? Then it's as if you'd dropped off the face of the earth! And for your information, it hasn't exactly been a Sunday school picnic around here, either."

"It may surprise you to learn that I have other things on my mind besides dealing with you and your grandfather."

"Implying I don't have anything to do with *my* time?"

"No," he said slowly. "Damn it, Janine, we're arguing again."

She sighed regretfully. "I know. We've got to stop this squabbling. It's counterproductive."

Zach's nod was curt and she saw that he was frowning. "What bothers me most is the way your grandfather found us the other day. We were standing so close and you were staring up at me, practically begging me to kiss you."

"I most certainly was not," she denied, knowing Zach was right. Her cheeks grew pink. She *had* wanted him to kiss her, but she hated having to admit that she would've walked into his arms without a second's hesitation. She decided to blame that unexpected longing on the exhausting flight home.

Zach shook his head and set his coffee cup carefully on the mantel. He thrust both hands into his pockets, still slouching against the fireplace wall. "The problem is, I was ready to do it. If your grandfather hadn't walked in when he did, I would've kissed you."

"You would?" she asked softly, feeling almost lightheaded at his words.

Zach straightened, and a nerve in his jaw pulsed, calling her attention to the strong chiseled lines of his face. "I'm only human," he said drly. "I'm as susceptible to a beautiful woman as the next man, especially when she all but asks me to take her in my arms."

That was too much. Janine pinched her lips together to keep from crying out in anger. Taking a moment to compose herself, she closed her eyes and drew in a deep breath. "Instead of blaming each other for something that *didn't* happen, could we please return to the subject at hand, which is my grandfather?"

"All right," Zach agreed. "I'm sorry. I shouldn't have said anything." He went to the leather wingback chair and sat down. Leaning forward, he rested his elbows on his knees. "What are you going to say to him?"

"Me? I thought… I'd hoped…you'd want to do the talking."

Zach shook his head. "Tact doesn't seem to be my strong point lately."

"Okay, okay, I'll do it, if that's what you really want." She gazed silently down at the richly patterned carpet, collecting her thoughts. "I think we should tell him how much we both love and respect him and that we realize his actions have been motivated by his concern for us both and his desire for our happiness. We might even go so far as to thank him—" She stopped abruptly when Zach gave a snort of laughter. "All right, if you think you can do better, you do the talking."

"If it was up to me, I'd just tell that meddling old fool to stay out of our lives."

"Your sensitivity is really heartwarming," she muttered. "At first, this whole thing was one big joke to you and you really enjoyed tormenting me."

"You're exaggerating."

"As I recall, you played that cow-and-ten-chickens business for all it was worth, but I notice you're singing a different tune now and frankly—"

The library door opened, interrupting her tirade. Her grandfather and his longtime friend, veterinarian Dr. Burt Coleman, walked into the room.

"Zach. Janine," Gramps said, grinning broadly.

"Gramps," Janine burst out, rushing to her feet. They weren't prepared for this, and Zach was being impossible, so she said the first thing that came to mind. Pointing at Zach, she cried, "I don't know how you could possibly expect me to marry that man. He's stubborn and rude and we're completely wrong for each other." She was trembling by the time she finished, and collapsed gracelessly into the nearest chair.

"In case you haven't figured it out yet, you're no angel yourself," Zach said, scowling at Janine.

"Children, please," Gramps implored, advancing into the library, hands held out in supplication. "What seems to be the problem?"

"I want this settled," Zach said forcefully. "I'm not about to be saddled with Janine for a wife."

"As if I want to be *your* wife? In your dreams, Zachary Thomas!"

"We realize you mean well," Zach added, his face looking pinched. He completely ignored Janine. "But neither of us appreciates your matchmaking efforts."

Gramps walked over to the leather chair recently occupied by Zach and sat down. He smiled weakly at each of them, his shoulders sagging. "I thought… I'd hoped you two would grow fond of each other."

"I'm sorry to disappoint you, Gramps, I really am," Janine said, feeling guilty. "But Zach and I don't even like each other. We can barely carry on a civil conversation. He's argumentative and unreasonable—"

"And she's illogical and stubborn."

"I don't think we need to trade insults to get our message across," Janine said. Her face was so hot, she felt as if her cheeks were on fire.

"There's no hope?" Anton asked quietly.

"None whatsoever," Zach said. "Janine will make some man a wonderful wife one day, but unfortunately, he won't be me."

Her grandfather slumped against the back of his chair. "You're sure?"

"Positive," Zach said, loudly enough to convince Mrs. McCormick who was working in the kitchen.

"I love you, Gramps," said Janine, "and I'd do almost anything you wanted, but I can't and won't marry Zach. We know you have our best interests at heart, but neither of us is romantically interested in the other."

Burt Coleman, who stood by the library doors, looked as if he'd rather be anyplace else. His discomfort at witnessing this family scene was obvious. "I think it'd be best if I came back another time," he murmured as he turned to leave.

"No," Anton said, gesturing his friend back. "Come in. You've met Zachary Thomas, haven't you?"

The two men nodded at each other, but Janine noticed how rigidly Zach held himself. This meeting with Gramps hadn't gone the way she'd planned. She'd wanted everything to be calm and rational, a discussion uncluttered by messy emotions. Instead they'd ended up practically attacking each other, and worse, Janine had been the one to throw the first punch.

Without asking, she walked over to the sideboard and poured Gramps and his friend a cup of coffee. Burt sat across from her grandfather, clearly ill at ease.

"I should be going," Zach said starkly. "Good to see you again, Dr. Coleman."

"You, too," Gramps's friend said, glancing briefly at Zach. His puzzled gaze quickly returned to Anton.

"I'll walk you to the front door," Janine offered, eager to make her own escape. She closed the library door behind her.

Both she and Zach paused in the entryway. Janine tried to smile, but Zach was studying her intently, and her heart clenched like a fist inside her chest. They'd done what they had to do; she should be experiencing relief that the confrontation she'd dreaded for days was finally over. Instead she felt a strange sadness, one she couldn't fully understand or explain.

"Do you think we convinced him?"

"I don't know," Zach answered, keeping his tone low. "Your grandfather's a difficult man to read. Maybe he'll never bring up the subject of our marrying again and we're home free. I'd like to believe that's the case. It's just as likely, though, that he'll give us a few days' peace while he regroups. I don't expect him to back off quite so easily."

"No, I don't suppose he will."

Zach looked at his watch. "I should be going," he said again.

Janine was reluctant to see him leave, but there was no reason to detain him. Her hand was on the doorknob when she suddenly hesitated and turned around. "I didn't mean what I said in there," she blurted in a frenzy of regret.

"You mean you do want us to get married?"

"No," she cried, aghast. "I'm talking about when I said you were stubborn and rude. That isn't really true, but I had to come up with some reason for finding you objectionable. I don't really believe it, though."

"It was the same with me. I don't think you're so intolerable, either. I was trusting that you knew it was all an act for your grandfather's sake."

"I did," she assured him, but her pride *had* been dented, although that wasn't anything new.

"The last four days have been difficult," Zach went on. "Not only was Anton gloating about Scotland, but like I told you, he's been giving me these amused looks and odd little smiles. A couple of times I heard him saying something in his native tongue—I'm afraid to guess what."

"Well, I know what he was saying, because he's been doing the same thing to me. He's talking about babies."

"Babies?" Zach echoed, his eyes startled.

"Ours in particular."

One corner of Zach's mouth lifted, as if he found the thought of them as parents amusing. Or unlikely.

"That was my reaction, too. Every time I've seen Gramps in the last few days, he's started talking about… well, you know."

Zach nodded. "I do know. The situation hasn't been pleasant for either of us."

"Setting Gramps straight was for the best." But if that was the case, why did she feel this terrible letdown? "If he accepts us at our word—and he just might—then I guess this is goodbye."

"Yes, I suppose it is," Zach responded, but he made no effort to leave.

Janine was glad, because these few moments gave her the opportunity to memorize his features. She stored them for the future, when there'd be no reason for her to have anything but the most infrequent and perfunctory contact with Zach.

"Unless, of course, your grandfather continues to throw us together."

"Of course," Janine added quickly, hating the way her heart soared at the prospect. "Naturally, we'd have to confront him again. We can't allow ourselves to be his pawns."

Zach was about to say something else when the library door flew open and Burt Coleman hurried out, the urgency on his face unmistakable. "Janine, I think we should call a doctor for your grandfather."

"What's wrong?"

"I'm not sure. He's very pale and he seems to be having trouble breathing. It might be his heart."

With Zach following, Janine ran into the library, her own heart in jeopardy. Dr. Coleman was right—she'd never seen her grandfather look worse. His breath came noisily and his eyes were closed as he rested his head against the back of the chair. He looked old, far older than she could ever remember seeing him. She felt a sense of panic as she raced across the room to the desk where there was a phone.

"I'm fine," Gramps said hoarsely, opening his eyes and slowly straightening. He raised his hand in an effort to stop Janine. "There's no need for everyone to go into a tizzy just because an old man wants to rest his eyes for a few minutes." His smile was weak, his complexion still pale. "Now don't go calling any doctor. I was in last week for a checkup and I'm fit as a fiddle."

"You don't look so fit," Zach countered and Janine noticed that his face seemed almost as ashen as her grandfather's. Kneeling beside him, Zach grasped his wrist and began to check his pulse.

"I'm fine," Gramps insisted again.

"Are you in any pain?"

Gramps's gaze moved from Zach to Janine. "None," he answered, dismissing their concern with a shake of his head.

"Dr. Coleman?" Janine turned to her grandfather's longtime friend. "Should I phone his doctor?"

"What does Burt know about an old man and his heart?" Gramps objected. "Burt's expertise is with horses."

"Call the doctor. Having him checked over isn't going to hurt," Burt said after a moment.

"Fiddlesticks," Gramps roared. "I'm in perfect health."

"Good," Janine said brightly. "But I'll just let Dr. Madison reassure me." She punched out the phone number and had to speak loudly in order to be heard over her grandfather's protests. A couple of minutes later, she replaced the receiver and told Zach, "Dr. Madison says we can bring him in now."

"I'm not going to waste valuable time traipsing downtown. Burt and I were going to play a few hands of cribbage."

"We can play tomorrow," Dr. Coleman said gruffly. "You keep forgetting, Anton, we're both retiring."

"I've got things to do at the office."

"No, you don't," Zach said firmly. "You've got a doctor's appointment. Janine and I are going to escort you there and we're not going to listen to a single argument. Do you understand?"

Gramps's eyes narrowed as if he were preparing a loud

rebuttal. But he apparently changed his mind, because he relaxed and nodded sluggishly, reluctantly. "All right, if it'll make you feel better. But I'm telling you right now, you're going to look like a fine pair of fools."

The next two hours felt like two years to Janine. While Dr. Madison examined Gramps, she and Zach paced the waiting room. Several patients came and went.

"What could be taking so long?" Janine asked, wringing her hands nervously. "Do you think we did the right thing bringing him here? I mean, should we have gone directly to the hospital emergency room instead?"

"I doubt he would have agreed to that," Zach said.

"Do you honestly believe I would've listened to him?" She sat on the edge of a chair, her hands clenched so tightly together her knuckles whitened. "It's ridiculous, but I've never thought of Gramps as old. He's always been so healthy, so alive. I've never once considered what would happen if he became ill."

"He's going to be fine, Janine."

"You saw him," she cried, struggling against the dread and horror that churned inside her.

Zach's hand clasped hers and the fears that had torn at her composure only seconds earlier seemed to abate with his touch. He lent her confidence and strength, and she was badly in need of both.

When the door leading to the doctor's office opened, they leapt to their feet. Zach's hand tightened around hers before he released it.

"Dr. Madison can talk to you now," the nurse told them briskly. She led them to a compact office and explained that the doctor would be with them in a few minutes. Janine sat in one of the cushioned chairs and studied the framed diplomas on the walls.

Dr. Madison came into the room moments later. He paused to shake hands with Janine and then with Zach. "So far, my tests don't show anything we need to be too concerned about," he said, shuffling through the papers on his desk.

"What happened? Why was he so pale? Why was he gasping like that?" Janine demanded.

Dr. Madison frowned and folded his hands. "I'm really not sure. He claims he hadn't been doing any strenuous exercise."

"No, he was drinking coffee and talking to a friend."

Dr. Madison nodded. "Did he recently receive any negative news regarding his business?"

"No," Janine replied, glancing at Zach. "If anything, the business is doing better than ever. Gramps is getting ready to retire. I hate the thought of anything happening to him now."

"I don't know what to tell you," Dr. Madison said thoughtfully. "He should take it easy for the next couple of days, but there's nothing to worry about that I can find."

Janine sighed and closed her eyes. "Thank God."

"Your grandfather's getting dressed now," Dr. Madison said. He stood, signaling the end of their interview. "He'll join you in a few minutes."

"Thank you, Doctor," Zach said fervently.

Relief washed through Janine like a tidal wave. She got up and smiled at Zach. It was a smile full of gratitude. A smile one might share with a good friend when something has gone unexpectedly right. The kind of smile a woman would share with her husband. The thought hit her full force and she quickly lowered her eyes to cover her reaction.

When Gramps joined them in the waiting room, he looked immeasurably better. His blue eyes were filled with indignation and his skin tone was a healthy pink. "I hope the two of you are satisfied," he said huskily, buttoning his coat. "Most of the afternoon was wasted with this nonsense."

"You were a hundred percent correct, Gramps," Janine said brightly. "You're as fit as a fiddle and we wasted valuable cribbage time dragging you down here."

"I should've been back at the office hours ago," Zach put in, sharing a smile with Janine.

"And whose fault is that?" Anton muttered. He brushed off his sleeves as though he'd been forced to pick himself up off the floor, thanks to them.

Once more Janine and Zach shared an intimate look. They both seemed to realize what they were doing at the same moment and abruptly glanced away.

Zach drove Gramps and Janine back to the house, Gramps protesting loudly all the while that they'd overreacted and ruined his afternoon. His first concern seemed to be rescheduling his cribbage game.

Afterward Janine walked Zach to his car. "Thanks for everything," she said, folding her arms to repress the sudden urge to hug him.

"If you're worried about anything, give me a call," Zach said as he opened the car door. He hesitated fractionally, then lifted his head and gazed directly into her eyes. "Goodbye, Janine."

She raised her hand in farewell as a sadness settled over her. "Goodbye, Zach," she said forcing a lightness into her voice. "Thanks again."

For the longest moment, he said nothing, although his eyes still held hers. Finally he repeated, "Call me if you need anything, all right?"

"I will."

But they both knew she wouldn't. It was best to end this now. Make a clean break.

Janine stood in the driveway until Zach's car was well out of sight. Only then did she return to the house.

"This is really good of you," Patty St. John whispered, handing the sleeping infant to Janine. "I don't know what I would've done if I'd had to drag Michael to the interview. I need this job so badly."

"I'm happy to help." Janine peered down at the sweet face of the sleeping six-month-old baby. "I apologize if it was inconvenient for you to bring Michael here, but I've been sticking close to the house for the past few days. My grandfather hasn't been feeling well."

"It wasn't any problem," Patty whispered, setting the diaper bag on the floor. She glanced around the house. "This place is really something. I didn't have any idea that you… well, you know, that you were so well off."

"This house belongs to my grandfather," Janine explained, gently rocking Michael in her arms. The warmth and tenderness she felt toward the baby was a revelation. She supposed it was understandable, though. Gramps had spent last week constantly telling her what remarkable babies she and Zach would have, and here she was with one in her arms. All the maternal instincts she didn't know she had came bubbling to the surface.

"I'll be back in about an hour," Patty said. She leaned over and kissed Michael's soft forehead. He didn't so much as stir.

Still carrying the baby, Janine walked to the door with her friend. "Good luck."

Patty gave a strained smile and crossed her fingers. "Thanks. Here's hoping."

No sooner had the door closed than Anton walked into the living room. He paused when he saw Janine rocking in the old chair that had once belonged to his wife. His face relaxed into a broad grin.

"Is that a baby you've got there?"

Janine smiled. "Nothing gets past you, does it, Gramps?"

He chuckled. "Who's he belong to?"

"Patty St. John. She's another volunteer at the Friendship Club. She quit her job when Michael was born, but now she'd like to find some part-time work."

"Are you volunteering to babysit for her?"

"Just for today," Janine explained. "Her regular sitter has the flu."

"I thought you were going out?" Gramps muttered with a slight frown. "You haven't left the house all week. Fact is, you're becoming a recluse."

"I've had other things to do," she returned, not raising her voice for fear of disturbing the baby.

"Right. The other things you had to do were keep an eye on your grandfather," he said. "You think I didn't notice? How long do you plan on being my shadow? You should be gadding about, doing the things you normally do, instead of worrying yourself sick over me. I'm fine, I tell you. When are you going to listen to me?"

"Dr. Madison said to watch you for a few days."

"It's been a week."

Janine was well aware of it. In fact, she was beginning to suffer from cabin fever. She'd hardly spoken to anyone all week. She hadn't heard from Zach, either. Not that she'd expected to. Perhaps Gramps had taken them at their word. Or else he was doing what Zach had suspected and simply regrouping for the next skirmish.

Michael stirred in her arms and she held him against her shoulder, rocking him back to sleep.

"I'm going to the office tomorrow," Gramps announced, eyeing her defiantly as though he anticipated a challenge.

"We'll see," she said, delaying the showdown.

Yawning, baby Michael raised his head and looked around. Gramps's weathered face broke into a tender smile. "All right," he agreed easily. "We'll see." He offered the little boy his finger and Michael gripped it firmly in his hand, then started to chew on it.

Janine laughed, enjoying her grandfather's reaction to the baby. After a couple of minutes, Michael grew tired of the game with Anton's finger and yawned again, arching his back. Janine decided it was time to check his diaper. She got up, reaching for the bag Patty had left.

"I'll be back in a minute," she told her grandfather.

She was halfway across the living room when Anton stopped her. "You look good with a baby in your arms. Natural."

Janine smiled. She didn't dare let him know it felt good, too.

While she was changing the baby, she heard the doorbell. Normally she would've answered it herself, but since she was busy, either Gramps or Mrs. McCormick would see to it.

Michael was happily investigating his toes and making cooing sounds as Janine pulled up his plastic pants. "You're going to have to be patient with me, kiddo," she told him, carefully untwisting the legs of his corduroy overalls and snapping them back in place. When she'd finished, she lifted him high above her head and laughed when Michael squealed delightedly. They were both smiling when she returned to the living room.

Gramps was sitting in the chair closest to the grand piano, and across from him sat Zach.

Janine's heart lurched as her eyes flew instantly to Zach's. "Hello, Zach," she said, striving to sound as nonchalant as possible, tucking Michael against her hip. She cast a suspicious glare at her grandfather, who smiled back, the picture of innocence.

"Zach brought some papers for me to sign," Gramps explained.

"I didn't mean to interrupt you," she apologized. Her eyes refused to leave Zach's. He smiled that slanted half-smile of his that wasn't really a smile at all. The one she'd always found so appealing. Something seemed to pass between them—a tenderness, a hunger.

"Janine's not interrupting anything, is she?" Gramps asked.

"No," Zach responded gruffly. He seemed to be taking in everything about her, from her worn jeans and oversize pink sweatshirt to the gurgling baby riding so casually on her hip.

Gramps cleared his throat. "If you'll excuse me a moment, I'll go get a pen," he said, leaving them alone together.

"How have you been?" Zach asked, his eyes riveted to her.

"Fine. Just fine."

"I see you haven't had any problems finding another admirer," he murmured, nodding at Michael.

Zach kept his tone light and teasing, and Janine followed his lead. "Michael St. John," she said, turning slightly to give Zach a better view of the baby, "meet Mr. Zachary Thomas."

"Hello," Zach said, holding up his palm. He seemed awkward around children. "I take it you're watching him for a friend."

"Yes, another volunteer. She's looking for a part-time job, but she's having a problem finding one with the right hours. She's at an interview."

"I see."

Janine sank down on the ottoman in front of Zach's chair and set Michael on her knee. She focused her attention on gently bouncing the baby. "Now that your life's back in order," she said playfully, glancing up at Zach, "have you discovered how much you miss me?"

He chuckled softly. "It's been how long since we last talked? Seven days? I'm telling you, Janine, I haven't had a single disagreement with anyone in all that time."

"That should make you happy."

"You're right. It should." He shook his head. "Unfortunately it doesn't. You know what, Janine? I was bored to death. So the answer is yes, I missed you."

Seven

Before Janine could respond, Gramps wandered back into the living room, pen in hand.

"So where are those papers you wanted me to sign?" he asked Zach.

With obvious reluctance, Zach tore his gaze from Janine's. He opened his briefcase and pulled out several papers. "Go ahead and read over these contracts."

"Do you need me to sign them or not?" her grandfather grumbled.

Once more Zach dragged his gaze away from Janine. "Please."

Muttering under his breath, Gramps took the documents to the small table, scanned them and quickly scrawled his name.

Janine knew she should leave; the two men probably had business to discuss. But she couldn't make herself stand up and walk away. Not when Zach had actually admitted that he'd missed her.

Gramps broke into her thoughts. "Janine, I—"

"I was just going," she said. She clambered to her feet, securing her hold on Michael.

But Gramps surprised her.

"I want you to stay," he declared. "I wanted to talk to you and Zach. Fact is, I owe you both an apology. Burt and I had a good long talk the other day and I told him how I'd tried to arrange a marriage between the two of you. He laughed and called me an old fool, said it was time I stepped out of the Dark Ages."

"Gramps," Janine began anxiously, unwilling to discuss the subject that had brought such contention, "Zach and I have already settled that issue. We understand why you did it and…and we've laid it to rest, so there's no need to apologize."

"I'm afraid there is," Gramps insisted. "Don't worry, Burt pointed out the error of my ways. Haven't got any new tricks up my sleeve." He rose to bring Zach the signed papers, then sat wearily in the chair across from them. He'd never looked so fragile, so old and beaten.

"Janine's a wonderful woman," Zach said unexpectedly. "I want you to know I realize that."

"She's got her faults," Gramps responded, pulling a cigar from his pocket, "but she's pretty enough to compensate."

"Thank you very much," Janine whispered sarcastically and was rewarded with a grin from Zach. Gramps didn't seem to hear her; if he had, he was ignoring her comment.

"I only want the best for my granddaughter, but when I approached her about marrying you, she made a big fuss. Fact is, it would've been easier to pluck a live chicken. She said she needed *romance*." Gramps pronounced the word as if it evoked instant amusement.

"There isn't a woman alive who doesn't need romance," she wailed, defending herself.

"I'm from the old country," Gramps continued. "Romance wasn't something I knew about from personal experience, and when I asked Janine to explain, she had some trouble defining it herself. Said it was a tryst on the moors and a bunch of other hogwash. That's the reason I sent you both to Scotland."

"We figured that out soon enough," Zach said dryly.

"As you'll recall," Janine found herself saying, "that definition was off the top of my head. Romance isn't easy to explain, especially to a man who scoffs at the entire idea."

Anton chuckled, moving the cigar to the side of his mouth. "It's unfortunate the two of you caught on to me so soon. I was looking forward to arranging the desperate passion part."

"Desperate passion?" Zach echoed.

"Yes. Janine said that was part of romance, too. I may be over seventy, but I know about passion. Oh, yes, Anna and I learned about that together." His blue eyes took on a faraway look and his lips curved in the gentlest of smiles. He glanced at Janine and his smile widened.

"I'm glad you find this so funny," Janine snapped.

Gramps dismissed her anger with a flick of his hand and turned to Zach. "I suppose you've discovered she's got something of a temper?"

"From the start!" Zach declared.

"It may come as a surprise to you, Zachary Thomas," Janine said, "but you're not exactly Mr. Perfect."

"No," Zach countered smoothly. "I suspect your grandfather was thinking more along the lines of Mr. Right."

"Oh, brother!"

"Now, children, I don't see that arguing will do any good. I've willingly accepted defeat. Trying to interest you in each other was an old man's way of setting his world right before he passes on."

The doorbell chimed and, grateful for an excuse to leave

the room, Janine hurried to answer it. Patty St. John stood there, her face cheerless, her posture forlorn.

"I wasn't expecting you back so soon."

"They'd already hired someone," Patty said, walking into the foyer and automatically taking her son from Janine. She held the infant close, as if his small warm body might absorb her disappointment. "I spent the whole day psyching myself up for this interview and it was all for nothing. Ah, well, who wants to be a receptionist at a dental clinic, anyway?"

"I'm so sorry," Janine murmured.

"Was Michael any problem?"

"None at all," Janine told her, wishing she could think of something encouraging to say. "I'll get his things for you."

It took Janine only a minute to collect Michael's diaper bag, but when she returned to the entryway, she discovered Zach talking to Patty. Janine saw him hand her friend a business card and overheard him suggesting she report to the Human Resources department early the following week.

"Thanks again," Patty said enthusiastically. She lifted Michael's hand. "Say bye-bye," she coaxed the baby, then raised his arm and moved it for him.

Janine let her out, with Zach standing next to her. Gramps had gone into the library, and Zach glanced anxiously in that direction before lowering his voice to a whisper. "Can you meet me later?"

"When?"

"In an hour." He checked his watch, then mentioned the number of a pier along the waterfront. Janine had just managed to clarify the location when Gramps came back.

Zach left the house soon afterward and Janine was able to invent an excuse half an hour later. Gramps was reading and didn't bother to look up from his mystery novel, although Janine thought she saw the hint of a smile, as if he knew full well what she was doing. She didn't linger to investigate. The last time she'd agreed to a clandestine meeting with Zach had been the night they'd met at the Italian restaurant, when she'd all but blurted out the arrangements to her grandfather.

Zach was waiting for her, grim-faced. He stood against the pier railing, the wind whipping his raincoat against his legs.

"I hope there's a good reason for this, because I don't think Gramps was fooled," Janine said when she joined him. "He'll figure out that I'm meeting you if I'm not back soon." She buried her hands in her pockets, turning away from the wind. The afternoon sky was gray, threatening rain.

"Am I interrupting anything important?"

"Not really." Janine wouldn't have minded listing several pressing engagements, but she'd canceled everything for the next two weeks, wanting to stay close to home in case her grandfather needed her.

Zach clasped his hands behind his back and started strolling down the pier, the wind ruffling his neatly trimmed hair. Janine followed. "I'm worried about Anton," he said suddenly, stopping and facing Janine.

"Why?" Perhaps there was something she didn't know about his health, something Dr. Madison hadn't told her.

"He doesn't look good."

"What do you mean?" Although she asked, she already knew the answer. She'd felt the same thing during the past few days. Gramps was aging right before her eyes.

"I think you know."

"I do," she admitted reluctantly.

"Furthermore I'm worried about you."

"Me?" she asked, her voice rising. "Whatever for?"

"If, God forbid, anything should happen to Anton," Zach said, drawing in a ragged breath, "what will happen to you? You don't have any other family, do you?"

"No," she told him, her chest tightening at the thought. "But I'm not worried about it. There are several friends who are very close to the family, Burt Coleman for one, so I wouldn't be cast into the streets like an orphan. I'll have the house and more than enough money to live on. There's no need for you to be concerned. I'm not."

"I see." Zach frowned as he walked to the farthest end of the pier, seeming to fix his gaze on the snow-capped peaks of the Olympic mountains far in the distance.

Janine hurried to catch up with him. "Why do you ask?" she demanded.

"He's always said he was concerned about your not having any other family. But it wasn't until recently that I really understood his motivation in trying to arrange a marriage between us."

"Good, then you can explain it to me, because frankly, I'm at a loss. He admitted he was wrong, but I don't think he's given up on the idea. He'd do just about anything to see the two of us together."

"I *know* he hasn't given up on us."

"What did he do? Up the ante?"

Zach chuckled and his features relaxed into a smile as he met her eyes. "Nothing so explicit. He simply told me that he's getting on in years and hates the thought of you being left so alone when he dies."

"I'll adjust. I'm not a child," she said, although her heart filled with dread at the thought of life without her cantankerous, generous, good-hearted grandfather.

"I don't doubt you would." Zach hesitated, then resumed

strolling, apparently taking it for granted that she'd continue to follow him.

"I have plenty of friends."

Zach nodded, although Janine wasn't certain he'd heard her. He stopped abruptly and turned to look at her. "What I'm about to say is going to shock you."

Janine stared up at him, not knowing what to expect.

"When you think about it, our getting married does make an odd kind of sense."

"What?" Janine couldn't believe he was saying this.

"From a practical point of view," he added quickly. "Since the business is in both our names, and we're both alone. I realize I'm not exactly Prince Charming..." Zach paused as if waiting for her to contradict him. When she didn't, he frowned but went on. "The problem has more to do with whether we can get along. I don't even know if we're capable of going an entire day without arguing."

"What are you suggesting?" Janine asked, wondering if she was reading more into this conversation than he intended.

"Nothing yet. I'm trying to be as open and as honest as I can." He gripped the railing with both hands and braced himself, as though expecting a fierce wind to uproot him.

"Are you saying that our getting married wouldn't be such a bad idea after all?" Janine ventured. Initially he'd made a joke of the whole thing. Then he'd seen it as an annoyance. Now he seemed to have changed his mind again.

"I...don't know yet. I'm mulling over my thoughts, which I'm willing to confess are hopelessly tangled at the moment."

"Mine aren't much better."

"Does this mean you'd consider the possibility?"

"I don't know, either." Janine had been so sure she was

in love with Brian. She remembered how he'd done everything a romantic hero should do. He'd sent her flowers, said all the things a woman longs to hear—and then he'd casually broken her heart. When she thought about it now, she couldn't really imagine herself married to Brian. But Zach, who'd never made any romantic gestures, somehow seemed to fit almost naturally into her life. And yet…

As she pondered these contradictions, Zach started walking again. "I'm not the kind of husband you want," he was saying, "and not nearly as good as you deserve. I'd like to be the man of your dreams, but I'm not. Nor am I likely to change at this stage of my life." He paused, chancing a look in her direction. "What are you thinking?"

Janine sighed and concentrated as hard as she could, but her mind was filled with so many questions, so many doubts. "Would you mind kissing me?"

Shock widened his dark eyes. He glanced around, then scowled. "Now? Right here?"

"Yes."

"There are people everywhere. Is this really necessary?"

"Would I ask you to do it if it wasn't?"

As he searched her face, she moistened her lips and looked up at him, tilting her head slightly. Zach slipped one arm around her waist and drew her close. Her heart reacted immediately, leaping into a hard fast rhythm that made her feel breathless. He lifted her chin with his free hand and slowly lowered his mouth to hers.

The instant his lips grazed hers, Janine was flooded with a sensual languor. It was as if they'd returned to the moors of Scotland with the full moon overhead, pouring magic onto their small corner of earth. Everything around them faded. No longer did Janine hear the sound of water slapping against the wooden columns of the pier. The blustery day went calm.

She supported her hands on his chest, breathing erratically, when he stopped kissing her. Neither spoke. Janine wanted to, but none of her faculties seemed to be working. She parted her lips and Zach lowered his mouth to hers again. Only this time it was a full-fledged kiss, deep and probing. His hands slid up her back as his mouth abandoned hers to explore the sweep of her neck.

Several glorious moments passed before he shuddered, raised his head and drew back, although he continued to hold her. "Does that answer your question?"

"No," she answered, hating the way her voice trembled. "I'm afraid it only raised more."

"I know what you mean," Zach admitted, briefly closing his eyes. "This last week apart was an eye-opener for me. I thought I'd be glad to put this matter between your grandfather and us to rest. If you want the truth, I thought I'd be glad to be rid of you. I was convinced you felt the same way." He paused, waiting for a response.

"The days seemed so empty," she whispered.

His eyes burned into hers, and he nodded. "You were constantly on my mind, and I found myself wishing you were there to talk to." He groaned. "Heaven knows you deserve a different kind of husband than I could possibly be."

"What about you? I've heard you say a hundred times that when it comes to finding a wife, you'll choose your own."

He blinked, as though he didn't recognize his words. Then he shrugged. "Once I got to know you, I realized you're not so bad."

"Thanks." So much for wine and roses and sweet nothings whispered in her ear. But then again, she'd had those things and they hadn't brought her happiness.

"Like I said—and I hate to admit it—our getting married makes sense. We seem to like each other well enough, and there's a certain…attraction." Zach was frowning a little as he spoke. "It would be a smart move for both of us from a financial viewpoint, as well." He took her by the shoulders and gazed into her eyes. "The question is, Janine, can I make you happy?"

Her heart melted at the way he said it, at the simplicity and sincerity of his words. "What about you?" she asked. "Will you be content being married to me?"

The apprehension in his face eased. "I think so. We'll be good for each other. This isn't any grand passion. But I'm fond of you and you're fond of me."

"Fond?" Janine repeated, breaking away.

"What's wrong with that?"

"I hate that word," Janine said through gritted teeth. "*Fond* sounds so…watered down. So weak. I'm not looking for a grand passion, as you put it, but I want a whole lot more than *fond*." She gestured dramatically with her hands. "A man is fond of his dog or a favorite place to eat, not his wife." She spoke so vehemently that she was starting to attract attention from other walkers. "Would it be too much for you to come up with another word?"

"Stop looking at me as if it were a matter of life and death," he said.

"It's important," she insisted.

Zach looked distinctly uncomfortable. "I run a business. There are more than three hundred outlets in fifty states. I know the office-supply business inside out, but I'm not good with words. If you don't like the word *fond,* you choose another one."

"All right," she said thoughtfully, biting the corner of one lip. Her eyes brightened. "How about *cherish?*"

"Cherish." Zach repeated it as if he'd never heard the word before. "Okay, it's a deal. I'll cherish you."

"And I'll cherish you," she said emphatically, nodding with satisfaction.

They walked along the pier until they came to a seafood stand, where Zach bought them each a cup of steaming clam chowder. They found an unoccupied picnic table and sat down, side by side.

Occasionally they stopped eating to smile at each other. An oddly exciting sensation attacked Janine's stomach whenever that happened. Finally, finishing her soup, she licked the back of her white plastic spoon. She kept her eyes carefully lowered as she said, "I want to make sure I understand. Did we or did we not just agree to get married?"

Zach hesitated, his spoon halfway between his cup and his mouth as an odd look crossed his face. He swallowed once. "We decided to go through with it, both accepting that this isn't the traditional love match, but one based on practical and financial advantages."

Janine dropped her spoon in the plastic cup. "If that's the case, the wedding is off."

Zach threw back his head and stared into the sky. "*Now* what did I say that was so terrible?"

"Financial and practical advantages! You make it sound about as appealing as a dentist appointment. There's got to be more of a reason than that for us to get married."

Shrugging, Zach gestured helplessly with his hands. "I already told you I wasn't any good at this. Perhaps we'd do better if you explained why you're willing to marry me."

Before she could prevent it, a smile tugged at her mouth. "You won't like my reason any better than I like yours." She looked around to ensure that no one could overhear, then leaned toward him. "When we kissed a few minutes ago, the earth moved. I know it's a dreadful cliché—the worst—but that's exactly what I felt."

"The earth moved," Zach repeated deadpan."Well, we are in an earthquake zone."

Janine rolled her eyes. "It happened when we were in Scotland, too. I don't know what's going on between us or even if we're doing the right thing, but there's definitely… something. Something special."

She wasn't surprised when Zach scowled. "You mean to say you're willing to marry me because I'm good at kissing?"

"It makes more sense to me than that stuff about financial advantages."

"You were absolutely correct," he said evenly. "I don't like your reason. Is there anything else that makes the prospect appealing?"

Janine giggled. "You know," she reflected, "Gramps was right. We're going to be good for each other."

A flash of light warmed his eyes and his hand reached for hers. He entwined their fingers as their eyes met. "Yes, we are."

The wedding was arranged so fast that Janine barely had time to reconsider their decision. They applied for a license that same afternoon. When they returned to the house, Gramps shouted for joy, slapped Zach on the back and repeatedly hugged Janine, whispering that she'd made an old man very happy.

Janine was so busy, the days and nights soon blended together and she lost all track of time. There were so many things to do—fittings and organizing caterers and inviting guests—that for the next five days she didn't talk to Zach even once.

The day before the ceremony, the garden was bustling with activity. Mrs. McCormick was supervising the men who were assembling the wedding canopy and setting up tables and chairs.

Exhausted, Janine wandered outside and glanced up at the bold blue sky, praying the sunshine would hold for at least another day. The lawn was lush and green, and freshly mowed. The roses were in bloom, perfuming the air with their rich fragrance.

"Janine."

She recognized his voice immediately. She turned to discover Zach striding purposefullly toward her, and her heart reacted of its own accord. Janine felt as though they'd been apart for a year instead of just a few days. She wore jeans and an old university sweatshirt and wished she'd chosen something less casual. In contrast, Zach was strikingly formal, dressed in a handsome pin-striped suit and dark tie. She was willing to admit she didn't know him as well as she should—as well as a woman who was about to become his wife. His habits, his likes and dislikes, were a mystery to her, yet those details seemed minor. It was the inner Zach she was coming to understand. Everything she'd learned assured her she'd made the right decision.

"Hello," she called, walking toward him. She saw that he looked as tired as she felt. Obviously he'd been busy, too, although the wedding preparations had been left to her.

They met halfway and stopped abruptly, gazing at each other. Zach didn't hug her or make any effort to touch her.

"How are you holding up?" he asked.

"Fine," she answered. "How about you?"

"I'll live." He glanced over at the activity near the rose garden and sighed. "Is there someplace we can talk privately?"

"Sure." Janine's heart leapt to her throat at his sober tone. "Is everything all right?"

He reassured her with a quick nod. "Of course."

"I don't think anyone's in the kitchen."

"Good." Hand at her elbow, he guided her toward the house. She pulled out a chair with trembling fingers and sat down at the oak table. As he lowered himself into a chair opposite her, she gripped the edge of the table. His eyes had never seemed darker. "Tomorrow's the day."

He said this as if he expected it to come as a shock to her. It didn't—but she understood what he was saying. Time was closing in on them, and if they wanted to back out, it would have to be now.

"Believe me, I know," she said, and her fingers tightened on the table. "Have you had a change of heart?"

"Have you?"

"No, but then again, I haven't had much time to think."

"I've done nothing *but* think about this wedding," Zach said, raking his hands through his hair.

"And?"

He shrugged. "We may both have been fools to agree to this."

"It all happened so fast," Janine said in a weak voice. "One minute we agreed on the word *cherish,* and the next thing I remember, we were deciding we'd be good for each other."

"Don't forget the kissing part," he added. "As I recall, that had quite a bit to do with this decision."

"If you're having second thoughts, I'd rather you said so now than after the ceremony."

His eyes narrowed fleetingly before he shook his head. "No."

"You're sure?"

He answered her by leaning forward, slipping his hand

behind her neck and kissing her soundly. Tenderly. When they broke apart, they were silent. Not talking, not wanting to.

Janine stared into his dark warm eyes and suddenly she could hardly breathe.

"This is going to be a real marriage," he said forcefully.

She nodded. "I certainly hope so, Mr. Thomas." And her voice was strong and clear.

Less than twenty-four hours later, Janine stood at Zach's side, prepared to pledge her life to his. She'd never felt more uncertain—or, at the same time, more confident—of anything she'd ever done.

Zach seemed to grasp what she was feeling. His eyes held hers as she repeated the words that would bind them.

When she'd finished, Zach slid his arm around her waist and drew her close. The pastor smiled down on them, then looked to the fifty or so family friends who'd gathered on Anton's lawn and said, "I present to you Mr. and Mrs. Zachary Thomas."

A burst of applause followed his words.

Before Janine fully realized what was happening, they were mingling with their guests. One minute she was standing in front of the pastor, trembling but unafraid, and the next she was a wife.

"Janine, Janine!" Pam rushed to her side before anyone else could. "You look so gorgeous," she said softly, and bright tears shone in her eyes.

Janine hugged her young friend. "Thank you, sweetheart."

Pam gazed up at Zach and shook her head. "He sure is handsome."

"I think so, too."

Zach arched his brows, cocked his head toward her and murmured, "You never told me that."

"There's no need for you to be so smug."

"My children," Gramps said, rejoining them. He hugged Janine, and she saw that his eyes were as bright as Pam's. "You've never been more beautiful. I swear you look more like my Anna every year."

It was the highest compliment Gramps could have paid her. From the pictures Gramps kept of his wife, Janine knew her grandmother had been exceptionally beautiful.

"Thank you," she said, kissing his cheek.

"I have something for you." Pam thrust a neatly wrapped box into Janine's hands. "I made them myself," she announced proudly. "I think Zach will like them, too."

"Oh, Pam, you shouldn't have," Janine murmured. Sitting on a cushioned folding chair, she peeled away the paper and lifted the lid. The moment she did, her breath jammed in her throat. Inside were the sheerest white baby-doll pajamas Janine had ever seen. Her smile faltered as she glanced up to see half a dozen people staring at her.

Zach's hand, resting at the nape of Janine's neck, tightened as he spoke, though his voice was warm and amused. "You're right, Pam. I like them very much."

Eight

Janine sat next to Zach in the front seat of his car. Dressed in a pink suit and matching broad-brimmed hat, she clutched her small floral bouquet. Although the wedding had been arranged in seven short days, it had been a lovely affair.

Zach had taken care of planning the short honeymoon. All he could spare was three days, so instead of scheduling anything elaborate, he'd suggested they go to his summer place in Ocean Shores, a coastal town two and a half hours from Seattle by car. Janine had happily agreed.

"So you think I'm handsome?" Zach asked, keeping his eyes on the road. Neither of them had said much since they'd set off.

"I knew if I told you, it'd go straight to your head, and obviously I was right," she answered. Then, unable to hold back a wide yawn, she pressed one hand to her mouth.

"You're exhausted."

"Are you always this astute?"

"Testy, too."

"I don't mean to be," she apologized. She'd been up since before five that morning and in fact, hadn't slept well all week. This wasn't exactly the ideal way to start a marriage. There was an added stress, too, that had to do with the honeymoon. Zach had made it understood that he intended their marriage to be real, but surely he didn't expect them to share a bed so soon. Or did he?

Every now and then as they drove, she glanced in his direction, wondering what, if anything, she should say. Even if she did decide to broach this delicate subject, she wasn't sure how.

"Go ahead and rest," Zach suggested. "I'll wake you when we arrive."

"It should be soon, shouldn't it?"

"Another fifteen minutes or so."

"Then I'll stay awake." Nervously, she twisted the small floral bouquet. Unwrapping Pam's gift had made her all the more apprehensive, but delaying the subject any longer was impossible.

"Zach…are we going to…you know…" she stammered, feeling like a naive schoolgirl.

"If you're referring to what I think you're referring to, the answer is no. So relax."

"No?" He didn't need to sound so casual about it, as if it hardly mattered one way or the other.

"Why do you ask, Janine? Are you having second thoughts about…that?"

"No. Just some reservations."

"Don't worry. When it happens, it happens. The last thing we need is that kind of pressure."

"You're right," she answered, relieved.

"We need some time to feel comfortable. There's no reason to rush into the physical aspect of our marriage, is there?"

"None whatsoever," she agreed quickly, perhaps too

quickly, because when she looked at him again, Zach was frowning. Yet he seemed so willing to wait, as though their lovemaking was of minor importance. But as he'd said, this marriage wasn't one of grand passion. Well, *that* was certainly true.

Before another five minutes had passed, Zach left the highway and drove into the resort town of Ocean Shores. He didn't stop in the business district, but headed down a side street toward the beach. The sun was setting as he pulled into a driveway and turned off the engine.

Janine was too enthralled with the house to say a word.

The wind whipped at them ferociously when they climbed out of the car. Janine held on to her hair with one hand, still clutching the flowers, and to Zach with the other. The sun cast a pink and gold reflection over the rolling hills of sand.

"Home, sweet home," Zach said, nudging her toward the house.

The front door opened before they reached it and a trim middle-aged man stepped onto the porch to greet them. He was grinning broadly. "Hello, Zach. I trust you had a safe trip."

"We did."

"Everything's ready. The cupboards are stocked. The firewood's stacked by the side of the house, and dinner's prepared."

"Wonderful, Harry, thanks." Zach placed his hand on Janine's shoulder. "This is my wife, Janine," he said. "We were married this afternoon."

"Your wife?" Harry repeated, looking more than a little surprised. "Why, that's fantastic. Congratulations to you both."

"Thank you," Janine said politely.

"Harry Gleason looks after the place for me when I'm not around."

"Pleased to meet you, Harry."

"So Zach got himself a wife," Harry said, rubbing his jaw in apparent disbelief. "I couldn't be more—"

"Delighted," a frowning Zach supplied for him, ushering Janine toward the front door.

"Right," Harry said. "I couldn't be more delighted."

Janine tilted back her head to survey the sprawling single-story house.

"Go on inside," Zach said. "I'll get the luggage."

Janine started to protest, suddenly wanting him to follow the traditional wedding custom of carrying her over the threshold. She paused, and Zach gave her a puzzled look. "Is something wrong?"

"No." She had no real grounds for complaint. She wasn't even sure why it mattered. Swallowing her disappointment, she made her way into the house. She stopped just inside the front door and gazed with wide-eyed wonder at the immense living room with its three long sofas and several upholstered chairs. A brick fireplace took up an entire wall; another was dominated by a floor-to-ceiling window that looked over the ocean. Drawn to it, Janine watched powerful waves crash against the shore.

Zach followed her inside, carrying their luggage, barely taking time to appreciate the scene before him. "Harry's putting the car away," he said.

"This place is incredible," Janine breathed, gesturing around her. She placed the flowers on the coffee table, then trailed after Zach into a hallway, off which were four bedrooms and an equal number of baths. At the back of the house, she found an exercise room, an office and an ultramodern kitchen where a pot of coq au vin was simmering.

In the formal dining room, the polished mahogany table was set for two. On the deck, designed to take advantage of the ocean view, she discovered a steaming hot tub, along with a bottle of French champagne on ice.

Zach returned as she wandered back into the kitchen and a strained silence fell between them. He was the first to speak. "I put your suitcases in the master bedroom," he said brusquely. "I'm in the one across the hall."

She nodded, not taking time to question her growing sense of disappointment. They'd agreed to delay their wedding night, hadn't they?

"Are you hungry?" he asked, walking to the stove and lifting the pot's lid, as she'd done earlier.

"Only a little. I was thinking about slipping into the hot tub, unless you want to eat first."

"Sure. The hot tub's fine. Whatever you want."

Janine unpacked and located her swimsuit, then changed into it quickly. The warm water sounded appealing. And maybe it would help her relax. Draping a beach towel over her arm, she hurried into the kitchen, but Zach was nowhere to be seen. Not waiting for him, she walked out to the deck and stepped gingerly into the hot tub. The water felt like a soothing liquid blanket and she slid down, letting it lap just under her breasts.

Zach sauntered onto the deck a minute later, still in his suit. He stopped short when he saw her. "I…didn't realize you'd be out so soon," he said, staring at her with undisguised appreciation. He inhaled sharply and occupied himself by uncorking the bottle of champagne, then pouring a liberal glass. When he'd gulped it down, he reached for a second one and filled it for Janine.

"You're coming in, aren't you?" she asked, when he handed her the crystal flute.

"No," he said abruptly. "I won't join you, after all. There were several things I wasn't able to finish at the office this week, and I thought I'd look over some papers. You go ahead and enjoy yourself."

He was going to *work* on their wedding night! But she didn't feel she had any right to comment or complain. She was determined to conceal her bitter disappointment.

"The water's wonderful," she said, as cheerfully as she could manage, hoping her words would convince him to join her.

Zach nodded, but his eyes now avoided Janine. "It looks…great." He strode to the end of the deck, ran his fingers through his hair, then twisted around to face her. He seemed about to say something, but evidently changed his mind.

Baffled by his odd behavior, Janine set aside her glass of champagne and stood up so abruptly that water sloshed over the edge of the tub. "You don't need to say it," she muttered, climbing out and grabbing her towel.

"Say what?"

"You warned me before the wedding, so I walked into this with my eyes wide open. Well, you needn't worry. I got the message the minute we arrived at the house."

"What message is that?"

"Never mind." Vigorously, she rubbed her arms with the towel.

"No," he said. "I want you to tell me."

Against her better judgment, she pointed a quaking finger at the front door. "You went out of your way to tell me how *fond* of me you were and how there wasn't going to be any grand passion. Great. Perfect. I agreed to those terms. That's all fine with me, but—"

"But what?"

Mutely, she shook her head.

He sighed. "Oh, great, we're fighting. I suppose you're going to ask for a divorce and make this the shortest marriage in Washington state history."

Janine paled. Divorce was such an ugly word, and it struck her as viciously as a slap. Despite her efforts, scalding tears spilled down her cheeks. With as much dignity as she could muster, which admittedly wasn't a lot, Janine went back inside the house, leaving a wet trail in her wake.

"Janine!" Zach shouted, following her into the kitchen. "Listen, Janine, I didn't intend to argue with you."

She turned abruptly. "This marriage doesn't mean anything to you, does it? You won't even interrupt your work long enough to…to act like a man who just got married."

With her head held high, she stared past him to a painting of yellow flowers on the dining room wall. When her tears blurred the flowers beyond recognition, she defiantly rubbed her eyes.

"I'm sorry," he whispered, reaching for her as if he needed to hold her. But then his arms fell to his sides. "I should've realized wedding traditions would be important to you. Like that carrying-you-over-the-threshold business. I'm sorry," he said again. "I completely forgot."

"It's not just that, it's everything. How many men bring a briefcase with them on their honeymoon? I feel like…like excess baggage in your life—and we haven't even been married for twenty-four hours."

Zach looked perplexed. "What does catching up on my reading have to do with any of this?"

His question only irritated her more. "You don't have the foggiest notion of how impossible you are, do you?"

He didn't answer right away, but seemed to be studying her, weighing his answer before he spoke. "I just thought

I might have a chance to read over some papers," he said slowly. "Apparently that bothers you."

Janine placed her hands on her hips. "Yes, it bothers me."

Zach frowned. "Since we've agreed to delay the honeymoon part, what would you suggest we do for the next three days?"

"Couldn't we spend the time having fun? Becoming better acquainted?"

"I guess I do seem like a stranger to you," he said. "No wonder you're so nervous."

"I am *not* nervous. Just tired and trying hard not to say or do anything that'll make you think of me as a…a nag."

"A nag?" Zach repeated incredulously. "I don't think of you as anything but lovely. The truth is, I'm having one heck of a time keeping my eyes off you."

"You are?" The towel she was holding slipped unnoticed to the floor. "I thought you said you didn't know how to say anything romantic."

"That was romantic?"

"And very sweet. I was beginning to think you didn't find me…attractive."

Astonished, Zach stared at her. "You've got to be kidding!"

"I'm not."

"I can see that the next few days are going to be difficult," he said. "You'll just need to be patient with me, all right?"

"All right." She nodded, already feeling worlds better.

"How about if I dish up dinner while you're changing?"

"Thanks," she said, smiling.

By the time she got back to the kitchen, wearing gray slacks and a sweater that was the color of fresh cream, Zach had served their meal and poured the wine. He stood behind her chair, waiting politely.

"Before we sit down, there's something I need to do."

The last thing Janine expected was to be lifted in his strong arms. A gasp of surprise lodged in her throat as her startled gaze met his.

"What are you doing?"

"It's tradition to carry the bride over the threshold, isn't it?"

"Yes, but you're doing it all wrong! You're supposed to carry me from the outside in—not the other way around."

Zach shrugged, unconcerned. "There's nothing traditional about this marriage. Why start now?" He made a show of pretending his knees were buckling under her weight as he staggered through the living room.

"This is supposed to be serious," she chastised him, but no matter how hard she tried, she couldn't keep the laughter out of her voice.

With a great deal of feigned effort, he managed to open the front door and then ceremoniously step onto the porch. Slowly he released her, letting her feet drop first, holding her upper body close against his chest for a long moment. The humor left his eyes. "There," he said tenderly. "Am I forgetting anything?"

It wouldn't hurt to kiss me, Janine told him in her heart, but the words didn't make it to her lips. When Zach kissed her again, she wanted it to be *his* idea.

"Janine?"

"Everything's perfect. Thank you."

"Not quite," he muttered. He turned her to face him, then covered her mouth with his own. Janine trembled, slipping her arms around his neck and giving herself completely to the kiss. She quivered at the heat that began to warm her from the inside out. This kiss was better than any they'd ever shared, something she hadn't thought possible. And what that meant, she had no idea.

Zach pulled his mouth abruptly from hers, but his eyes remained closed. Almost visibly he composed himself, and when he broke away he seemed in control of his emotions once again. Janine sighed inwardly, unsure of what she'd expected.

The next two days flew past. They took long walks on the shore, collecting shells. They rented mopeds and raced along the beach. They launched kites into the sky and delighted in their colorful dipping and soaring. The day before they were scheduled to return to Seattle, Zach declared that he intended to cook dinner. With that announcement, he informed her he had to go into town to buy the necessary groceries. After the first night, he'd given Harry a week off, and Janine had been fixing simple meals for them.

"What are you serving?" she wanted to know when he pulled into the parking lot of the town's only grocery store. "Tell me so I can buy an appropriate wine."

"Wine," he muttered under his breath. "I don't normally serve wine with this dish."

She followed him in, but when he discovered her trailing down the aisle after him, he gripped her by the shoulders and directed her back outside. "I am an artist, and I insist upon working alone."

Janine had a difficult time not laughing outright.

"In order to make this dinner as perfect as possible, I must concentrate completely on the selection of ingredients. You, my dear wife," he said, pressing his index finger to the tip of her nose, "are too much of a distraction. A lovely one, but nevertheless a distraction."

Janine smiled, her heart singing. Zach wasn't free with his compliments, and she found herself prizing each one.

While Zach was busy in the grocery store, Janine wandered around town. She bought a lifelike ceramic sea gull, which she promptly named Chester, and a bag of saltwater taffy. Then on impulse, she purchased a bottle of sun lotion in case they decided to lie outside, tempting a tan.

When she returned to the car, Zach was already there, waiting for her. She was licking a double-decker chocolate ice-cream cone and feeling incredibly happy.

"Did the master chef find everything he needed?" she asked. Two brown paper bags were sitting on the floor and she restrained herself from peeking inside.

"Our meal tonight will be one you'll long remember, I promise you."

"I'm glad to hear it." Holding out her ice-cream cone, she asked. "Do you want a taste?"

"Please." He rejected the offer of the cone itself and instead bent forward and lowered his mouth to hers. As she gazed into his dark heavy-lidded eyes her heartbeat accelerated and she was filled with a sudden intense longing. Janine wasn't sure what was happening between them, but it felt, quite simply, right.

Although the kiss was fleeting, a shiver of awareness twisted its way through her. Neither of them spoke or moved. He'd meant the kiss to be gentle and teasing, but it had quickly assumed another purpose. For a breathless second, the smile faded from his eyes. He continued to hold her, his breathing rapid.

After nearly two full days alone together, Janine found it amusing that when he finally chose to kiss her, he'd do it in a crowded parking lot.

"I don't remember chocolate being quite that rich," he

murmured. He strove for a casual tone, but Janine wasn't fooled. He was as affected by their kiss as she was, and struggling just as hard to disguise it.

They were uncharacteristically quiet on the short drive back to the house. Until the kiss, they'd spent companionable days together, enjoying each other's company. Then, in the space of no more than a few seconds, all that had changed.

"Am I banished from the kitchen?" Janine asked once they were inside the house, forcing an airy note into her voice.

"Not entirely," Zach surprised her by saying. "I'll need you later to wash the dishes."

Janine laughed and pulled her suntan lotion out of her bag. While Zach puttered around inside, she put on her swimsuit, then dragged the lounge chair into the sun to soak up the last of the afternoon's rays.

Zach soon joined her, carrying a tall glass of iced tea. "You look like you could use this."

"Thanks. If I'd known how handy you were in the kitchen, I'd have let you take over long before now."

He set the glass down beside her and headed back to the kitchen. "You'd be amazed by the list of my talents," he threw over his shoulder.

Kissing was certainly one of them, she thought. The sample he'd given her earlier had created a sharp need for more. If she was a sophisticated, experienced kind of woman, she wouldn't have any problem finding her way back into his arms. It would all appear so effortless and casual. He'd kiss her, and she'd kiss him, and then... They'd truly be husband and wife.

Lying on her back with her eyes closed, Janine imagined

how wonderful it would be if Zach were to take her in his arms and make love to her....

She awoke from her doze with a start. She hurried inside to change, and as soon as she was ready, Zach announced that dinner was about to be served. He'd set the patio table so they could eat on the deck.

"Do you need any help?" she asked, trying to peek inside the kitchen.

"None. Sit down before everything cools." He pointed to the chair and waited until she was comfortable.

"I only have a spoon," she said, after unfolding the napkin on her lap. He must have made a mistake.

"A spoon is all you need," he shouted to her from the kitchen.

Playfully she asked, "You went to all this trouble for soup?"

"Wait and see. I'll be there in a minute."

He sounded so serious, Janine had to smile. She was running through a list of words to praise his efforts—"deliciously unique," "refreshingly different"—when Zach walked onto the deck, carrying a tin can with a pair of tongs.

"Good grief, what's that?" she asked in dismay.

"Dinner," he said. "The only real cooking I ever did was while I belonged to the Boy Scouts."

As though he was presenting lobster bisque, he set the steaming can in front of her. Janine leaned forward, almost afraid to examine its contents.

"Barbecued beans. With sliced hot dogs," he said proudly.

"And to think I doubted you."

Her reservations vanished, however, the moment she tasted his specialty. The beans were actually quite appetizing. He surprised her, too, by bringing out dessert, a concoction consisting of graham crackers covered with melted chocolate and marshmallows. He'd warmed them in the oven and served them on a cookie sheet.

Janine ate four of what Zach called "s'mores." He explained that once they'd been tasted, everyone asked for "some more."

"I don't know how you've managed to stay single all these years," she teased, forgetting for the moment that they were married. "If the news about your talent in the kitchen got out, women would be knocking at your door."

Zach chuckled, looking extraordinarily pleased with himself.

An unexpected thought entered Janine's mind, filling her with curiosity. She was astonished that she'd never asked Zach about other women in his life. It would be naive to assume there hadn't been any. She'd had her relationship with Brian; surely there were women in Zach's past.

She waited until later that night when they were sipping wine and listening to classical music in front of the fireplace. Zach seemed relaxed, sitting with one knee raised and the other leg stretched out. Janine lay on her stomach, staring into the fire.

"Have you ever been in love?" She was trying for a casual tone.

Zach didn't answer her right away. "Would you be jealous if I said I had?"

"No." She sounded more confident than she felt.

"I didn't think so. What about you?"

She took her time answering, too. She'd thought she was in love with Brian. It wasn't until later, after the pain of Brian's rejection had eased, that she realized she'd been in love with the *idea* of being in love.

"No," she said, completely honest in her response. What

she felt for Zach, whom she was only beginning to know, was already a thousand times stronger than what she'd ever felt for any other man. She didn't know how to explain it, so she avoided the issue by reminding him, "I asked you first."

"I'm a married man. Naturally I'm in love."

"You're fond of me, remember?"

"I thought you detested that word."

"I do. Now stop tiptoeing around the subject. Have you ever *really* been in love—I mean head over heels in love? You don't need to go into any details—a simple yes or no will suffice."

"A desperate-passion kind of love?"

"Yes," she told him impatiently. "Don't make fun of me and please don't give me a list of all the women you've been *fond* of."

He grew so quiet and so intense that her smile began to fade. She pulled herself into a sitting position and looped her arms around her bent knees.

Zach stared at her. As she watched the harsh pain move into his eyes, Janine felt her chest tighten.

"Yes," he answered in a hoarse whisper. "I've been in love."

Nine

"Her name was Marie."

"Marie," Janine repeated the name as though she'd never heard it before.

"We met in Europe when I was on assignment with the armed forces. She spoke five languages fluently and helped me learn my way around two of them in the time we worked together."

"She was in the military with you?"

"I was army, she worked for the secret service. We were thrown together for a top-secret project that was only supposed to last a few days and instead dragged on for weeks."

"This was when you fell in love with her?" The ache inside her chest wouldn't go away. Her heart felt weighed down with the pain.

"We both were aware that the assignment was a dangerous one, and our working closely together was essential." He paused, sighing deeply. "To make a long story short, I fell in love with her. But she didn't love me."

"Then what?"

"I wanted her to leave the secret service and marry me. She wasn't interested. If you insist on knowing the details, I'll give them to you."

"No."

Zach took a sip of his wine. "I left the army soon after that. I didn't have the heart for it anymore. Unlike Marie—her work, with all its risks, was her whole life. She was the bravest and most dedicated woman I've ever known. Although it was painful at the time, she was right to turn down my proposal. Marriage and a family would have bored her within a year. It *was* painful, don't misunderstand me. I loved her more than I thought possible."

They both were silent for a moment, then Janine asked, "What did you do once you left the army?"

"Over the years, I'd managed to put aside some money, make a few investments. Once I was on my own, I decided to go into business for myself. I read everything I could get my hands on about the business-supply field and modeled the way I dealt with my clients and accounts after your grandfather's enterprise. Within five years, I was his major competitor. We met at a conference last year, and decided that instead of competing with each other, we'd join forces. And as they say, the rest is history."

"Was she pretty?" Even as she asked the question, Janine knew it was ridiculous. What difference would it make if his Marie was a former Miss America or had a face like a gorilla? None. Zach had loved Marie. Loved her as he'd probably never love again. Loved her more than he'd thought possible. By comparison, what he felt for her, Janine, was indeed only fondness.

"She was blond and, yes, she was beautiful."

Janine made a feeble attempt at a smile. "Somehow I knew that."

Zach shook himself lightly as if dragging himself back to the present and away from the powerful lure of the past. "You don't need to worry. It was a long time ago."

"I wasn't worried," Janine muttered. She got to her feet and collected their wineglasses. "I'm a little tired. If you don't mind, I'll go to bed now."

Zach was still staring into the fire and Janine doubted he'd even heard her. She didn't need a crystal ball to know he was thinking of the beautiful Marie.

No more than ten minutes after she'd turned off her bedroom light, Janine heard Zach move down the hallway to his room. For a moment she thought he'd hesitated in front of her door, but Janine convinced herself that was just wishful thinking.

From the second Zach had told her about the one great love of his life, Janine had felt as if a lump were building inside her. A huge lump of disillusionment that seemed to be located somewhere between her heart and her stomach. With every breath she took, it grew larger. But why should she care about Marie? Zach had never confessed to any deep feeling for *her.* He hadn't cheated Janine out of anything that was her right.

An hour later, she lay on her side, wide awake, her hands pressed to her stomach. She didn't mind that Zach had loved another woman so deeply, but what did hurt was that he could never love her with the same intensity. Marrying her, he'd claimed, made practical and financial sense. He was *fond* of her.

Like a romantic idiot, Janine had been frolicking through their short marriage, confident that they'd soon be in love with each other and live happily ever after with their two-point-five children in their perfect little home with the white picket fence.

Zach had loved Marie, who'd dedicated herself to her country.

The most patriotic thing Janine had ever done was cast

her vote at election time. She didn't think she should include the two occasions she'd made coffee at Red Cross meetings.

Marie was a linguist. After two years of high-school French, Janine wasn't bad at conjugating verbs, but got hopelessly lost in real conversations.

"I had to ask," she groaned to herself. She was almost certain that Zach would never have mentioned Marie if she hadn't forced the subject. How blissful her ignorance had been. How comfortable.

She could never be the great love of his life and would always remain in the background. Far in the background…

When Janine heard Zach moving around the house a few hours later, she rolled over and glanced at the clock, assuming it was the middle of the night. Then she noticed it was midmorning; they'd planned to be on the road before now. Tossing aside the blankets, she stumbled out of bed and reached blindly for her robe. But she wasn't paying attention. She collided with the wall and gave a shout of pain. She cupped her hand over her nose and closed her eyes. Tears rolled slowly down her cheeks.

"Janine." Zach pounded on the door. "Are you all right?"

"No," she cried, still holding her nose. She looked in the mirror and lowered her hand. Just as she'd suspected, her nose was bleeding.

"Can I come in?" Zach asked next.

"No…go away." She hurried to the adjoining bathroom, tilting back her head and clamping both hands over her nose.

"You sound funny. I'm coming in."

"No," she hollered again. "Go away." She groped for a washcloth. The tears rained down now, more from humiliation than pain.

"I'm coming in," Zach shouted, his voice distinctly irritated.

Before Janine could protest, the bedroom door flew open and Zach stalked inside. He stopped in the bathroom doorway. "What happened?"

Pressing the cold cloth over the lower half of her face with one hand, Janine gestured violently with the other, demanding that he leave.

"Let me look at that," he said, obviously determined to deal with her bloody nose, as well as her anger. He pushed gently against her shoulders, lowering her onto the edge of the tub, and carefully removed the cloth.

"What did you do? Meet up with a prizefighter?"

"Don't you dare make fun of me!" The tears ran down her cheeks again and plummeted on her silk collar.

It took only a minute or so to control the bleeding. Zach seemed to know exactly what to do. Janine no longer had any desire to fight, and she allowed him to do what he wanted.

Zach wiped the tears from her cheeks. "Do you want me to kiss it and make it better?"

Without waiting for an answer, Zach brought his mouth to hers. Janine felt herself go completely and utterly still. Her heart started to explode and before she realized what she was doing, she'd linked her arms around his neck and was clinging to him helplessly. Zach kissed her forehead and her eyes. His thumbs brushed the remaining tears from her cheeks. Then he nuzzled her neck. Trembling, she immersed herself in his tenderness. No matter what had happened in the past, Zach was hers for this minute, this day.

He lifted Janine to her feet and seemed to be leading her toward the bed. She might have been tempted to let him if she hadn't learned about his love for Marie. Knowing she'd always place a remote second in his affections was a crippling blow to her pride—and her heart. It would take time and effort to accept that she could never be the woman who evoked an all-consuming passion in him.

With that thought in mind, she pushed him away, needing to put some distance between them before it was too late.

Accepting Janine's decision, Zach dropped his arms and moved to lean against the doorjamb, as if he needed its support to remain upright.

Janine couldn't look at him, couldn't speak. She began fumbling with her clothes.

"I'll give you a few minutes to dress while I begin loading the car," Zach said a moment later, sounding oddly unlike himself.

Janine nodded miserably. There was nothing she could say. Nothing she could do. He'd wanted to make love to her, and she'd turned him away.

While he packed the car, Janine dressed. She met him fifteen minutes later, her suitcase in hand. She was determined to act cool toward him. But not too cool. Friendly, she decided, but not excessively so.

"I'm ready," she announced, with her most cheerful smile.

Zach locked the house, and they were on their way. Pretending there was nothing out of the ordinary, Janine chatted amicably during the drive home. If Zach noticed anything amiss, he didn't comment. For his part, he seemed as hesitant as she was to talk about what had happened. They seemed to be of one mind about the morning's incident. The whole thing was best forgotten.

Only once did Zach refer to it. He asked her if her nose was causing her any pain, but she quickly assured him she was fine. She flashed a smile bright enough to blind him and immediately changed the subject.

The Seattle sky was gray and drizzling rain when they pulled into the parking garage at the downtown condominium owned by Zach. Silently, she helped him unload the car. They were both unusually quiet as they rode the elevator to the tenth floor.

Zach paused outside his door and eyed her skeptically. "Am I obliged to haul you over the threshold again, or is once enough?"

"Once is enough."

"Good." He grinned and unlocked the door, then pushed it open for her to precede him. Curious, she quickened her pace as she walked inside. The living room was a warm mixture of leather and wood, and its wide window offered a breathtaking view of the Seattle skyline.

"It's lovely."

He nodded, seeming pleased at her reaction. "If you prefer, we can move. I suppose now that we're married, we should think about purchasing a house."

"Why?" she inquired innocently.

"I'm hoping we'll have children someday. Whenever you're ready, that is. There's no pressure, Janine."

"I…know that." She looked past him at the panoramic view, and wrapped her arms around herself, her heart speeding up at his words.

Walking to his desk, Zach listened to his voice mail messages; apparently there were a lot.

While he did that, Janine wandered from room to room, eager to see her new home. In the hallway, she noted that Zach had diplomatically left her luggage on the carpet between the two bedrooms. His was in the master. In his own way, he was telling her that where she slept would be her decision. If she wished to become his wife in the fullest sense, all she had to do was place her suitcase in the master bedroom. Nothing more needed to be said.

It didn't take Janine long to decide. She pulled her suitcase toward the guest room. When she looked up, Zach was standing in the hall, studying her, his expression aggrieved.

"Unless you need me for anything, I'm going to the office," he said gruffly.

"See you tonight."

His gaze moved past her and rested briefly on the bed in the guest room. He cocked one eyebrow questioningly, as though to give her the opportunity to reconsider. "Are you sure you'd rather sleep in here?" he asked.

"I'm sure."

Zach raked his fingers through his hair. "I was afraid of that."

A minute later, he was gone.

Zach didn't come home for dinner that night. Janine had been in the bathroom when the phone rang; Zach had left her a message saying he'd be late. So she ate by herself in front of the television, feeling abandoned and unloved. She was just putting the dishes in the dishwasher when he came home.

"Sorry I'm late."

"That's okay," she lied, never having felt more alone.

Zach glanced through the mail on his desk, although Janine was sure he'd looked at it earlier. "You got the message I wouldn't be home for dinner?"

"Yes. Did you want anything to eat? I could fix you something."

"I ate earlier. Thanks, anyway."

They watched an hour's worth of television and then decided to go to bed.

Janine changed into her pajamas—the same no-nonsense type she'd been wearing all week, since she couldn't bring herself to wear the baby-dolls Pam had given her—and had just finished washing her face. She was coming out of the bathroom, her toothbrush between her teeth, when she nearly collided with Zach in the hallway. She'd forgotten her slippers and was going to her bedroom to retrieve them. They'd already said their good-nights, and Janine hadn't expected to see him again until morning. She wasn't prepared for this encounter, and the air between them crackled with tension.

She had to force herself not to throw her toothbrush aside. Not to tell him that she longed for him to love her with the same passion he'd felt for Marie.

His hands reached out to steady her, and when she didn't immediately move away, he ran the tips of his fingers down her thick brown hair, edging her bangs to the side of her face so he could gaze into her eyes.

Janine lowered her head. "Esh-coo me," she managed, but it was difficult to speak with a toothbrush poking out of her mouth.

"Pardon?"

Janine hurried back to the bathroom and rinsed out her mouth. Turning, she braced her hands on the sink. "I said excuse me for bumping into you."

"Will you be comfortable in the guest room?"

"Yes, I'll be fine."

He held a blanket in his arms. "I thought you might need this."

"Thanks," she said as smoothly as possible, coming out

of the bathroom to take the blanket from him. She wanted to be swept off her feet. She wanted love. She wanted passion.

He was offering a warm blanket.

"I…phoned Gramps," she said, looking for a way to delay their parting and cursing herself for her weakness.

"I intended to call him myself, but got sidetracked."

"He sounded good. Dr. Coleman and a couple of his other friends were at the house and the four of them were playing pinochle."

"I'm glad to hear he's enjoying his semi-retirement."

"I am, too."

A short silence followed.

"Good night, Janine," Zach said after a moment. He glanced, frowning, into the guest room.

"Good night," she said awkwardly.

Janine was sure neither of them slept a wink that night. They were across the hall from each other, but might as well have been on opposite sides of the state, so great was the emotional distance between them.

In the morning, Zach's alarm rang at seven, but Janine was already awake. She threw back her covers, dressed and had coffee waiting when he entered the kitchen.

Zach seemed surprised to see her. "Thanks," he murmured as she handed him a cup. "That's a very…wifely thing to do."

"What? Make coffee?"

"Get up to see your husband off to work."

"I happened to be awake and figured I should get out of bed and do something useful."

He opened the refrigerator, took out the orange juice and poured himself a glass. "I see." He replaced the carton and leaned against the counter. "You did agree that our marriage would be a real one."

"Yes, I did," she said somewhat defensively. But that agreement had been before she'd learned about the one great love of his life. Zach had warned her their marriage would be advantageous for a variety of reasons, the least of which was love. At the time, Janine had agreed, convinced their relationship would find a storybook ending nonetheless—convinced that one day they'd realize they were in love. Now she understood that would never happen. And she didn't know if she could stand it.

"Janine," Zach said, distracting her, "what's wrong?"

"What could possibly be wrong?"

"Obviously something's bothering you. You look like you've lost your best friend."

"You should've told me," she burst out, running from the kitchen.

"Told you what?" Zach shouted, following her down the hall.

Furious, she hurried into her room and sat on the end of the bed, her hands in tight fists at her sides.

"What are you talking about?" he demanded, blocking the doorway.

"About…this woman you loved."

"Marie? What about her? What's she got to do with you and me?"

"You loved her more than…more than you thought possible. She was brave and wonderful, and I'm none of those things. I don't deal with pain very well and… I'd like to be patriotic but all I do is vote and all I know in French are verbs."

"What's any of that got to do with you and me?" Zach repeated hoarsely, then threw his hands in the air. "What's it got to do with *anything?*"

Knowing she'd never be able to explain, Janine shook

her head, sending her bangs fanning out in several directions. "All you are is *fond* of me."

"Correction," Zach said as he stepped into the bedroom. "I *cherish* you."

"It isn't enough," she said, feeling miserable and wretched and unworthy.

"What do you mean, it isn't enough? According to you the only reason you married me was that I was a good kisser, so you can't fault me for *my* reasons."

"I don't, it's just that you…you never told me about loving someone else. Not only that, you *admired* her—she was a hero. All you feel for me is fondness. Well, I don't want your fondness, Zachary Thomas!" She leapt to her feet, trying to collect her scattered thoughts. "If you cared for me, you would've told me about Marie before. Not mentioning her was a form of dishonesty. You were completely… unfair."

"And you weren't?" Zach's expression darkened and he buried his hands in his pockets. "You didn't say one word to me about Brian."

Janine was so shocked she sank back onto the bed. Zach still glared at her, challenging her to contradict him. Slowly gathering her composure, she stood, her eyes narrowing as she studied her husband. "Who told you about Brian?"

"Your grandfather."

"How did he know? I never said a word to him about Brian. Not one solitary word."

"But obviously he knew."

"Obviously." Janine had never felt more like weeping. "I suppose he told you Brian lied to me and claimed to love me when all the while he was seeing someone else." Another, more troubling thought entered her mind. "I…bet

Gramps told you that to make you feel sorry for me, sorry enough to marry me."

"Janine, no."

She hid her face in both hands, humiliation burning her cheeks. It was all so much worse than she'd imagined. "You felt sorry for me, didn't you?"

Zach paced the length of the bedroom. "I'm not going to lie to you, although I suspect it would be better if I did. Your grandfather didn't mention that you'd fallen in love with Brian until after the day we took him to the doctor."

"He waited until we got to know each other a little," Janine whispered, staggered by the realization that her grandfather had known about Brian all along.

"By then I'd discovered I liked you."

"The word *like* is possibly even worse than *fond*," she muttered.

"Just hear me out, would you?"

"All right," she sighed, fearing that nothing he said now mattered, anyway. Her pride had suffered another major blow. The one love of his life had been this marvelous patriot, while Janine had fallen for a weak-willed womanizer.

"It isn't as bad as it seems," Zach tried to assure her.

"I can just imagine what Gramps told you."

"All he said was that he was afraid you'd never learn to trust your own judgment again. For quite a while now, he's watched you avoid any hint of a relationship. It was as though you'd retreated from men and were content just to lick your wounds."

"That's not true! I was seeing Peter Donahue on a regular basis."

"Safe dates with safe men. There was never any likelihood that you'd fall in love with Peter, and you knew it. It was the only reason you went out with him."

"Is…is what happened with Brian why Gramps decided to play matchmaker?"

"I suspect that was part of it. Also his concern for your future. But I don't fully understand his intentions even now. I don't think it matters, though. He wanted you to be happy and secure. Anton knew I'd never purposely hurt you. And in his eyes, the two of us were perfect for each other." Zach sat down next to her and reached for her hand, lacing her fingers with his own. "*Does* it matter? We're married now."

She looked away from him and swallowed hard. "I…may not be blond and gorgeous or brave, but I deserve a husband who'll love me. You and Gramps both failed to take that into account. I don't want your pity, Zach."

"Good, because I don't pity you. You're my wife, and frankly, I'm happy about it. We can have a good life if you'll put this nonsense behind you."

"You'd never have chosen me on your own. I knew what you thought of me from the moment we met. You assumed I was a rich spoiled woman who'd never had anything real to worry about. I bet you thought I'd consider a broken nail a major disaster."

"All right, I'll admit I had the wrong impression, but that was before," Zach insisted.

"Before what?"

"Before I got to know you."

Janine's shoulders heaved with barely suppressed emotion. "As I recall, the reason you were willing to marry me was because I wasn't so bad. And let's not forget the financial benefits," she added sarcastically.

Zach's sigh was filled with frustration. "I told you I wasn't ever going to say the stuff you women like to hear. I don't know a thing about romance. But I care about you, Janine, I honestly care. Isn't that enough?"

"I need more than that," she said miserably. It was the promise of their future, the promise of learning about love together, that had intrigued her.

Zach frowned. "You told me even before we were married that you didn't need romantic words. You were content before I mentioned Marie. Why should my telling you change anything?"

She saw that Zach was losing his patience with her. She stared down at the thick carpet. "I really wish I could explain, but it does make a difference. I'm sorry, Zach, I really am."

A lifetime seemed to pass before he spoke again. "So am I," he whispered before turning away. A moment later the front door opened and almost immediately closed again. Zach had left.

"What did you expect?" she wailed, covering her face with both hands. "Did you think he was going to fall at your knees and declare his undying love?" The picture of the proud and mighty Zach Thomas playing the role of besotted husband was actually comical. If he'd done that for any woman, it would've been the brave and beautiful Marie. Not Janine.

After that disastrous morning, their relationship grew more strained than ever. Zach went to work early every day and returned late, usually past dinnertime. Janine never questioned where he was or who he was with, although she had to bite her tongue to keep from asking.

Zach proved to be a model housemate, if not a husband—cordial, courteous and remote. For her part, she threw herself into her volunteer work at the Friendship Club, spending hours each week with the children. She did her best to hide her unhappiness from her grandfather, although that was difficult.

"You look pale," he told her when she joined him for lunch one afternoon, several days after her return from Ocean Shores. "Are you losing weight?"

"I wish," she said, attempting to make a joke of it. They sat in the dining room, with Mrs. McCormick wandering in and out, casting Janine concerned glances. Janine resisted the urge to leap up and do aerobic exercises to demonstrate that she was in perfect health.

"You can't afford to get much thinner," Gramps said, eyeing her solemnly. He placed a dinner roll on the side of her plate and plunked the butter dish down in front of her.

"I'm not losing weight," she told him, spreading butter on the roll in order to please him.

"I took that sea gull you gave me into the office," Gramps said as he continued to study her. "Zach asked me where I got it. When I told him, he didn't say anything, but I could tell he wasn't pleased. Do you want it back?"

"No, of course not." Janine dropped her gaze. She'd never intended for Gramps to take Chester into the office. On impulse, she'd given him the ceramic bird, reluctant to have it around the condominium to remind her of those first glorious days with Zach.

"I wish I knew what was wrong with you two," Gramps blurted out in an uncharacteristic display of frustration. He tossed his napkin onto his dinner plate. "You should be happy! Instead, the pair of you look like you're recovering from a bad bout of flu. Zach's working so many hours it's a wonder he doesn't fall over from sheer exhaustion."

Janine carefully tore her roll into pieces. She toyed with the idea of bringing up the subject of Brian, but in the end, she didn't.

"So you say you're fine, and there's nothing wrong between you and Zach," Gramps said sarcastically. "Funny, that's exactly what he said when I asked him. Except he also told me to mind my own business—not quite in those words, but I got the message. The thing is, he looks as pathetic as you do. I can't understand it—you're perfect for each other!"

Gramps reached into his pocket for a cigar. "I'll be seeing Zach this afternoon and I intend to give that boy a piece of my mind. By all rights, you should be a happy bride." He tapped one end of the cigar against the table.

"We'll be fine, Gramps. Please stay out of it."

For a long moment, he said nothing; he only stared at the cigar between his fingers. "You're sure you don't want me to talk some sense into the boy?" he finally asked.

The mental picture of him trying to do so brought a quivering smile to her lips. "I'm sure," she said, then glanced at her watch. Pam would be waiting for her. "But since you're seeing Zach, would you please let him know I'll probably be late for dinner? He...should go ahead and eat without me."

"Do you do this often?" His question was an accusation.

"No," she replied, shaking her head. "This is the first time. Pam needs my help with a school project and I don't know when we'll be finished."

Gramps glowered as he lit his cigar, puffing mightily before he spoke. "I'll tell him."

As it turned out, Janine spent longer with Pam than she'd expected. The homework assignment wasn't difficult, but Pam begged Janine to stay with her. Pam's father was working late and the girl seemed to need Janine more than ever. They made dinner together, then ate in the kitchen while Pam chatted about her friends and life in general.

It was almost nine by the time Janine pulled into the parking garage. The first thing she noticed was Zach's car. The atmosphere had been so falsely courteous between them that she dreaded each encounter, however brief. Since that first morning, Zach hadn't made any effort to talk about her role in his life. Janine wasn't looking for a long flowery declaration of love. Just a word or two more profound than *fond* or *like* to let her know she was important to him.

Drawing a deep breath, she headed for the condominium.

She'd just unlocked the door when Zach stormed into the room like a Minnesota blizzard. "Where the hell have you been?" he demanded.

Janine was so shocked by his fierce anger that she said nothing.

"I demand to know exactly where you were!"

She removed her sweater, hanging it carefully in the entry closet, along with her purse. Zach scowled at her silence, fists clenched at his sides. "Do you have any idea of the time? Did it even cross your mind that I might've been concerned about you? Your cell phone was off and you didn't return any calls."

"I'm sorry." Janine turned to face him. "But you knew where I was," she said calmly.

"All Anton said was that you'd be late. Not where you were going or who you were with. So naturally I was worried."

"I'm sorry. Next time I'll tell you myself." Janine yawned; the day had been exhausting. "If you don't mind, I think I'll go to bed now. Unless there's anything else you'd like to know?"

He glared at her, then shook his head. Wheeling around abruptly, he walked away.

Hours later, Janine was awakened by a gruff sobbing sound coming from the other room. It took her a moment to realize it was Zach. Was he having a nightmare?

Folding back the covers, she got out of bed and hurried into his room. The cries of anguish grew louder. In the light from the hallway, she could see him thrashing about, the bedding in disarray.

"Zach," she cried, rushing to his side. She sat on the edge of the bed and placed her hands gently on his shoulders. "Wake up. You're having a dream. Just a dream. It's okay…."

Zach's eyes slowly opened. "Janine." He ground out her name as though in torment and reached for her, hauling her into his arms with such force that he left her breathless. "Janine," he said, his voice so husky she could barely understand him. "I thought I'd lost you."

Ten

"Zach, I'm fine," Janine whispered. Emotion clogged her throat at the hungry way his eyes roamed her face. He seemed to have difficulty believing, even now, that she was unhurt.

"It was so real," he continued, his chest heaving. He hid his face as if to block out the vivid images the dream had induced. Making room in the large bed, he pulled her down beside him. His hands stroked her hair as he released several jagged breaths. "We were at the ocean," he told her, "and although I'd warned you against it, you decided to swim. A huge wave knocked you off your feet and you were drowning. Heaven help me, I tried, but I couldn't get to you fast enough." He shut his eyes briefly. "You kept calling out to me and I couldn't find you. I just couldn't get to you fast enough."

"Zach," she whispered, her mouth so close to his that their breath mingled, "I'm right here. It was only a dream. It wasn't real."

He nodded, but his eyes still seemed troubled, refusing to leave her face. Then ever so slowly, as though he expected her to object, he moved his mouth even closer to hers. "I couldn't bear to lose you. I'd rather die myself."

Helpless to deny him anything, Janine turned her face to receive his kiss.

His hands tangled in her thick dark hair, effectively holding her captive, while his mouth seized hers in a kiss that sent her senses swirling. Nothing mattered except his touch. Overcome for a moment by the fierce tenderness she felt in him, Janine eagerly fed his need.

"Janine, oh, my dear sweet Janine. I couldn't bear to lose you."

"I'm here… I'm here." Melting against him, she molded her body to the unyielding contours of his, offering her lips and her heart to his loving possession. Again and again, he kissed her. Janine slid her hands up his chest and twined them around his neck. This was what she'd longed for from the first, the knowledge that he needed her, and she gloried in the sensation.

With a groan, he reluctantly pulled his mouth from hers. He held her firmly to his chest, his breathing harsh and rapid. Peace combined with a delirious sense of happiness, and Janine released a deep sigh. Pressing her ear to his chest, she listened, content, to the heavy pounding of his heart.

"Did I frighten you?" he asked after a minute.

"No," she whispered.

He resumed stroking her hair as she nestled more securely in his arms. Zach had made her feel wondrous, exciting things every time he kissed her, but the way he held and touched her now went far beyond those kisses. She'd experienced a bonding with Zach, a true joining of spirits that had been missing until now. He had told her he'd cherish her, but she hadn't believed it until this moment. Tears clouded her eyes and she struggled to restrain them.

For a long while neither of them spoke. But Janine didn't need words. Her eyes were closed as she savored this precious time.

When Zach did speak, his voice was little more than a hoarse whisper. "I had a sister who drowned. Her name was Beth Ann. I'd promised I'd always be there for her—but I failed her. I couldn't bear to lose you, too."

Janine tightened her hold, knowing how difficult it must be for him to speak of his sister.

"I never forgave myself." His body tensed and his fingers dug roughly into her shoulder. "Losing Beth Ann still haunts me. She wouldn't have drowned if I'd been with her. She—"

Lifting her head slightly, Janine's misty gaze met his. "It wasn't your fault. How could it have been?"

"But I was responsible for her," he returned harshly.

Janine suspected that Zach had rarely, if ever, shared his sorrow or his guilt over his sister's death with anyone. A low groan worked its way through him and he squeezed his eyes tightly shut. "For years, I've drummed out the memories of Beth Ann's death. The nightmare was so real, only this time it wasn't her—it was you."

"But I'm safe and sound. See?" She pressed her hands to both sides of his face, smiling down on him.

He sighed and smiled back, a little uncertainly. "I'm all right now. I shouldn't have burdened you with this."

"It wasn't a burden."

His arms tightened around her, and he inhaled deeply as if absorbing her scent. "Stay with me?"

She nodded, grateful that he needed her.

Within minutes, Janine felt herself drifting into drowsiness. From Zach's relaxed, even breathing, she knew he was already asleep.

When Janine next stirred, she was lying on her side, and Zach was cuddling her spoon fashion, his arm about her waist. At some point during the night, she'd slipped under the covers, but she had no recollection of doing so. A small satisfied smile touched the edges of her mouth. She rolled carefully onto her back so as not to disturb Zach, and wondered what she should do. When Zach woke and found her in bed with him, she was afraid he might regret what had happened, regret asking her to stay. He might feel embarrassed that he'd told her about his sister's death and the guilt he still felt.

Closing her eyes, Janine debated with herself. If she left his bed and returned to her own room, he might think she was rejecting him, shocked by his heart-wrenching account of Beth Ann's death.

"Janine?" He whispered her name, his voice husky with sleep.

Her eyes flew open. "I…we fell asleep. What time is it?"

"Early. The alarm won't go off for another couple of hours."

She nodded, hoping to disguise any hint of disappointment in her voice. He didn't want her with him, she was sure of it. He was embarrassed to find her still in his bed. "I'll leave now if you want."

"No."

The single word was filled with such longing that Janine thought she'd misunderstood him. She tipped her head back to meet his gaze. The light from the hall allowed her to see the passion smoldering in his dark eyes. Turning onto her side, Janine lovingly traced the lines of his face.

"I'm sorry about the way I behaved over… Marie," she whispered. "I was jealous and I knew I was being ridiculous, but I couldn't help myself."

The corners of his eyes crinkled with his smile. "I'll forgive you if you're willing to overlook the way I behaved when you got home last night."

She answered him with a light kiss, and he hugged her to him. Janine surrendered to the sheer pleasure of being in Zach's arms, savoring the rush of warm sensations that sprang to life inside her.

"I don't know how to say all the words you deserve to hear, but I know one thing, Janine. I love you. It happened without my even being aware of it. One day I woke up and realized how important you'd become to me. It wasn't the grand passion you wanted, and I'm sorry for that. The love I feel for you is the quiet steady kind. It's buried deep in my heart, but trust me, it's there. You're the most important person in my life."

"Oh, Zach, I love you so much."

"You love me?"

"I have for weeks, even before we were married. That's what bothered me so much when I learned about Marie. I wanted you to love *me* with the same intensity that you felt for her…that I feel for you."

"It isn't like that. It never was. Marie was as brave as she was beautiful, but what we shared was never meant to last. And she was smart enough to understand that. I fell in love with her, but she was too much of a professional to involve her heart. She was the kind of person who thrives on excitement and danger. It wasn't until you and I met that I realized if I were ever to marry, it would be to someone like you."

"Someone like me?"

He kissed her briefly. "A woman who's warm and gentle and caring. Someone unselfish and—" he hesitated "—desirable."

Her throat tightened with emotion, and it was all she could do to meet his gaze. Zach found her desirable. He wanted to make love to her. He didn't need to say it; the message was there for her to read in his eyes. It wasn't the desperate passion she'd once craved, but his love, his need to have her in his life, was far more potent than any action he could have taken, any words he could have said.

"Love me, Zach," she whispered simply.

Zach's mouth touched hers with a sweet desperate ardor. If she had any lingering doubts they vanished like mist in the sun as his lips took hers, twisting her into tight knots of desire.

His arms locked around her and he rolled onto his back, pulling her with him. His hands outlined her face as though he half expected her to stop him.

"Make me your wife," she said, bending forward to brush her moist mouth over his.

Zach groaned, and then he did the strangest, most wonderful thing. He laughed. The robust sound echoed across the room and was so infectious that it made Janine laugh, too.

"My sweet Janine," he said. "You've changed my life." And then he kissed her again, leaving her with no doubts at all.

For a long time afterward, their happiness could be heard in their sighs and gasps and whispered words of love....

The buzzing sound refused to go away. Janine moaned softly and flung out her hand, hoping to find the source of the distraction. But before she could locate it, the noise ceased abruptly.

"Good morning, wife," Zach whispered.

Her eyes remained closed as she smiled leisurely. “Good morning, husband.” Rolling onto her back, she held her arms open to him. “I had the most marvelous dream last night.”

Zach chuckled softly. “That wasn’t any dream.”

“But it must’ve been,” she said, slipping her arms around his neck and smiling lazily. “Nothing could be that incredible in real life.”

“I didn’t think so, either, but you proved me wrong.” He kissed her tenderly, and then so thoroughly that by the time he lifted his head, Janine was breathless.

Slowly, almost against her will, her eyes drifted open. His were dark with desire. “You’ll be late for work,” she warned him.

His smile was sensuous. “Who cares?”

“Not me,” she murmured. And with a small cry of pleasure, she willingly gave herself to her husband.

Zach was already an hour late for the office when he dragged himself out of bed and headed for the shower. Wearing her husband’s pajama top, Janine wandered into the kitchen and prepared a pot of coffee. She leaned against the counter and smiled into space, hardly aware of the passage of time.

A few minutes later—or perhaps it was longer—Zach stepped behind her and slid his arms around her waist, nuzzling her neck.

“Zach,” she protested, but not too strenuously. She closed her eyes and cradled her arms over his, leaning back against his solid strength. “You’re already late.”

“I know,” he murmured. “If I didn’t have an important meeting this morning, I’d skip work altogether.”

Turning in his arms, Janine tilted back her head to gaze into his eyes. “You’ll be home for dinner?”

"Keep looking at me like that and I'll be home for lunch."

Janine smiled. "It's almost that time now."

"I know," he growled, reluctantly pulling away from her. "We'll go out to dinner tonight," he said, kissing her again. His mouth was hot on her own, feverish with demand and passion and need. He raised his head, but his eyes remained shut. "Then we'll come home and celebrate."

Janine sighed. Married life was beginning to agree with her.

At precisely five, Zach was back. He stood by the door, loosening his tie, when Janine appeared. A smile traveled to his mouth as their eyes met. Neither moved. They stared at each other as if they'd spent years apart instead of a few short hours.

Janine was feeling distinctly light-headed. "Hi," she managed to say, shocked that her voice sounded more like a hoarse whisper than the cheery greeting she'd intended. "How'd the meeting go?"

"Bad."

"Bad?"

He nodded slowly and stepped forward, placing his briefcase on the desk. "I was supposed to be listening to an important financial report, but unfortunately all I could do was wonder how much longer the thing would take so I could get home to my wife."

"Oh." That wasn't the most intelligent bit of conversation she'd ever delivered, but just looking at Zach was enough to wipe out all her normal thought processes.

"It got to be almost embarrassing." His look was intimate and loving as he advanced two more steps toward her. "In the middle of it, I started smiling, and then I embarrassed myself further by laughing outright."

"Laughing? Something was funny?"

"I was thinking about your definition of romance. The tryst on the moors was supplied by your grandfather. The walk along the beach, hand in hand, was supplied by me after the wedding. But the desperate passion, my dear sweet wife, was something we found together."

Her eyes filled with tears.

"I love you."

They moved toward each other then, but stopped abruptly when the doorbell chimed. Zach's questioning eyes met hers. Janine shrugged, not knowing who it could possibly be.

The second Zach answered the door, Anton flew into the room, looking more determined than Janine had ever seen him.

"All right, you two, sit down," he ordered, waving them in the direction of the sofa.

"Gramps?"

"Anton?"

Janine glanced at Zach, but he looked as mystified as she did. So she just shrugged and complied with her grandfather's demand. Zach sat down next to her.

Gramps paced the carpet directly in front of them. "Janine and I had lunch the other day," he said, speaking to Zach. "Two things became clear to me then. First and foremost, she's crazy in love with you, but I doubt she's told you that."

"Gramps—" Janine began, but her grandfather silenced her with a single look.

"The next thing I realized is that she's unhappy. Terribly unhappy. Being in love is difficult enough but—"

"Anton," Zach broke in, "if you'd—"

Gramps cut him off with the same laser-eyed look he'd scnt Janinc.

"Don't interrupt me, boy. I'm on a roll and I'm not about to stop now. If I noticed Janine was a little melancholy at lunch, it was nothing compared to what I've been noticing about you." Suddenly he ceased his pacing and planted himself squarely in front of Zach. "All week I've been hearing complaints and rumors about you. Folks in the office claim you're there all hours of the day and night, working until you're ready to drop." He paused. "I know you, Zach, probably better than anyone else does. You're in love with my granddaughter, and it's got you all tangled up inside."

"Gramps—"

"Shh." He dismissed Janine with a shake of his head. "Now, I may be an old man, but I'm not stupid. Maybe the way I went about bringing the two of you together wasn't the smartest, or the most conventional, but by golly it worked." He hesitated long enough to smile proudly. "In the beginning I had my doubts. Janine put up a bit of a fuss."

"I believe you said something about how it's easier to pluck a live chicken," Zach inserted, slanting a secret smile at Janine.

"True enough. I never knew that girl had so much spunk. But the fact is, Zachary, as you'll recall, you weren't all that keen on the idea yourself. You both think because I'm an old man, I don't see things. But I do. You were two lonely people, filling up your lives with unimportant relationships, avoiding love, avoiding life. I care about you. Too much to sit back and do nothing."

"It worked out," Janine said, wanting to reassure him.

"At first I thought it had. I arranged the trip to Scotland and it looked like everything was falling neatly into place, like in one of those old movies. I couldn't have been more pleased when you announced that you were going to get married. It was sooner than I'd expected, but I assumed that meant things were progressing nicely. Apparently I was wrong. Now I'm worried."

"You don't need to be."

"That's not the way I see it," Gramps said with a fierce glare. "Tell him you love him, Janine. Look Zach in the eye and put aside that silly pride of yours. He needs to know it. He needs to hear it. I told you from the first that he wasn't going to be an easy man to know, and that you'd have to be patient with him. What I didn't count on was that damnable pride of yours."

"You want me to tell Zach I love him? Here? Now?"

"Yes!"

Janine turned to her husband and, feeling a little self-conscious, lowered her eyes.

"Tell him," Gramps barked.

"I love you, Zach," she said softly. "I really do."

Gramps gave a loud satisfied sigh. "Good, good. Okay, Zach, it's your turn."

"My turn?"

"Tell Janine what you feel and don't go all arrogant on me."

Zach reached for Janine's hand. He lifted her palm to his mouth and brushed his lips against it. "I love you," he whispered.

"Add something else," Gramps instructed, gesturing toward him. "Something like...you'd be a lost and lonely soul without her. Women are impressed by that sort of thing. Damn foolishness, I know, but necessary."

"I'd be a lost and lonely soul without you," Zach repeated, then looked back at Janine's grandfather. "How'd I do?"

"Better than most. Is there anything else you'd like him to say, Janine?"

She gave an expressive sigh. "I don't think so."

"Good. Now I want the two of you to kiss."

"Here? In front of you?"

"Yes," Gramps insisted.

Janine slipped into Zach's arms. The smile he shared with her was so devastating that she felt her heart race with anticipation. Her eyes fluttered closed as his mouth settled on hers, thrilling her with promises for all the years to come.

Gently, provocatively, Zach moved his mouth over hers, ending his kiss far too soon to suit Janine. From the shudder that coursed through him, Janine knew it was too soon for him, too. Reluctantly they drew apart. Zach gazed into her eyes, and Janine responded with a soft smile.

"Excellent, excellent."

Janine had all but forgotten her grandfather's presence. When she turned away from Zach, she discovered Gramps sitting across from them, his hands on the arms of the leather chair. He looked exceedingly proud of himself. "Are you two going to be all right now?"

"Yes, sir," Zach answered for them both, his eyes hazy with desire as he smiled at Janine. She could feel herself blushing, and knew her eyes were foggy with the same longing.

"Good!" Gramps declared, nodding once for emphasis. A slow grin overtook his mouth. "I knew all the two of you needed was a little assistance from me." He inhaled deeply. "Since you're getting along so well, maybe now would be the time to bring up the subject of children."

"Anton," Zach said, rising to his feet. He strode across the room and opened the door. "If you don't mind, I'll take care of that myself."

"Soon?" Gramps wanted to know.

Zach's eyes met Janine's. "Soon," he promised.

* * * * *

If you enjoyed this story, you won't want to miss New York Times *bestselling author Brenda Novak's Silver Springs series, about a picturesque small town in Southern California where even the hardest hearts can learn to love again...*

Turn the page for a sneak peek at the newest book in the series, Keep Me Warm at Christmas, *available now!*

One

Thursday, December 16

Tia Beckett ran a finger along the jagged scar on her cheek as she gazed into the mirror above the contemporary console on the living-room wall. She'd taken down almost every mirror in her own house as soon as she came home from the hospital—broken them all and tossed them out. But she couldn't do the same here. This wasn't her home, and there seemed to be mirrors everywhere, each one projecting the same tragic image.

She leaned closer. It must've been the windshield that nearly destroyed her face.

She dropped her hand. After a month, her cheek was still tender, but she continued to examine her reflection. The woman in the mirror was a complete stranger. If she turned her head to the left, she could find herself again. The shiny black hair that framed an oval face. The smooth and creamy olive-colored skin. The bottle-green eyes with long, thick eyelashes. The full lips, which were her own, not a product of Botox injections. All the beauty that'd helped her land the leading role in Hollywood's latest blockbuster was still there.

But when she turned her head to the right…

Her stomach soured as she studied the raised, pink flesh that slanted in a zigzag fashion from the edge of her eye almost to her mouth. The doctor had had to piece that side of her face back together like a quilt. He'd said there was a possibility that cosmetic surgery could improve the scars later, but that wasn't an option right now. After what she'd been through already, she couldn't even contemplate another surgery. It'd be too late to save her career by then, anyway.

Who was this poor, unfortunate creature?

Her agent, her fellow cast members for *Expect the Worst*, the romantic comedy in which she costarred with box-office hit Christian Allen, and the friends she'd made since moving to LA said she was lucky to have survived the accident. And maybe that was true. But it was difficult to *feel* lucky when she'd lost all hope of maintaining her career just as it was beginning to skyrocket.

A knock at the front door startled her. Who could that be? She didn't want to see anyone, not even her friends—and especially not the press. They'd been hounding her since the accident, trying to snap a picture of her damaged face and demanding an answer as to whether she would quit acting. That was part of the reason she'd readily accepted when Maxi Cohen, the producer of her one and only film, offered to let her stay at his massive estate in Silver Springs, ninety minutes northwest of LA. He and his family would be in Israel for the holidays, so he needed someone to house-sit. That was what he'd said. What she'd heard was that she could hide out for a month and be completely *alone*. And she wouldn't even have to pay for the privilege. She just had to care for the houseplants, feed and play with Kiki, the parrot, occasionally drive each of the six vehicles parked in the airplane-hangar-sized garage and make sure nothing went wrong.

She also turned on the lights in the main house at night—Maxi didn't yet have them set up on a timer, like those in his yard—so that it looked occupied since she was staying in the guesthouse, which was smaller and more comfortable. But that was probably unnecessary. There wasn't a lot of crime in Silver Springs. Known for its boutique hotels, recreational opportunities and local, organic produce, it was sort of like Santa Barbara, only forty minutes away and closer to the coast, in that there were plenty of movie moguls and the like who had second homes here.

Still, he couldn't have left Kiki without a caretaker. And safe was always better than sorry. He also owned an extensive art collection that could never be replaced, so she figured he was wise to have someone watch over it, just in case.

Whoever was at the door rapped again, more insistently. Maxi had given the housekeeper and other staff a paid holiday. Even the gardeners were off, since the yard didn't grow much during the cold, rainy season. The entire estate was essentially in mothballs until Maxi returned. And no one Tia knew could say exactly where she was. So why was someone at her door? How had whoever it was gotten onto the property? The front gate required a code.

"Hello? Anyone home?" A man's strident voice came through the panel. "Maxi said you'd be in the guesthouse."

Damn. Those words suggested whoever it was had a right to be here, or at least permission. She was going to have to answer the door.

"Coming," she called. "Just…give me a minute." She hurried into the bedroom, where her suitcase lay open on the floor. She'd arrived in Silver Springs two days ago but hadn't bothered to unpack. There hadn't seemed to be much point. There didn't seem to be much point in doing anything anymore. She hadn't bothered to shower or dress this morning, either, and she was wearing the same sweat bottoms, T-shirt and socks she'd had on yesterday.

Yanking off her clothes, she pulled on a robe so that there'd be no expectation of hospitality as she scurried back through the living room. Still reluctant to speak to anyone, she peered through the peephole.

A tall, slender man—six-two, maybe taller—stood on the stoop. His dark hair had outgrown its last haircut and stuck out beneath a red beanie, he had a marked five-o'clock shadow, suggesting he hadn't shaved for a couple of days, and a cleft chin almost as pronounced as that of Henry Cavill. He was a total stranger to her, but he had to be one of Maxi's friends or associates, and she should treat him as such.

Bracing herself—human interaction was something she now avoided whenever possible—she took a deep breath. *Please, God, don't let him recognize me or have anything to do with the media.*

The blinds were already pulled, so she turned off the lights and cracked the door barely wide enough to be able to peek out with her good side. "What can I do for you?"

His scowl darkened as his gaze swept over what he could see of her. He must've realized she was wearing a robe, because he said, "I hate to drag you out of bed at—" he checked his watch "—two in the afternoon. But could you let me into the main house before I freeze my—" Catching himself, he cleared his throat and finished with "Before I freeze out here?"

Assuming he was a worker of some sort—she couldn't imagine why he'd be here, bothering her, otherwise—she couldn't help retorting, "Sure. As long as you tell me why I should care whether you freeze or not."

The widening of his eyes gave her the distinct impression that he wasn't used to having someone snap back at him. So…maybe he wasn't a worker.

"Because Maxi has offered to let me stay in *his* home, and he indicated you'd let me in," he responded with exaggerated patience. "He didn't text you?"

"No, I haven't heard from him." And surely, what this man said couldn't be right. Maxi had told her that she'd have the run of the place. She'd thought she'd be able to stay here without fear of bumping into anyone. She'd been counting on it.

"He was just getting on a plane," he explained. "Maybe he had to turn off his phone."

"Okay. If you want to give me your number, I'll text you as soon as I hear from him."

He cocked his head. "You'll…what?"

"I'm afraid you'll have to come back later."

"I don't want to come back," he said. "I just drove six hours, all the way from the Bay Area, after working through the night. I'm exhausted, and I'd like to get some sleep. Can you help me out here?"

His impatience irritated her. But since the accident, she'd been so filled with rage she was almost relieved he was willing to give her a target. "No, I'm afraid I can't."

He stiffened. "Excuse me?"

"I can't let some stranger into the house, not unless Maxi specifically asks me to." Even if this guy was telling the truth, forcing him to leave would not only bring her great pleasure, it would give her a chance to feed Maxi's parrot before hiding the key under the mat. Then there would be no need for further interaction. He wouldn't see her, and she wouldn't have to watch the shock, recognition and pity cross his face.

Pity was by far the worst, but none of it was fun.

"If I have the code to the gate, I must've gotten it from somewhere, right?" he argued. "Isn't it logical to assume that Maxi is the one who gave it to me?"

"That's a possibility, but there are other possibilities."

"Like..."

"Maybe you hopped the fence or got it from one of the staff?"

His chest lifted in an obvious effort to gather what little patience he had left. "I assure you, if I was a thief, I would not present myself at your door."

"I can appreciate why. But I'm responsible for what goes on here right now, which means I can't take any chances."

"You won't be taking any chances!" he argued in exasperation. "If anything goes missing or gets damaged, I'll replace it."

What was there to guarantee that? "The art Maxi owns can't be replaced," she said and thought she had him. Maxi had told her so himself. But this stranger said the only thing that could trump her statement.

"Except by me, since I'm the one who created most of it in the first place," he said drily.

"You're an artist?" she asked but only to buy a second or two while she came to grips with a few other things that had just become apparent. If he was one of the artists Maxi collected, he wasn't some obscure talent. Yet...he couldn't be more than thirty. And he certainly didn't look too important shivering in a stretched-out T-shirt, on which the word *Perspective* was inverted, and jeans that had holes down the front.

"I am," he replied. "And you are…the house sitter, I presume?"

She heard his disparaging tone. He wondered who the hell she was to tell him what to do. He thought he mattered more than she did. But that came as no surprise: she'd already pegged him as arrogant. She was more concerned about the fact that Maxi might've referred to her as a menial laborer. Is that the way her former producer thought of her now? It was only a few months ago that she'd been the most promising actress in Hollywood. Certainly she'd attained more fame than this snooty artist—when it came to having her name recognized by the general public, anyway.

But what did it matter how high she'd climbed? She'd fallen back to earth so hard she felt as though she'd broken every bone in her body, even though the damage to her face was the only lingering injury she'd sustained in the accident. "I'm house-sitting, yes. But, like you, I'm a friend of Maxi's," she said vaguely.

Fortunately, he didn't seem interested enough to press her for more detailed information. She was glad of that.

"Fine. Look, *friend*." He produced his phone. "I have proof. This is the text exchange I had with Maxi just before his plane took off. As you can see, he says he has someone—*you*—staying in the guesthouse, but the main house is available, and I'm welcome to it. If you'll notice the time, you'll see that these texts took place just this morning."

Her heart sank as she read what he showed her: I have someone in the guesthouse. Just get the key from her.

"How long are you planning on being here?" she asked.

"Does it matter?" he replied.

It *did* matter. But this was Maxi's estate, and they were both his guests, so she had an obligation to treat him as well as he was accustomed to being treated. "Just a minute," she said and muttered a curse after she closed the door. *There goes all my privacy.*

She got the key from the kitchen drawer before cracking the door open just wide enough to slip her hand through. "Here you go, but I'll need your phone number so I can coordinate getting inside the house when I need to."

"The main house? Why would you need to get inside that?"

"I take care of the plants. As easy as that may sound, in a house that's over fourteen thousand square feet, it's no small job. And I have to take care of Kiki."

"Kiki?"

"Maxi's parrot."

"Maxi didn't say anything about a parrot."

"Well, he has one, and parrot-sitting requires more than throwing a handful of birdseed in a bowl." Maxi had taught her how to take care of Kiki the day before he left. Then he'd observed her for several hours, just to be sure she could do the job. Parrots could be finicky, and he knew Kiki wouldn't like him leaving. "I was also going to dust and vacuum once a week to keep things up, since the housekeeper is on holiday. But if you'd rather take over those chores, I can show you how to do it all."

"Nice try," he said. "Who are you—Tom Sawyer's sister? I'll let you handle the parrot and the rest of it. And don't worry. I won't get in your way."

She continued to hang back so he couldn't see her face. "You'd rather have me invade your space?"

"I won't mind as long as you're quiet. That bird isn't going to be too loud, is it? Because I typically work at night and sleep during the day."

She barely refrained from rolling her eyes. The tortured artist was such a cliché. "She sleeps at night, so she should be quiet while you create your latest masterpiece. During the day you might hear her speak or squawk or whatever."

"She speaks?"

"She says a few phrases. Maxi used to have a dog, so she learned to bark, too."

He narrowed his eyes as if he wasn't quite sure she was being straight with him. "Sounds annoying."

"It's the reason he didn't replace his dog once it passed. But you don't have anything to worry about. She lives in an aviary in the middle of the house that goes up through both stories. The plants and the glass walls capture most of the noise, so you shouldn't hear much—not unless she's upset."

"How often does that happen?"

"She's an animal. Emotional episodes aren't scheduled. If we keep her happy, it might not happen at all."

"Good to know. I'll make you a copy of the key." He turned to go but she spoke again.

"You don't feel it would be presumptuous to copy someone else's house key?"

"Not if I'm going to be staying for a few months. I consider it a practical matter. Why? Would you rather try to pass it back and forth between us?"

Her heart sank at learning he'd be living on the premises for more than just the weekend, but she tried to focus on the coordination sharing a key might require. "No. A copy will be fine."

"That's what I thought," he said and cracked the first smile she'd seen him wear. He was getting in the house right away and would have his own key, and she'd be taking care of the bird. That he was gloating annoyed her, but she had to admit that his smile absolutely transformed his face. He was much more handsome than she'd wanted to acknowledge—in a dark-lord-of-the-underworld sort of way.

She thought of all the beautiful people she'd encountered in Los Angeles and believed he could easily hold his own.

She'd been able to compete in that arena once, too. As far back as she could remember, people outside the tight-knit Mennonite community in which she'd been raised had gushed about her beauty, even though her parents had done everything they could to downplay it. They and the other members of their church believed it put her at risk of losing her soul through the sin of vanity. But she didn't have to worry about that anymore. She'd lost all the beauty she'd once had.

"Welcome to Silver Springs," she said, her voice as frigid as the wind whipping at his clothes. He hadn't bothered to put on a coat before climbing out of the car. Getting the key hadn't been as quick as he'd obviously expected.

Instead of being offended by her response, he chuckled as he strode off. She didn't even know his name. But that was fine with her. If he did anything wrong, Maxi could deal with it. She didn't plan on interacting with him again.

His presence only meant there was now someone on the property she'd try to avoid.